Please turn to the back of the book
for an interview with Harry Harrison.

Praise for Harry Harrison's
The Hammer and the Cross

"In this rich and exciting alternate history, Harrison evokes
the spirit and atmosphere of the so-called Dark Ages with
wit, sensitivity, and impeccable research."
—*Publishers Weekly*

"Fascinating, sinewy, brutal, and fine ... Few historicals
are as powerfully evocative of time and place as Harrison's
tremendous saga."
—*Kirkus Reviews*

STARS & STRIPES FOREVER

Harry Harrison

A Del Rey® Book

THE BALLANTINE PUBLISHING GROUP · NEW YORK

A Del Rey® Book
Published by The Ballantine Publishing Group
Copyright © 1998 by Harry Harrison
Illustrations © David A. Hardy

www.randomhouse.com/delrey/

Library of Congress Catalog Card Number: 99-90611

ISBN 0-345-40934-5

Manufactured in the United States of America

First Ballantine Books Hardcover Edition: October 1998
First Ballantine Books Mass Market Edition: October 1999

10   9   8   7   6   5   4   3   2   1

For Nat Sobel—
with immense thanks

There is no privileged past . . . There is an infinitude of Pasts, all equally valid . . . At each and every instant of Time, however brief you suppose it, the line of events forks like the stem of a tree putting forth twin branches.

—André Maurois

A LOOK AT WHAT
MIGHT HAVE BEEN

There, in the center of London, his statue sits in Imperial Roman splendor, toga-garbed and carved in finest marble. Prince Albert, consort to Queen Victoria, his memory enshrined in what is probably the ugliest monument in the world; the Albert Memorial.

He was a kind man and much loved by the Queen; he brought her true happiness. But did this Saxon prince, who never lost his thick German accent, ever do anything of any importance? Other than father the future king.

He certainly did. He averted war with the United States.

In 1861 the American Civil War was still in its first murderous year. Britain and France, to the dismay of the North, were planning to recognize the South as a separate nation. Now the British steam packet *Trent* was taking the two newly appointed Confederate commissioners, James M. Mason and John Slidell, to England to represent President Jefferson Davis.

On the eighth of November 1861 the *Trent* was stopped at sea by the USS *San Jacinto*. When her commanding officer, Captain Wilkes, found that there were two rebels aboard the *Trent* he had them arrested on the spot and removed from the British ship.

England was aroused, furious. The War of 1812, when Britain had been at war with the newly established United States of America, was still fresh in memory. With the Northern blockade of the Confederate ports biting deep, there was little cotton from the South and the weaving mills of the

North were facing bankruptcy. The Prime Minister, Lord Palmerston, saw the boarding of a British ship and the seizing of the passengers as a deliberate insult to Britain's sovereignty. The Foreign Minister, Lord John Russell, echoed the public sentiment when he sent a dispatch to President Lincoln ordering him to release the men immediately—or suffer the consequences. British troops and thousands of rifles were dispatched to Canada and troops massed on the United States border.

Enter the peaceful Prince Albert. Already terminally ill with lung congestion—which was in reality typhoid fever caught from the foul water supply and drains of Windsor Castle—he did a rewrite of the dispatch, ameliorating the language and giving Lincoln a face-saving way out. Queen Victoria approved of the changes and it was sent to Washington.

On December 26 President Lincoln ordered that the two Confederate commissioners be released.

Sadly, Prince Albert would never know that he had averted what very well could have

V & A Picture Library

**ALBERT AND
THE TRENT ULTIMATUM**

been a tragic confrontation. He had died on the fourteenth of the same month.

But consider for a moment what would have happened if he had not changed the fatal dispatch.

What if Lincoln had been forced by the strong language to ignore the ultimatum?

What if the British invasion of the United States had gone forward?

What if there had been war?

STARS & STRIPES
FOREVER

NOVEMBER 8, 1861

The USS *San Jacinto* rocked gently in the calm seas of the South Atlantic; blue water below, blue sky above. The fire in her boiler was banked and only a trickle of smoke rose up from her high funnel. The Bahama Channel was only fifteen miles wide at this point, near the Parador del Grande lighthouse, a bottleneck through which all the island traffic funneled. Captain Charles D. Wilkes stood on the bridge of the American warship, hands clasped behind his back, staring grimly toward the west.

"Smoke in sight," the lookout stationed in the crow's nest called out. "East southeast."

The captain did not move as Lieutenant Fairfax repeated the sighting. The ship that he was waiting for would be coming from the west—should be coming soon if his calculations were correct. If the reports from the Union spies in Cuba could be believed, the men he was seeking should be on board. The chase so far had been a frustrating one; all about the Caribbean. The wanted men had been one step ahead of him ever since he had sailed from Florida. This would be his last chance to apprehend them. If he were wrong, and the *Trent* did not take this passage between the islands, she would now be safely on her way back to England and the pair would have escaped.

The decision he had made to station his ship here in the Old Bahama Channel was based completely on speculation. If the two men had indeed boarded the *Trent*, and if the steam packet had left Havana as scheduled—and if she took this course to St. Thomas, why then she should be here by noon at the latest. He started to reach for his watch, then stopped, not wanting to reveal eagerness or doubt before the crew. Instead he squinted up at the sun; surely it was close to the meridian. He clasped his hands even tighter behind his back and the scowl deepened on his face.

Five minutes went by—they could have been five hours—before the lookout called out again.

"Steamer ahoy! Just off the port bow."

"Raise steam," the captain ordered. He slammed his fist on the rail. "That's the *Trent*, I *know* that is the *Trent*. Have the drums beat to quarters."

Lieutenant Fairfax repeated the commands. In the engine room the boiler doors clanged open and the stokers hurled shovel load after shovel load of coal onto the fire. The deck thudded with the sound of running feet. Fairfax relaxed a little when he saw the slightest of smiles on the captain's lips. Wilkes was a hard man to serve under at any time, gruff and bad-tempered at being passed over so often for command. Sixty-two years old and seemingly doomed to remain forever behind his desk as chairman of the Lighthouse Board. Only the outbreak of war had saved him from that. Dispatched to Fernando Po to bring back this veteran wooden steamer to the Philadelphia Naval Yard, he had violated his orders as soon as they had reached Florida and heard about the search that was going on. He never for an instant considered going to the navy yard, not while two traitors were still at large! He needed no orders to apprehend them—just as he had needed no orders from his superiors in the long-gone days when he explored and mapped the frozen Antarctic wilderness. He had little faith in the official chain of command and was always happier working alone.

The deck vibrated as the screw turned and a small wave foamed at the bow. Fairfax had his glass pointed at the approaching ship, hesitated to speak until he was absolutely sure.

"That is the *Trent*, sir, I know her lines well. And it is just as you said, eleven-forty, just before noon." There was more than a little awe in his voice; Wilkes nodded.

"Our English cousins are good at punctuality, Lieutenant. They are not good at much else." He had been a fourteen-year-old midshipman when the British *Shannon* had half destroyed the first ship he ever sailed in, the *Chesapeake*. Captain Lawrence, mortally wounded by musket fire, had died in his arms. He had never forgotten the dying man's last words—"Don't give up the ship." Yet despite the captain's order the colors had been struck and the ship had surrendered so that he, and the surviving crew members, ended up in a filthy British jail. He had never lost his hatred of the British since then.

"Hoist the flag," he ordered. "As soon as they can see it signal her to stop engines and prepare for boarding."

The helmsman brought the ship about in a smooth turn until they were sailing on a parallel course close to the steam packet.

"She's not slowing, sir," Fairfax said.

"A solid shot across her bows should induce her master to take proper action."

Moments later the gun boomed out; the *Trent* had to have seen it but they chose to ignore it.

"Very well," Captain Wilkes said. "Fire the pivot gun."

This gun was loaded with an explosive shell that burst close beside the British packet's bow. As the white cloud of smoke dispersed the bow wave on the *Trent* died away as her engines stopped. Captain Wilkes nodded grim approval.

"Lower the boat, Lieutenant Fairfax. You will take a squad of marines with you, muskets and bayonets. Use them if needs be. You know whom we are looking for."

"I do indeed, sir."

Wilkes watched in silence as the oars dipped and the boat pulled smartly toward the other ship. He betrayed none of the doubts that racked him. The broken orders, the desperate pursuit, the guesses and decisions, were part of the past. But everything he had done would be worth it if the wanted men were aboard. If they weren't . . . He preferred not to think of the consequences.

As soon as the boarding ladder was dropped, Fairfax climbed up to the *Trent*'s deck. Wilkes could clearly see him talking to an officer there. Then he turned about to face the American warship and took a white kerchief from his sleeve.

Moved it in the agreed signal from chin to waist and back again.

They were aboard!

Eustin pushed through the cabin door and slammed it behind him.

"What is happening?" Madam Slidell asked. He just shook his head and ran across the cabin to the adjoining chamber, pushed into it.

"It's us—the Yankees are after us!" He stammered as he spoke, face pale with fear.

"Did they mention our names?"

"They did, Sir, said they were after John Slidell and William Murray Mason. Didn't mention me nor Macfarland. But the officer, he did talk some about you gentlemen's assistants so they know that we're aboard."

Slidell did not like this. He rubbed at his big, red nose angrily, stomped the length of the cabin and back. "They just can't do this, stop a British ship at sea, board her—this sort of behavior—it cannot be done."

JOHN SLIDELL   WILLIAM MURRAY MASON

"Easy to say, John," Mason said. "But as I live and breathe it sure looks like it has been done. Now we must think of the papers we are carrying, our warrants—the letters from Jefferson Davis. All the letters to the English and Scotch shipyards about the privateers they are building for us. Remember that we also have personal letters to the Queen and Louis Napoleon. They must not be taken!"

"Throw them overboard!" Slidell said.

"Too late for that—there is the good possibility that they would float, be seen. We need a better plan. And I have it." The first fear was gone and Mason was his old and arrogant self again, brushing the back of his hand across his gray, bushy brows in a gesture long familiar to his fellow senators in Washington.

"John, you will stay here with your family and buy us time—a holding action."

"Why?"

"Because I know what to do with the papers. Give yours to Eustin immediately. Macfarland, get to my cabin and get the lot. We will meet in the mail room. Go!"

They went. Mason paused before he followed them, waiting as Slidell threw papers onto the bed in a flurry of activity. "You must think of something, stall them somehow—you are a politician so that pontification, obfuscation and filibustering should come naturally. And lock this door behind me. I am well acquainted with the Mail Officer, and am aware of the fact that he is a retired Royal Navy commander. A real old salt. We have talked long over whiskey and cigars and I have heard many a nautical tale. And he dislikes the Yankees as much as we do. I am sure that he will aid us."

He followed Eustin, heavily laden with the documents, out of the door and heard the key turn in the lock behind him. Eustin stumbled and a sheaf of papers fell to the companionway floor.

"Steady, man," Mason said. "No, leave them, I'll pick them up. Go ahead."

Macfarland was waiting at the Mail Room door, his face drawn and white.

"It's locked!"

"Bang on it, you idiot!" He thrust the papers he was carrying into the other man's arm and hammered on the door with his fist, stepped back when it opened.

"Why Mr. Mason—what is it?" The door was opened by an elderly man with white mutton-chop whiskers, his face tanned by a lifetime at sea.

"Yankees, sir. They have fired at this ship, stopped her, sir."

"But—why?"

"It is their expressed desire to makes us their prisoners, to seize us against our will, clap us in irons and carry us off to some foul cell. And perhaps even worse. But you can help us."

The officer's face tightened in grim anger. "Of course—but what can I do? If you hide—"

"That would be cowardly, and we would be found." Mason seized a handful of papers and held them out. "It is not our fate that can be altered. But here are our credentials, our documents, our secrets. It would be disaster if the Yankees seized them. Would you preserve them for us?"

"Of course. Bring them inside."

He led the way across the room to a massive safe, took a key from his pocket and unlocked it.

"Put them in here, with the government post and specie."

When this was done, the safe door swung shut and was locked. The Mail Officer returned the key to his pocket and patted it.

"Gentlemen, though I am retired now I have never turned from my duty as a naval officer. I am now a bulldog in your defense. Threats of death will not sway me. I will keep this key in my pocket and it will not come out until we are in safe harbor in England. They must pass over my body before they enter this room. Your papers are as safe as the letters of the Royal Mail."

"I thank you, sir. You are an officer and a gentleman."

"I am but doing my duty . . ." He looked up at the sound of muffled shouting from the deck above, and the march of heavy boots. "I must lock the door."

"Hurry," Mason said. "And we must get to the cabin before the bluebellies do."

"I must protest this action, protest it strongly," Captain James Moir said. "You have fired on a British ship, halted her at sea at gunpoint, piracy—"

"This is not piracy, Captain," Fairfax broke in. "My country is at war and I am diligent in her service, sir. You have informed me that the two traitors, Mason and Slidell, are aboard this vessel. You will see that I am unarmed. I ask only to satisfy myself of their presence."

"And then?"

The American did not respond, knowing full well that anything he said would only add to the English captain's seething anger. This situation was too delicate, too laden with the possibility of international complications, for him to make any mistakes. The captain would have to decide for himself.

"Midshipman!" Moir snapped, turning his back rudely on the lieutenant. "Take this person below. Show him to the cabin of his countrymen."

Fairfax contained his own anger at this ungentlemanly behavior and followed the lad belowdecks. The steam packet was spacious and comfortable. Dark wood paneling lined the companionway and there were brass fittings on the cabin doors. The midshipman pointed to the nearest one.

"This will be it, sir. American gentleman name of Slidell, him and his family."

"Family?"

"Wife, sir, and son. Three daughters."

Fairfax hesitated only for an instant. The presence of Slidell's family made no difference; there could be no going back. He knocked loudly.

"John Slidell—are you there?"

He could hear whispered voices through the door, people moving about. He tried the handle. It was locked.

"I call to you again, sir. I am Lieutenant Fairfax of the United States Navy. I call upon you to open this door at once."

Silence was his only answer. He hammered again on the door so that it shook in its frame. It did not open and there was still no response.

"The responsibility lies with you, Slidell. I am a military officer doing his duty. I have orders to follow and follow them I will."

When there was still no response Fairfax turned and stamped angrily away, the midshipman scurrying ahead as he went back on deck. A group of passengers had come on deck as well and stared at him as he crossed to the rail and leaned over to shout his orders down to the boat.

"Sergeant—I want your men up here at once. All of them."

"I protest!" Captain Moir called out.

"Noted," Fairfax said turning his back on the man, treating the captain just as he had been treated.

Heavy boots slammed on the decking as the blue-clad marines scrambled aboard.

"Right shoulder . . . shift!" the sergeant bellowed and the muskets slammed into position.

"Sergeant, have your men fix their bayonets," was Fairfax's next command. He needed as strong a show of force as possible, hoping to avoid any untoward incidents this way. The sergeant shouted the commands and sharp steel glittered in the sunlight. The watching sailors shuffled back at the sight of it: even the captain was silent now. Only the Southern passengers who had now come on deck displayed their feelings.

"Pirates!" one of the men shouted as he shook his fist. "Murderous Yankee bastards." Others joined the shouting and started forward.

"Stop there!" Lieutenant Fairfax ordered. "Sergeant—have your men prepare to fire if these people get any closer."

This threat damped down the Southern enthusiasm. There were muttered complaints as they moved slowly back from the leveled bayonets. Fairfax nodded.

"See you stay that way. I'll take the corporal and two men below, Sergeant."

Marine boots thundered on the steps, stamped down the passageway. Fairfax led them forward, pointed to the cabin door.

"Use your musket butt, Corporal. Don't break it down yet—but I damn well want them to know that we are here."

Once, twice, thrice, the butt slammed thunderously on the thin wood before Fairfax waved him aside, called out loudly.

"I have armed marines here and they will do their duty if this door is not unlocked at once. I understand there are women in there so I do not wish to use violence. But I will use force to enter this cabin—if the door is not unsealed instantly. The choice is yours."

The heavy breathing of the waiting men was the only sound to break the silence. Fairfax felt his patience was at an end and had just opened his mouth to give the order when there was a rattling at the door. It opened a scant inch—then stopped.

"Ready your weapons," Fairfax ordered. "Use them only if we meet resistance. Follow me." He threw the door wide and went in. Halted abruptly at the sound of the shrill screaming.

"Stop right there!" the angry woman called out, holding the three girls to her ample bosom. A boy was at her side, shivering with fear.

"I mean you no harm," Fairfax said. The screaming died away to mournful sobbing. "Are you Mrs. Slidell?" Her answer was only a quick, angry nod. He looked about the luxurious cabin, saw the other door and pointed toward it. "It is your husband I wish to address. Is he there?"

John Slidell had his ear pressed hard against the panel in the door. He turned as there was a soft knock on the door across the cabin from him that led to the companionway. He hurried to it, whispered hoarsely.

"Yes?"

"It's us, John—unlock this thing at once."

Mason pushed his way in, Eustin and Macfarland hurrying after him. "What is happening?" Mason asked.

"They are inside with my family. A naval officer, armed marines, we delayed them as long as we could. The papers . . . ?"

"Are in safe hands. Your delaying action was vital for our one small victory in this battle at sea. The Mail Officer, a retired Royal Navy commander as I told you, has taken the papers under his personal control. Locked them away and says he will not take out the key to his safe until he sees England's shores. He even said that threat of death itself would not sway him. Our papers are as safe as the letters in the Royal Mail."

"Good. Let us go in there now. My family has suffered enough indignity as it is."

The sobbing died away when the connecting door opened. A marine pointed his bayonet and stepped forward; Lieutenant Fairfax waved him back.

"There is no need for violence—as long as the traitors obey orders."

Fairfax watched coldly as the four men entered the room. The first man through called out to the huddle of women.

"L'est-ce que tout va bien?"

"Oui, ça va."

"Are you John Slidell?" Lieutenant Fairfax said. His only answer was a curt nod. "Mr. Slidell it is my understanding that you have been appointed as the special Rebel commissioner to France . . ."

"Your language is insulting, young man. I am indeed a member of the government of the Confederacy."

The lieutenant ignored his protestations, turned to the other politician. "And you will be James Murray Mason sent to the United Kingdom on the same mission. You will both accompany me, your assistants as well . . ."

"You have no right to do this!" Mason boomed out.

"Every right, sir. You as a former member of the American government know that very well. You have all rebelled against your flag and country. You are all traitors and are all under arrest. You will come with me."

It was not an easy thing to do. Slidell had an endless and emotional conversation in French with his Louisiana Creole wife, filled with tearful interruptions by his daughters. Their son fell back against the wall, pale and trembling, looking ready to faint. Mason made a thundering protest that no one listened to. The matter continued this way until almost an hour had passed and there was still no end in sight. Fairfax's anger grew until he shouted aloud for silence.

"This most grave matter is descending into a carnival and I will not allow it. You will all follow my orders. Corporal— have your marines accompany these two men, Eustin and Macfarland, to their cabins. There they will each pack one bag of their clothing and possessions and will be taken on deck at once. Have them ferried across to the *San Jacinto*. When the boat returns the other prisoners will be waiting on deck."

The logjam was broken—but it was mid-afternoon before the transfers were completed. Mason and Slidell were escorted up to the deck, but would not leave the ship until all their personal effects were packed and brought to them. In addition to their clothes they insisted upon taking the thousands of cigars that they had purchased in Cuba. While these were being transferred Captain Moir insisted that they would need dozens of bottles of sherry, pitchers and basins and other conveniences of the toilet that would not be found aboard a man-of-war. There was even more delay as these items were found and brought on deck.

It was after four in the afternoon before the prisoners and their belongings had been transferred to the *San Jacinto*. The warship raised steam and turned west toward the American shore.

When Captain Moir on the *Trent* had seen his remaining passengers safely in their cabins he mounted to the bridge and ordered his ship under way again. The American warcraft was only a dot on the horizon now and he had to resist the urge to shake his fist in her direction.

"This has been a bad day's work," he said to his first officer. "England will not be humiliated by this rebellious colony. Something has begun here that will not be easily stopped."

He did not realize how very prophetic his words would prove to be.

THE EXECUTIVE MANSION, WASHINGTON

NOVEMBER 15, 1861

Wind-driven rain splattered against the office window; a cold draft of air whistled in around its ancient frame. John Hay, Abraham Lincoln's secretary, added more coal to the fire and stirred it until the flames blazed high. The President looked up from his paper-strewn desk and nodded approvingly.

"A cold day, John—but not half as chill, I believe, as last evening at General McClellan's home."

"That man, sir, something must be done—" Hay was spluttering with rage.

"There is very little to be done that I can think of. Even generals cannot be shot for impoliteness."

"This was more than impoliteness—it was a downright insult to his Commander-in-Chief. While we sat in that room waiting for his return he *did* come back and went directly upstairs. Refusing to see you, the President!"

"I am indeed the President, yes, but not an absolute monarch, not quite yet. And not even an absolute President, since you will remember, as the Democratic politicians are so fond of reminding me, that I was elected with a minority of the popular vote. At times it appears that I have more opposition in Congress than I do in Richmond. Dealing with the quarrelsome Senate and House is very close to a full-time job."

Lincoln ran his fingers through his thick mane of hair, looked out gloomily at the driving rain. "You must remember

14

that first things come first—and the firstest thing of all is this terrible conflict that we are so deeply engaged in. In order to win this unhappy war I must rely on the generals and soldiers. It is a time for a great deal of patience and an even greater amount of sagacity—particularly with this young McClellan, General-in-Chief who is also Commander of the Army of the Potomac, which stands between this city and the enemy forces."

"Stands is indeed the correct word. An army which drills and drills and gets more troops—and goes absolutely nowhere at a glacial speed."

"Perfectly true. This war seems to have ground to a halt. It has been six months since the Rebels captured Fort Sumter and hostilities began. Since then only the success of the blockading squadrons gives me cheer. This year began with feelings of enmity and apprehension. We are building our army—and the Seces-

PRESIDENT LINCOLN

sionists are doing the same. Since the battles of Bull Run and Ball's Bluff there have only been minor skirmishes. Yet the tension continues to build. This war will not end easily and I fear the dreadful battles that are sure to come." He looked up as the office door opened.

"Mr. President, I'm sorry to interrupt you," his other secretary, John Nicolay, said. "But the Secretary of the Navy is here."

Abraham Lincoln was tired, very tired. The papers on his desk and filling its pigeonholes multiplied daily. For every problem that was resolved two more seemed to spring up in its place. He had rested his hand on his head, and his long fingers were heedlessly rumpling his hair. He was glad of the distraction. "It's no interruption, John. Send him through."

"And the reports are here that you asked for—as well as these letters for you to sign."

Lincoln sighed and pointed at the cluttered pigeonholes in the tall desk. "In with the rest, Nico, and I promise that they shall have my attention."

He stood and stretched wearily, shuffling past the stern portrait of Andrew Jackson and over to the marble fireplace. He had his coattails lifted and was warming himself before the fire when Hay left and Secretary Welles came in; the President pointed at the paper he was carrying.

"I imagine that is a dispatch of some importance that you are holding in your hand," Lincoln said.

Gideon Welles, the Secretary of the Navy, hid a shrewd brain behind his abundant chin whiskers and exotic wig. "Some exciting and interesting news has just arrived by military telegraph from Hampton Roads." He started to pass over the sheet of paper but Lincoln held up a halting hand.

"Please then, tell me about it and save my weary eyes."

"Simple enough to do, Mr. President. The screw sloop *San Jacinto* stopped in the port at Hampton Roads to refuel and the captain sent this message. They have Mason and Slidell aboard."

"Now that is the kind of good news that is pretty rare around here." The battered maplewood armchair creaked as Lincoln settled into it and leaned back, tenting his long fingers together. "I do believe that we will all sleep the better these nights with the knowledge that those two are not conspiring right across Europe, causing fierce kinds of mischief."

"I'm afraid that the situation is not all that simple. As you know, since they escaped from the South and ran the blockade in the *Gordon*, they have been one step ahead of us all of the way. First in the Bahamas, then in Cuba. We have had a small fleet of ships tracking them down."

"And now they have succeeded."

"Indeed they have. However there is a complication. The rebels were not arrested on land, or taken from a Confederate vessel. That would have been perfectly legal during the present state of war. It appears however that they were taken from a British mail packet, the *Trent*. Which was stopped at sea."

Lincoln thought deeply about this, then sighed. Like dragon's teeth his troubles did multiply. "We must send for Seward. The Secretary of State will want to know about this at once. But how could this happen? Weren't there orders issued about halting neutral ships at sea?"

"There were. But the captain of the *San Jacinto* never received them—and it appears that he had different orders altogether. He has been at sea some time and was supposed to return with his ship from Fernando Po, bring it to the navy yard. Nothing more. He must have heard of the chase when he returned and refueled. Since then he has proceeded on his own."

"It shows an independence of spirit—though perhaps a bit misplaced."

"Yes. I am given to understand that Captain Wilkes has a very independent spirit. In fact some in the navy call it insubordination and bad temper."

The door opened and Seward came in.

"Read this, William," the President said. "Then we will decide what must be done."

The Secretary of State quickly scanned the dispatch, frowning as he did so. Always a cautious man, and one not given to precipitate decisions, he read it again, more slowly this time. Then tapped it with his index finger.

"Two things strike me at once. Firstly these traitors must be secured safely under lock and key. We have them now and we do not want to lose them. I suggest, Gideon, that you telegraph the *San Jacinto*'s commander that as soon as his vessel has refueled he is to proceed at once to New York City. Further instructions will await him there."

Lincoln nodded. "I agree. While he is making his passage we can give serious thought as to what we should do with these men now that we have them in our hands."

"I am in complete agreement as well," Welles said, then hurried to give the order.

There was a sudden loud barking from under the President's desk and Welles started. Lincoln smiled at him.

"Have no fear—this dog does not bite," he said as the boy burst from his hiding place, grinning from ear to ear as he hugged his father's long legs.

"Our Willie is a great lad," Lincoln said as the boy ran happily from the room. "Some day he will be a great man—I feel that in my bones." His smile faded away. "But those same bones are feeling a certain disquiet over this *Trent* affair." The President's first pleasure at hearing the news now gave way to a feeling of dark premonition. "I can well imagine what your second consideration is going to be. What repercussions must we look forward to when word reaches London? Our friends the British are already bothered about this war of rebellion, as they tell us quite often."

"That was indeed my very thought. Troubles will have to be faced as they arise. But at least we have the rebel troublemakers now."

"We do indeed. Two birds in the hand. I imagine that diplomatic complaints and discussions will proceed at their usual snail-like pace. Protests carried across the Atlantic by ship, responses sent back by even slower ones. Diplomacy always takes time. Perhaps if enough time passes with questions and answers and replies, why the matter might soon be forgotten."

"I pray that you are correct, Mr. President. But as you are well aware there is already much agitation among the British about the present conflict. They side with the rebellious states and bitterly resent the disruption in cotton shipments caused by our blockade. There are reports that some Lancashire mills are closing. I am afraid that this country of ours is not very popular at this time, in Britain, or even elsewhere on the continent."

"There are a lot worse things on the earth than not being popular. Like the story about the rabbit who got angry at the old hounddog and he went and got all the other rabbits to get together with him and give the hounddog a good hiding. Not that the hounddog minded—he hadn't et that well in years."

"The English are not rabbits, Mr. Lincoln."

"Indeed they are not. But this particular old hounddog is going to worry about trouble only when it comes. Meanwhile two very painful thorns have been removed from our hide. We must now find a secure container to put them in, lock them away out of sight and then, hopefully, forget all about them. Perhaps this entire matter might blow over and be forgotten as well."

"God blast and damn every one of those poxy Yankees!"

Lord Palmerston, the Prime Minister of Britain, stamped the length of his office, then back again. The dispatch from Southampton was lying on his desk. He seized it up and read it again; his large nostrils flared with rage, big as cannon muzzles. His lordship's temper was not very good at the best of times; now it was fully on the boil. Lord John Russell just sat quietly and waited, preferring not to be noticed. Alas, this was not to be.

Lord Palmerston crumpled the sheet, hurled it from him, turned on Russell and stabbed out a finger that trembled with rage. "You are the Foreign Minister, which means that this matter is your responsibility. Now, sir—what do you intend to do about it?"

"Protest, of course. My secretary is already preparing a draft. I will then consult with you—"

"Not bloody good enough. Give those rebellious Yankees an inch and they'll want an ell. What we must do is get them by the scruff and give them a sound shaking. Like a terrier with a rat. This has been an infamous deed that must be answered instantly——and with great firmness. I shall remove you of the responsibility and shall take care of this matter myself. It is my firm intention to get off a dispatch that will blow the Yankees right out of the water."

"I am sure that there are precedents, sir. And then we must consult with the Queen . . ."

"Damn the precedents and—of course, yes, we surely must bring this matter to the attention of the Queen. Though I dread the thought of another meeting with her so soon. The last time I was at Buckingham Palace she was in the middle of one of those screaming fits, flying through the corridors. At least this nasty bit of news will draw her attention. But I am sure that she will be even more than outraged about this than we are, doesn't like those Americans at all."

"There would be no need to meet with the Queen if we were more circumspect. Perhaps it would not be so wise as to fire all of our batteries at once at the Yankees? There is a case to be made that we first go through the correct channels. Begin with a protest, then a reply. Then if they don't accede to our polite requests we forget all kindness and sweet reason. We stop asking them. We tell them what they must do."

"Perhaps, perhaps," Palmerston muttered. "I will take that under consideration when the cabinet convenes. It has become imperative that we have a cabinet meeting at once."

The secretary knocked lightly, then came in.

"Admiral Milne, sir. He would like to know if he could see you."

"Of course, show him in."

Lord Palmerston stood and took the admiral's hand when he entered. "I imagine that this is no courtesy call, Admiral?"

"Hardly, sir. May I sit?"

"Of course. The wound—?"

"Well healed, but I'm still not as strong as I should be." He sat and came straight to the point. "I have been too long on the shore, gentlemen. This sudden development has forcefully reminded me of that fact."

"The *Trent*?" Russell said.

"The *Trent* indeed! A ship flying British colors—stopped at sea by an alien warship . . . words do fail me."

"Not I sir, not I!" Palmerston's anger surged again. "I see this action through your eyes and understand your passion. You have fought honorably for your country, have been wounded in her service in China. You are an Admiral of the Fleet in the most powerful navy the world has ever seen. And this matter, I know how you must feel . . ."

Milne had found his words now, shook with anger as they tumbled out. "Humiliation, Your Lordship. Humiliation and rage. Those raggle-taggle colonists must be taught a lesson. They cannot fire on a British ship, a Royal Mail packet by God, and not face the consequences of this despicable act."

"What do you think the consequences should be?" Palmerston asked.

"That is not for me to say. It is for you gentlemen to decide the proper course to take in these matters. But I want you to know that every manjack in the Royal Navy is behind you, every foot of the way."

"You feel they share your outrage?"

"Not feel—*know!* From the lowest matelot on the gun deck to the highest rank in the admiralty there will be disgust and anger. And the keen desire to follow where you lead."

Palmerston nodded slowly. "Thank you, Admiral for your frankness. You have given new fiber to our determination. The Cabinet will meet at once. Be assured that action will be taken this very day. And I am sure that your return to active service will be appreciated and your offer accepted."

"There is an officer from the *Trent* here, sir," the secretary said as soon as the admiral had been ushered out. "He is seeking instruction as to the dispersal of certain documents he is holding."

"What documents?"

"It seems that he took under his care all of the papers and documents that Messrs Mason and Slidell wished to conceal from the American government. They were safely concealed and now he wishes instruction as to their disposal."

"Capital! Have them in and we shall see just why the Yankees were in such a hurry to nobble these two men."

As the *San Jacinto* steamed north toward New York City the weather deteriorated. Captain Wilkes stood on the weather deck, rain lashing against his oilskins. The sea was getting up and there was snow now mixed in with the rain. He turned as Lieutenant Fairfax came out on deck.

"Engineer reports that we are taking in some water, sir. Seams working in this cross sea."

"Pumps holding?"

"Very well, Captain. But he wants to reduce the revolutions to ease the strain on the hull. This ship has seen a lot of service."

"Indeed she has. All right, 80 revolutions—but no less than that. Our orders are quite explicit."

At the slower speed the leaking abated so much that the pumping could be stopped for a few minutes so that the water level could be sounded in the well. There proved to have been a great improvement. Nevertheless the wind was getting up and the *San Jacinto* rolled heavily. It was not a comfortable voyage. By the time she arrived in New York visibility was almost zero in the blinding snowstorm, now mixed with lashing hail. Her arrival had been expected and she was met by a tugboat in the Narrows.

His face buried in the collar of his greatcoat, Captain Wilkes watched from the bridge. Lines were thrown and the tug was secured to their side. Two uniformed men climbed the rope ladder with some difficulty, then waited on deck as their leather bags were passed up to them. Lieutenant Fairfax reported to the bridge.

"They are Federal marshals, Captain. With orders to report to you."

"Good. See that they are taken to my cabin. How are our prisoners?"

"Protesting mightily about the weather and the conditions of their quarters."

"That is of no importance. Are they secure under lock and key?"

"They are, sir. With guards outside their door right around the clock."

"See that it remains that way."

The captain went to his cabin where he awaited the Federal marshals. They stamped in, big, burly men; snow melted on their heavy coats.

"You have new orders for me?"

The marshal in charge passed over the leather wallet. Wilkes took out the document and scanned it briefly. "You know what these orders are?"

"We do, Captain. We are to remain aboard and mount a close guard over your prisoners. Then this ship is to proceed directly to Fort Warren in Boston harbor. The only concern of the Navy Department was that you might not have enough coal."

"My bunkers are nearly full. We sail at once."

Once out of the shelter of the harbor the full strength of the storm hit them. Waves crashed over the decks and water foamed in the scuppers. The *San Jacinto* rolled and pitched so badly that, when the waves passed under her stern, the screw lifted briefly out of the water. It was a hard night even for the veteran sailors; disaster for the landsmen. The four prisoners were devastatingly ill with seasickness, as were the Federal marshals. Slidell groaned aloud, praying that their vessel either arrive in safe harbor—or sink. Anything to end the torment.

It was not until the afternoon of the second day that the storm-battered *San Jacinto* sailed into the smoother waters of Boston harbor and tied up at the wharf on Fort Warren. The exhausted prisoners were led away by an armed squad of soldiers, the Federal marshals stumbling in their wake. Lieutenant Fairfax supervised the unloading of their luggage and their supplies from the *Trent*. Fort Warren was a secure prison, the fort's high stone walls running right around the tiny island. When Fairfax returned to the ship he brought the day's newspapers to the captain's cabin.

"The entire country is jubilant, Sir. They hail you as the savior of the nation."

Wilkes did not reveal the pleasure he felt at this news. He had only done his duty as he saw it—though the naval authorities might not have seen it in quite the same way. But nothing succeeds like success. He almost smiled at the good news. His superior officers would find it hard, in the light of public jubilation, to find a way for him to be reproved for his actions. He read the headlines with grim satisfaction.

"Apparently, Lieutenant Fairfax, there is no love lost in this country for our prisoners. Look here. Mason is called a knave, a coward and a bully ... dear, dear. And even more—a pompous snob as well as being a conceited and shallow traitor."

Fairfax was also reading the papers. "Slidell is treated the same way here in *The Globe*. They see him as cold, clever, selfish, rapacious and corrupt."

"And we thought we were just seizing a brace of traitorous

politicians. I wonder if the English newspapers will see this matter in the same light?"

"I very much doubt that, Captain."

Lord Palmerston read the London newspapers as he waited for his Cabinet to assemble, nodding with grim agreement at the bombast and rage.

"I concur with every word, gentlemen, every word," he said, waving a handful of the journals across the Cabinet table. "The country is with us, the public outraged. We must act with deliberate speed lest these rebellious colonials believe their cowardly act will go unremarked. Now—have you all had a chance to look at the documents from the *Trent*?"

"I have gone through them quite carefully," William Gladstone said. "Except, of course, for the personal communications for the Queen and the French Emperor."

Palmerston nodded. "These will be sent on."

"As for the instructions to the dockyards and other documents, they are full proof of the legitimacy of these ambassadors. I know not how the French will respond—but I for one am amazed at the Yankee gall in this seaborne capture."

"I share your feelings," Palmerston said.

"Then your proposed action, my lord?" Russell asked.

"After due consideration, and in the light of public support, I feel that something drastic must be done, firm action taken. I have a draft of the dispatch here before me," Palmerston answered, tapping the letter on the desk in front of him. "Originally I thought that a protest through normal diplomatic channels would suffice, which is why I have called you together. But I have since come to believe that this universal outpouring of rage cannot be ignored. We must speak for the country—and speak with most righteous indignation. I have prepared a dispatch for the American government, and have couched it in the strongest terms. I have given instructions that the mail steamer is to be held in Southampton awaiting the arrival of this communication. The Queen will see it today and will undoubtedly agree with every word. When she approves—then off it will go."

"Sir?"

"Yes Mr. Gladstone," Palmerston responded, smiling. William Gladstone, his Chancellor of the Exchequer, was a rock of support in trying times.

"It is my pleasure to inform you that my wife and I are dining with the Queen and Prince Albert this evening. Perhaps I might then present her with the dispatch and impress upon her the unanimity of her government in this matter."

"Splendid!" Palmerston was relieved, almost wanted to pat Gladstone on the back, pleased that he could avoid a meeting with the Queen. "We are all in your debt for this undertaking. The memorandum is yours."

Though Gladstone left the cabinet meeting in the best of humors, eager to be of some aid in his party and his country's service, he lost a good deal of his enthusiasm when he took the time to read the document he had so readily volunteered to endorse. Later that evening, as their carriage rattled across the cobblestones and through the entrance to Buckingham Palace, his wife noted with some concern the dour set to his features.

"Is there something wrong, William? I have not seen you look so grim since we were in that dreadful Kingdom of Naples."

"I must apologize. I am most sorry to bring my troubles with me." He took and pressed her gloved hand. "As in Napoli it is affairs of state that disturb me so. But we shall not let it spoil this evening. I know how much you have been looking forward to this dinner with Her Majesty."

"As indeed I have." Her voice broke a bit as she spoke. Hesitantly she asked, "The Queen has, I sincerely hope, been very well of late? There has been talk, not that I believe it of course, about her, well . . . state of mind. After all, she is the granddaughter of Mad King George."

"You must not concern yourself my dear with rumors worded about by idle riff-raff. She is, after all, the Queen."

They were shown into the sitting room, where they bowed and curtsied to Queen Victoria.

"Albert will be with us momentarily, Mr. Gladstone. He is resting now. I am afraid that the dear man has been terribly fagged for some time."

"I am devastated to hear that, ma'am. But I am sure that he is getting the best of care."

"Of course! Sir James Clarke sees him daily. Today he prescribed ether and Hoffman's drops. But do help yourself. There is sherry on the sideboard if you wish."

"Thank you, ma'am." Indeed he did wish for he was not at ease; he patted his chest where the document resided in the inner pocket. He was just pouring the sherry when Prince Albert came in.

"Mr. Gladstone, I wish a very good evening to you."

"And to you, sir. Health and happiness."

Happiness the Prince certainly had, with his adoring wife and ample family. But he could certainly use every wish for good health—since he looked decidedly ill. The years had not been kind to him. The elegant and graceful youth was now paunchy, balding, prematurely middle-aged. His skin was pale and damp, and there were dark circles under his eyes. He held shakily to the arms of the chair as he dropped into it. The Queen looked at him worriedly but he waved away her concern.

"It is the lung congestion you know, it comes and goes. It will be much better after a good dinner. Please, do not be concerned."

With this reassurance the Queen turned to other matters. "Mr. Gladstone, my secretary informs me that there are affairs of state that you wish to address to us."

"A dispatch that the Prime Minister intends to send to the Americans, ma'am, about the *Trent* Affair. With your approval, of course. But I am sure that it can wait until after we dine."

"Perhaps. Nevertheless we shall see it now. I am most disturbed about this matter—more than disturbed, horrified I should say. We do not take lightly the fact that a British ship has not only been stopped, but boarded at sea."

She pointed to the Prince Consort when Gladstone drew out the letter. "Albert will read it. I would not even consider writing a letter without consulting him. He is of the greatest support to me in this and many other matters."

Lord Russell bowed in agreement, well aware of the common knowledge that the Queen would not even dress without consulting him. He passed the envelope to Prince Albert.

The Prince unfolded the sheet of paper and turned it to face the light, then read aloud.

" 'As regards the matter of the forced removal of four passengers from a British vessel on the high seas. Her Majesty's government are unwilling to imagine that the United States government will not of their own accord be anxious to afford ample reparation for this act of folly. The Queen's ministers expect the following. One. The liberation of all four captured gentlemen and delivery to the Lord Lyons, the British ambassador in Washington. Two. An apology for the insult offered to the British flag. Three . . .' "

He coughed deeply. "Excuse me. This is very strong language and there is more like this I am afraid. Most strongly worded."

"As it should be," the Queen said with marked indignation. "I do not admire the Americans—and I despise that Mr. Seward who has made so many untruthful remarks about this country. But, still, if you feel there are changes needed, *Liebchen*."

Albert's drawn face was drawn into a quick smile at the German term of endearment. He believed that his wife was *Vortrefflichste*, a matchless woman, mother, queen. Moody perhaps, one day screaming at him, the next most affectionate. And he felt the need to advise her at all times. Only his ill health had prevented him from being of greater aid to her in her unceasing labors as ruling monarch. Now this. Palmerston had made his demands in a most bellicose and threatening manner. Any head of state would be greatly offended by the manner as well as the message.

"Not so much changes," he said, "for the Prime Minister is quite correct in his demands. An international crime has been committed, there is no doubt about that. But perhaps the captain of the American ship is to blame for the incident. We must determine exactly what has happened, and why, before threats are made. This matter must not be allowed to get out of hand. Therefore I believe that perhaps some alterations are in order. Not so much in the contents but in the tone. A sovereign country cannot be ordered about like a willful child." He climbed to his feet shakily. "I think perhaps I should write a bit on it now. At the present I am not hungry. I will eat later if you will excuse me."

"Are you not well?" the Queen asked, half-rising from her chair.

"A slight malaise, nothing, please do not let me the dinner disturb."

Prince Albert climbed shakily to his feet, trying to smile. He started forward—then appeared to stumble. Bending at the knees, collapsing. Striking his head sharply on the floor.

"Albert!" the Queen cried.

Gladstone was instantly at his side, turning the Prince, touching the pale skin.

"He is unconscious, ma'am, but breathing quite steadily. Perhaps the physician . . ."

The Queen needed no encouragement in ordering assistance to her dear Albert. Servants appeared in great numbers, rushed to find a rug, covered his legs, put a pillow beneath his head, searched for a stretcher, sent a footman running for Sir James. The Queen wrung her hands and was beyond speech now. Gladstone looked down at the unconscious Albert and noticed for the first time that the dispatch was still clutched in his tightened fist.

"If I may, ma'am," he whispered, as he knelt and gently pulled it free. He hesitated. This was neither the time nor the place. Nevertheless he felt that he was forced to mention it.

"This dispatch, tomorrow perhaps?"

"No! Take it away. Look what it has contrived to do! The wretched thing has done this to my dear Albert. It disturbed him, you saw that. In his delicate state it was just too much for him. It is the Americans again, this is all their fault. Poor man, he was so concerned . . . take it from my sight. Do what you will with it. At last—the doctor!"

There was no further mention of dinner. The Queen exited with the Prince. When the door had closed behind her Gladstone called for their coats and asked for his carriage to be brought around.

It had not been a good evening.

The dispatch would go out just as it had been written.

The die had been cast.

ARMS OF WAR

When the presidential train had stopped to fill the engine's water tanks in Jersey City, the latest messages and reports were put aboard: the President's personal secretary brought them to him. Abraham Lincoln, away from the constant press and demands of the White House, stared out at the frosty winter beauty of the Hudson River. A radiant coal stove kept the cold at bay. Simon Cameron, the Secretary of War, dozed in the seat opposite. This was a peaceful refuge from the White House where favor seekers besieged him every moment of the day. He was relaxed and at ease for the first time in weeks. Even the sight of the thick bundle of paper did not disturb him.

"I see that the war still follows me everywhere, Nicolay."

"The war with the Secesh and with the Congress. I sometimes think that the latter is worse. The congressmen in . . ."

"Spare me the politicians for the moment. Shot and shell seem kindlier."

John Nicolay nodded agreement and shuffled through the new reports that Hay passed over to him. "Now here is one that should please you. The landings on Tybee Island in the Savannah River were most successful. The commander says that Fort Pulaski will be attacked next. Once that is reduced, Savannah will surely be taken. Next, our undercover agent in Norfolk reports that more armor plate for the *Merrimack* has arrived. Guns as well. They've renamed the ship CSS *Virginia*."

"We won't worry about her for awhile yet. But see that a copy of the report gets to the Monitor people. That should keep them working around the clock."

The President leafed through the newspapers. The press

30

seemed to be uniformly against him and his administration these days. The abolitionists were in full bay after him again—anything short of killing every Southerner and freeing every slave was a worthless goal. An item caught his eye and he smiled as he read it, then smacked the paper with his hand.

"Now this is real journalism, Nicolay. Our guardians of law and order have made a famous victory on a steamer at Baltimore. Listen . . . 'Their suspicions were aroused by a lady who appeared nervous and desirous of avoiding them. When her reticule was searched a quantity of gloves, stockings and letters were found, all intended to the South. As well a small boy was discovered to be carrying a quantity of quinine. Both were allowed to pass after their cargo had been confiscated.' Our protectors never sleep."

By the time they had gone through the files the train was pulling into the West Point station, the locomotive's steam whistle announcing their arrival. Lincoln pulled on coat and scarf, clapped his stovepipe hat onto his head before descending to meet the army officers and foundry officials. Cameron and his secretaries followed. They all walked together to the ferry that would take them across the river to Cold Spring. It was a chill but brief crossing and carriages were waiting for them at the dock when they disembarked. The horses were stamping their hooves, with their breath rising like smoke in the still, cold air. A serious, frockcoated man stood beside the first carriage as they approached.

"Mr. President," Cameron said, "may I introduce Mr. Robert Parker Parrott, inventor and gunsmith, proprietor of the West Point Foundry."

Lincoln nodded as Parrott shook his hand, then Cameron's.

"A great pleasure, Mr. Lincoln, to have you visit my foundry and see for yourself what we are doing here."

"I could not refuse the opportunity, Mr. Parrott. My commanders cry for guns and more guns and their wishes must be respected."

"We are doing our best here to grant those wishes. I've prepared a test of our newly completed 300-pounder. If you find it agreeable we will go to the test site first—then on to the cannon works. I can assure you that this gun is the most impressive and powerful that I have ever built."

And indeed it was. Secured firmly to the massive cannon-testing platform, it was a black and ominous brute. Lincoln nodded in appreciation as he paced the length of the weapon and, despite his great height, he could barely see into the gun's muzzle to make out the lands and grooves of the rifling inside.

"Charged and loaded, Mr. President," Parrott said. "If you will retire a short distance away you will see what this gun can do."

When the party was safely out of range of any accident the command was given and the firing mechanism activated.

The ground shook with the strength of the explosion and, even with their hands clasped hard over their ears, the spectators found that the sound was deafening. An immense gout of flame seared from the muzzle and Lincoln, standing to the rear of the weapon, saw the pencil-like dark trace of the shell hurtle across the river. An instant later there was an explosion among the trees on the range on the other bank. Smoke billowed high among the splintered branches and some seconds later the sound of the blast reached their ears.

"An impressive sight, Mr. Parrott," Lincoln said, "and one that I shall never forget. Now you must tell me more about your work here—but in the warmth of the foundry if you please."

It was a short drive from the test site and they hurried into the beckoning heat that emanated from the roaring furnaces. An army lieutenant was waiting there; he saluted when they approached.

"General Ripley sent me ahead, Mr. President. He regrets that duties at West Point prevented him from joining you earlier. However he is on his way now."

Lincoln nodded. Brigadier General James W. Ripley was head of the Ordnance Department and was responsible not only for the production of weapons, but also for the introduction of new designs. At the President's insistence he had reluctantly agreed to leave his paperwork and join the party at the foundry.

With Parrott leading the way, the presidential inspection party toured the foundry. Work did not stop: the men laboring over the molten iron could not spare the time to even look up at their distinguished visitors. Cannon of all sizes filled the score of buildings, in all stages of production from rough castings to final assembly. All stamped with the initials WPF and RPP. West Point Foundry and Robert Parker Parrott. Lincoln slapped his hand against the cascabel of a 30-pounder.

"My engineers tell me that banding the breech of your guns is responsible for their success. Is that true?"

"In a sense, yes, but the matter is quite technical, Mr. President."

"Do not hesitate to inform me in detail, Mr. Parrott. You must remember that before I was a politician I was a surveyor and very keen on mathematics. I understand that rifling the cannon is the source of the current problems."

"You are completely correct, sir. Smoothbore cannon are now a thing of the past. The twisted rifling spins the shell as it emerges, giving far better accuracy and range. But this also causes problems. Rifled shells seal in the explosion far more than solid shot does, which is what causes the great increase in range. Alas, this greater pressure can also cause the gun to explode. For this reason an iron reinforcing ring is fitted around the breech to accommodate the higher pressure. Using rings in this way is not new. However my invention lies in the construction of a better and far stronger ring, as I shall now demonstrate. If you will, sir, over here."

The newly forged and rifled barrel of the 20-pounder rested on metal rollers, with its breech projecting to the side. At Parrott's signal two mighty blacksmiths took their tongs and seized a white-hot iron band from inside a roaring furnace. With skilled movements they slipped it over the breech of the waiting gun. It was only slightly larger than the gun and they grunted with effort as they struggled and hammered it into place.

"That's done it—start her turning!"

As the newly banded gun began to rotate, a hollow rod was pushed into the barrel of the gun and water pumped in to cool it from the inside.

"Metal expands when heated," Parrott explained. "That band is larger in circumference now than it was before heating. As you can see the water is cooling the breech and the band in turn. As the band cools it contracts evenly and grips the barrel tightly around its entire circumference. Previous to this the usual practice of banding reinforced cannon was not as efficient or as strong. The barrel would be gripped unevenly and in just a few spots. Barrels made in that fashion would be forced to use much smaller charges or they would have exploded."

"I am impressed. And how many of these new guns are you producing at this time?"

"At present we complete ten heavy guns every week. Along with two thousand shells for them."

"In your letter you said that you could increase that?"

"I can—and I will. With new furnaces and lathes I can expand within three months so that I will be able to produce at least twenty-five guns and seven thousand shells every week." Parrott hesitated a moment and looked disturbed. "The details have been worked out and are ready for your inspection. However, would it be possible . . . to talk to you in private?"

"Mr. Cameron and my secretaries share my every confidence."

Parrott was sweating now—and not from the foundry's heat. "I am sure that they do. But this is a matter of great secrecy, individuals . . ."

His voice died away and he glanced at the floor, struggling to compose himself. Lincoln stroked his beard in thought, then turned to Cameron and his secretaries. "Would you gentleman excuse us for a few moments."

With great relief Parrott led the President to his office and sealed the door behind them. As they crossed the room Lincoln stopped before a framed drawing on the wall. "Mr. Parrott, a moment if you please. What in tarnation is this incredible machine?"

"That is a copy of the drawing that accompanied a certain patent application. I make it a point of checking all patent applications that might be relevant to my work. I found this on a visit to London some years ago. In 1855 two gentlemen, named Cowen and Sweetlong, if memory serves me right, attempted to patent this armored fighting wagon."

"It appears to be formidable enough, bristling with cannon and spikes."

"But highly impractical, Mr. President. With all those guns and the weight of armorplate it would take a steam engine bigger than the wagon itself to make it move. I attempted to revise the design, with a single gun and lighter plating, but it still was not practical."

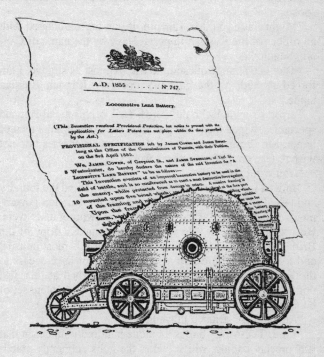

THE BRITISH LAND BATTERY

"Thank the Lord for that. War is hellish enough now without devilish designs like this to make it even worse. Though it might mean the end of all warfare if something like this appeared on the battlefield. But you said they would be impossible to build?"

"At the present time, yes. But steam engines are getting smaller and more powerful at the same time—and I have read of successful oil-fired engines. So I would not rule out the possibility that some day an armored battle wagon like this might be built."

"May that black and evil day never come. But you did not ask me here to discuss this strange device?"

Parrott looked worried again. When they were seated he spoke.

"Might I ask you, Mr. Lincoln, if you are acquainted with an officer of the Russian Imperial Navy by the name of Captain Schultz?"

"That is a strange question to ask. Almost as strange, I am forced to add, as the captain's not very Russian Russian name."

Parrott struggled with his words. Took off his metal-rimmed spectacles, wiped them and put them back on. "I am a man of honor, Mr. President, and while I enjoy my successes I do not wish to take credit for another's work."

"You will explain?"

"Indeed I will. Last year this gentleman visited the foundry and asked if I would make a cannon for the Russian government. I agreed and asked him what his requirements were. He was most precise. He wanted me to make a copy of the British Armstrong rifled cannon. I thought this most unusual and told him so. Told him also that I did not have access to the Britons' secret plans. He was not disturbed at this, just nodded agreement—and turned over to me a complete set of blueprints for the Armstrong."

"And you constructed this gun?"

"I did. The Armstrong is a unique hundred-pounder in that it is breech-loading, which makes the guns eminently practical for sea warfare."

"And why is that?"

"If you will compare the differences between a gun on land and a gun at sea you will understand. On land, after a gun is fired, the gunners step forward and swab out the barrel and reload. But in a ship, the gun is fired through a gun port, an opening in the hull. So after each shot the gun must be run back, tons of metal you realize, swabbed out and reloaded. Then with great effort on the tackles it is run forward again into firing position."

"I am beginning to understand."

"Exactly. If the gun is a breechloader it will not be necessary for it to be run back inside the ship and out again with every shot. This is fine in theory, but the breech on this particular cannon sealed badly, leaking gas, and was unreliable as well. If you will look at these drawings you will see why.

"It is most cumbersome to load. Firstly, this breech screw must be slackened off to relieve the pressure on the vent piece. This is a strong metal plate that seals the open breech of the gun barrel. It is very heavy and it requires the strength of two burly men to grasp the handles and swing it up onto the saddle. After the bore is sponged out and the vent in the vent piece cleared, and reloaded with a new firing tube, a projectile is loaded through the hollow breech. A lubricator is fitted behind it that contains the black powder charge. Next the vent piece is lowered into place and the breech screw tightened. The gun is now ready to fire."

"Complex, I agree, but surely a great advantage over the practice of running the gun back and then into position again."

"I agree, sir, but difficulties soon arise. After a few shots the gun heats up and the parts expand. Burnt powder accumulates and the vent piece jams and leaks quantities of burning gas. After very few shots the gun becomes inoperable. After testing this weapon before delivering it to the Russians I am forced to believe that this is not the path to a successful breech-loading weapon. However there was another improvement on this gun that drew my attention. It had a banded breech to reinforce the loading mechanism. The drawings contained detailed instruction on how this banding was done."

Parrott started to rise, thought better of it and sat again. His hands twisted together on the desk before him as he struggled to get out the words.

"It was . . . a few weeks later that I personally took out the patents on the first Parrott gun."

Lincoln leaned forward and rested his hand lightly on the troubled man's arm.

"You have nothing to berate yourself for. You did the right and correct thing. There are many ways to serve one's government. Particularly in the time of war."

"Then—you knew?"

"Let us say that Captain Schultz is known to the proper people. So I think we had better let the matter rest there if you please."

"But . . ."

"You serve your country well, Mr Parrott. If you profit from that service it is all the better. And you may be interested to know that the British have withdrawn the Armstrong guns from service for the same reason you just mentioned."

"I am sure that they did. However I have been improving on the design of a locking breech with what I call an interrupted thread. My first experiments have been most successful."

"You have dispensed with the vent piece?"

"I have. Consider, if you would, how secure a breech would be if a breech-block could be screwed into place. The screw threads, in breech and block, would fit tightly against one another along a great length and contain both pressure and gas."

"It sounds eminently practical. But would not great effort be needed to screw this large piece of metal in and out?"

"You are absolutely correct! That is why I have devised what I call an interrupted thread. Matching grooves are cut in both breech-block and breech. In operation the breech-block is slid into position—then twisted to lock."

"Does the device work?"

"I am sure that it will—but machining is difficult and construction still at an early stage."

"Continue your efforts by all means. And keep me informed of any future developments. Now—we will rejoin the others. I am told that you are perfecting the fuses for your explosive shells to ensure greater accuracy in timing . . ."

The inspection tour had scarcely begun again when an army officer hurried in and took Nicolay aside, spoke to him quickly. Parrott was explaining the operation of the new fuse when Lincoln's secretary interrupted him.

"I'm sorry, sir, but there has been an accident. To General Ripley, Mr. President. This officer has no details, but he does forward a request for your presence at the military hospital."

"Of course. We'll go now. Thank you for everything, Mr. Parrott—*everything*."

The ferry had been held awaiting their arrival. Two carriages were standing on the dock. In the first one the commander of West Point, Lieutenant General Winfield Scott, was waiting to escort them to the hospital. Cameron and his secretaries took the second carriage. There was an embarrassing moment when the President climbed awkwardly through the door of Scott's carriage.

"How are you, Winfield?"

"As well as might be expected at my age, Mr. Lincoln."

The former General-in-Chief of the Union Army, who had been replaced by the younger and more energetic McClellan, could not keep a thin bite of anger from his words as he looked grimly at the man who had ordered that replacement. Heroically fat and gray of hair, he had served his country well for many decades and through many wars. He had chosen command of West Point instead of retirement, but well knew that his years of service had effectively ended. And the tall, ungainly man in the ugly tall hat who clambered into the carriage across from him was the power that had engineered that fall.

"Tell me about Ripley," Lincoln said as the carriage started forward.

"A tragic accident without sense or reason. He was mounted and riding toward the ferry, to join you—or so he informed me. The road he took crosses the railway tracks close to the station. Apparently a train was about to pull out and, as he approached, the driver blew the whistle for departure. The general's horse was startled and reared up, throwing him from the saddle. He fell on the tracks and was gravely injured. I am no medical man, as you well know, so we will leave it for the head surgeon to explain. He is waiting for you in his office in the hospital." Scott looked at Lincoln with a very penetrating eye. "How goes the war? I assume that your generals are drawing the ever tighter noose of my anaconda around the Rebels?"

"I sincerely hope so. Though of course the winter weather makes operations most difficult."

"And gives Little Napoleon another excuse to vacillate."

His voice was sour, his anger ill-concealed. Since McClellan had replaced him in command of the Army of the Potomac all forward movements had ceased, all attacks had crawled to a stop. Scott's every word and gesture suggested that if the army were still under his command they would be in Richmond by now. Lincoln would not be drawn into speculation about this.

"Winter is a bad season for soldiering. Ahh, there is the hospital at last."

"My aide will take you inside."

Scott was so fat that it took three men to lift him into his carriage; he was certainly not capable of climbing the hospital steps.

"It has been good to see you again, Winfield."

The general did not respond when the President climbed down and joined the others as they followed the waiting officer into the hospital. The surgeon was an elderly man with a great white beard, which he pulled at abstractedly as he spoke.

"A traumatic blow to the spine, here." He reached over his shoulder and tapped between his shoulder blades. "The general appears to have landed on his back across the rail track. I estimate that that would be a very strong blow, somewhat like being struck in the spine with a sledgehammer. At least two of the vertebrae appear to be broken—but that is not the cause of the general's condition. It is his spinal cord that has been crushed, the nerves severed. This causes a paralysis which we are well acquainted with." He sighed.

"The body is paralyzed, the limbs will not move, and he breathes only with great difficulty. Though it is usually possible to feed patients in this condition, in most cases it is not enough to sustain life.

"Perhaps it is a blessing that patients with this type of injury inevitably die."

* * *

The visit to West Point that had begun so well ended with deep unhappiness. They sat in silence as the train pulled out of the station. Cameron sat with his back to the engine, looking out at the snow-covered countryside streaming by. Lincoln sat opposite him, looking out as well but seeing only the endless problems of this war that assailed him at all times. His secretaries sat across the aisle going through a sheaf of records from the arms factory.

"General Ripley was not the easiest man to get along with," Lincoln said, long minutes after their train had pulled out of the station. Stanton nodded silent agreement. "But he had an awesome responsibility which he labored at professionally. He told me that he had to supply cartridges and shells for over sixty different types of weapons. That we are fighting, and hopefully winning, this war is in many ways due to his labors. What will happen now?"

"General Ramsay has been his assistant for some time," the Secretary of War said. Lincoln nodded.

"I met him once. A responsible officer. But is he qualified for this position?"

"More than qualified," Cameron said. "In my contacts with him at the War Department I have seen all of his reports and have passed them on to you when they were relevant. Please don't think me to be presumptuous—or to be speaking ill of the dead—but Ramsay is a modern soldier of the modern school."

"While Ripley was most conservative, as we all know."

"More than conservative. He looked with great suspicion at any new weapon or invention. He knew what guns were like and how they were used. Knew that wars have been fought and won with these weapons and he was satisfied by that. I don't believe he liked change of any kind. But you must meet General Ramsay before you decide, Mr. Lincoln. Make your mind up then. I think you will be more than interested in his approach."

"Talk to my secretary and arrange it then. For tomorrow. This important post shall not remain vacant for an instant longer than is necessary."

AN ULTIMATUM
FROM BRITAIN

"Mrs. Lincoln said you had no dinner to speak of last night—and that you were to come down to breakfast now."

Keckley was more than a Negro servant these days; the President could hear a ready echo of his wife's voice in her words. Mary had originally hired her as a seamstress but that relationship had shifted and changed to an ambiguous but important place in the family.

"I'll be there in just a minute . . ."

"She said that you would say that too and I shouldn't believe it."

Keckley stood in the open doorway silent and unmoving. Lincoln sighed and stood. "Lead the way. I trust you will take the word of the President that I am right behind you."

As always the hall was filled with petitioners seeking jobs in the government. Lincoln thrust his way through them, as though wading through an angry sea. If he addressed one he must address them all. Not for the first time he wondered at the long-established policy that allowed anyone—and his brother—easy access to the Presidential Mansion. Of course, America was an egalitarian society. But there were, he was beginning to think, certain demerits in complete openness. He sighed and opened the door to the dining room, closing it behind him with a satisfactory thud.

The table was already laid when he came in; buttermilk cakes with honey, always a family favorite.

"You start with that, Father," Mary said. There was a thunder of feet as the boys rushed in.

42

"Paw, Paw!" Tad shouted as he rushed at his father and seized him around the leg. Willie, always more restrained, seated himself at the table.

"Tad—you stop that," Mary ordered, but was completely ignored. The boy climbed his father as though he were a tree, wrinkling his already wrinkled trousers and jacket in the process. He did not stop until he was perched triumphantly on his father's shoulder. Lincoln marched twice around the table while Tad screeched with pleasure, before he lowered the boy into his chair. Willie had already poured honey on his cakes and was chewing an immense mouthful.

Keckley and Mary were bringing in more food, as well as hot freshly brewed coffee. Lincoln poured a cup and sipped it as the table slowly filled with more and more attractive dishes. Under Mary's watchful eye he forked a spicy Virginia sausage onto his plate, took some hominy grits and poured some red-eye gravy over them. He ate slowly, his thoughts a hundred miles from this warm domestic scene. The war, the endless dreadful war. Mary saw this clearly, pressed her hand to his shoulder in silence, then joined them at the table. She ate well, too well if the tightness of her dress meant anything.

She went to fetch more milk for the boys and he was gone when she returned, his plate scarcely touched. He worked too hard and ate too little she thought. And he was losing weight steadily. The war was eating him up. He would be back in his office now and it might be another day before she saw him again.

"John," Lincoln said, "I want you to write a letter for me."

Hay used his own system of shorthand to record Lincoln's dictation. Now it was yet another memorandum from the President to General McClellan asking some sharply pointed questions about a possible forward movement of the Army of the Potomac. There was exasperation in Lincoln's voice as he concluded.

" 'And how *long* would it require to actually get into motion? You have the army and you have the recruits and all are well trained, if I can believe the reports. But to win this war this army must be used in battle and Richmond must be taken.' End there and have that telegraphed to him at once. Now cheer me up, John. Tell me some good news from the morning reports."

"Good news indeed, sir. We now occupy Ship Island and all resistance is ended. The mouth of the Mississippi is close to this island so that part of the blockading fleet will be well supported and supplied. More news at sea. The USS *Santiago de Cuba* has halted a British schooner, the *Eugenia Smith*, near the mouth of the Rio Grande River."

"Are any reasons given why?"

"Indeed. Commander Daniel Ridgely has explained that the British vessel had called at a Texas port. His suspicions were confirmed when a well-known Confederate purchasing agent was found aboard. J. W. Zacharie, a merchant from New Orleans. He was removed from the schooner which was then allowed to proceed."

Lincoln shook his head wearily. "This will only add fuel to the fire we are having over the *Trent*. Is that all?"

"No, sir. The Rebels are so sure that Savannah will shortly fall to our troops that they are burning all of the cotton on the docks and in the fields. At sea the gunboat *Penguin* has captured a blockade runner trying to get to Charleston. A rich cargo indeed. The manifest lists small arms, ammunition, salt, provisions of all kinds. Not only fancy fabrics from France but saddles, bridles and cavalry equipment which is valued at $100,000."

"Capital. Their loss, our gain. Is the Attorney General here yet?"

"I'll go and see."

Lincoln looked up from the sprawled papers on his desk when Edward Bates came in.

"I would like a moment of your time," Lincoln said. "I must give my State of the Union address to Congress tomorrow. That the State is perilous they must know, but I must extend some hope for the future. May I read you some of what I plan to say to them and seek your opinion?"

"A responsibility that I willingly accept."

The President coughed lightly, then began.

" 'The Union must be preserved, and hence, all indispensable means must be employed. We should not be in haste to determine that radical and extreme measures, which may reach the loyal as well as the disloyal, are indispensable. To continue and to fight this war the raising of funds is as inevitable as it is necessary." Lincoln looked up and Bates nodded.

"I agree. Taxes, I imagine. To fund this war they must be raised yet again. And more men must be raised for the army. Despite the draft rioting among the Irish immigrants in New York you must press on."

"I appreciate your endorsement. I must also dwell some on popular institutions for we must be always aware of the reasons we are fighting this war." The President turned to the next page. " 'Labor is prior to, and independent of, capital. Capital is only the fruit of Labor, and would never have existed if Labor had not first existed. But Capital has its rights, which are as worthy of protection as any other rights.' "

Bates, a shrewd politician himself, knew that all sides must be pacified. The workers, who gave their labor and their bodies to the war effort, certainly must have these efforts acknowledged. But, at the same time, businessmen must not feel that they were bearing the sole burden of taxes for the war effort. But when Lincoln read on about the Negro problem he shook his head in disagreement and interrupted.

"You know my feelings on this matter, Mr. President. I see the Colonization of free Negroes as a very remote possibility."

"You shouldn't. A location could be found, perhaps in the Americas to the south, where an independent colony could be founded. With the Negroes removed from the equation there would be no reason left to continue the war."

"But I have talked to free Negroes here in the North and they think this ill-advised. They consider themselves as American as we do and feel no desire to depart to some distant shore. When you met the delegation of free Negroes it is my understanding that they told you the same thing."

Before Lincoln could respond Nicolay knocked and entered.

"Sorry to interrupt, but General Ramsay has arrived. You asked to meet with him as soon as possible. He is waiting outside."

"Fine. As soon as we are finished here have him sent in."
He turned to the Attorney General. "We must discuss this in
greater detail later. I am firm in my resolve that this is a real
solution to our problems."

"I find this difficult to say, Mr. President. But in this matter I
think that you are alone. Perhaps it would be a good idea to
found these colonies—but who would go there? The Negroes
will not volunteer, there seems to be complete agreement upon
that. But can we ship them there in shackles? That would be
equal, or worse, than the slave trade that brought them to this
country in the first place. I ask you to reconsider this matter,
with deepest respect, consider it in all its aspects."

When Bates had gone out Ramsay was ushered in. The
general was an impressive man, tall and erect. However he
wore a simple blue uniform with none of the braid and deco-
rations that the other staff officers seemed to prefer. He was
an engineer and technician and it was obvious that he thought
more of that, and the war, than he did of a glittering uniform.
He stood at attention and only sat down when Lincoln waved
him to a chair.

"This accident of Ripley's is a tragic thing, General, most
tragic."

Ramsay nodded and thought a moment before he spoke.
He was a man of firm decisions but never of hasty ones. "He
was a good officer, Mr. President, and a brave fighting soldier
as well. This is not the way he would have chosen to go."

"I am sure not. Is there any more news of his condition?"

"Only that he is weakening and cannot breathe well. The
doctors do not give him too much time."

"I am most sorry to hear that. Yet despite our casualties the
war must go on. And General Ripley's most vital work must
continue to be done. You have been aide to the general for
some time?"

"I have."

"Then there is nothing I can tell you about the importance
of the Bureau of Ordnance, nor how vital to our country it is?"

"Nothing, Mr. President. We both know that the war could
not be fought without a constant flow of weaponry and ammu-

nition. We are better supplied than the enemy at all times and that must never change if we are to have victory."

Lincoln nodded solemnly. "May it always be thus. Now I have been consulting with my Cabinet about this matter. Secretary of War Cameron speaks very highly of you. He feels you are ideally suited to head the Bureau of Ordnance. What do you think?"

"I know that I can do the work, sir. But before any appointment is approved I think you must know that General Ripley and I did not see eye-to-eye on a number of things. Most importantly we differed completely on at least one matter of some gravity. When I was his subordinate I was honor bound not to mention this. But I feel I must do so now. I do not speak in anger or envy. I feel that I was a good and loyal lieutenant to the general. While he was alive I never considered speaking aloud of our differences. But everything is changed now. If I am to occupy this position I must make the changes that I believe in."

"I admire your honesty in coming forward with this. What was this major bone of contention?"

For long seconds the officer looked discomfited. Looking first at the floor, then out of the window. Then he sat even more erect and sterned himself to speak.

"The general was a firm believer in the virtues of standard muzzle-loading rifles. They are proven and reliable and with proper training can deliver a good rate of fire."

"And you don't agree with this?"

"Of course I agree, Mr. President. But we live in an age of progress. I see new inventions almost every day. I believe in examining all these inventions—but more strongly I also believe in the virtues of breech-loading rifles. We have put numberless samples to the test and frankly most of them were useless. They jam and explode, break down very often and are difficult to maintain. But there are two breech-loaders that we have examined and fired at length, two remarkable weapons that stand out from all the others. The Spencer rifle and the Sharps. I wished to order a good quantity of them, but General Ripley disagreed strongly. Therefore nothing was done."

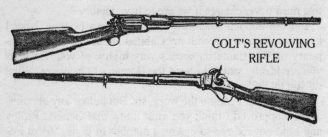

COLT'S REVOLVING
RIFLE

SHARP'S RIFLE

"Did he say why he disagreed?"

Ramsay hesitated to answer. When he did not speak Lincoln broke the silence. "I appreciate your loyalty to your superior officer. But by speaking honestly and frankly now you do him no harm—and you will be aiding the great effort that we are all so deeply involved in. If it helps I, as your Commander-in-Chief, can order you to tell me what you know."

Ramsay responded with great difficulty. "That will not be needed, sir. It was a matter of, well, opinion. The general felt that using breech-loaders would encourage the soldiers to waste ammunition. I do not think it a waste because the role of a soldier is to fire at the enemy."

"I agree, Ramsay, I do agree. You must arrange a demonstration of your wonderful rifles at the earliest opportunity. That will be your first order of business as our new Chief of Ordnance. Is there anything else that I should know about?"

"Well—it's Colonel Berdan and his regiment of sharpshooters. You have heard of him?"

"A memorandum in my desk somewhere. Didn't he use his own money to organize the regiment? With every man an expert shot."

"He did indeed. But here, again, and I do not blame General Ripley for having firmly held values. But Berdan's men have been lumbered with the Colt revolving rifle. The thing is like a revolver pistol with a long barrel. They misfire and, well, there is nothing really good that can be said about them.

It was a bad second choice. What they want, what they need, is the Sharps breech-loading rifle. A precision instrument in a marksman's hands."

"See that it is done."

The general saluted and left. Ramsay was a good man and would do an excellent job. Lincoln brushed away the unkind thought that General Ripley's tragic accident might have been a work of God. An intervention by Him who ruled all, an intercession in this war. One man's death to save countless others. But if the Supreme Being really were on his side he, for one, surely would not mind. Being President of the United States had endless burdens, not the least of which was this great war that had started as soon as he had been elected. Fighting and winning the war was the first priority and any aid—particularly that of the Almighty—would be greatly appreciated.

Sixty short miles away, in the city of Richmond, Virginia, the President of the Confederacy was weighted down by the same intractable problems and priorities as the President of the United States. But Jefferson Davis did not have the advantages of Lincoln's strength and stamina. Always weak in the aftermath of severe pneumonia years earlier, his eyes ravaged by snow blindness. Each day was a battle to be fought against unending pain. But no one had ever heard a word of complaint from him. A gentleman does not humble himself before any man. Today an ear infection troubled his concentration and he fought to quell any visible reaction to the enduring pain.

The South was as ill as their President. It was a cold winter and supplies of everything were running low. And the list of the dead in battle mounted. But the Southerners tried not to notice, tried to keep their hopes and their morale high. There were songs and rallies and it seemed to help. But the blockade had bitten deep and there was a shortage of everything, everything except valor.

Davis had a new Secretary of War, whom he hoped would help him cope with the endless struggle to supply the fighting forces. Jefferson Davis tapped on the thick sheaf of paper that rested on the desk before him.

"Judah—do you know why I had you appointed to replace LeRoy Walker?"

Judah P. Benjamin took the question to be a rhetorical one so he simply smiled in response and waited patiently for the answer, his folded hands resting lightly on his ample waistline.

"LeRoy is an excellent man and a hard worker. But he made too many enemies in government. I think he had to spend more time fighting them than he did fighting the Yankees. Here." Davis pushed the file across the desk. "Address yourself to these and see if the new Secretary of War can come up with some new answers. That's why you have the job. You are a patient man, Judah, an elder statesman who has many friends. You can stop the bickering and see that everyone in harness pulls in the same direction. When you look at these reports you will see that we are short of everything—but mostly short of guns and powder. If we were not a rural nation we would be in a dreadful pickle. As it is almost every volunteer brings along his own gun when he joins up. But it is more than muskets that we need. We must find cannon—and gunpowder—if we are going to win this war."

"It is my understanding, Mr. President, that a quantity of supplies was captured after the battle of Ball's Bluff."

"Indeed. It was a great victory and the bluebellies threw their guns away when they retreated. Our first victory since Bull Run. That helped—but not for long. There are also reports of Yankee foraging parties being captured, all good— but still not good enough. We can't expect the North to be our sole source of supplies. The military front is very static for the moment and we must take advantage of this lull in the fighting. McClellan's Yankee armies are being held at bay, but we can certainly look forward to some action there in the peninsula in the spring. But it is the naval blockade that is hurting us, hurting real bad. That is why we have been diverting all our resources to readying the ironclad *Virginia* for battle. When she sails our prayers go with her to break the blockade and sink the Northern fleet. When that happens we can bring in supplies by the boatload. Our cotton is eagerly sought in

Britain and the funds from that will buy the gunpowder, cannon and supplies that we so desperately need."

Benjamin had been leafing slowly through the file while the President talked. He pulled out a handful of newspaper clippings.

"They're from the North," Jefferson Davis said. "They are crowing like cockerels up there, all puffed with victory, over the imprisonment of Mason and Slidell. Let them gloat. I'm beginning to feel that this may all be a blessing in disguise. I do declare that those two Southern gentleman are doing more for the Confederacy sitting in that Yankee prison then they ever could have done in Europe. The British are all het up at this violation of their territory. I believe that every shipyard over there is building a blockade runner or a raider for us. And the wonderful part is that the Yankees did this to themselves. Nothing that we might have done could have been of greater aid to our cause."

"I agree Mr. President, agree strongly. Our ambassadors to Boston are doing wonderfully fine there. Let us thank the Lord and pray to Him that they remain in that prison while the British get themselves more and more irritated. They should be congratulated on their sagacity in being captured by the Yankees."

Lord Palmerston was seated in the wingchair before the glowing coal fire, his right leg extended and resting on a mound of cushions. His eyes were closed and ringed with lines of pain. He opened them slowly when the butler announced Lord John Russell.

"Ah, John, do come in. Pour yourself a port—and one for me if you please. A large one if you would be so kind."

He sipped and smacked his lips with pleasure, then grimaced and pointed to his supported foot.

"Gout. Infernal bloody nuisance. Hurts like the very blazes of hell. Quacks can't do a thing about it. I drink their foul nostrums and nothing improves in the slightest. They try to blame the port for the condition, simpering nonces. Port's the only thing that seems to help in the slightest. But enough of that.

Of greater importance. You must tell me. How did it go at the palace?"

"Wonderfully. Her Majesty agreed that we should make all preparations to increase the pressure on the Americans—even before they have had a chance to respond to our ultimatum. Prince Albert is doing very poorly, I regret to report. The physicians now are sure that his lung congestion is far more serious than they had previously determined. They believe that he has all the symptoms of the typhoid fever."

"I say! But he has not been in the south, has not left London."

"He doesn't need to. You've smelled the drains in Windsor Castle. Mephitic! Anything could lurk in their bowels. Nothing has ever been done to improve the various closets and sinks there. Noxious effluvia escape from the old drain—the stench of the cesspools make parts of the Castle almost uninhabitable. I am surprised that more are not felled by the miasma."

"Poor Albert, poor man."

"If there is any good to come of his illness it is the Queen's anger. She feels that, in his weakened condition, he should not have attempted to work on our dispatch. She is positive that he gave his strength for his country, and she fears he may perhaps, terrible thought, even give his life. She blames the Americans for everything, everything. No action we take will be too severe."

"Such a fine woman—and a veritable dragon in defense of St. George. So what shall we do first?"

"First we demonstrate to the Yankees the firmness of our will."

"Which is indeed of the firmest."

"We reconsider our neutrality in supplying military supplies to both antagonists in this conflict. We can order an embargo on all shipments of saltpeter to the North—the vital ingredient of gunpowder."

"A fine beginning. And if we do that we must also forbid shipment of munitions and all other warlike instruments. We shall hit them where it hurts."

"And we must prepare ourselves to show our warlike mettle as well. Two troop vessels have sailed for Canada this very day. Quite a spirited departure I am told with the bands playing 'The British Grenadiers' followed by 'Dixie.' But there has been another slight hold up. You will recall that we have another regiment and an artillery battery that were to be transferred to Canada."

"I do," Palmerston said, frowning. "But I assumed they were seaborne or in the province by now."

"They are still in barracks. The Canadians say they have no quarters or tents for them . . ."

"Nonsense! These are hardened troops capable of living and fighting in any extremity. Have the orders issued for their transferral at once. And I suggest that we don't wait for the navy and their transports. I can hear their delaying arguments already. Hire a Cunard steamer. What is the strength of our forces in Canada?"

"I am afraid that we have only five thousand regulars stationed there at the present time."

"That must change. By God we should have finished the colonials off in 1814. We had the strength to do it. Burnt their cities of Buffalo and Washington as well, didn't we? Would have won if it hadn't been for the French. Well, spilt milk and all that. How about our situation now at sea? What is the condition of our fleet at the North American station?"

"Quite adequate, well over thirty vessels. There are three battleships, as well as frigates and corvettes."

"Good, but not good enough. They must be reinforced with more capital ships. The Americans must see that we are very serious in this matter. The two Southern representatives must be returned, an apology must be made. On this we are adamant. With the country united behind us we can not be seen to be weak or pusillanimous. What is today's date?"

"The twenty-first of December."

"The very day that Lord Lyons is to present our dispatch to the Americans. I am sure that it was a singularly momentous occasion. Now, some more port, if you please."

Lord Lyons hated the Washington weather. Tropically hot and humid in summer, arctic in winter. His carriage had bumped and slithered over the ice and slush, shaking him about like a pea in a pod. Finally back at his home he descended from the carriage and tramped through the wet snow, slammed the front door behind him. His manservant took his snow-whitened coat and opened the door to the study where a fire crackled on the hearth.

"William," Lyons called out as he warmed his hands before the flames. His secretary slipped in silently. "Bring pen, ink and paper for yourself. I have met with the Americans and must write a report at once to Lord Palmerston. It has been a dreadful morning. That Seward is a cold fish indeed. He read our dispatch without moving a muscle at the demands and commands it contained. Even managed to look bored when I told him we must have an answer within a week. If our demands are not met, I assured him that I would remove my passports and return to Britain. He smiled at that—as though he enjoyed the idea!"

His secretary nodded understandingly, knowing that he was but a witness not a participant in the conversation.

Lyons walked back and forth before the fireplace, composing his words carefully. He was a small and plump man, with a smoothness of manner that hid the subtlety of his nature. William sat in silence, quill pen poised over paper.

"Usual honorifics, you know. Then—I have this day handed over to Secretary of State Seward your demands for the release of the Confederate commissioners Messrs Mason and Slidell. I am convinced that unless we give our friends here a good lesson this time, we shall have the same trouble with them again very soon. They will soon see the folly of their ways when they read this ultimatum. Surrender or war will have a very salutary effect upon them. Though I must say that our demands were met with a very cool reception."

The fire crackled; the only other sound the scratch of the pen on paper. Lyons warmed his hands, aware of a sudden chill. Would there be war? Would it come to that in the end?

It was an exhilarating albeit a most depressing thought. War against aborigines was one thing. Against an armed and dangerous foe was another. But this was a country divided and the Union was already battling for its life. While Britain, at peace with the rest of the world, could draw upon the mighty strength of her Empire if it came to battle. The richest Empire the world had ever seen. America had managed to slip from the British grasp—but that could be rectified. There was a continent brimming with wealth here that would only add greater luster to the Empire.

Perhaps a war would not be such a bad idea after all.

ON THE BRINK

Dr. Jenner closed the door to Prince Albert's bedroom as quietly as he could, turning the handle as he shut it so there would not be the slightest click of metal on metal. Queen Victoria watched him, eyes wide with fright and apprehension; the flame on the candlestick in her trembling hand wavered and smoked.

"Tell me . . ." she said, almost breathlessly.

"Sleeping," the doctor said. "A very good sign."

"It is, of course!" Victoria felt the slightest lift of spirits. "It has been, I don't know how long, days, nights since he has slept a little, or not at all."

"Nor you either, for that matter."

She dismissed this with a disdainful wave of her small and chubby hand. "I am not ill, he is the one whom you and Sir James must be concerned about. I have been sleeping on that makeshift bed in his dressing room. But he walks about, does not lie down—and he is so thin. Some nights I do not believe he sleeps at all. Nor does he eat! It tears at my heart to see him like this."

"His gastric fever must run its course so we must be patient. You can be of immense help by doing what no one else can do. You must see that he eats something every day. Even if only gruel, his body must need all the help to fight this disease." Jenner took the candle from her trembling hand and placed it on the table next to the couch. "You had best sit, ma'am."

Victoria sat as bid, spreading her skirts wide. Trying to fold her hands steady on her lap, but kneading them ceaselessly instead.

"I saw Lord Palmerston today," Jenner said. "He was most concerned about the Prince's health and had what I consider to be a most worthwhile suggestion. I am of course most qualified, but I see no reason that other physicians might—"

"He has talked to me too. You need not go on."

"But his suggestion may be a wise one. I would certainly not take umbrage if another physician, or even more, were consulted."

"No. I do not like Palmerston's interference. You are my dear husband's doctor and so you shall remain. This hasty feverish sort of influenza and deranged stomach will soon pass as it has done so before. At least he is resting now, sleeping."

"The best medicine in the world for him in his condition . . ."

As if to deny his words the candle flame guttered as the door to the bedroom opened. Albert stood there in his dressing gown, clutching the fabric to his chest, his pale skin stretched taut across his cheekbones.

"I awoke—" he said weakly, then coughed, a racking cough that shook his frail body.

Jenner sprang to his feet. "You must return to your bed—this is most imperative. The chill of the night alone!"

"Why?" Albert asked in tones of deepest despair. "I know how ill I am. I know this fever, an old enemy—and knowing it I know that I shall not ever recover."

"Never!" Victoria cried. "Come dearest, come to bed. I shall read to you until you fall asleep."

Albert was too weak to protest, merely shaking his head with Teutonic despair. Leaning on her arm he shuffled across the room. He was not wearing his slippers, but the long underwear he insisted on using had fabric feet sewed to them, offering some protection against the cold. Dr. Jenner lit the bedside lamp as Victoria saw her husband back to bed. Carefully walking backward, Dr. Jenner bowed and left.

"You will sleep now," she said.

"I cannot."

"Then I will read to you. Your favorite, Walter Scott."

"Some other time. Tell me—is there still talk of war with the Americans?"

"You must not disturb yourself with politics. Let others concern themselves now with affairs of state."

"I should have done more. That ultimatum should not have been sent."

"Hush, my dearest. If I cannot read to you from Scott—why then you have always been fond of the writings of von Ense."

Albert nodded agreement and she fetched the book from the shelf. The memoirs of Varnhagen von Ense, the famous soldier and diplomat, indeed was his favorite. And hearing her read in German seemed to soothe him somewhat. After some time his breathing steadied and she saw that he was asleep. Lowering the lamp she found her way by the light of the flickering fire, in the grate to his dressing room, and to her improvised bed.

The next day was December eleventh and the coldest day of this coldest month on record. England and London were in the grip of the deepest of deep frosts. Here, in this stone castle, if possible the chill and dank corridors of Windsor Palace were colder than ever before. The servants stoked the many fires, yet still the cold prevailed.

At noon Albert was still in his bed, still asleep. Victoria's daughter, Alice, was at her side when Dr. Jenner came to examine his patient.

"He is sleeping well, isn't he?" the Queen asked with some apprehension. "This is a change for the better?"

The doctor nodded, but did not speak. He touched his hand to his patient's forehead before taking his pulse.

"This is a turning point," Jenner said with an inadvertent air of deepest gloom. "But he is very weak you must remember—"

"What are you saying? Are you giving up hope?"

The doctor's silence was answer enough.

Victoria no longer protested at additional medical support. There were other doctors in attendance now, five specialists who aided Jenner, who spoke to each other in murmured whispers that the Queen could not hear. When she became upset Alice led her gently from the room, sent for tea.

For two days the Prince lay very still, his face ashen, his breathing labored. Victoria never left his side, holding his pale hand with its weakening pulse. In mid-afternoon of the second day clouds broke and a ray of golden sunlight illuminated the room, touching his face with a sheen of color. His eyes opened and he looked up at her.

"The *Trent* Affair . . ." he whispered, but could not go on. Victoria wept silently, clasping his cold and limp hand.

At sunset the children were brought in to see their father. Beatrice was too young to be allowed to attend this depressing scene, but Lenchen, Louise, Alice and Arthur were all there. Even Bertie came by train from Cambridge for a final visit to his father. Unhappily Alfie and Leopold were traveling abroad and could not be reached. Vickie, pregnant again, could not make the exhausting trip from Berlin. Still, four of their children were present in the sick room, clutching hands, trying to fathom what was happening to their father. Even Bertie, always at odds with his father, was silent now.

The following morning, in bright sunlight, a military band playing faintly in the distance, Albert sank into a final coma, Victoria still at his side. His eyes were open now, but he did not move or speak. Her vigil lasted all of that day and into evening and night.

At a little before eleven o'clock he drew several long breaths. Victoria clutched at his hand as his breathing ceased.

"Oh! My dear darling!" she cried aloud as she dropped to her knees in distracted despair. "My Angel has gone to rest with the angels."

She leaned over to kiss his cold forehead one last time. And unbidden the last words he had spoken sprang poisonously to her mind.

"The *Trent* Affair. Those Americans did this. They have killed my love."

She screamed aloud, tore at her clothing, screamed again and again and again.

Across the Atlantic the winter was just as bad as that in England. There were thick sheets of ice in the river water that were struck aside by the ferry boat's bow, to thud and hammer down her sides. It was a slow passage from the island of

Manhattan. When the ship finally tied up in its slip on the Brooklyn shore of the East River, the two men quickly went from the ferry and hurried to the first carriage in the row of waiting cabs.

"Do you know where the Continental Ironworks is?" Cornelius Bushnell asked.

"I do, Your Honor—if that is indeed the one on the river in Greenpoint."

"Surely it is. Take us there."

Gustavus Fox opened the door and let the older man precede him. The cab, stinking of horse, was damp and cold. But both men were warmly dressed for this was indeed a bitter winter.

"Have you met John Ericsson before?" Bushnell asked. They had met at the ferry and had had little chance to talk before in private.

"Just the once, when he was called in by the Secretary of the Navy. But only to shake his hand—I had to miss the meeting, another urgent matter."

Bushnell, although chairman of the navy committee funding the ironclad, knew better than to ask what the urgent matter was. Fox was more than the Assistant Secretary of the Navy; he had other duties that took him to the Presidential Mansion quite often. "He is a mechanical genius . . . but," Bushnell seemed reluctant to go on. "But he can be difficult at times."

"Unhappily this is not new information. I have heard that said of him."

"But we need his genius. When he first presented his model to my Naval Committee I knew he was the man to solve the problem that is troubling us all."

"You of course mean the ironclad that the South is building on the hull of the *Merrimack*?"

"I do indeed. When the Confederates finish her and she sails—it will be a disaster. Our entire blockading fleet will be in the gravest danger. Why she could even attack Washington and bombard the city!"

"Hardly that. And not that soon as well. I have it on good authority that while her hull and engines have been rebuilt in the drydock, there is a serious shortage of iron plate for her armor. There is no iron in the South and they are desperate. They are melting down gates and fences, even tearing up disused railroad sidings. But they need six hundred tons of iron plate for that single ship, and that is far from easy to obtain in this manner. I have men reporting from inside the Tredegar Iron Works in Richmond, the only place in the South where armor plate is rolled. There is not only a shortage of iron—but a shortage of transportation as well. The finished plates just lie there, rusting, until railroad transportation can be arranged."

"That is most gratifying to hear. We must have our own vessel ready before she is launched, to stand between her and our vulnerable fleet."

The cab stopped and the driver climbed down to open the door. "Here she is, the ironworks."

A clerk took them to the office where Thomas Fitch Roland, owner of the Continental Ironworks, awaited them.

"Mr. Roland," Bushnell said, "this is Mr. Gustavus Fox who is Assistant Secretary of the Navy."

"Welcome, Mr. Fox. I imagine that you are here to see what progress we are making on Captain Ericsson's floating battery."

"I am indeed most interested in that."

"Work goes according to plan. The keel plates have already been passed through the rolling mill. But you must realize that a craft of this type has never been built before. And, even as we begin to assemble the ship, Mr. Ericsson is still working on the drawings. That is why I asked Mr. Bushnell's committee for just a bit more time."

"That will not be a problem," Bushnell said. "I always felt that three months, from design to completion, was very little time. Are you sure that ten more days will be enough?"

"Ericsson says that she will be launched after one hundred days—and I have never known him to be wrong."

"That is good news indeed. And now—may we see this remarkable vessel?"

"That will be a little difficult. The hull is still under construction and there is very little that can be seen at the present time. I feel that if you will look at these drawings you will understand something more of this wonderful invention." He spread the large sheets out on the table. "The bottom of the hull is made of iron plate and is 124 feet long and eighteen feet wide. It is stiffened with angle iron and transverse timber beams to support the decking above which is much bigger, all of 172 feet long and forty-one feet abeam. And armored, heavily armored on top and on the sides that extend below the water to protect the thin hull. Engines here in the hold to drive the propeller screw. And all of this has but a single purpose— to bring this turret into battle."

"I am sure of that," Fox said, turning the drawings about. "But I must admit that my experience in understanding the designer's craft is less than perfect. The ship is apparently made of iron, with some wood to reinforce it. But is not iron heavier than water? Will it not sink when launched?"

"Have no fear of that. There are a number of iron ships afloat—and iron warships as well. The French have one—the British too. The hull will certainly support the massive firepower of the turret, the new engines will bring it into battle."

"Then we shall see the turret itself—and the man who designed it."

The large building echoed with the clamor of metal on metal. Overhead winches swayed up a load of plate iron to be fitted onto the growing hull. Following Roland they made their way toward the rear of the hall where the circular form of the turret was beginning to take shape. A tall, gray-haired man with mutton-chop whiskers was supervising the assembly of a small steam engine. Although he was almost sixty years old Ericsson's strength was still phenomenal; he easily lifted and slid into place a rocker beam that weighed over ninety pounds. He nodded to his visitors and wiped the grease from his hands with a rag.

"Und so, Bushnell, you come to see what you spending the navy's $275,000 on." Although he had been an American citizen for many years he had not lost his thick Swedish accent.

"I do indeed, John. You have met Mr. Fox before?"

"I have. In the office of the Secretary of the Navy—and joost the man I want to see. I want my money!"

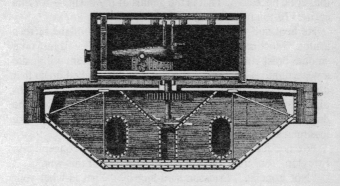

MONITOR'S TURRET

"I am afraid that appropriations are not my responsibility, Mr. Ericsson."

"Then talk to someone to pay up. My good friend Cornelius here has received nothing—even though he is building my ship! He pays for the iron plate out of his own pocket. This is a situation that should not be. The navy commissions this battery so the navy must pay."

"I promise to talk to my superiors and do what I can to alleviate the situation." Not that it will do much good, he thought to himself. The navy was tight-fisted and loath to pay any debts that could be avoided. "But for the moment I would dearly like to discover how this vessel's marvelous turret will operate."

"It will operate in a manner never seen before, I assure you." Ericsson patted the black metal affectionately, financial matters forgotten for the moment. "Deadly and impenetrable. This armor is eight inches thick and the gun has not been made that can send a shell through that much iron. Now around here—you see these openings. Through them will fire two 11-inch Dahlgren guns. Remember—this vessel has been designed to work in the coastal waters of the South, to penetrate up narrow rivers in search of its prey. Turning the entire ship to fire the guns, the way navy ships are built now, will no longer be necessary. That is the genius of my design—for this entire 120-ton turret *revolves*!"

He bent and ran his hand along the bottom of the turret's armor. "Machined flat as you can see. At sea it will rest on a smooth brass ring in the deck—and its great weight will make a watertight seal. In action the turret will be jacked up so that it will rest on these wheels. Below it is this steam donkey engine that will drive this circular gear situated right below the deck—operated by a lever in the turret of course. It will take less than a minute for a complete revolution."

Fox nodded with appreciation. "It is a great concept, Mr. Ericsson. Your ironclad will change the face of this war."

"Not ironclad," Ericsson said angrily. "That is what your idiots in the Navy Department do not realize. This is a machine, the creation of an engineer, an iron, steam-powered vessel of war. A fabricated iron hull filled with complex machinery that bears no similarity to the wooden sailing ships of the past. Yet in the specifications your people say, a moment, I have it here." He took a wrinkled and much-folded sheet of paper from his pocket and read it aloud.

"They want me to . . . here it is. 'To furnish *Masts*, *Spars*, *Sails* and *Rigging* of sufficient dimension to drive the vessel at the rate of *Six knots* per hour in a fair breeze of wind.' Impossible! The power is steam and steam only as I have said many times in the past. No masts, no sails, no ropes. Steam! And the cretin who wrote this proves that he knows nothing of ships when he writes of 'knots per hour'! One knot means that a vessel covers a distance of one nautical mile in one hour as you know."

"I do indeed," Fox said and hurried to change the subject. "Have you a name for your floating battery?"

"I have been giving that a good deal of thought. Consider that the impregnable and aggressive character of this structure will admonish the leaders of the Southern Rebellion that their batteries on the banks of their rivers will no longer present barriers to the entrance of our Union forces. This iron-clad intruder will thus prove a severe monitor to those leaders. But there are other leaders who will also be startled and admonished by the booming of the guns from this impregnable iron turret. Downing Street will hardly view with indifference this last Yankee notion, this monitor. On these and many similar grounds, I propose to name the new battery *Monitor*."

"A most excellent point," Bushnell said, "and I shall recommend it to my committee."

"I concur," Fox said. "I will put it to the Secretary of the Navy as well. Now if you gentlemen will excuse us for a few minutes, I need to have a few words about naval matters with Mr. Roland."

In the ironworks owner's office, Fox got right to the important matter at hand.

"It has been pointed out to me that in addition to your being an entrepreneur, you are also an engineer of experience, not only in ship building but in the construction of marine steam machinery as well."

"I am indeed. In the past I have submitted designs to your Navy Department." He pointed to the wooden model on his desk. "This was one of them. A twin screw ironclad with twin rotating turrets."

"The design was not accepted?"

"It was not! I was told it would not bear the weight and provide stability."

"But will it?"

"Of course. I have discussed it with John Ericsson, who did the mathematic equations to analyze its design. He has proven that the weight of the engines in the hold will counterbalance the weight of the turrets above. He also suggested design changes in the hull that will make for higher speed." He opened a drawer in his desk and took out a set of drawings.

"A week after our talk John gave me these. He designed a new kind of boiler that he calls a surface condenser, where steam is condensed in an evaporator consisting of horizontal copper pipes. With his newly designed engines he estimates the ship will do fifteen knots."

"This will be a larger ship than the *Monitor*, more seaworthy?"

"It will indeed. This ship is designed for deep water, to stay at sea to defend our coasts." Roland looked curiously at Fox. "There is some meaning behind these questions, sir?"

"There is. Before *Monitor* is completed we would like full details of your ship. I can guarantee approval this time."

Fox leaned over and touched the model.

"Then, as soon as *Monitor* is launched, we want you to begin construction of this ship."

"It will be far bigger than the *Monitor*, so it cannot be built in this building. But it will be spring by then and I can use the outside slipway."

"Even better. The navy would also like you to start building a second ship of the *Monitor* class here as soon as the first one is launched. The first of many if I have my way."

DRIFT TOWARDS WAR

The Cabinet members were at loggerheads and arguing violently. So involved were they that they did not even notice when the door opened and the President appeared. Abraham Lincoln looked on in silence for a moment, hearing the raised voices, seeing the fists clenched tight in anger. He sat by the door and listened closely to the arguments and counter-arguments, but did not speak himself. Minutes passed before he was noticed and his presence acknowledged. He stood and joined the others at the table. When the arguments broke out again he spoke loudly enough to silence the contention.

"It is Christmas Day, gentlemen, Christmas Day. Best wishes to you all."

There were muttered thanks as he changed his chair to his rightful place at the head of the table. He waited patiently until he had their attention before he spoke again.

"I know that this is the day when you all wish to be with your families—as I with mine. Nevertheless I have called you here because this must also be a day of decision. Tomorrow morning a message will be sent to Lord Lyons about the *Trent* Affair. We are now gathered to decide just what that message will be. Mr. Cameron—you look disturbed."

"I am, Mr. President. As Secretary of War I am charged with the defense of the country and the subjugation of the enemy. As you well know we have had our successes and we have had our failures. We must look forward only to a future of great sacrifices if our cause is to succeed. It will not be an easy one. For victory in this struggle we will need every man in the army that we can find. Every factory must work at full output. Therefore I believe that it would be folly beyond belief

67

if, in the middle of a war against a determined enemy, we would be so unwise as to risk the possibility of a second war at the same time."

"There is no such possibility!" Attorney General Bates shouted. "Even the dunderhead British are not so stupid as to go to war over a matter so petty as this one. They have received no harm, suffered no losses. They are just in a pique. In 1812 we went to war because we had just cause. They were stopping our ships and impressing our seamen. Even though we were sorely tried we still did not then rush into war but tried to avoid it. We suffered humiliation time and time again and did not declare war until there was no alternative, no other choice. Now we have a most minor affair with one ship halted, two enemies of our country taken, the ship released. This is a tempest in a teapot and will eventually die away as all storms, no matter how fierce, eventually do. It is impossible that this incident could lead to a war with Britain. Impossible!"

"I agree with you completely," Gideon Welles said. "As Secretary of the Navy I was charged with capturing these traitors before they could do harm to our country. Acting in the finest tradition of this service Captain Wilkes did just that. The American people consider him a hero and have been feting him with honors. Do we turn their joy to Dead Sea ash at the command of a foreign power? Do we knuckle under to threats and commands to our sovereign state? Do we betray this great sailor's labors in his country's cause? The public and the newspapers would not permit it. I say that we should not, will not, and cannot!"

"I would go even beyond that," Seward said. "As Secretary of State I have long suggested the possibility of a diversionary foreign war to reunite this divided country. Now we have one being forced upon us and we would be wise not to oppose it."

Lincoln shook his head. "I have never agreed with you on this matter, as you know. Even if we consider the possibility, I find that going to war with some small Central American country is a far different matter from being involved in a war with a powerful country that is supported by a world-spanning

Empire. We must find better reasons than this if we are to halt a spreading fire of hatred."

Voices were raised in anger and only Lincoln grew silent. He listened to what was being said until he had heard the opposing arguments in greatest detail. Only then did he speak.

"Gentlemen—I regret to say that we have reached a stalemate. If I were to take a vote now on a course of action, by my observation we would be a house divided. But we must be unanimous in our decision. Therefore I suggest a compromise. We will send a message to the British that we will not be bullied. We will tell them that we appreciate their position and respect it. We will consider releasing those men to continue their voyage—but only if the threats and commands are removed from their dispatch. We will suggest that Lord Palmerston meet with Charles Adams, our much-respected minister in London, in a concerted effort to reach agreement on the wording. If this is done, honor will be served and peace confirmed. What say you to this proposal?"

Stanton hurried to speak as other voices were raised. "I for one say yes. A copy of our message should go to Adams as soon as possible, along with various drafts and proposals that we here do agree to. War will be averted and honor saved. Let us subscribe to this proposal with a single voice—then return to our loved ones on this most sacred of family days."

One by one the doubters were convinced, drawn to a mutual and satisfactory conclusion.

"A day's work well done," Lincoln said, smiling for the first time this day. "Hay and Nicolay will draw up the documents and present them to us tomorrow morning for approval. I am sure that this compromise will satisfy all the parties concerned."

Lord Lyons, the British representative in the American capital, glowered at the communication and was not satisfied in the slightest. He stood at the window staring out in anger at the frozen and repellent landscape and the endless falling snow. This response was neither flesh nor fowl nor good red herring. It neither accepted nor rejected the ultimatum. Instead it suggested a third and contentious rejoinder. However, since the demands had not been rejected out of hand, he could not hand over his passports as he had been ordered to do. The matter was still far from being settled. He must present this response to Lord Palmerston and could already feel that individual's wrathful reaction. He rang for his servant.

"Pack my bags for a sea voyage."

"You will remember, sir, you asked me to do that some days ago."

"Did I? By Jove I do believe that you are right. Did I not ask you as well to keep record of ship movements?"

"You did indeed, your Lordship. There is a Belgian barque, the *Marie Celestine*, now taking on cargo in the port of Baltimore. She will be departing for the port of Ostend in two days time."

"Excellent. I will take the cars to Baltimore in the morning. Arrange it."

He must return to London at once; he had no other choice. But there was the ameliorating factor that at least he would be out of this backwoods capital and, for a time at least, in the clement city at the heart of the mightiest Empire on earth. One whose drastic displeasure these frontiersmen must be ready to suffer if their truculence prevailed.

Lord Lyons was indeed correct, at least about the weather in Britain. It was a weak and watery sun which shone on London this same December day—but at least it shone. Charles Francis Adams, the United States Ambassador to the Court of St. James, was happy to be outdoors and away from the endless paperwork and the smoky fires. The servants in the homes he passed must have been up at dawn to sweep and wash the Mayfair pavements: the walk was a pleasant one. He turned off Brook Street and into Grosvenor Square, climbed the familiar steps of number 2 and tapped lightly on the door with the handle of his walking stick. The manservant opened it and ushered him through to the magnificent sitting room where his friend awaited him.

"Charles—how kind of you to accept my invitation."

"Your invitation to dine with you, Amory, was as a rainbow from heaven."

They were close friends, part of the small number of Americans resident in London. Amory Cabot was a Boston merchant who had made his fortune in the English trade. He had been a young man when he had first come to this city to represent the family business. The temporary position had become permanent when he had married here, his wife a member of a prominent Birmingham manufacturing family. Now, alas, his wife was dead, the children far from the family seat. But London was his home and Boston a distant part of the world. Now in his eighties, he watched his business with a benign eye and let others do the hard work. While devoting most of his attention to whist and other civilized diversions. The servants brought pipes and mulled ale as the friends talked idly. Only when the door had closed did Cabot's features darken with worry.

"Is there any new word of the crisis?"

"None. I do know that the newspapers and public opinion at home is still very firm on the matter. The traitors are in our hands and there they must stay. Setting them free would be unthinkable. There has been no response from Washington as yet to the *Trent* memorandum. My hands are tied—there is nothing that I can do on my own—and I have no instructions. Yet still this crisis must be averted."

Cabot sighed. "I could not agree more. But can it be done? Our countrymen are incensed but, as you well know, matters are no better here in London. Friends I have known for years shut their doors to me, harden their faces should we meet. I'll tell you something—it is like the War of 1812 all over again. I was here then as well, kept my head down and rode it out. But even then most of my friends and associates did not turn on me as they are doing now. They felt that war had been forced upon them and they fought it with great reluctance. Why a few, the more liberal of them, even sympathized with our cause and thought it to be a singularly stupid war. Not brought about by circumstance but by arrogance and stupidity. No shortage of that at any time. But it is far different now. Now the anger and hatred are fierce. And the newspapers! Did you read what the *Times* wrote?"

"Indeed I did, the so-called 'City Intelligence.' Said outright that Lincoln and Seward were attempting to hide the spectacle of their internal condition by embarking on a foreign war. Utter hogwash!"

"As indeed it is. But the *Daily News* is even worse. They write that all Englishmen believe that Seward, in some manner they did not reveal, had arranged the entire *Trent* Affair himself."

Adams's pipe had gone out. He rose and used a spill to relight it from the fire, exhaled pungent Virginia smoke. "What bothers me more than the newspapers are the politicians. The traditional Whig elite, like our mutual acquaintance the Earl of Clarendon, actually hate democracy. They feel it threatens their class system and their power. To them the Unites States is the bastion of the devil, a perversion that is best wiped out before it can contaminate the underclasses here. They would cheerfully welcome a war against our country."

"The Queen as well," Cabot said glumly, taking a long swig from his tankard as though to wash some bad taste from his mouth. "She approves of all this, actually predicts the utter destruction of the Yankees. She blames us for Prince Albert's death, you know, irrational as the thought is."

"It goes beyond words. I walked along the Thames on Christmas Day. Even on that feast day they were working flat out at the Tower of London—packing firearms. I counted eight barges that were filled that single morning."

"Can nothing more be done? Must we sit by helplessly while the United States and Great Britain march to their doom? Is foreign intervention not possible?"

"Would that it were," Adams sighed. "The Emperor Louis Napoleon has quite charmed Queen Victoria. And he agrees with her that America must bend the knee. The French are at least behind him in this. They see Britain as the traditional enemy and welcome any trouble here. Then of course there is Prussia and the other German states. All related some way or other to the Queen. They will do nothing. Russia holds no love for the British after the Crimean War—but the Czar will not intervene on America's behalf. He is too stupid in any case. No, I am afraid that we are alone in the world and can expect no outside help. Something terrible is happening and no one seems to have discovered a way to avoid it."

Black clouds had come up to obscure the sun and the room grew dark. Obscured their spirits as well and they could only sit in silence. Where would it end, where would it end?

A brisk walk from this house on Grosvenor Square to Park Lane would take one to the most famous address in London. Appsley House. Number 1, London. The carriage from Whitehall stopped there and the footman opened the door. Grunting with the effort, wincing with the pain from his gouty foot, Lord Palmerston clambered down and hobbled into the house. A servant took his coat and the butler opened the door and admitted him to the presence.

Lord Wellesley, the Duke of Wellington, perhaps the most famous man in England; surely the most famous general alive.

"Come in, Henry, come in," the voice said from the wingchair before the fire. A thin voice, high-pitched with age, yet nevertheless still containing echoes of the firmness of command.

"Thank you, Arthur. It has been quite a time."

Lord Palmerston eased himself into the chair with a sigh. "You are looking good," he said.

Wellington laughed reedily. "When one is ninety-two it does not matter how one looks, rather that it is of paramount importance that one is there to be looked at at all."

Thin, yes, the skin drawn back over the bones of his skull to further accent the mighty Wellington nose. Conky, his troops had called him affectionately. All dead now, all in their graves, the hundreds of thousands of them. When one reaches the ninth decade one finds that there are very few peers left.

There was a slight click as a silent servant placed a glass on the table at Palmerston's elbow.

"The last bottle of the last case of the '28 port," Wellington said. "Been saving it for you. Knew you would be around here one of these days."

Palmerston sipped and sighed. "By gad that is music, heavenly music not drink. To your continued good health."

"May your toast be a true one. 1828, you remember that year?"

"Hard to forget. You were Prime Minister and I was the new boy in the Cabinet. I'm afraid that I was not as cooperative as I should have been at the time . . ."

"Water under the bridge. When one slowly approaches the century mark many things become no longer important. Since my illness in 'fifty-two I have the feeling that I am living on borrowed time and I mean to enjoy it."

"It was a time of great concern—"

"For me as well, I assure you. I was at death's door—but that dread portal never opened. Now, to business. It cannot be the port nor the reminiscences that bring you here today. In your note you said that it was a matter of some importance."

"It is. I assume that you read the newspapers?"

"You assume wrong. But my secretary does read to me from most of them. I imagine that you are referring to this matter with the Americans?"

"Indeed I am."

"Then why are you here?'

"I have been asked to come. By the Queen herself."

"Ahh," Wellington said, stirring in the chair, pulling at the rug with skeletal hands where it had slid down. "My dear Victoria. She was quite an attractive child, you know. Round-faced and pink and bubbling with energy. She often came to me for advice, even after her marriage and coronation. For one with so little promise, with such a strange childhood, she has outdone herself. I believe that she has become a Queen in deed as well as name. What does she wish of me now?"

"Some sage advice, I believe. She is battered from all sides by conflicting opinions as to how the Americans must be treated. She herself believes that they are responsible for Albert's death. But she also fears to let her emotions rule her head."

"She is alone in that," Wellington said with some warmth. "There is far too much hysteria about. Too much hysterical emotion and no attempt at logical thought. People, the press, the politicians. They all clamor for war. During my military career I always considered politicians to be self-serving and more loyal to their party than they were to their country. When I began my political career I discovered that my earlier opinion was far more correct than I could have possibly imagined. Now they bay for a reckless and needless war."

"And you do not? Viscount Wellington and Baron Duoro."

"Baron Duoro, conferred after Talavera. Only victors receive titles. You are deliberate in your choice of titles and remind me of my military career."

"I do."

"I prefer to remember my political career when considering this matter before me. I have always been for non-intervention in foreign affairs, you know that. It is terribly easy to begin wars, terribly difficult to stop them. We have not been invaded, none of our countrymen has been hurt, none of our property destroyed."

"An English ship was stopped on the high seas. A most illegal act—and two foreign nationals taken from her."

"I agree—a most illegal act. By international law the packet should have been taken to a neutral port. There it would be determined what the correct procedure would be. The two countries concerned would have their day in court. If this had been done, and the two men handed over to the Americans, why you would have no case at all against them. So why not let the lawyers in? If illegality is what we are talking about. There are enough of them around and I am sure that they would love to have a go at this one."

"Is that what you want me to tell the Queen?"

"Not at all. I am sure that the time is too late for lawyers. Someone should have thought about this a very long time ago."

"What would you have me tell her then?"

Wellington settled back into his chair, breathed out a low sigh.

"What indeed. On all sides the good and the great, as well as the low and the stupid, bay for war. It will be hard for her to go against that tide, particularly since she is inclined that way herself. And you have told me that she blames the Americans and this *Trent* Affair for her husband's death."

"She does indeed."

"She was always good at languages. But other than that she was not a very bright little girl. Breaking into tears quite often and quite prone to give in to emotional fits. You must tell her to look into her heart and think of the countless thousands now alive who will die if war comes. Tell her to put rational thought ahead of emotion. Not that I think she will listen. Tell her to seek peace with honor if she can."

"It will be difficult."

"Nothing in warfare or politics is easy, Lord Palmerston. You shall tell Her Majesty that she must think most seriously of the consequences, if this matter is allowed to proceed in the future as it has in the past. I have seen too much of battle and death to take relish in it. Here, have another glass of port before you leave. You'll not taste wine like that again in your lifetime."

The old man's eyes closed and his breath was a soft sighing. Palmerston finished the last of the port, sighed as well himself at pleasures spent. Then rose, quietly as he could, and saw himself out.

VICTORIOUS IN BATTLE

General William Tecumseh Sherman had woken at dawn, as he did most days, and watched the sky brighten outside the hotel window. Ellen was sleeping soundly, her even breathing almost a slight snore. He rose quietly, dressed and let himself out. The hotel lobby was empty except for the night porter who was dozing in a chair. He jumped to his feet when he heard Sherman's boots on the marble floor.

"Mornin' General. Looks to be a nice day." He unlocked the front door and raised his hand in a most unmilitary salute. Sherman was barely aware of his presence. William's Hotel was just across from the Presidential Mansion and he walked that way. The blue-clad soldiers at the end of the drive snapped to attention when he passed and he returned the salute. It was going to be a fine day.

The weather, that is. How fine it would be for him depended upon the man in the White House. He walked faster, as though to get away from his thoughts. Stopped for a moment to watch a flock of crows swirling about the stub of the unfinished Washington Monument, tried to think about anything except his approaching meeting with the President. He knew himself, knew how easy it would be to fall into the black humor that dogged his existence. Not now. Not today. He turned abruptly and retraced his path. Walking at a brisk military pace, staring straight ahead, fighting to keep his thoughts under tight control.

He smelled fresh coffee as he approached the hotel, went through to the bar, talked to the waiter there. The moment of blackness had passed; the coffee was very good and he had a second cup.

Ellen was seated before the vanity when he came back to their room, brushing her long black hair.

"You are up and about early, Cump," she said.

"Once I woke up and started thinking . . ."

"Then you started to fuss yourself and worry, that's what you did. But not today."

"But today is so important . . ."

"Every day is important now. You must forget what happened in Kentucky. Since then you have done work that General Halleck is proud of. He is your supporter, as is your friend Grant."

"I let them down once, I can't forget that."

She turned and took his hands, pressed them firmly between hers as if to add physical support as well. He tried to smile but could not. She stood and clasped his thin body to her.

"Who knows you better than I? We have known each other since I was ten years old. Since we have been married, so many years now, you have never failed me or the children."

"I failed in the bank in California—and in the army in Kentucky."

"Halleck does not think so—or he would not have reinstated you in command. And you have paid all your debts in San Francisco—none of which you had to."

"But I did. The bank failure was not caused by me. But I did encourage fellow officers to invest in the bank. That was my doing. When they lost their money—why I had a debt of honor to repay them. Every cent."

"Yes, you have done that, and I am proud of you. But there was a cost. Living so far apart for so long. Life has not been easy, I am the first to admit that, and we have been separated too much. And it has been lonely."

GENERAL WILLIAM TECUMSEH SHERMAN

"For me as well," he said, pulling away and sitting on the

edge of the bed. "I have kept it to myself but, more than once—I have felt so—suicidal. But for you and the children . . . Only seeing Minnie and Lizzie and Willy, thinking of them . . . without that I could have cast myself into the Mississippi."

Ellen knew that when he was in this black mood there was no reasoning with him. She glanced down at the watch pinned to her dress.

"Today is too important for you to get yourself all worked up. What time is John meeting you?"

"Nine o'clock, he said, in the lobby downstairs."

"More than time enough to change your shirt then. And while you are doing that I'll give that coat a good brushing."

Sherman sighed deeply and climbed to his feet, straightened his back. "You are right, of course. A war is being fought and I am a soldier and I do not fear battle. In fact I welcome it. And the first battle is to put these dark thoughts behind me now and think only of this meeting. My future depends upon its success."

Senator John Sherman was smoking his first cigar of the day when he saw the couple come down the stairs. He stubbed it out and crossed the lobby to give his sister-in-law a fraternal kiss on the cheek. Turned, smiling with pleasure, to greet his brother.

"You're looking fit as a fiddle, Cump. Ready to meet with the railsplitter?"

Sherman smiled, but his eyes remained icy cold. Today's meeting was too important to make jokes about.

"Can't these job seekers wait? Must everyone who wants a government appointment come to see me personally?" the President asked, lifting the thick sheaf of papers unread, letters unsigned, urgent matters unresolved.

"I've kept the ones that are not urgent waiting, for weeks some of them, and have dissuaded or canceled the very worst of them," Nicolay said. "But you made this appointment yourself, with Senator John Sherman. And he wants you to meet his brother, General Sherman."

Lincoln sighed deeply and let the papers drop back onto the desk. "Well—it is politics that keeps this war going, so politics it will be. See them in."

They were not a very prepossessing pair. The Senator was young and already balding. General Sherman had a wiry red beard and a short but tough body, although he did have the erect and military bearing of a West Point graduate. His eyes were as cold and empty as those of a bird of prey. Unless he was addressed directly he did not speak. Instead he sat quietly, looking out the window at the Potomac River and past that to the plowed fields of Virginia on the far side. Apparently having no interest at all in the political conversation. Lincoln watched him out of the corners of his eyes, struggling with a memory that was just below the surface. Of course!

"Well Senator," the President cut in, interrupting what was turning into an all too familiar abolitionist speech, "what you say has a lot of good reason to it. All I have to say is what the girl said when she put her foot into the stocking, 'It strikes me that there is something in it'. I shall keep your thoughts in mind. But now I would also like to have a word or two with your brother." He turned in his chair to face Sherman. "General, stop me if I am wrong, but didn't we meet at least once before?"

Sherman nodded. "We have, Mr. Lincoln. It was soon after the Battle of Bull Run."

"That's it, of course, a little matter of discipline with one of your Irish regiments as I recall."

"You might say that. As I remember it happened soon before you arrived. A captain, a lawyer if you will excuse my saying so, came up to me and spoke while a number of his soldiers were within earshot. In no uncertain terms he told me that his three-month term was up and he was going home. I was not going to abide by this, not in front of the men."

Sherman's face was rigid with anger as he relived the moment. "This kind of thing has to be stopped the instant it starts. Particularly in front of men who have already fled once from battle. So I reached inside my overcoat and said, 'If you attempt to leave without orders, it will be mutiny, and I will shoot you like a dog'. The matter ended there."

"Not quite," Lincoln said, smiling at the memory. "It must have been later that same day when I was riding through the encampment with Secretary of State Seward when this same captain comes up and points at you and says, 'Mr. President, I have a cause of grievance. This morning I went to speak to Colonel Sherman, and he threatened to shoot me'."

Always savoring a good story, Lincoln leaned back while he hesitated a dramatic moment before going on.

"I waited a bit, then leaned down and whispered to him in what I believe they call a stage whisper. I said, 'Well, if I were you, and he threatened to shoot, I would not trust him for I believe he would do it!' "

They laughed together because it was a good story well told.

"Of course," Lincoln added, "I only discovered what it was all about after Colonel Sherman, as he was at that time, explained. My feeling was that since I did not know anything about it, I did still feel that you knew your own business best."

"Morale was not good after our defeat at Bull Run so any talk like that had to be stopped at once."

"In the West Point manner."

"That is correct."

"After leaving West Point were you not also at one time superintendent of the Louisiana State Military Academy? Is that true?"

"I had that honor."

"Cump is too reluctant by far," John said. "He founded that academy, practically built it by himself. Started with an empty field, designed the buildings and had the school up and running within two months."

The President nodded. "With a responsible post like that you must have had many friends in the South?"

"I had—and perhaps still have some of them. During my service I grew to know the men of the South. I had personal friends there whom I admired as men. But for their attitude toward the Negroes they enslave I have no respect at all. If a man goes forth and no matter how well dressed and well spoken he is, he is a man like any other. However if a man goes forth and is followed by a slave who attends him, why in the South he is looked upon as something else again. A man who enslaves other men—and is proud of it to boot. In many other ways they can be fine and honorable people. If trained, they make good soldiers. They are a military people with a strong military tradition."

Lincoln nodded. "Unhappily that is so. Far too many of your West Point comrades are fighting on the other side."

"The Southerners make good fighting men. But at times they are immune to simple logic. I know, for I have attempted to make them see reason. At one time I even attempted to warn them, the officers teaching in the academy, of their certain fate, of what the future positively held in store for them. I am afraid they did not listen for they are a most firm-minded lot."

The President was puzzled. "You have me there, General. What was it you wanted to warn them about?"

"This was after the Southern states began to secede. It was a time of great concern. All of the instructors in the academy were serving officers in the United States Army. They were torn by loyalty to the government and loyalty to their states. I tried to reason with them. To tell them about the disastrous war that was certainly coming, Mr. President. I tried to tell them of their folly for I could see that our country would be drenched in blood if they persevered along this road to civil war. Drenched in their own blood. I could not convince them that the peaceful people of the North would fight if they had to. They would fight and they would win."

"You speak with great conviction. You felt the fighting spirit of the North would eventually prevail against that of the South?"

"Not at all. The Southerner has always been military-minded, that is why so many of them have gone to West Point. Because of that they think themselves superior in many ways. But we are all Americans, North and South, and react to conflict in an identical manner. But it is not the fighting spirit that will win this war. In the end it is the machinery of warfare that will prevail. The South cannot build a locomotive or a railway car. Or anything else needed to fight a war and pursue it to final victory. They will win battles—they are very brave people—but they do not have the resources to win a war. When I told them this they smiled at me as though I were soft."

Sherman paused for a moment looking out of the window with his cold, empty eyes. Looking across the dividing Potomac at the enemy land. Seeing events past—perhaps seeing events to come.

"After that I had no choice. The only course open to me was to leave the South and join the Union cause. Of course my words were rejected and quickly forgotten—and we were swept into this war. But I knew them as kind good friends. To this day I cannot think of them as rebels or traitors. They are fighting in defense of their country, their houses and families, against what they see as invaders."

Lincoln was impressed; a fighting man who was a serious thinker as well. Too many of his generals were full of fight and very little else. And some of them didn't even have that fighting spirit. General McClellan had spent five months doing absolutely nothing. Now he was in hospital with fever and the President had taken over his command. In the west Halleck appeared to be stalemated. Soldiers were dying but nothing seemed to be happening despite this. Only at sea was the blockade succeeding. Blockade runners were seized almost every day, supplies in the South running out. But this was a stalemate. The war could not be won by simply standing back and hoping the Rebels would starve themselves to death. If this General Sherman had a higher command he might be able to do something about that. Not right now, but he would keep him in mind.

"You will go far, General. Indeed I wish I had a dozen like you. If I did this war would be over by next spring. It is my understanding that it is your wish to take up a command under General Halleck?"

"It is. If the Commander-in-Chief is in agreement he wishes me to have a division under General Grant."

"Then it is done! The order will be issued and I wish you every success."

Nicolay, with true secretarial precision appeared at that moment, opened the door and ushered them out. Only when the door was closed did he speak.

"Mrs. Lincoln has asked that you see her in Willie's room."

Lincoln's face was gray under his dark skin. "Any change?"

"I don't know. That was all she said."

Lincoln hurried out. Mary was standing by the door looking at the bed. She turned when he touched her arm.

"He is so cold," she said.

One of Willie's playmates was sitting by the great bed, solemnly upright. Willie's eyes were shut.

"Has he spoken?" Lincoln asked the boy.

"No, sir, not today. But I am sure he knows that I am here, for he squeezes my hand."

They pulled up chairs next to the boy and sat in silence. There was nothing that they could say, nothing that they could do. The doctor came and looked at the silent child, touched his forehead—then shook his head. This was more expressive than words could ever be.

It was a good hour before Lincoln returned to his desk. He dropped wearily into his armchair, turned at the sound of a voice.

"He has done it, Mr. Lincoln, Grant has done it again!"

The Secretary of War hurried into the room waving the dispatch like a battle flag. So excited was he that he did not notice the President's drawn face, his expression of blank despair. Cameron turned to the map of the United States on the wall and tapped his finger on the state of Tennessee.

"Fort Donelson has fallen and it is indeed a mighty victory." He read from the paper in his hand. " 'February 16th . . . the Confederate army has surrendered . . . fifteen thousand of them captured.' And here is the best—proof that we have a mighty fighting general in Grant. When General Buckner asked Grant for terms, you know what Grant said?" He found the quote on the paper, raised his finger dramatically as he spoke.

" 'No terms except unconditional and immediate surrender can be accepted. I propose to move immediately upon your works'." He was jubilant. "I do believe, if I have your permission, that we should promote Grant to Major General."

Lincoln nodded slowly. Cameron turned back to the map.

"First the fall of Fort Henry, now Fort Donelson in turn, a

catastrophe for the enemy. The Cumberland and the Tennessee, the two most important rivers in the southwest are in our hands. The state of Tennessee is now ours while Kentucky is wide open before us. The South can only despair. They are surrounded and under attack." He addressed the map again, stabbing at it.

"Our armies are here in Virginia, near Washington, and here at Harper's Ferry. On the Peninsula at Fort Monroe as well—ready to strike at Richmond and Norfolk. A ring of steel, that is what it is! Our men are at Port Royal aiming at Savannah and Charleston. Down on the Gulf Coast we are poised at the gates of Mobile and New Orleans. And here on the Mississippi, on the Cumberland and the Tennessee."

Exhausted and elated he dropped into a chair. "And all along the rebel coast the blockade is now no longer just a nuisance to Johnny Reb but a fully developed danger. I will be surprised if the war lasts until the end of this year. Eighteen sixty-two will be our *annus mirabilis*, our year of victory."

"I pray it will be so, Cameron. I pray that all the death and destruction will finally come to an end and that this beleaguered country will be one again. But a wounded beast will turn and rend—and the South has been well wounded. We must keep ever-watchful guard. And most important of all is the blockade. It must be maintained and strengthened. We must cut off all source of outside supplies. Without supplies and the military wherewithal the South cannot succeed in the field. In the end their armies will be defeated."

Although the words were optimistic they were spoken in tones of leaden gloom. So sorrowing were they that Cameron for the first time noticed the President's obvious distress.

"Sir—you are not ill?"

"No, I am not. But the one I love is. My son, little Willie, just twelve years old. Mortally ill the doctors say. The typhoid. They doubt he will live out the day."

Stricken by the President's pain and suffering, Cameron could not speak. He rose, head shaking with remorse, and slowly left the room.

*　*　*

The James River cuts through Virginia, the heart of the Confederacy. After leaving Richmond, the Confederate capital, it rolls slowly through the rich countryside toward the sea. It is joined by the Elizabeth River just before it flows into the wide estuary known as Hampton Roads.

A chill mist rose from the surface of the Elizabeth River this March morning, the first light of dawn barely penetrating. Gaunt trees lined the riverbanks; a bluejay sat on a limb overhanging the water, singing coarsely—then was suddenly silent. Disturbed by the dark form that had appeared out of the mist below he took fright and flew off. Birdsong was replaced by a gasping sound, like the breath of some water monster. The monster itself slid slowly into sight, its breath the puffing of a steam engine, dark smoke roiling up from a single, tall funnel.

It was steel-plated, slant-sided, slow and ungainly, its forward motion barely able to stir ripples from the river's glassy surface. As it slipped by it could be seen that its gray armored flanks were pierced with gun ports, now shut and sealed; an immense ram was fixed to the ship's bow. An armored pilot house was on the foredeck just above the four-foot iron beak. Inside the pilot house the ship's commanding officer, Flag Officer Franklin Buchanan, stood behind the helmsman at the wheel.

He was not a happy man. His ship was a clobbered together collection of compromises. Her wooden hull was the burnt shell of the USS *Merrimack*, fired by the Yankees when they had retreated from Norfolk and the great naval yard there. That sodden hull was supposed to be the salvation of the Confederacy. The burnt strakes and hull had been cut away until sound wood was reached. Onto this hull had been constructed an armored superstructure of pine and oak, covered with iron cladding, to shield the ten large guns that she carried. Now the *Merrimack*, renamed the CSS *Virginia*, was going into battle for the first time. And painfully slowly. The single-cylinder engine, always feeble and under-powered, had been under water for a long time before the hull was raised and it was salvaged. The engine was old and badly maintained to begin with, it had suffered no good during its immersion. Nor was the engine equal to the task of moving the heavy craft at more than the feeble speed of five knots.

But they were at least under way at last and the ship would soon taste battle. They would have attacked earlier but severe spring storms had lashed the coast for days, sending mountainous seas rolling across the bay and crashing into the shore. The shallow draft *Virginia* would never have survived. But now the storm had ended, the waves died down during the night—and the ironclad could finally be put to the test.

Flag Officer Buchanan turned and clambered partway down the steps to the engine room, called out loudly above the clanking and hiss of steam.

"Too slow, Lieutenant Jones, too slow by far. Can we not raise more steam?" The grease-covered officer shouted back.

"No, sir. This is the most we can do. I have too much pressure as it is—any more and something will blow."

Buchanan went back to his station. As they clanked slowly out into the James River they were joined by four small wooden sidewheel gunboats. The *Patrick Henry* was the largest, mounting a total of six guns, but the tiny *Teaser* had only a single gun.

This was the force that was to challenge the might of the warships of the United States Navy.

The mist was gone now as they slowly chugged out into the open waters of Hampton Roads. Once past Norfolk they would be in the open sea.

Where they would face the blockading Yankee warships, for here was where the throttling blockade began. So vital was this entrance to the heart of the Confederacy that a small fleet of Union ships was stationed here. Buchanan had never seen them, but he had received daily reports of their strength and condition.

Here were the 40-gun steam frigates *Roanoke* and *Minnesota*. Accompanying them were the sailing frigates the 50-gun *Congress* and *Cumberland* with 24 guns. Over 150 cannon in complete control of the entrance to the Charles River. He knew that it would take at least another small fleet to defeat them. The South did not have a fleet.

All that they had was this single, botched together and untried ironclad. And four tiny, unarmored steamboats.

Never tested in battle, ludicrous and rumbling, almost leisurely, the CSS *Virginia* steered for the blockading ships.

"Ports open," Buchanan shouted. "Prepare for action!"

The lookout on the USS *Mount Vernon*, the ship closest to shore, saw smoke appear above Sewall's Point and thought a fire had been lit. He was about to report it when the dark shape emerged into view. A ship, but what kind of a ship? Its length shortened as the bow swung toward him and he raised the alarm. He may not have seen a vessel like this before—but he could recognize the Confederate flag at her stern. This could very well be the armorclad craft they had all been expecting, the ship that was supposed to bring victory to the South.

THE IRONCLAD *VIRGINIA* STRIKES!

The *Mount Vernon* raised a signal flag to alert the fleet. It was not noticed. Her captain ordered a gun to be fired at the approaching ironclad. This single shot was the first shot fired in the Battle of Hampton Roads.

Puffing leisurely up the South Channel toward the anchored warships the *Virginia* looked more ridiculous than menacing.

Until her gun ports opened and the black muzzles of her guns appeared. Buchanan singled out *Cumberland* for his first attack. Still a mile away she opened fire with the bow gun loaded with grape shot that killed or wounded the crew at the pivot gun.

The drums sounded beat to quarters on the Northern frigate and the crew ran to their stations. But the attack was so sudden and unexpected that they even had washing suspended from the rigging. They did their best. The crew swarmed aloft to set sail while the guncrews leaned into the tackle. Within scant minutes the *Cumberland*'s guns roared their first broadside. The attacker was closer now and the broadside of solid shot crashed into *Virginia*'s armor plating, four inches of thick iron that was backed by two feet of pine and oak.

The shot hit—and bounced away. None penetrated the armor nor did they slow in any way her steady and ponderous approach.

"Steady," Buchanan said to the coxswain, "steady." The ironclad's armor rang like a giant bell as the round shot struck and screamed away. "Hold her there—I want to hit the hull midship."

Before the frigate's guns could be loaded again the ram struck *Cumberland* with a tremendous crash, driving into her wooden hull and through it. Water gushed in through the immense opening and the ship commenced to sink—threatening to drag the ironclad down with her.

"Full speed astern!"

The threat was a real one and the *Virginia*'s forward deck was already under water. There was the constant crack of lead on iron as marksmen on the *Cumberland* fired their muskets at point-blank range. They were no more effective than the cannon had been.

But the *Virginia* had condemned herself. Her feeble engine could not drag her free of the sinking ship. Water was already flooding onto her deck, splashing through ventilation openings under her armor. The hope of the South was being destroyed in her first ship action.

But the strain on the ram was too much—it broke off and the ironclad was free. As the *Virginia* backed away the ocean poured through the gaping opening in the other ship's hull. The attacker turned its attention toward the rest of the fleet.

But *Cumberland* did not strike her colors—nor did she stop firing. Because of this *Virginia* stayed beside her, firing steadily despite the solid shot that clanged impotently against her armor, fired until the Yankee warship was burning, sinking. Yet the surviving gun crews stayed at their stations, still firing. The crash of iron on steel sounded one last time before she sank.

Then the armorclad was into the Union fleet. During the attack on the *Cumberland*, *Congress* had set sail and with the aid of the tugboat, *Zouave*, had run ashore. Trapped there she was being pounded by the small Confederate gunboats. Now *Virginia* joined them in the attack. Crossing the frigate's stern *Virginia* sent round after round through her frail wooden hull until it was ablaze from stem to stern.

Hot, exhausted, filthy—the crew of the ironclad still raised a victorious cheer as their ship turned toward the rest of the blockading fleet.

The steam-powered *Minnesota* could have escaped from the slow and ponderous attacker. Her commander and her crew did not see it that way. Using her greater mobility she circled the *Virginia* trying to press any advantage. There was none. Her cannonballs caused no damage, while her own wooden hull was penetrated again and again. By afternoon she was badly damaged and run aground. Only the turn of the tide saved her. *Virginia* had to stay in the deep channel or she would be aground as well.

"Break off the engagement," Buchanan ordered, peering out at the setting sun and the turning tide. "Set course back to the river."

As darkness began to fall the ironclad Confederate steamship, slightly damaged, with few wounded, chugged back into harbor. Buchanan and his crew celebrated, looking forward to the morning when they would bring their ship out again to destroy the beached *Minnesota*. And any other wooden ship of the Union navy. The fleet would be destroyed, the blockade lifted, the South saved.

Iron had triumphed over wood. Sail had given way to

steam. Nor was this message lost to the world, for this battle had long been anticipated, the existence of the *Virginia* a badly-kept secret. There were French and British ships standing out to sea that had been waiting for this encounter. They had watched closely the events of the day and fully expected the total destruction of the blockading fleet in the morning.

This was a new kind of war at sea. The sun set on a day of Southern victory.

IRON OF THE NORTH

The same storm that had kept the *Virginia* in port had prevented the *Monitor* from leaving the Brooklyn Navy Yard. Days and weeks of frustrating delays had followed her launching in mid-February. Ericsson's design was magnificent; her construction from keel to completion in 101 days was a mechanical miracle. It was the human factor that could not have been allowed for in the drawings.

The metal ship had a single-screw propeller that was turned by a powerful two-cylinder engine—also of Ericsson's design. However the engineers who had fitted the propeller had made a single major mistake. They had assumed that the drive shaft rotated in one direction—when in fact it rotated the opposite way. So when the first sea tests were begun and her commander, Lieutenant John Worden, ordered half-speed ahead, the craft shuddered and went backward and slammed into the dock.

"What is happening?" he called down to Chief Engineer Alban Stimers. The engineer's profane reply could luckily not be heard above the clank of machinery. This died away and Stimers went forward to the pilothouse and called up to Worden.

"No one ever seems to have asked if the propeller is left-handed or right-handed. When you want to go forward it goes into reverse."

"Can a new propeller be fitted?"

"No. This was one was specially designed and made to order. I don't know how long it would take to manufacture a new one, but I know it could not be done very quickly. And she would have to go back into drydock to have it replaced, which would take even more time."

"Damnation! What about running the engine in reverse then? That would certainly make her go forward."

Stimers shook his head gloomily, mopping his sopping face with a rag that only spread more grease across his skin. "We could. But we wouldn't get more than two or three knots—not her design speed of seven."

Worden climbed down from the armored pilothouse. "Why? I don't understand."

"Well you have to know something about engines to get the drift. You see each slide valve is driven by a loose eccentric which is shifted part way around to get into reverse. This gives the best result in one position—not the other."

"The answer then?"

"The entire engine must be taken down and the eccentrics repositioned."

Worden knew that time was growing short. The newspapers, both North and South, were filled with reports that the Southern ironclad was nearing completion. He had also had more specific intelligence reports that it would be a matter of weeks, possibly days, before the enemy ship came out to tackle the blockading fleet. Every day wasted was a day lost. But the propeller had to be put right. They were not going to backwater stern first into battle!

"Start on it at once."

It was not until February 19 that ablebodied seamen and officers were mustered and *Monitor* was finally towed by a tug for the short trip from Greenpoint to the Brooklyn Navy Yard, where the monster pair of guns were lowered into place. They were 11-inch smoothbore Dahlgren cannon capable of firing a solid shot weighing 166 pounds. Stores were loaded aboard as well, along with a supply of powder, shot, shell, grape and canister. The iron ship was going to war.

Though not quite yet.

Engineer Stimers had the responsibility of test-firing the guns, although he had never seen a recoil mechanism like theirs before. After the guns were fired the recoil ran them back along a metal track. When this happened the guns were slowed by friction plates that were clamped tightly to the track. But Stimers turned the friction recoil wheel the wrong way—loosening rather than tightening the clamps.

When the first gun was test-fired it flew back at great speed and was only stopped by the cascabel striking the interior of the turret. This sheared off several bolts that secured the bearings of the guide-rollers to the carriage. These were hard to get to and it took a long time to drill them out and replace them.

The human element again. Stimers was so upset by the incident that he made the same mistake with the second gun. Which had to be repaired in the same manner. Ericsson himself supervised the repairs, staring angrily at the shamed engineer, muttering darkly in Swedish until the job had been done to his satisfaction.

It wasn't until February 26 that all the repairs had been made. The following morning at 7 A.M., cold and dark and with a fierce snowstorm blowing, the *Monitor* let go her lines. Her destination Hampton Roads and the blockading Union fleet. The longshoremen headed for shelter and only John Ericsson and Thomas Fitch Roland, owner of the ironworks where the ship had been made, remained on the dock.

"At last," Roland said. "Now the Ericsson battery will prove its worth. It is a wonderful machine that you have invented and it is a matter of great pride to me that we have completed it to everyone's satisfaction."

"It will do what it has been designed to do. You have my word on that." Then he gasped. "But—what is happening?"

Monitor had turned her bow suddenly towards the bank of the narrow, choppy channel. A collision seemed certain—however just before she struck the bank the bow swung out—toward the other side. Slower and slower the iron ship continued, corkscrewing from side to side until she finally hit a flimsy dock, almost demolishing it, and stopped.

Ericsson was almost dancing with rage. "Get a tug," he said through tight-clamped teeth. "Get her back to the dock."

"I couldn't hold her," the abashed helmsman explained. "Once I turned the rudder to one side, I had to fight to get it back. Even with Lieutenant Worden helping me it was almost physically impossible to do. Then, once I got it over it would go to the other side and the same thing would happen."

Ericsson insisted on making the examination himself, inspecting the tiller ropes and linkage to the rudder. Sailors relayed instructions from him to turn the wheel first one way, then the other. It was more than an hour before he emerged, trousers soaked from the bilges, filthy and grease-covered but unaware of it.

"The rudder is overbalanced," he said. "We must increase the purchase of the connecting linkage. Double it if needs be."

It look less than a day to accomplish this. But three days later the *Monitor* was still tied up at her docking berth. The crew restless and upset. They knew that their craft had been designed to fight the *Virginia*, which was nearing completion according to the continual reports in the newspapers. Yet they could do nothing. A heavy storm was hitting the coast; great waves breaking on the shore. *Monitor* was designed for shoal water and rivers. Her low freeboard and shallow draft made her most unseaworthy even in a slight swell.

On March 6 there was a clear sky, a slight wind—and a smooth sea. It had been decided that, since the *Monitor*'s top speed was only seven knots, she would be towed to her destination. A heavy line was passed from the tug *Seth Low* and, accompanied by the steam gunboats *Currituck* and *Sachem*, *Monitor* finally headed out to sea.

The day passed easily enough and the crew were getting used to their new charge. They had boiled beef and potatoes for dinner and those off duty retired peacefully for the night. They did not get much sleep. The wind grew stronger, the seas heavier, and by morning the good weather had ended and a dreadful journey had begun.

Green seas broke right across the tiny ship, coming under the turret in waterfalls. The waves rolled right over the pilothouse, jetting in through the narrow eyeholes with such force that it knocked the helmsman off the wheel.

Even worse were the waves that passed over the vital blower pipes. These protruded above the deck, high enough to stay above the water in a normal sea for they supplied air to the steam engines deep in the hold below. Water inundated the blower engines, wetting the leather straps that turned them, stopping them from functioning. Without air the fires died; without blowers to pump it out the engineroom filled with poisonous, acid gas that nearly killed the men there.

MONITOR BATTLES THE WAVES

The bravery of the crew was not in doubt. Volunteers entered the engineroom, at the risk of their own lives, and carried out the unconscious men. They were dragged out to the top of the turret in the fresh air. After some time they recovered—but the ship was still in great danger. With the fires damped, the engineroom was now filled with carbonic acid gas from the coal fumes. With no steam the bilge pumps were put out of action. The tow rope still held, pulling them through the crashing seas—but the ship was slowly filling with water. Hand pumps were tried but to no avail. The men fought the many leaks—and still the water rose. When each wave broke more water was forced in through the hawse pipe.

It was a terrible night, of exhaustion and seasickness. Few men had the strength to climb to the top of the turret and vomit over the side. Belowdecks, lit by the feeble oil lights, was a scene of crashing filthy water, floating debris, endless labor to save the ship.

It wasn't until just before daylight that the storm blew itself out and the waves died down. The poisonous gas had dissipated during the night, so now the sodden ashes could be shoveled from the boilers and fresh fires lit. When the head of steam built up the blower engines began to turn. There was a spontaneous cheer throughout the ship as the first gouts of bilge water jetted over the side.

No one had slept. Cooking was impossible, so that those who could manage to eat had only cheese and crackers, with fresh water from the condenser to drink.

The second day was slightly better than the first, but the weary, wet men were not aware of the difference. Yet they were getting close to their destination. By four in the afternoon Fortress Monroe, the Union fort guarding the entrance to Hampton Roads, was in sight.

And clouds of billowing smoke as well. Dark streaks of cannon projectiles could be seen, exploding into white smoke. Lieutenant Worden climbed to the top of the turret for a better view.

"Might be a Secesh ship trying to run the blockade," one of the sailors said; little hope in his voice. Worden shook his head in a silent no.

"Too much, too much firing from too many ships. The *Virginia* must be out and among the fleet. Iron against wood—they don't have a chance."

"That's our job to take her on—that's what we have to do!" one of the men shouted.

"We'll never get there before dark," a sailor said, looking up at the sky, then at the horizon.

"Then we will be there in the morning," Lieutenant Worden said grimly. "If that ironclad is among our fleet, and she survives this day, she will surely be back in the morning. But when dawn breaks and *Virginia* appears, we are going to be there waiting for her. It will be iron against iron this time. Then those Rebels will know that they have been in a fight."

Standing out to sea, at the mouth of Hampton Roads, the

watching French and British were unaware of the small, black, ugly vessel that had dropped anchor after dark at Fortress Monroe, the Union bastion on the other side of the Roads. What they had witnessed that day when *Virginia* had attacked the Northern fleet had been more of a massacre than a battle. In the morning they expected more of the same.

But would it be different when the untested *Monitor* faced up to the battle-proven *Virginia* in the morning?

Monitor raised her anchor in the night and steamed out into Hampton Roads. The warm spring night was lit by the newly-risen moon—but far brighter was the glare from the burning *Congress*. Explosions racked her as loaded guns and powder magazines exploded. The crew of *Monitor* had been told of the day's disastrous events; the reality was far more shocking than words could ever be. By ten o'clock she had stationed herself between the badly damaged *Minnesota* and the shore. Her crew waited sleepless throughout the night while steam tugs tried to free the stranded warship. Though stranded and vulnerable by daylight, *Minnesota* had not given up the fight. She took aboard more cannon balls and powder from the fort during the night.

At two in the morning the battleship was refloated—but soon grounded again. The *Monitor* approached her and dropped anchor. Worden sent Lieutenant Greene aboard to talk to her commander.

"Thank God that you have arrived," Captain Van Brunt said, pointing to the still-burning *Congress*. "That will be us in the morning if we don't get out of these shallows. Our guns can't make a dent in that infernal contraption, though we will keep on trying."

"Perhaps ours can. In any case we will station ourselves between your ship and the enemy. She will have to get by us to reach you and that will take some doing."

At a little after nine o'clock next morning the history of naval warfare changed forever. Modern warfare began. When the *Virginia* made her leisurely way toward the stranded Union warship, *Monitor* was placed squarely between the ironclad and her prey.

Aboard the *Virginia* the sailors cleared for action once again. But Lieutenant Jones was unhappy.

"What's happening there?" he called out, his view restricted by the armored eyeslit. Midshipman Littlepage climbed up the armor to see better.

"The tugs are leaving. But there is a raft of some kind close to her. Something on it—as though they were taking her boilers and machinery ashore."

"Nonsense! Not at this time." He pulled himself up to see better and grimaced with anger. "Damnation! That's no raft—and that is a monstrous gun turret. It must be Ericsson's battery."

It could not have come at a worse time. His plans to finish off the *Minnesota* then disperse the rest of the blockading fleet were in peril.

A FIERCE STRUGGLE—IRON AGAINST IRON

Virginia was determined to finish off the wounded ship. At the range of a mile she fired at the stranded ship and saw some of her shells strike home. But the small iron ship could not be long ignored. Puffing clouds of smoke it drove directly toward its larger opponent until it was just alongside.

"Stop engines," Worden ordered. "Commence firing."

The first gun crew heaved the swinging shield away from the gunport, ran the gun out and Greene pulled the lockstring. The gun boomed out, deafening the men, doing more harm inside the turret by its blast than it inflicted on its target. The cannon ball hit the other's armor and bounced away.

The *Virginia* fired her broadside and the battle of iron against iron was begun.

The *Monitor* rode so low in the ocean that her decks were awash. All that could be seen above water, other than a small armored pilothouse, was her immense central turret. Both targets were almost impossible to hit. The few balls that hit their target merely ricocheted away.

And every three minutes the 120-ton structure was rotated by its steam engine so that the two immense guns housed inside could be brought to bear. Their large target could not be missed. Agile and under perfect control, the smaller ship darted about the clumsy, almost uncontrollable Southern ironclad.

For two hours, the muzzles of their guns almost touching, the two warships hammered solid shell into each other. Disaster almost struck the *Virginia* when her prow grounded in a mudbank. For a quarter of an hour her feeble engine struggled to free her while *Monitor* moved about her firing steadily. Soon the larger ship's funnel was so holed with shot and disabled that there was scarcely any draft for her engine. Solid shot had blown off the ends of the muzzles of two of her guns. They could still fire but when they did so the flames of the discharge set fire to the wooden surrounds.

The *Monitor* however did suffer one casualty. Her commander was looking through the armored slit in the pilothouse when a cannon ball struck squarely against it. He screamed with pain when fragments of paint and metal were blown into his eyes. He was taken below where the ship's doctor did what he could to repair the damage. He saved one eye—but Worden was blinded in the other.

The battle continued, and ended only when the tide began to turn. The sluggish *Virginia* broke contact and made her way slowly back up the channel while her undefeated opponent still remained on guard between her and her prey.

Virginia returned to her base while *Monitor* waited like a bulldog at the gate for her to return.

She never did. The tall funnel was riddled with holes, while some of the armor plate was hanging free. Her faulty engines were beyond repair, her weight was so great that her draft was too deep for her to do battle anywhere except in the calm waters of Hampton Roads.

The warship that had forever changed naval warfare would never fight again.

The blockade was once again sound. The noose was again tightening about the South.

There were optimists in the North who felt that the war was as good as won.

SHILOH

Confederate General Albert Sidney Johnston was of course a gentleman, as well as being a not unkind man. He wished for a moment that he was not a gentleman, so he would not have to see Matilda Mason. There was a war to be fought after all. No, that wouldn't cut. All the orders had been issued, the troops deployed, so there was really nothing more for him to do until the attack began. She had been waiting to see him for two days now and he knew he could not put the meeting off any longer for he had run out of excuses. It was undeniable that she was indeed a close friend of his family so if word got back that he had refused to see her . . .

"Sergeant, show the lady in. Then bring a pot of coffee for some refreshment."

The tent flap lifted and he climbed to his feet and took her hand. "It has surely been a long time, Matty."

"A lot longer than it *should* have been, Sidney." Still an impressive woman even though her hair was going gray. She sniffed, then crumpled into the canvas chair. "I am sorry, I should not speak like that. Lord knows you have the war to fight and more important things to do than see an old busybody."

"That's certainly not you!"

"Well indeed it is. You see, I am so worried about John, chained in that prison in the North, like some kind of trapped animal. We are so desperate. You know the right people, being a general now and all, so you can surely do something to help."

Johnston did not say so—but he had very little sympathy for the imprisoned John Mason. He was reported to be living in some comfort, with all the best food—and he would surely never run out of cigars.

"I can do nothing until the politicians can come to some agreement. But look at it this way, Matty. There is a war on and we all must serve, one way or the other. Right now, in that Yankee prison, John and Slidell are worth a division or more to the Southern cause. The British are still fuming and fussing about the incident and making all sorts of warlike sounds. So you have to understand that anything that is bad for the North is good for us. The war is not going as well as we might like."

"You will hear no complaints from me, or anyone else for that matter. You soldiers are fighting, doing the best you can, we know that. At home we all also do what we can to support the war. There is not an iron fence left in our town, all sent away to melt down for armor for the ironclads. If the vittles aren't as good as we like that is no sacrifice in the light of what the boys in gray are doing. I'm not complaining for myself. I do believe that we are doing our part."

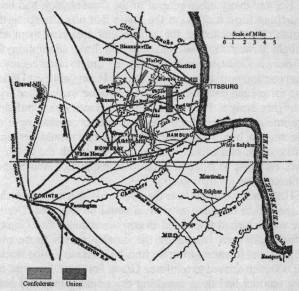

THE SHILOH BATTLEFIELD

"You don't know how delighted I am to hear those words, Matty. I will tell you that it is no secret that the South is surrounded. What I want to do now is break through the Yankee armies that are choking us. I have had the army marching for days to face the enemy. And the attack begins tomorrow. Now that is a secret . . ."

"I'll not tell!"

"I know that, or I wouldn't be talking to you. I do this so that you will see that John, who is in reality quite comfortable where he is, is doing far more for the war where he is than he could in any other place. So please don't trouble yourself . . ."

He looked up as his aide opened the tent flap and saluted. "Urgent dispatches, General."

"Bring them in. You must excuse me, Matty."

She left in silence, the lift of her chin revealing what she thought of this sudden interruption; planned no doubt. In truth it had not been, but Johnston was still grateful. He took a swig of the coffee and opened the leather case.

He, and every other general of the Confederacy, had been searching for a way to cut the noose that was strangling the South. They looked at the armies that encircled them and sought a way to break out. He had little admiration for Ulysses S. Grant, nevertheless he knew him to be an enemy of purpose and will. His victories at Fort Henry and Fort Donelson threatened continuing disaster. Now he was camped with a mighty army at Pittsburg Landing in Tennessee. Confederate intelligence had discovered that reinforcements were on the way to him. When they arrived Grant would certainly strike south into Mississippi in an effort to cut the South in two. He must be stopped before that happened. And Sidney Johnston was the man to do it.

His attack would be later than planned—but other than that it seemed to be going as well as could be expected. During the winter he had assembled an army even larger than Grant's, which had been judged by the cavalry scouts to be over 35,000, and he meant to strike first, before Don Carlos Buell's 30,000 men arrived to reinforce Grant. For three days now his raw recruits had been marching the muddy lanes and back roads of Mississippi, their weary columns converging on

Pittsburg Landing. Now it was time for a final meeting with his officers.

They filed in one by one, drawing up chairs, pouring themselves coffee when he waved to the pot. He waited until they were all there before he spoke.

"There will be no more delays. We attack at daylight tomorrow, Sunday morning."

His second-in-command, General P.G.T. Beauregard, was not quite so sure. "There is no longer the possibility of a surprise. They'll be entrenched to the eyes. And our men, they're just raw recruits and most of them had never heard a gun fired in anger."

"We know that—but we also know that tired as they are from the march they are still filled with enthusiasm. I would fight the enemy even if they were a million. The attack goes on."

"Do you have the time, Thomas? My watch has stopped," General Sherman said. His orderly shook his head and smiled.

"Could never afford no watch, General," Thomas D. Holliday said. "I'll ask one of the officers."

Brigadier General William T. Sherman and his staff were riding out in front of their camp, near Shiloh Church, on the banks of the Tennessee River. The morning mist had not lifted, so little could be seen under the trees and hedges. But the rain had stopped during the night and it promised to be a fine day. Sherman was worried, not happy at all with Grant's decision not to have the troops dig in.

"Their morale is high, Cump," Grant had said, "and I want it to stay that way. If they dig those holes and hide in them they are going to start worrying. We best let them be."

Sherman still did not like it. There had been reports of movement on their front which had not disturbed Grant in the slightest. Nevertheless Sherman had led his staff out at dawn to see if there was any truth in the reports of the pickets that they had heard movement in the night.

Holliday turned his horse and trotted back to the general's side.

"Just gone seven," he said. And died.

The sudden volley of fire from the unseen Confederate

pickets hit Holliday, blowing him off his horse and killing him instantly.

"Follow me!" Sherman shouted, turning and galloping toward their own lines. A Union picket burst out of the thicket ahead and called out.

"General—the Rebs is out there thicker than fleas on a hounddog's back!"

It was true. They were three battle lines deep and were attacking all along the front. A victorious Rebel yell rose up as they crashed into the unprepared Northern positions, forced them back under a withering fire from their guns. Caught out by the surprise attack the soldiers wavered, favoring retreat to standing up to the hail of bullets.

SHILOH—THE BLOODIEST BATTLE OF THE WAR

Then, riding between the enemy and his own lines, General Sherman appeared. He seemed oblivious to the bullets now streaking past him as he stood in his stirrups and waved his sword.

"Soldiers—form a line, rally on me. Fire, load and fire. Stand firm. Load and fire!"

The General's fervor could not be denied; his cries inspired the soldiers, who moments before had been about to run.

They stayed at their positions, firing into the attacking troops. Load and fire, load and fire.

It was desperately hard and deadly work. This was the most exposed flank of the Union army and the heaviest attacks hit here. Sherman had eight thousand men to begin with—but their numbers withered steadily under the Confederate attack. Yet the Northern line still held. Sherman's regiments took the brunt of the attack—but they did not retreat. And the general stayed in the midst of the battle, leading them from the front, seemingly oblivious to the storm of bullets about him.

When his horse was shot from under him he fought on foot until another mount was found and brought up.

Within minutes this horse was also killed while the general was leading a counterattack, and later on a third one that he was riding was shot dead as well.

It was a hot, hard, dirty and deadly engagement. The green Confederate troops, those who survived the bloody opening of battle, were learning to fight. Again and again they were rallied and sent forward to attack. The Union lines were driven back slowly, fighting every foot of the way, taking great losses—but still they held. And Sherman was always there, rallying the defenders from the fore. Men fell on all sides but still his troops held their positions.

Nor was he immune from injury; later in the day he was wounded himself, shot in the hand. He wrapped a handkerchief about the torn flesh and fought on.

A fragment of shell took off part of the brim of his hat. Despite this, despite the casualties, he stayed in command of his troops and managed to stabilize their positions. Three hours after the battle had begun Sherman had lost over half of his men. Four thousand dead. But the line held. Their powder and ball were so low that they had to plunder the supplies of the fallen. The wounded, who had not stumbled, or been carried, to the rear, loaded weapons for the men who fought on. Then, during a hiatus in the battle while the enemy regrouped, Sherman heard someone calling his name. The captain on the exhausted horse threw a rough salute.

"Orders from General Grant, sir. You are to fall back to the River Road."

"I will not retreat."

"This is not a retreat, sir. We have dug in on the River Road, positions that can be better defended."

"I'll leave skirmishers here. Keep them firing as long as they can. In the smoke they could slow the next attack some. Tell the general that I am falling back now."

It was a fighting retreat. Disengaging from a determined enemy can be as difficult as holding them at bay. Men fell, but almost all of the survivors reached the River Road through the smoke and thunder of cannon.

"Them's our guns, General," one of the soldiers cried out.

"They are indeed," Sherman said. "They are indeed."

This was the first day of the Battle of Shiloh. The carnage was incredible. Despite their mounting losses the Confederate advance continued, slow and deadly. It wasn't until five-thirty in the afternoon that the Union left was finally penetrated— but by then it was too late. General Grant had managed to establish a defensive line, studded with cannon, just before Pittsburg Landing. With the help of cannon fire from the gunboats tied up at the landing the last Confederate attack was thrown back. As this was happening Grant's defenders were reinforced by the fresh troops of Don Carlos Buell who began to arrive on the other bank of the river.

The Confederate forces were bloodied and exhausted and no match for the strengthened Northern divisions.

The counterattack began the next day at dawn and by afternoon all of the lost ground had been recaptured.

If there was any victor in this carnage it had to be the North. They were now reinforced and back in their original defensive positions—but the cost had been terrible. There were 10,700 Confederate casualties, including their commander General Johnston, who had been shot and had bled to death because the doctor who might have saved him was treating the Union wounded. 13,000 Union troops were dead as well. Despite the courage, despite the sacrifices and the dead, the South had proved itself incapable of breaking out of the ring of steel that was closing around them.

Grant and Sherman were the heroes of the day. Sherman

who had held the line despite his personal injuries and the terrible losses his troops had suffered.

"He must be rewarded for his bravery," Lincoln said when he had read the final reports of the battle. "John, get a letter to the War Department and tell them that I strongly recommend that Sherman be promoted to major general, in acknowledgment of his bravery and strength of command. Talent like this should not go unacknowledged. And have the promotion dated back to April seventh, the day the battle was fought."

"Yes, sir, I'll do that at once. Will you be able to see Gustavus Fox now?"

"By all means. Show him in."

Assistant Secretary of the Navy Gustavus Fox was a very talented man. He was familiar with the White House because Lincoln's secretaries lived across the hall from the President's office and he was a frequent visitor there. This apparent socializing provided an unquestioned cover for his visits. For Gustavus Fox had authority and commissions that only those in the highest echelon of government knew anything about.

"Good morning, Gus. Do you have any reports of interest to me?" the President asked.

"A good deal since last we met. My agents in Canada and the British West Indies have been quite diligent."

"Is one of them Captain Schultz of the Russian Navy?"

Lincoln's smile was mirrored on Fox's face. "Not this time, Mr. President—he is busy elsewhere. But before I report on the British—I must tell you that my trip to Brooklyn was a great success. After the victory of the *Monitor* in Hampton Roads, and the navy's agreement to put more money into iron warships, Mr. Ericsson was more than eager to proceed. Construction on the second *Monitor*-class ironclad is proceeding as planned. Very smoothly in fact since the ironworkers are now experienced with this particular kind of construction. Ericsson is now devoting his time to improving the design and construction of a larger iron ship with two turrets. Much more seaworthy and with greater range. The man is a demon for work—the keel was laid that very day for the USS *Thor*."

"I doubt that the navy will approve of a pagan deity in their fleet."

"They didn't. They withheld their first payment until Thor went back to Valhalla and *Avenger* emerged in his place."

He took a sheet of paper from an inner pocket and unfolded it. His secret agents in the field had been busy indeed. Here were the names and strengths of the regiments of British troops newly arrived in Canada, as well as the number of guns unloaded on the docks of Montreal.

The President looked grim. "That sounds like a powerful lot of soldiers to be sending over here."

"More than an army corps. And I have some reports that more are on the way, but I haven't confirmed them yet. The British Navy has been busy too."

He read from the list of navy warships based in the British West Indies, as well as giving an account of newly arrived reinforcements to the marines also based there. The President never asked who the men and women were who sent in these reports, while Fox never volunteered the information. If a report was doubtful, or possibly false, he would say so. The rest of the information had always proven to be correct.

"You are my eyes and ears," Lincoln said. "I wish that you could find a way to convince Mr. Pinkerton that your reports are far more reliable than those furnished by his agents in the South."

"I have tried many times, in roundabout ways, but he is a very stubborn man."

"General McClellan believes in him."

"General McClellan also believes in the inflated figures for Southern troops that Pinkerton comes up with. The real number is a third, at most a half of what he reports."

"But McClellan remains sure that the numbers are correct and once more finds a reason to avoid action. But he is my responsibility and not yours. So, tell me—what conclusions do you draw from all these facts about the British that you have just presented?"

Fox thought carefully before he spoke, summoning up his conclusions. "The country is preparing for war in North

America. They have the men, the weapons, the supplies and the ships to wage a major war on this continent. Most important of all is the fact that there are no voices of dissent. The newspapers call for war to teach us a lesson. Whigs and Tories unite in Parliament baying for blood. The Queen now believes it as a certainty that we killed Prince Albert."

"Certainly that is absurd."

"To us perhaps. But I am reliably informed that there is worry about her sanity, that she has sudden vicious obsessions that she cannot control."

"Are there no sane voices to be heard?"

"It is imprudent to go against the public will. A certain baronet in the House of Lords was so unwise as to speak of a possible search for peace. He was not only shouted down but physically assaulted."

"This is hard to believe, but I suppose I must. But will they do it? Take the final step?"

"You can answer that far better than I can, Mr. President. You are privy to the negotiations over their ultimatum, while I am not."

"There is little I can tell you that you don't already know. We want to talk, but I fear that they do not want to listen. And I am beginning to think that we have run out of options. Our newspapers and theirs are filled with fire and brimstone. Their ministers are just as ardent. Lord Lyons has given us his passports and vacated our shores. Our minister Charles Adams does his best to have London accept a rewording of their dispatch, but they agree to nothing. Now Lord Palmerston keeps him at bay and will not admit him to his house, although Adams has called repeatedly at that gentleman's door. The lord pleads gout as the reason. I believe in the gout but not the excuse."

Fox nodded agreement. "Meanwhile the cause of all this, Mason and Slidell, live a life of great luxury in their prison cells. Ordering the best food and wine from Boston and smoking their way through their bottomless supply of Havana cigars."

"Luxury it may be—but they are still imprisoned. And as

long as they are the Britons will remain adamant in their condemnation of this country. Find me a way out of this impasse, Mr. Fox, and I will bestow upon you the highest rewards this country can offer."

"I wish that I could sir, how I wish that I could."

BRINK OF WAR

Although it was the first day of May, it felt more like winter here in the northern hills of Vermont. Cold rain lashed the pine trees, turning the little-used track into adhesive mud. The horses walked slowly, heads down with weariness, and had to be urged on constantly by pulling on their reins. Both of the men who were leading them were as weary as the horses, yet they never for an instant thought of riding. That would have meant that their mounts would have to carry heavier loads. That was not possible. The reason for this long and exhausting journey was there in the barrels on the horses' backs.

Jacques squinted up at the sky, then wiped his streaming face with the back of his hand. Only the rich could afford to buy a watch—and he was anything but that. But he knew by the steadily darkening sky that it was close to sunset.

"Soon, Phillipe, soon," he shouted back in Canadian-accented French. "We will stop before we cross the ridge. Then go on after dark."

His brother answered something, but his words were drowned out by a sharp crack of thunder. They plodded on, then turned from the track to seek some shelter under the branches of an ancient stand of oak trees. The horses found clumps of fresh grass to graze upon while the men slumped down with their backs against the thick trunks. Jacques took the cork from his water bottle and drank deep, smacking his lips as he sealed it again. It was filled with a strong mixture of whiskey and water. Phillipe watched this and frowned.

Jacques saw his expression and laughed aloud—revealing a mouthful of broken and blackened teeth. "You disapprove of

113

my drinking, little brother. You should have been a priest. Then you could tell others what they should and should not do. It helps the fatigue and warms the bones."

"And destroys the internal organs and the body."

"That too, I am sure. But we must enjoy life as well as we can."

Phillipe squeezed water from his thin, dark beard, and looked at the squat, strong body of his older brother. Just like their father. While he took after their mother, everyone said. He had never known her: she had died when he had been born.

"I don't want to do this anymore," Phillipe said. "It is dangerous—and some day we will be caught."

"No we won't. No one knows these hills as I do. Our good father, may he rest in peace with the angels, worked the stones of our farm until he died. I am sure that the endless toil killed him. Like the other farmers. But we have a choice, do we not? We can do this wonderful work to aid our neighbors. Remember—if you don't do this—what will you do? You are like me, like the rest of us—an uneducated Quebecois. I can barely sign my name—I cannot read nor write."

"But I can. You left school, the chance was there."

"For you perhaps, I for one have no patience with the schoolroom. And if you remember our father was ill then. Someone had to work the farm. So you stayed in school and were educated. To what end? No one will hire you in the city, you have no skills—and you don't even speak the filthy language of the English."

"There is no need for English. Since the Act of Union Lower Canada has been recognized, our language is French—"

"And our freedom is zero. We are a colony of the English, ruled by an English governor. Our legislature may sit in Montreal but it is the English Queen who has the power. So you can read, dear brother, and write as well. Where is the one who will hire you for these skills? It is your destiny that you must stay in Coaticook where there is nothing to do except farm the tired land—and drink strong whiskey to numb the pain of existence. Let the rest stay with the farming—and we will take care of the supplying of the other."

He looked at the four barrels the horses were carrying and

smiled his broken smile. Good Yankee whiskey, untaxed and purchased with gold. When they crossed back into Canada its value would double, so greedy were the English with their endless taxes. Oh yes, Her Majesty's Customs men were active and eager enough, but they would never be woodsmen enough to catch a Dieumegard who had spent his life in these hills. He pressed his hand against the large outer pocket of his leather coat, felt the welcome outline of his pistol.

"Phillipe—" he called out. "You have kept your powder dry?"

"Yes, of course, the gun is wrapped in oilskin. But I don't like it . . ."

"You have to like it," Jacques snarled. "It's our lives that depend upon this whiskey—they shall not take it from us. That is why we need these guns. Nor shall they take me either. I would rather die here in the forest than rot in some English jail. We did not ask for this life or to be born in our miserable village. We have no choice so we must make the best of it."

After this they were silent as day darkened slowly into night. The rain still fell, but not as heavily as earlier in the day.

"Time to go," Jacques said, climbing stiffly to his feet. "One more hour and we will be across the border and in the hut. Nice and dry. Come on."

He pulled on the horse's reins and led the way. Phillipe leading the other horse, following their shapes barely visible in the darkness ahead.

There was no physical boundary between Canada and the United States here in the hills, no fence or marking. In daylight surveyors' markers might be found, but not too easily. This track was used only by the animals, deer for the most part. And smugglers.

They crossed the low ridge and went slowly down the other side. The border was somewhere around here, no one was quite sure. Jacques stopped suddenly and cocked his head. Phillipe came up beside him.

"What is it?"

"Be quiet!" his brother whispered hoarsely. "There is something out there—I heard a noise."

A DEADLY SURPRISE IN THE FOREST

"Deer—"

"Deer don't rattle, *crétin*. There again, a clinking."

Phillipe heard it too, but before he could speak dark forms loomed up before them. Mounted men.

"*Merde*! Customs—a patrol!"

Jacques cursed under his breath as he struggled his revolver from his pocket. His much-treasured Lefaucheaux pinfire caliber .41. He pointed it at the group ahead and pulled the trigger.

Again and again.

Stabs of flame in the darkness. One, two, three, four shots—before the inevitable misfire. He jammed the gun into his pocket, turned and ran, pulling the horse after him.

"Don't stand there, you idiot. Back, we go back! They cannot follow us across the border. Even if they do we can get away from them. Then later get around them, use the other trail. It's longer—but it will get us there."

Slipping and tugging at the horses they made their way down the hill and vanished into the safety of the forest.

There was panic in the cavalry patrol. None of them had ventured into this part of the mountains before and the track was ill-marked. Heads down to escape the rain, no one had noticed when the corporal had missed the turning. By the time it grew dark they knew that they were lost. When they stopped to rest the horses, and stretch their legs, Jean-Louis approached the corporal who commanded the patrol.

"Marcel—are we lost?"

"Corporal Durand, that is what you must say."

"Marcel, I have known you since you peed yourself in bed at night. Where are we?"

Durand's shrug went unseen in the darkness. "I don't know."

"Then we must turn about and return the way we came. If we go on like this who knows where we will end up."

After much shouted argument, name-calling and insults, they were all from the same village, the decision was made.

"Unless anyone knows a better route, we go back," Corporal Durand said. "Mount up."

They were milling about in the darkness when the firing began. The sudden flashes of fire unmanned them. Someone screamed and the panic grew worse. Their guns were wrapped about to keep them dry; there was no time to do anything.

"Ambush!"

"I am shot! Mother of God, they have shot me!"

This was too much. Uphill they fled, away from the gunfire. Corporal Durand could not stop them, rally them, not until the tired horses stumbled to a halt. He finally assembled most of them in the darkness, shouted loudly so the stragglers would find them.

"Who was shot?"

"It was Pierre who got it."

"Pierre—where are you?"

"Here. My leg. A pain like fire."

"We must bandage it. Get you to a doctor."

The rain was ending and the moon could be seen dimly through the clouds. They were all countrymen and this was the only clue they needed to find their way back to camp. Exhausted and frightened they made their way down from the hills. Pierre's dramatic moaning hurrying them on their way.

"Lieutenant, wake up sir. I'm sorry—but you must wake up."

Lieutenant Saxby Athelstane did not like being disturbed. He was a heavy sleeper and difficult to waken at the best of times. At the worst of times, sodden with drink like this, it was next to impossible to stir him. But it had to be done. Sergeant Sleat was getting desperate. He pulled the officer into a sitting position, the blanket fell to the ground, and with a heave he swung him about so that the lieutenant's feet were on the cold ground.

"Wha . . . what?" Athelstane said in a blurred voice. Shuddered and came awake and realized what was happening. "Take your sodding paws off of me! I'll have you hung for this . . ."

Sleat stepped back, desperate, the words stumbling from his mouth as he rushed to explain.

"It's them, sir, the Canadian militia patrol, they're back . . ."

"What are you babbling about? Why in Hades should I care at this time of night?"

"They was shot at, Lieutenant. Shot at by the Yankees. One of them is wounded."

Athelstane was wide-awake now. Struggling into his boots, grabbing at his jacket, then stumbling out of his tent into the driving rain. There was a lantern in the mess tent which was now crowded with gabbling men. A few of the volunteer militia could speak some broken English, the rest none at all. They were backwoods peasants and totally useless. He pushed through them, thrusting them aside, until he reached the mess table. One of their number was lying on the table, a filthy cloth tied about his leg.

"Will someone bloody well tell me what happened," Athelstane snarled. Corporal Durand stepped forward, saluted clumsily.

"Eet was my patrol, sir, the one you ordered out that we should scout along the Yankee border. We rode as you told us to, but took too long. The weather it was very bad . . ."

"I don't want the history of your sodding life—just tell me what you found."

"We were at the border when it happened, many Yankees, they attacked suddenly, fired at us. Pierre here is wounded. We fought back, fired at them and drove them back. Then they went away, we came back here."

"You say you were at the border—you are sure?"

"*Sans doute*! My men know this country well. We were very close to the border when the attack she came."

"Inside Canada?"

"*Oui.*"

"You have no doubt that the bloody Yankees invaded this country?"

"No doubt, sir."

Lieutenant Athelstane went to the wounded militiaman and unwrapped the rag from his leg; he groaned hoarsely. There was a bloody three-inch-long gash in his thigh.

"Shut your miserable mouth!" Athelstane shouted. "I've cut myself worse while shaving. Sergeant—get someone to wash this wound out and bandage it correctly. Then bring the corporal to my tent. We'll see if we can't make some kind of sense of this entire affair. I'll take the report to the colonel myself."

Lieutenant Athelstane actually smiled as he walked back through the lines. It would be jolly nice to get away from the frog militia for a bit, back in the mess with his friends. That was something to look forward to. He hadn't bought this commission with his inheritance just to be buried out here in the forest. He would write a detailed report of this night's business that would get the colonel's attention and approval. Invasion from the United States. Cowardly attack. Fighting defense. It would be a very good report indeed. He would show them the kind of job he could do. Yes, indeed. This really was worth looking forward to.

* * *

"A word, sir, if I could," Harvey Preston said.

Charles Francis Adams looked up from the papers on his desk with irritation, his concentration broken. "Not now, Preston—you can see that I am working."

"It is about the servants, sir."

"Well, yes, of course. Best to close the door."

When Secretary of State Seward had secured for Adams the position of minister to Great Britain it was Abraham Lincoln himself who offered him congratulations. Adams was no stranger to the Presidential Mansion—after all his father had been President—and his grandfather as well. But this had been a very different occasion. Lincoln had introduced him to an Assistant Secretary of the Navy, one Gustavus Fox. For a navy man Fox had a great interest in matters of security. English servants, important papers, state secrets and the like. He had recommended the appointment of Preston, "A former military man" as house manager. Or butler, or major-domo. His exact role remained unclear. Yes, he did indeed manage Adams's house, keeping an eye on the cook and hiring the servants.

But he did a lot more than that. He knew far more about affairs of state in London, Court gossip, even matters of the military, than Adams himself did. And his information always proved accurate. After a few months Adams began to rely on the facts he assembled, using some of them as the basis of reports to Washington. The reference to *servants* meant that he had information to reveal.

"Something very important is happening in Whitehall," Preston said as soon as the door was closed.

"What?"

"I don't know yet. My informant, who is a junior clerk in one of the departments, would not tell me without payment of a sum of money."

"Don't you usually pay for information?"

"Of course—but just a few shillings at a time. This time it is different. He wants twenty guineas, and I don't have that sum available."

"That is a lot of money!"

"I agree. But he has never failed me before."

"What do you suggest?"

"Pay him. We must take the chance."

Adams thought for a moment, then nodded. "I will get it from the safe. How do you meet him?"

"He comes to the carriage house at a prearranged time."

"I must be there," Adams said firmly.

"He must not see you." Preston chewed his lip in thought. "It could be done. Get there early, sit in the carriage in the dark. I'll keep him at the door."

"Let us do it."

Adams waited in the carriage, growing more and more unsure of his decision. The man was late, the whole thing might be a plot to embarrass him. He was definitely not acquainted with this kind of occasion. His thoughts spinning, he jumped when there was a sudden loud knocking on the door. He pushed back against the seat, trying to get as close as he could without being seen. There was the squeak of rusty hinges.

"Do you 'ave it?" a cockney voice whispered.

"I do—and it had better be worth it."

"It is, sir—I swear on my mother's soul. But let me see it first."

There was the dull clink of gold against gold and the man's gasp.

"That's it, yes it is. You must tell your master that there is an uproar in Parliament, the military, everyone. I hear that they may go to the Queen."

"About what?"

"We're not supposed to know, but clerks talk. It seems that the American army has invaded Canada, shot up some soldiers there. There is even talk of war."

"Names, places?"

"I'll get them, sir. Tomorrow at this time."

"Then here is half the money. The rest when we have the details."

The door closed and Adams emerged from the carriage. "Is he speaking the truth?"

"Undoubtedly."

Adams was at a loss. "This could not happen, the army would not do a thing like that."

"The British *believe* that it happened, that is all we have to know."

Adams started toward the house, turned back. "Find out when the next mail packet sails. We must get a full report of this to the State Department. As soon as we can."

The emergency meeting of the British Cabinet lasted until late afternoon. There was a constant coming and going between Downing Street and the House of Commons, high-ranking officers, generals and admirals for the most part. When a decision was finally reached the order was passed and Lord Palmerston's carriage clattered on the cobbles up to the main entrance of the House of Commons. Palmerston was carried out of the building by four strong servants, who lifted him carefully through the carriage door. Not carefully enough for he cried out in pain, then cursed his bearers when his bandaged foot struck against the frame. Lord John Russell climbed in and joined him for the short ride down Whitehall, then along the Mall to Buckingham Palace. Word had been sent ahead of this momentous visit and the Queen was waiting for them when they were ushered into her presence. She was dressed entirely in black, still in mourning for Albert, a period of mourning that would last her lifetime.

Lord Palmerston was eased into a chair. The pain was clear on his face but he struggled against it and spoke.

"Your Majesty. Your cabinet has been assembled this entire day in solemn conference. We have consulted with responsible members of the armed forces before reaching a decision. You will of course have seen the dispatch from Canada?"

"Report?" she said vaguely. Her eyes were misted and red with weeping. Since Albert's death she had barely been able to function. At times she tried; most of the time she refused to leave her private chambers. Today, with great effort, she had emerged to meet with Palmerston. "Yes, I think that I read it. Very confused."

"Apologies, ma'am. Written in the heat of action no doubt. If I could elucidate. Our cavalry is thinly stretched along the length of the Canadian border. We have limited troops there so, in order to keep close and continuous watch, it is my understanding that the local militia has been deployed. Commanded by British officers of course. It was one of these patrols that was stationed near the Quebec village of Coaticook that came under attack."

"My soldiers—attacked!" Her attention was attracted at last. Her voice rose to a shrill screech. "This is a grave matter, Lord Palmerston. Terrible! Terrible!"

"Grave indeed, ma'am. It appears that a road of some sort crosses the border here leading to Derby, in the American state of Vermont. Lord Russell, if I could have the map."

Russell opened the map on an end table and the servants carried it over and placed it before the Queen. She looked around unseeingly, finally bent over it as Palmerston tapped it with his finger.

"The border between Canada and the United States is ill marked and runs through some very rugged country, or so I have been told. Apparently a party of American cavalry had crossed the border here and was apprehended by our patrol. Surprised in their trespass they opened fire in a most cowardly fashion, completely without warning. The militia, although only Colonials, fought back bravely and succeeded in repelling the invasion—though not without losses. A brave soldier wounded by gunfire is now at death's door."

"This is shocking, shocking."

Queen Victoria was terribly upset, fanning her bright red face with her kerchief. She signaled to a lady-in-waiting and spoke to her. Lady Kathleen Shiel hurried away and returned with a glass of beer from which the Queen drank deep. This was some mark of her distress at the news, since she loved beer but rarely drank it with others present. Somewhat restored she sipped again from the glass and felt the anger rise within her.

"Are you informing me that my province has been invaded, one of our subjects killed by the Americans?" She shouted out the words.

"Indeed invaded. Certainly shot but . . ."

"I will not have this!" She was almost screaming now, infused by an intense rage. "There must be an answer to this crime. Something must be done. You say you discussed this all day. Too much talk. There must be some action."

"There will be, ma'am."

"What will it be? What has my cabinet decided?"

"With your permission, ma'am, we wish to send the Americans an ultimatum . . ."

"We have had enough of these ultimatums. We write and we write and they do exactly what they please."

"Not this time. They will have seven days to respond. Their response must be the immediate release of the two Confederate commissioners and their aides. We also demand that we receive a letter of apology for this incursion into Your Majesty's sovereign territory, as well as the attempted murder of one of Your Majesty's subjects. Lord Lyons will

VICTORIA'S FATEFUL DECISION

personally carry this communication to Washington City and remain there for a week and no longer. We are firm in this intention. At the end of this period he will leave, with the response or without it, and return on the same steam packet that will convey him there. When he arrives in Southampton the response will be cabled to Whitehall."

These firm words had calmed the Queen somewhat. Her mouth worked as she spoke wordlessly to herself. Finally she nodded in agreement and patted her damp face with her black kerchief.

"It is too fair—more than fair considering what has been done. They deserve worse. And what if the response is in the negative? If they refuse a reply and do not release the prisoners? What will my bold ministers do then?"

Lord Palmerston tried to ignore her agitated state. His voice was grave, yet very firm, when he responded.

"If the Americans do not accede to these reasonable demands all responsibility will lie with them. A state of war will then be deemed to exist between the United States of America and the United Kingdom of Great Britain and Ireland."

The silence that fell upon the room was more revealing of the feelings of those gathered there than any cry or spoken word might have been. All present had heard, all present understood the somber and momentous decision that must be made. All waited in deep silence for Queen Victoria to respond.

She sat stiffly in her chair, her hands lying on the black silk of her gown. Lady Shiel rustled forward and took the glass from her when she held it out. With a great effort the Queen drew herself together, forced herself to concentrate upon the matters to hand. She rested her hands on the arms of the chair, sat up straighter. And spoke.

"Lord Palmerston, this is a grave responsibility and decision that my ministers have placed before me. But we cannot shrink from the truth, nor can we shy away from the conclusions that must then be reached." She paused abstractedly before she spoke again.

"We are not pleased by what the Americans have done to our honor and our person. They will be punished.

"Send the ultimatum."

THE ROAD TO WAR

The governor of the state of Louisiana, Thomas O. Moore, was a very worried man. He did not have to be reminded of this by higher authorities. He had sent for General Mansfield Lovell as soon as he had received the letter—and he waved it at him when the general entered the room.

"Lovell, we have Jefferson Davis himself worrying over our plight. He expresses great concern over the city of New Orleans and the threat against this city from two directions. Listen to this—'The wooden vessels are below, the iron boats are above; the forts should destroy the former if they attempt to ascend. The *Louisiana* may be indispensable to check the descent of the iron boats. The purpose is to defend the city and valley; the only question is as to the best mode of effecting the object.' "

"Does the President offer any suggestions as to what this best mode might be?" The general had a deep voice and a rich Louisiana drawl, sounding very much like the distant steam whistle of a riverboat.

"No he does not! Nor does he send any aid, troops, weapons or military supplies all of which we are in short supply. How goes the work on the *Louisiana*?"

"Slow, sir, mighty slow. It is the severe shortage of iron plate that is holding her back. But when she is done she will knock the living hell out of those bitty Yankee ironclads."

"*If* she is ever completed." Moore opened the jar on his desk and took out a cigar, sniffed it then bit off the end. Almost as an afterthought he passed one over to Lovell. "And if the bluebellies don't attack first. I'm strongly minded of old General Winfield Scott's anaconda speech. The Union will

126

encircle the South like a great anaconda snake, encircle, squeeze and crush it. Well, I'll tell you, Thomas, I'm feeling a tad crushed right about now. With those gunboats upriver just waiting for the chance to swoop down on us. The Feds have built up their forces on Ship Island at the mouth of the river, they're in the passes and the river below Fort Jackson and Fort St. Philip. A whole fleet of Yankee warships is out there downstream from New Orleans, along with a goodly number of transports filled with troops."

"They won't get past the forts, Governor."

"Well they are trying hard enough. How many days now? Five at least that they been dropping mortar shells into those forts."

"Hasn't done the job yet, might never. And then there is the barrier."

"A passel of old boats and a lot of chain across the river. Not much to put your faith in. Yankees upriver, Yankees downriver—and old Jeff Davis telling us to stand to our defenses, but without any help from him. I guess that I've seen blacker days, though I don't rightly remember when."

They puffed on their cigars until a cloud of blue smoke drifted across the desk. In silence, for there was little else that could be said.

Flag Officer David Glasgow Farragut did not put much faith in the barrier either. But he didn't like it there blocking his fleet from ascending the Mississippi. Porter's mortar ships had been assailing the forts for five days now with no visible success. Farragut, never a patient man at the best of times, felt that his patience was now at an end. He had promised Porter six days to subdue the forts and the time was almost up. And the forts were still there. As was the barrier.

But at least he was doing something about that. It was now after midnight; he should try to get some sleep but knew that he could not. Brave men were out there in the night risking their lives. He paced the length of the USS *Hartford*'s deck towards the stern. Wheeled about to face the bow—just as the sky upriver lit up with a sudden burst of light. Seconds later the sound of the explosion reached their ears.

"By God they've done it!" He banged his fist on the rail.

They were the volunteers from *Itasca* and *Pinola* who had slipped upriver with explosives—but without weapons to defend themselves. They had counted upon darkness—and silence—to protect them. They had rowed away with muffled oars, their target the barrier in the river. If all went well they intended to plant their charges on the hulks there—hopefully without alerting the guards on the banks—set the fuses and get out. The fuses had obviously worked—pray the boats were out of reach before the powder had exploded. Farragut had a sudden vision of those brave young men, all dead. Volunteers, yes, and happy to go. But the plan had been his and he felt the weight of a terrible responsibility.

A long time passed, far too long Farragut thought, before they heard the creaking of oars in oarlocks and the dark form of a ship's boat emerged out of the darkness. The boat from the *Pinola* drew up at the gangway and an officer hurried on deck.

"A success, sir. The charges were planted without the men being apprehended. The fuses were lit and all the boats were well clear before the explosions."

"Any casualties?"

"None. A perfect operation."

"A good night's work indeed. My congratulations to them all."

Unhappily, when the sun rose, the barrier was still there.

"But definitely weakened, sir. At dawn one of our boats got close enough to see that there are big chunks blown out of it. Hit it hard enough and it will give way."

"I only hope that you are right, Lieutenant."

Farragut went down to the wardroom where Porter and Butler were waiting.

"This is the sixth day, Porter, and your mortars appear not to have done the job. The forts are still there, their guns still covering the approach to New Orleans by river."

"Just a little more time, sir—"

"There is no more time. I said that you could have six days and you have had them. We must reach the city by other means. General Butler, you have had your scouts out there on both sides of the river. What do they report?"

General Benjamin F. Butler did not easily admit defeat. He scowled and bit down on an already well-chewed cigar. Then shook his head in a lugubrious no.

"There is just no way through. Water on all sides, all of the land low-lying and swampy. Then, just when you think you're getting somewhere, you'll come onto a waterway you can't cross. Critters and bugs, snakes, gators, you name it. They thrive out there—but my soldiers don't. Sorry."

"Not your fault, nothing to be sorry for. You too, Porter. Your big mortars just aren't big enough. Do either of you gentlemen see a way out of this impasse?"

"We could continue with the mortar attack on the forts . . ."

"That has proven not to be the answer. General Butler?"

"I would like to have some scouts take a closer look at those forts. They are the key to this entire engagement. If we could assess their strengths—and weaknesses—there might just be a less defended aspect. Using small boats we could land my troops at night, surprise and take the forts."

Farragut shook his head in a slow no. "I think General, with no disrespect, that you have had little experience in landing troops. If you had you would recognize the folly of an undertaking like this. Landing soldiers from small craft, even on an undefended shore in daylight, is time-consuming and fraught with difficulties. I dare not consider the consequences of nighttime landings against defended positions. Are there any other suggestions? In that case we will just have to get to New Orleans in the only way that remains. Tonight we run the flotilla by the forts."

"Wooden ships against iron guns!" Porter gasped.

"We will get by."

"But the barricade across the river." Butler shook his head.

"We will break it. We sail at two in the morning. We will move in two divisions. I will take the *Hartford* through last in the second division. The signal to begin will be two red lanterns on my mizzen peak. Here are the ship assignments to each of the divisions."

The officers present looked at each other but did not speak. Duty called. It would be a brave attempt, some might even say foolhardy, but Farragut was in command and he would be obeyed.

Every ship had a full head of steam by two in the morning, ready to move when the signal was given. Telescopes were trained on the *Hartford* and the instant the two red lights appeared the attack began.

It was a dark night, with some low clouds, as the ships of the first division moved upriver. They revealed no lights and, at low speed, their engines were as silent as they could possibly be. The longer they proceeded without their presence being observed—the less time they would be under fire.

There was some trepidation as the barrier appeared ahead, pale against the dark river. The bow of the first gunboat sliced into it, carried it forward slowing the ship.

Then it broke and the joined, crushed hulks drifted away.

They were through the barrier, but the armed enemy was still waiting for them. Dimly seen against the night sky the dark masses of the two forts appeared ahead.

The quiet rush of water along the hull, the deep heartbeat of the engines was all that could be heard. One by one the ships of the first division slipped by the dark and silent forts and moved on towards New Orleans.

Without a shot being fired.

The second division was not as lucky. They had just reached the forts when the moon rose at three-forty. Unvigilant as the guards had been up until this moment, they could not miss seeing the ships in the bright moonlight. A shot was fired, then another and the alarm was raised.

"Full steam ahead," Farragut ordered. "Signal all ships." The sound of the engines would not matter now.

Both forts suddenly blossomed with fire and the cannonballs streaked across the river. There were some hits, but most of them skipped across the water in the darkness. The ships fired in return, flare of gunfire lighting up the night. Now the Union mortars added their thunderous roar and thick clouds of smoked drifted low across the river. It was a gauntlet of confusion and death, made even more menacing when Confederate fire rafts were launched against the Union's wooden ships.

Yet in the end all of the ships made it past the forts into the silent waters beyond. There was some damage and three of the smaller vessels were badly disabled. *Hartford* was the last through. She had been hit but was still sound. Farragut watched with great satisfaction as the firing died away behind them. He had taken the risk—and he had won.

"Signal to all ships, well done. And I'll want damage reports as soon as possible after we make anchor."

Governor Moore did not sleep well that night. Worrying about the fate of the city had led him into drinking just a little bit more corn whiskey than he was used to. Then, when he had finally dropped off, thunder had awakened him. He had gone to the window to close it but there had been no sign of rain. The thunder was to the south; perhaps it was raining there. Could it have been gunfire? He tried not to consider this option.

A DARING NIGHT ATTACK

He awoke at first light. There were carriages going by in the street outside and someone was shouting. A churchbell rang—yet this wasn't Sunday. He went to the window and stared out at the ships tied up in the Mississippi River.

Looked past their masts and spars, looked in horror at the Union fleet in the river before him.

Then the ultimate shock, the ultimate despair. Not only was the Yankee fleet at their gates he realized, but the *Louisiana*, the ironclad that was being built to defeat these same Yankee ships, would never be launched to perform this vital task. She would be a great prize if she were taken by the Yankees. This had not been allowed to happen.

Instead of coming to the aid of New Orleans, she now floated, burning furiously, past the city and downriver towards the sea. The ironclad would never be launched, never fulfill her vital defending role he realized. All that effort, all that work, all for nothing.

She would soon sink, steaming and bubbling, to the bottom of the river that she was supposed to defend.

Scott's anaconda, he realized, had tightened that little bit more.

"This is indeed wonderful news, Mr. President," Hay said, smiling as he watched Lincoln read the telegram.

Lincoln smiled ever so slightly but did not speak. Since the death of little Willie something seemed to have gone out of him. A dreadful lassitude had overcome him and everything was a far greater effort than it had ever been before. He struggled against it, forced himself to read the telegram again and make some sense of it.

"I agree wholeheartedly, John. Wonderful news." He spoke the words well enough, but there was no real sincerity in his voice. "Taking New Orleans is a stab right into the heartland of the Confederacy. From its sources to the sea the Mississippi River is now ours. I would almost tempt fate by saying that we are on the way to winning this war. I would be the happiest President in the White House if it weren't for our British cousins and their stubbornness."

Lincoln shook his head wearily and ran his fingers through his dark beard, the way he did when something was bothering him. Hay slipped out of the room. The President's dead son was ever present in spirit.

The May evening was warm and comfortable, with only a slight suggestion of the damp, hot summer to come. The door to the balcony was open and Lincoln stepped through it and rested his hand on the railing, looking out at the city. He turned when he heard his wife call his name.

"Out here," he said.

Mary Todd Lincoln joined him, clutched tightly to his arm when she saw the torchlit crowd in the street outside. She had kept very much to herself after little Willie's death and rarely left her room. At times it appeared to be more than melancholia, when she talked to herself and pulled at her clothing. The doctors were very guarded in their appraisals of her condition and Lincoln had real fear for her sanity. He mentioned this to no one. Now he put his arm about her but said nothing. The pain of the child's parting was still so great that they could not talk about it. There was a stirring in the mob as some people left, others joined, and the sound of raised voices and an occasional shout.

"Do you know what they are saying?" she asked.

"Probably the same thing they have been shouting for days now. No surrender. Remember the Revolution and 1812. If the British want war—they got it. Things like that."

"Father . . . what's going to happen?"

"We pray for peace. And prepare for war."

"Is there no way of stopping this?"

"I don't know, Mother. It's like an avalanche just rushing downhill, faster and faster. Get in front of it and try to stop and you will just get crushed. If I ordered Mason and Slidell released now I would be impeached or just plain lynched. That's the mood of the day. While the newspapers add fuel to the fire daily, and every congressman has a speech to make about international affairs. They say that the war against the South is good as won, that we can fight them and anyone else who comes around looking for trouble."

"But the English, will they really do this terrible thing?"

"You read their ultimatum, the whole world did when the newspapers published it. Our hands are tied. I did send back proposals for peace with Lyons—but they were rejected out of hand. We had to agree to their terms, nothing else. With Congress and the people in a stew like this, if I had agreed to the British demands I might as well just have fitted a noose around my neck.

"And their newspapers are worse than ours. They threw our minister, Adams, right out of the country. Told him not to come back without accepting their terms. He brought with him a bundle of London newspapers. No doubts expressed whatsoever. The gamblers over there are putting bets on the day when war will start and how long it will take to whup us. I feel that their politicians are in the same fix I am. Riding the whirlwind."

"And the South . . . ?"

"Jubilant. They have an immense lust for this new war and see Mason and Slidell as holy martyrs. Britain has already recognized the Confederacy as a free and sovereign nation. There is already talk of military aid on both sides."

There was a burst of noise from the crowd now, and more torches as well, that lit up the file of soldiers guarding the White House. The lanterns of guard ships were visible in the Potomac, lights of other ships and boats beyond them.

"I'm going inside," Mary said. "It is foolish I know, the night is so warm, but I'm shivering."

"Unhappily, there is much to shiver about. Let me take you inside."

Secretary of the Navy Welles was waiting inside, straightening his wig in the mirror. Mary slipped by him without a word.

"I assume the navy is doing well—as always," Lincoln said.

"As always, the blockade is in place and drawing ever tighter. I just heard the word that the ex–Secretary of War had boarded ship for the long voyage to Moscow."

"I thought he would be a fine man to represent this government in the Russian court."

Welles laughed aloud. "He will soon be selling watered stock to the Czar, if he runs true to form. I wonder what they will make of the crookedest politician in these United States."

"I wouldn't assign him that prize too readily. There are an awful lot of others vying for that title."

John Nicolay looked in. "The Secretary of War is outside, sir. He wonders if he could see you for a few minutes?"

"Of course." He turned to Mary who smiled as she pressed his hand, then left the room. War and talk of war were just too much for her tonight.

"No bad news for me Mr. Stanton?" Lincoln asked his new cabinet member. He and Stanton rarely saw eye-to-eye—but Edwin M. Stanton was a wonder of efficiency after his incompetent predecessor, Simon Cameron.

"Happily not. I've just left a meeting of my staff and thought you should know the results. Until we know more of the British plans there is little we can do. Being in a state of war already I imagine we are about as prepared as we could possibly be. However we are taking special precautions in the north. It is a long border and scarcely defended. The militia that is not already serving has been called out and put on the alert. Welles will know more about the situation at sea."

"Like you we are already at full alert. The only fact in this black world that pleases me is that the British have allowed their navy to run down since the Crimean War."

"Have you heard from General Halleck?" the President asked.

"We have indeed. He has telegraphed that he has now taken up his new post in command of the Department of the North in New York City. As agreed General Grant has taken over Halleck's post in the Department of the Mississippi. Sherman is with him and together their armies form a substantial barrier against any Rebel incursions."

"And now we wait."

"We do indeed . . ."

Running footsteps sounded down the corridor outside and, without knocking, John Hay burst through the door.

"Mr. President, a communication from . . . from Plattsburgh, New York. It has been delayed, the telegraph wires south of that city have been cut."

"What does it say?"

Hay read from the paper in his hand, choked at the words, finally got them out.

"I am . . . under attack by British troops. Colonel Yandell, Plattsburgh Militia Volunteers."

INVASION!

The troops must have marched all night. Because there they were, trampling across the field of young wheat, just as the sun rose. A sentry called out for the colonel who appeared, sleepy-eyed and rubbing at his face.

"Redcoats!" The colonel snapped his mouth shut, realizing that he was goggling at them like a teenage girl. In double rank they marched slowly across the field toward the American defenses, then halted upon command. Their pickets were out ahead of the lines, shielding behind trees and dips in the ground. Groups of cavalry were stationed on either flank, while field guns were visible, coming up the road to their rear. Colonel Yandell snapped himself out of the paralysis and shouted.

"Sergeant—turn out the company! I want a message off to . . ."

"Can't do it, sir," the sergeant said grimly. "Tried to telegraph as soon as we saw them, but the wire must be down. Plenty of cavalry out there. Could easily have got around us in the night and cut the wire."

"Something has to be done. Washington has got to know what is happening here. Get someone, get Anders, he knows the country around here. Use my horse, it's the best we got."

The colonel scrawled a quick note on his message pad, tore it off and passed it to the soldier.

"Get this to the railway station in Keeseville, to the telegraph there. Send it to Washington. Tell them to spread the word that we're under attack."

Colonel Yandell looked around grimly at his men. His volunteers were green and young and they were frightened. The

137

mere sight of the army before them seemed to have stripped most of them of their senses. Some were starting to shuffle toward the rear; one private was loading his musket, although he already had loaded it with two charges. Colonel Yandell's snapped commands had exacted numbed and reluctant obedience.

"Colonel, sir, peers like someone's comin' this way."

Yandell looked through the nearest gun port and saw a mounted officer, resplendent in red uniform and gold braid, trotting toward the battlement. A sergeant walked beside him with his pike raised, a white flag tied on its end. Yandell climbed up to the top of the wall and watched their slow approach in silence.

"That's far enough," he called out when they had reached the bottom of the slope before him. "What do you want?"

"Are you the commanding officer here?"

"I am. Colonel Yandell."

"Captain Cartledge, Seaforth Highlanders. I have a message from General Peter Champion, our commanding officer. He informs you that at midnight a declaration of war was issued by the British government. A state of war now exists between your country and mine. He orders you to surrender your weapons and guns. If you comply with his commands you have his word of honor that none of you will be harmed."

The officer drawled out the words with bored arrogance, one hand on his hip the other resting on the hilt of his sword. His uniform was festooned in gold bullion; rows of shining buttons ran the length of his jacket. Yandell was suddenly aware of his own dusty blue coat, his homespun trousers with a great patch in the seat. His temper flared.

"Now you just tell your general that he can go plumb to hell. We're Americans here and we don't take orders from the likes of you. Git!"

He turned to the nearest militiaman, a beardless youth who clutched a musket that must have been older than he was.

"Silas—stop gaping and cock your gun. Put a shot over their heads. Don't aim at them. I just want to see them skedaddle."

The single shot cracked out and a small cloud of smoke drifted away in the morning air. The sergeant began to run and the officer pulled at his reins and spurred his horse back toward the British lines.

The first shot of the Battle of Plattsburgh had been fired.

A new war had begun.

The British did not waste any time. As soon as the officer had galloped back to the lines a bugle sounded, loud and clear. Its sound was instantly lost in the boom of the cannon that stood behind the troops, almost hub to hub.

The first shells exploded in the bank below the fortifications. Others, too high, screamed by overhead. The defenders clutched the ground as the gunners corrected their range and shells began to explode on the battlement.

When the firing suddenly stopped the day became so still that the men on the battlement could hear the shouted orders, the quick rattle of a drum. Then, with a single movement, in perfect unison, the two lines of soldiers started forward. Their muskets slanted across their chests, their feet slamming down to the beat of the drums. Suddenly there was a hideous squealing sound that pierced the air. These New York farmers had never heard its like before, had never heard the mad skirl of the bagpipes.

The attackers were halfway across the field before the stunned Americans realized it, struggled to their feet to man the crumbled defenses.

The first line was almost upon them. The Seaforth Highlanders. Big men from the glens, their kilts swirling about their legs as they marched. Closer and closer with the cold precision of a machine.

"Hold your fire until I give the order," Colonel Yandell shouted as the frightened militiamen began to pop off shots at the attackers. "Wait until they're closer. Don't waste your ammunition. Load up."

Closer, steadily closer the enemy came until the soldiers were almost at the foot of the grassy ramp that led up to battlements.

"Fire!"

It was a ragged volley, but a volley nevertheless. Many of the bullets were too high and whistled over the heads of the ranked soldiers. But these men, boys, were hunters and a rabbit or squirrel was sometimes the only meat they had. Lead bullets thudded home, and big men slumped forward into the grass leaving holes in the ranks.

A TREACHEROUS ATTACK FROM CANADA

The response to the American volley was devastating and fast. The front rank of soldiers kneeled as one, raised their guns as one—and fired.

The second rank fired an instant later and it was as though the angel of death had swept across the battlements. Men screamed and died, the survivors looked on, frozen, as the red-clad soldiers, with bayonets fixed, stormed forward. The second rank had reloaded and now fired at anyone who attempted to fire back.

Then their ranks parted and the scaling parties ran through them, slammed their long ladders against the crumbled defenses. With a roar the Highlanders attacked. Up and over and into the lines of the outnumbered defenders.

Colonel Yandell had just formed a second line to the rear, to guard the few guns mounted there. He could only look on in horror as his men were overrun and butchered.

"Hold your fire," he ordered. "You'll only kill our own boys. Wait until they form up for the attack. Then shoot and don't miss. You, Caleb, run back and tell the guns to do the same thing. Hold their fire until they are sure of their targets."

It was careful butchery, too terrible to watch. Very few Americans survived the attack to join the defenders in the second line.

Again the drums rolled and the big men in their strange uniforms lined up in perfect rows. And came forward. Their lines thinned as the Americans fired. Thinned but did not stop, formed up again as men moved into the gaps.

Colonel Yandell emptied his pistol at the attacking men, fumbled to reload it when he was addressed.

"Colonel Yandell. It is ungentlemanly to fire at an officer under a flag of truce."

Yandell looked up to see Captain Cartledge standing before him. His uniform had been blackened by smoke, as had his face. He stepped forward and raised his long sword in mocking salute.

Colonel Yandell pointed the pistol and fired. Saw the bullet strike the other man's arm. The English officer stumbled back under the impact, shifted the sword to his left hand and stepped forward.

Yandell clicked the trigger again and again—but he had only had time to load the one chamber.

The sword plunged into his chest and he fell.

One more dying American, one more victim of this new war.

The regimental carpenter had planed the plank smooth, then tacked on the sheet of white cartridge paper with a couple of nails. It made a rough but serviceable drawing board. A charcoal willow twig was a suitable drawing instrument. Sherman sat outside his tent concentrating on the drawing he was making of the landing and the steamboats behind. He turned when he heard the footsteps approach.

"Didn't know that you could draw, Cump," Grant said.

"It snuck up on me and I learned to like it. Did a lot of engineering drawings at the Point and just sort of fell into sketching. I find it relaxing."

"I could use some of that myself," Grant said, taking a camp chair from the tent and dropping into it. He pulled a long black cigar from his jacket pocket and lit it. "Never did like waiting. Johnny Reb is quiet—and the British! Why we just don't know do we. I feel like latching onto a jug of corn likker . . ."

Sherman turned quickly from the drawing, his face suddenly drawn. Grant smiled.

"Not that I will, mind you," he said. "That's all behind me now that there is a war on. I don't think either of us did well as we should when we were out of the army. But at least you were a bank president in California—while I was hauling timber with a team of mules and burying my face in the booze every night."

"But the bank failed," Sherman said grimly. "I lost everything, house, land, everything I had worked for all those years." He hesitated and went on, his voice lowered. "Lost my sanity, felt that way at times."

"But you came out of it, Cump—just the way I came out of the bottle. I guess war is our only trade."

"And you are good at it, Ulysses. I meant it when I wrote that letter. I have faith in you. Command me in any way."

Grant looked a little discomfited. "Not just me. Halleck said you should have the command under me. I was more than happy to oblige. You have good friends in this army, that's what it comes down to."

"General Grant, sir," a voice called out and they turned to see the sergeant on the bank above. "Telegraph message coming through from the east. About the British the operator said."

"This could be it," Grant said, jumping to his feet.

"I'll put this away. Be right with you."

The military telegraph was still clicking out its message when General Grant came into the tent. He stood behind the operator, reading over his shoulder as he wrote. Seized up the paper when he was finished. He clamped down hard on his long cigar, then puffed a cloud of smoke over the operator's head.

"Stuart," he called out, and his aide hurried over. "Get my staff together. Meeting in my tent in half an hour. If they want to know what it is about, just tell them that we got a second war on our hands."

"The British?"

"Damned right."

Grant walked slowly back to his tent, chewing on his cigar and planning out just what he had to do. Sherman was already there, pacing back and forth. As Grant stamped into the tent he knew exactly what orders had to be issued, what actions taken.

Grant poured out a glass of whiskey from the stone crock and passed it over to Sherman. Looked at the jug and smiled grimly; then pushed the corn cob back into its neck.

"They've done it, Cump, actually gone and done it. We are at war again with the British. Without much reason this time. I don't see how stopping one ship and taking some prisoners could lead to this."

"I don't think that there has ever been much reason for most wars. Since Victoria has been on the throne there has always been a war going on somewhere around the world for the British."

"Little ones maybe, but this is sure going to be a big one." Grant went over and tapped his index finger against the map that was spread across the sawhorse-supported table. "They invaded New York State right up here and attacked the fortifications at Plattsburgh."

Sherman looked at the site of the attack, just south of Lake Champlain, and shook his head in disbelief, took a sip of his whiskey. "Who would have thunk it. The British always seem ready to fight the last war when the new one begins."

"Or even the one before it. Stop me if I am wrong—but didn't General Burgoyne come that way when he invaded the colonies in 1777?"

"He surely did. And that's not all. Just to prove that the

British never learn anything by experience, General Provost in 1814 did exactly the same thing and attacked in exactly the same way. Got whupped though and lost all of his supplies. Maybe that can happen again."

Grant shook his head glumly. "Not this time, I'm afraid." He sat back in his field chair and puffed on his cigar until the tip glowed red. He pointed the cigar at his fellow general and close friend.

"Won't be as easy this time as it was before. All we got in front of them now is some militia with a couple of old cannon. The British field guns and their regulars will run right over those poor boys. The way I see it, it is not a matter of will they lose, but just how long they will be able to hold out."

Sherman traced his finger down the map. "Once past Plattsburgh the invading army will have a clear track right down the Hudson Valley. If they're not stopped they'll go straight through Albany and West Point and the next thing you know they will be knocking on the door in New York City."

Grant shook his head. "Except it is not going to be that easy. Halleck has already got his troops loaded onto the New York Central Railroad and is heading north even while we speak. As far as we can tell the enemy has not yet penetrated further south than Plattsburgh. A lot depends on how long the militia there can hold on. Halleck hopes to draw the line north of Albany. If he does I will join him there. He wants me to entrain with as many regiments as we can spare from here and come and support him."

"How many are we taking?"

"No we, Cump. He is putting you in command when I am gone. How many troops will you need if Beauregard tries another attack at Pittsburg Landing?"

Sherman thought long and hard before he spoke. "For defense I'll have the cannon on the gunboats that are still tied up on the riverbank. So I can fall back as far as the landing and make a stand there. If you can leave me four batteries and a minimum of two regiments I'll say that we can hold the line. We can always cross back over the river if we have to. Beauregard won't get through us. After Shiloh we're not giving away an inch."

"I think you had better have three regiments. The Rebs still have a sizable army out there."

"That will do fine. Are hard times coming, Ulysses?"

Grant drew heavily on his cigar. "Can't lie and say that things are going to be easy. Johnny Reb may be down but he is surely not out. And they'll just love to see us being kicked up the behind by the lobsterbacks. But I don't think that the Rebs will try anything for awhile. Why should they?"

Sherman nodded solemn agreement. "You're absolutely right. They'll let the British do their fighting for them. While their scouts watch our troop movements and keep track of us, they will have plenty of time to regroup. Then, when we're tied up on the new fronts, why they can then just pick and choose exactly where they want to attack in force. I cannot lie. Far from being almost won, our war with the Secesh is about to begin to go very badly."

"I'm afraid that you are right. They've got spies everywhere—just like us. They'll know where we are weakening the line, and they will also know just what their friends the British are doing. Then, soon as they catch us looking away for a moment—bang—and the battle is on."

Grant was silent for a moment, weighing their problems. "Cump, we have both had our problems in the past—in the army and out of it. Mostly out of it. I used whiskey to drown my problems, as you know."

Sherman's face was grim. "Like you, life has not been easy. All of the things I did when I left the army suddenly don't seem that important. Before the battles started I was fearful and upset. Saw troubles where none existed. That's all over. But funny enough, it is all a lot easier now. There seems to be clarity in war, a fulfillment in battle. I feel that I am in the right place at last."

Grant stood and seized his friend's hand, took him by the arm as well. "You speak the truth far better than you know. I have to tell you that. Some people's facilities slow down and go numb when faced with battle. Others sharpen and quicken. You are one of those. They are rare. You held my right flank at Shiloh and you never wavered. Got a lot of good horseflesh shot out from under you too, but you never hesitated, not for one second. Now you have to do it again. Hold the line here, Cump, I know you can do it. Do it better than anyone else in this world."

DEATH IN THE SOUTH

Alexander Milne, admiral of the British Navy, was a courageous and bold fighting man—when it was time to be courageous and bold. He had always been bold in battle, had been badly wounded in his country's cause. When the Americans had seized a British ship and taken prisoners from it, he had gone at once to the Prime Minister and requested active service once again. This had been the right and bold thing to do.

He was also cautious when it was necessary to be cautious. Now he knew, as the squadron plowed ahead through the warm, star-filled night, that this was indeed a time for caution. They had been out of sight of land ever since his flotilla had sailed from the Bahamas at dusk two weeks ago, on a northerly course. The islands reeked with spies and his departure would surely be noted and transmitted to the Americans. Only when night had fallen and they were out of sight of land had the squadron turned south.

It had been dead reckoning ever since then, without a sight of land since Andros Island; a quick inspection at dusk of its prominent landmarks in order to check their position. It was good navigation training for the officers. They had sailed south almost to the Tropic of Cancer before they had altered course west through the Straits of Florida. They had held to this course since then, far out from the American coast and well clear of any coastal shipping. In all this sailing they had seen no other vessel, had assumed they had gone undetected as well.

It wasn't until the noon sun observations agreed with the ship's chronometer that they had indeed reached eighty-eight degrees west longitude that they had altered course for the last time. Sailed due north toward the Gulf Coast of the United States.

WARRIOR AT SEA

Admiral Milne flew his flag from the ironclad *Warrior*. He stood now on her bridge, besides Captain Roland who was her commander.

"How many knots, Captain?" he asked.

"Still six knots, sir."

"Good. If the calculations are correct that should have us off the coast at dawn."

Milne climbed up onto the after bridge and looked back at the ships keeping station astern. First were the two ships of the line, *Caledonia* and *Royal Oak*. Beyond them, just blurs in the darkness were the transports. Out of sight to their stern he knew were the other ships of the line, the frigates and corvettes. The largest British fleet that had been to sea since 1817.

But he was still not pleased. That a force this size had to circle out of sight of land—then slip in at night like a blockade runner—was a humiliating thing to have to do. Britain had ruled the waves for centuries and had won all of her wars that had been fought at sea. But the Americans had a large fleet guarding this coast and it must be avoided at all cost. Not because of fear of battle, but out of necessity of keeping their presence in these waters a secret.

Captain Nicholas Roland had joined him. "Clouding up ahead, sir," he said. "Too late for the rainy season, but the weather can be foul along this coast at any time of the year."

They stood in silence, each wrapped in his own thoughts, the only sound the metronome-like *thud thud* of the ship's engines. Ahead of them the brilliant stars were vanishing behind the rising darkness of the approaching cloud. Out here, where the watch officer and the helmsman could not hear them, they could speak together as they could not in the crowded ship.

Roland was married to the admiral's niece. Their homes in Saltash were quite close and he had seen a good deal of both of them when he had been recuperating from the wound that he had received in China, at the Battle of the Peio River. He and Roland had struck up an easy friendship despite their difference in years.

"I'm not sure, Nicholas, that I like the way warfare at sea is developing. We always seem to be a little bit late with engineering advances, too prone to let others lead the way."

"I cannot believe that is true, sir. We are now standing on the bridge of the most advanced warship ever seen. Built of iron, steam-powered, with twenty-six 68-pounders, not to mention ten 100-pounders. A forty gun ship with guns of the largest caliber, unbeatable, unsinkable. We know that the senior service must be conservative, sir. But once we get our teeth into something we are a bulldog."

"I agree. But far too often we tend to fight present wars with the skills of the past war. There is a weight of tradition and a tendency to suspect innovation that I feel will cost us dear."

"That is possibly true, sir, but I am too far down the ladder to have an opinion. But surely you exaggerate. Just look at this ship. As soon as the navy discovered that the French were building *La Gloire*, an iron warship, there was the instant decision by the Secretary to the Admiralty to build an iron-belted frigate. Two of them in fact to go the French one better. Like our sister ship, *Black Prince,* we make the most of the modern science of the sea. We have sail as well as steam so we can stay at sea longer. I am most proud to command her."

"You should be. But do you remember what I said when word reached us about the battle between *Virginia* and *Monitor*?"

"I can never forget it. We had just finished dining and you were passing the port. Robinson was deck officer and he came in holding the report, read it aloud to all of us. Some of the officers called it colonial tomfoolery but you would have none of that. You sobered them up quite quickly. 'Gentlemen', you said, 'we have just entered a new age. This morning, when I awoke, the British navy had 142 warships. When I retire tonight we will have but two. *Warrior* and *Black Prince*.' "

"What I said then is still very true. Just as the steam engine put paid to the sailing ship, so shall the ironclad eliminate the wooden ship from the navies of the world. Which is why we are entering battle through the rear door, so to speak. The Yankee blockading fleet has effectively sealed off the southern coastline from any commerce by sea. Now I intend to break through that blockade and I have no intention of meeting any of the blockading fleet except under my terms. It is sheer bad luck that *Black Prince* is having her boilers repaired at this time. I would feel much better if she were at our side."

Roland stamped his heel hard on the iron plating of the after bridge. "An iron ship that can carry the largest guns made. In her I dread naught."

"I agree, a fine ship. But I wish her designers had not been so condescending to the Admiralty old guard. Sail or steam, I say. One or the other and not a mixture of the two. With masts and sail we must have an enormous crew to tend them. To raise sail by hand, to even raise the screw by hand—needs two hundred hands to do that job. Where one steam winch would have sufficed."

Captain Roland coughed politely, then got up the nerve to ask the question that had been bothering him since he had first been appointed to command this ship.

"Sir, perhaps it is out of place, but I must admit that I have always been bothered by this. After all, the merchant ships use steam winches . . ." His words ran out as he blushed, unseen in the darkness, sure that he had spoken out of turn. The admiral was aware of this, but took pity.

"We have been friends, my boy, for some time. And I can well understand your worries about your charge. And I know that you have a sound enough head not to repeat anything that I tell you in confidence."

"Indeed, sir! Of course."

"I was part of the committee that approved *Warrior* and her sister ship. Although I protested I was overruled. I said that the navy would rather look backward than forge ahead. My suggestions were overruled. All of the others believed that the sailors would be spoiled and grow lazy if machines did their work for them. Besides, it was felt, the exercise would keep them healthy!"

Captain Roland could only gape. He was almost sorry that he had asked. The ship's bell sounded the change of watch. He went down to the upper deck, to the rifle-proof conning tower.

On the deck below George William Frederick Charles, the Duke of Cambridge, stirred in his berth when he heard the bell, wide-awake and cursing it. When he closed his eyes instead of blissful darkness and the Lethe of sleep he saw divisions of soldiers, batteries of cannon, military stores, plans—all the paraphernalia of war that had occupied his mind for weeks—months now. The steel box of a cabin closed in on him. He did not consider for a moment the ship's Master who had been moved out of this cabin, now sharing an even smaller cabin with the Commander—or the hundreds of ratings who swung their hammocks in the even darker, closer, noisome chambers belowdeck. Rank had its place—and his was at the very top. The Duke of Cambridge, Commander-in-Chief of the British Army, cousin to the Queen, was not used to physical discomfort, in the field or off it.

When he sat up his head struck the candle holder above the bed and he cursed it soundly. When he opened the cabin door enough light came in from the passageway for him to find his clothes. Pulling on jacket and trousers he went out of the cabin, turned right and went into the captain's day room; a spacious area lit by a gimballed kerosene light and airy from the scuttle in the ceiling above. Still resting on the sideboard was the excellent brandy he had sampled after dinner: he poured himself a good measure. He had just dropped into the leather armchair when the door opened and Bullers looked in.

"I'm sorry, sir, didn't mean to disturb you."

He started to withdraw but the duke called after him. "Come in, Bullers, do come in—not able to sleep?"

"The truth indeed. Soldiers at sea are about as useful as teats on a boar."

"Well said. Enter and address the brandy, there's a good fellow."

Major General Bullers was commander of the infantry, next in rank below the duke. Both were fighting soldiers who had served in Ireland, then in the Crimea.

"Bloody hot," Bullers said.

"Drink up and you won't notice it." He sipped from his glass. "Champion should be well on his way to New York City by now."

"He should indeed. With his divisions and guns there is no force in the Americas that can stand in his way."

"Let it be so. God knows we spent enough time in planning and outfitting the expedition."

"You should have commanded it—to ensure success."

"Nice of you to say so, Bullers—but General Champion is more than able to handle a straightforward attack like the one from Canada. This one is where certain other skills will be needed."

As one their eyes turned to look at the maps strewn on the mahogany table. Although they had gone over the plans for the attack countless times before, the maps drew them back, like iron filings to a magnet. They stood, taking their drinks with them, and strode across the room.

"The Gulf Coast of America," the Duke of Cambridge said. "Yankee naval bases here and here and here. A fleet at sea guarding every harbor and inlet. While here at Hampton Roads I am sure that the *Monitor* and her attendant ships of the line still guard the bolt hole where the *Virginia* must still lie at rest. Admiral Milne has insisted that we avoid that bit of coast like the plague—and I couldn't agree more. That fleet is less than six hundred miles away and I want it to stay that way. Of course there is this small naval force blockading Mobile

Bay not more than fifty miles away. But they are of no threat to our superior force." He tapped the chart lightly.

"But *here* is the enemy's Achilles heel. Deer Island off the coast of the state of Mississippi. Invaded and seized by the North and now a base for their blockading fleet. That is our destination. At dawn we shall attack and destroy them with a naval bombardment. Then your regiments, and the marines, will land and seize the fortifications. The blockade will be broken. The navy shall remain on station there, protected by the shore batteries, to make sure that the blockade in this area is not restored. As soon as our landings are successful I'll take a troop of cavalry and contact the Confederates—and Jefferson Davis in Richmond. The Queen herself has messages for him and I am sure that our welcome will be of the warmest. After that our merchant fleet will get cotton here, bring in military supplies in return. The South will grow strong—and very soon will be victorious. Our armies still attack in the North so the Yankees must divide their strength if they attempt to pry us from this base. Divide and fall, defeated. They cannot long survive. Between our invading armies and a rejuvenated Southern army. Might will prevail."

Bullers shared his enthusiasm. "It will be over by winter, God willing. The United States of America will cease to exist and the Confederate States of America will be the legitimate government."

"A worthy aim and a happy conclusion," the duke said. "I care little what the politicians do with the spoils. I just know that a victorious army will prove Britain's might to the world. Then our navy will also be able to expand its ironclad fleet, until once again mastery of the world's oceans shall be ours."

At dawn, as planned, the commanders of the landing party were rowed to *Warrior*. Their boats appeared suddenly out of the sea mist and the officers climbed most carefully aboard, since every rope and piece of wood or decking was slick from the fog and gently falling rain.

The coastline was in sight now, flat and featureless and barely visible in the falling rain.

"It all looks the same," the Duke of Cambridge said. "No obvious landmarks that I can make out."

"It was a good landfall," the admiral said. "After sailing by dead reckoning, for so long out of sight of land, I would say it was excellent navigation. The frigates are scouting both east and west and the island will soon be found."

But it was noon before *Clam* came bustling back from her search. The fog had persisted and the drizzle still continued, which made her signals hard to read at a distance.

"Deer Island sighted. No ships at anchor," the signal officer finally said.

"Capital," the Duke of Cambridge said, feeling some of the tension drain away now that the final phase of the operation was about to begin. "Commander Tredegar, your marines will secure the landing beaches. As soon as you are ashore General Bullers will begin landing his men. Victory here, gentlemen, will be the first combined naval and army engagement that will lead inexorably to the final defeat of the enemy."

As the ships approached the gray coastline the battlements of the shore defenses became more clearly seen. Admiral Milne had his telescope trained on them. The image was blurred by raindrops, so much so that he had to take it from his eye and wipe the object lens with his kerchief. When he looked again he laughed sharply.

"By George, there they are, sir. The Yankees, their flag."

The Duke of Cambridge looked through his telescope at the stars and stripes above the ramparts. Red, white and blue.

"Send the order to begin firing as soon as the fortifications are within range. The boats will land under our covering fire."

But it took time, too much time. No time was wasted by Tredegar's experienced marines who were swiftly ashore and running up the beaches. But the soldiers of the regular army had no experience of beach landings and their attempts were glacial in the extreme. While the marines were attacking there was chaos among the army troops. The overloaded boats ran into each other, one capsized and the men had to be rescued and dragged from the sea. It was growing dark before the last of them were ashore and beaten into some kind of order by the sergeants. Major General Sir Robert Bullers used the flat of his sword against more than one of the dullards before he was satisfied enough to order his troops into the attack.

It proved to be desperately hard work. It was growing dark and the marines were still stalled before the earthen breast-works, the bodies of those who had fallen in the attack litter-ing the sodden ground.

It was left to the 67th South Hampshire to do the job. They had been stationed on the island of Trinidad long enough for them to be able to work and fight in the clammy heat. Their sergeants had chivvied them into two lines now, muskets loaded, bayonets fixed.

"Hampshire Tigers—follow me!" General Bullers shouted and waved his sword as he started forward. With a roar of hoarse voices they charged past the colonel and into a hail of lead.

The standard bearer, just in front of the general, was thrown back as a minié bullet caught him in the stomach and doubled him over. Before his body fell the general had seized the regi-mental flag and saved it from falling into the bloody mud. He shouted encouragement, flag in one hand, sword in the other, until a corporal took the standard from him and charged on.

Although they were badly outnumbered the defenders still put up a stiff resistance. Two field guns had been landed and dragged into position. Under their merciless fire the ramparts were finally breached. But more good men fell in the attack that followed. It was a bloody business with hand-to-hand fighting at the very end.

Night had fallen before the rampart was finally taken—at a terrible price. The torn bodies of Bullers's men and soldiers of the 56th West Essex mingled with the corpses of the de-fenders. A lamp was lit to look for survivors. There were very few. Blood and mud colored all of the uniforms, though it could be seen that the Americans were motley clad, not only in blue but with many other rags of uniform. Ill-uniformed or not—they could fight. And run—but not far. They must have formed a second line because gunfire crackled again and the air screamed with bullets. The lantern was quickly doused.

"They'll rue this day's work," Bullers said through tight-clamped teeth, as his officers and noncoms ordered their lines. Some of the wounded were sitting up while others were lying in the mud with empty eyes; the walking wounded stumbled to the rear.

"Fire when you are sure of your target—then it is the bayonet. Forward!"

Men died in the night of fierce hand-to-hand combat. The Yankees would not retreat and every yard of advance had to be fought for. Men struggled in the mud and drowned in water-filled muddy ruts. In the end the relentless pressure of the British was too much for the outnumbered defenders and the survivors were forced to fall back. But it was not a rout. They kept firing as they retreated and held onto their guns.

The officers had put out pickets and, tired as he was, the general made the rounds with the sergeant major to be sure they were alert. The desperately tired soldiers drank from their water bottles and ate what bits of food they had in their packs. Fell asleep in the warm rain, clutching their muskets to their chests.

Just before dawn the cries of the pickets and a sudden crackle of gunfire heralded a counterattack. The weary soldiers rolled over and once again fought for their lives.

Surprisingly, the attack was quickly broken, a last weary attempt by the defenders. But the British soldiers after days at sea, a night of fighting and dying, little water and less sleep, would not be stopped now. Anger replaced fatigue and they pursued the running enemy in the gray dawn. Bayoneting them in the back as they fled. Chased them into the buildings beyond.

And found drink there. Large stone jugs of potent spirits that tore at their throats and burned in their guts. But there were barrels of beer as well to wash away the burn. And even better.

Women. Hiding, running, screaming. The trained British troops rarely broke down. But when they did so—as they did during the Indian Mutiny—the results were drastic and deadly. Now inflamed by drink and exhaustion, angry at the deaths of their comrades, the beast was released. The clothes were torn from the women's bodies and they were pressed down into the mud and taken with fierce violence. And these soldiers, consumed by lust and drink, could not be easily stopped. One sergeant who attempted to intervene got a bayonet through his kidneys; the drunken men roared with laughter as he writhed in twisted death agony.

General Bullers did not really care. He ordered his officers not to intervene lest they risk their own destruction. The soldiers would fall down drunk soon, unconscious and stuporous. It had happened before; the British common soldier could not be trusted with drink. It had happened in India during the Mutiny—and even in Crimea. Now they would drink themselves stupid. In the morning the sergeants and the few teetotalers in the regiment would drag them under cover until they came around. To face whatever punishment he decreed. Lights appeared as bandsmen with lanterns came searching for survivors among the dead.

The general shook his head, realizing suddenly that he was close to exhaustion. A South Hampshire private stumbled out of a shed in front of him, stopped and drank from the crock of spirits that he had found. He dropped, stunned unconscious, when Bullers caught him a mighty blow on the neck with his fist. The general picked the jug out of the mud and drank deep and shuddered. Good whisky from the Scottish isles it was not. But it had an undeniable potency that was needed right now. Bullers swayed and sat down suddenly on the remains of a rampart, pushing aside a corpse to do so. The whiskey was tasting better with each swallow.

The dead soldier had been lying on a flag, clutching it in clawed fingers, perhaps trying to shield it from the carnage. General Bullers pulled it up and wiped some of the mud from it. Saw in the light of a passing lantern its colors. Red, white and blue. He grunted and dropped it back onto the corpse. Red, white and blue, the colors of the flag of the United States of America. Yes, but somehow different. What? He seized it up again and spread it on the rampart.

The correct colors all right. But differently shaped, arranged. This was not the stars and stripes he had seen flying from Yankee ships in Kingston harbor. This one had a few stars on a blue field, and only a few large horizontal stripes.

The flag moved in his hands and he started. Blinked and

saw that the dead man's eyes were open—mortally wounded perhaps, but not yet dead.

"This flag, what is it?" Bullers asked. The wounded man's eyes misted so he shook him cruelly. "Speak up man, this flag, this is the stars and stripes?"

The dying soldier strained to speak, squeezing out the words and the colonel had to lean close to hear them.

"Not . . . damned Yankee flag. This . . . is the stars and bars . . . flag of the South."

That was all he said as he died. General Bullers was stunned. For a single horrified moment he believed the man, believed that this was the flag of the Confederacy.

Had he attacked the wrong side? That could not be possible. He knew the flag of the Confederacy with its crossed blue bands with white stars on a red background. He had seen it on blockade runners tied up at the Pool in London. And this was certainly not the same.

And no country, even these miserable colonials, could possibly have two flags. Or could it? No! The man had lied, lied with his dying breath, may he burn in Hades for that. He held the flag in his hand and turned it about. Then hurled it into a mud-filled puddle and ground it under his heel.

What the hell difference did it really make, either way? North or South they were all filthy backwoodsmen. Sons and grandsons of the colonial revolutionaries who had had the temerity to fight and kill good Englishmen. Including his good father, Lieutenant General Bullers, who had fallen at the Battle of New Orleans.

He drank heavily from the stone crock and twisted his boot back and forth until the last scrap of flag had disappeared in the filthy mud.

Then sighed—and pulled it out again. Whatever flag it was, whatever had happened here, the Duke of Cambridge would have to know about it.

The duke had moved his headquarters to a stone blockhouse, close to the beach, that had been part of the defending gun battery. He was shuffling through a handful of half-burned reports when Bullers came in with the flag.

THE STARS AND BARS

"Most strange," the duke said. "These reports are all headed CSA—not USA. What the devil is going on here?"

Bullers held out the battered flag. "I think—Your Grace—I think that a terrible mistake has been made. There are no Yankees here. For some reason, I don't know, we have been fighting and killing Southerners."

"Good God!" The duke's fingers opened and the papers fell to the floor. "Is that true? Are you sure of it?"

Bullers bent and picked up the papers, shuffled through them. "These are all addressed to the forces in Biloxi. A coastal city in Mississippi."

"Damn and blast!" The duke's amazement was replaced by a boiling rage. "The navy! The senior service with their much-vaunted skills of navigation. Couldn't even find the right bloody place to attack. So where does that leave us, Bullers? With egg on our face. Their mistake—our blame."

He began to pace the length of the room and back. "So what do we do? Retire and apologize? Not my way, General, not my way at all. Crawl away with tail between legs?"

"The alternative . . ."

"Is to carry on. We have the men and the determination. Instead of aiding this nauseous slaveocracy we shall defeat it. Strike north to Canada and destroy everything in our path. Defeat this divided and weak country, countries, now and bring them all back into the Empire where they belong.

"Strike and strike hard, Bullers. That is our only salvation."

A MUTUAL ENEMY

After the first year of the Civil War both sides in the conflict had learned how important it was to dig in—and dig quickly. Standing up and firing shoulder-to-shoulder, Continental style, had proven to be only a recipe for suicide. If there were any possibility of an attack the defenders dug in. With shovels if they were available. With bayonets, mess kits, anything if they were not. They became very good at it. In no time at all trenches were dug and dirt ramparts thrown up that would stop bullets and send cannonballs bouncing to the rear.

With memories of the blood-drenched Battle of Shiloh still fresh in their minds, the survivors dug. The 53rd Ohio were now entrenched on top of the high bluff above Pittsburg Landing. Chunks of branches and trees, blasted during the fighting there, were embedded in the red dirt of the rampart.

Knowing how weak his manpower was, now that General Grant had taken the bulk of the army east to face the British invasion, General Sherman had done his best to reinforce the defenses. He had mounted all of his guns forward so they could spray any attack with canister shot, tin canisters of grapeshot that burst in the air over the enemy. This line would have to be held against the far superior force of the Confederates. He wondered how long it would take them to discover his diminished strength; not long, he was sure.

At least he could rely on the gunboats tied up at the landing. He and his signals officer had spent long hours with the captains of the vessels to ensure that covering fire would be fast and accurate. He felt that he had done all that he could do in the situation.

Now that the spring floods were over, the Tennessee River

had fallen, exposing sandbanks and meadows beside the landing. Sherman had put up tents and made his headquarters there beside the river. The messenger found him in his tent.

"Colonel says to come and git you at once, General. Something's happening out where the Rebs is camped."

Sherman climbed the high bank and found Colonel Appler waiting there for him. "Some kind of parlay going on, General. Three Secesh on horses out there. One blowing a bugle and the other waving a white flag. Third one got plenty of gold chicken guts on his sleeve, ranking officer for sure."

Sherman clambered up onto the parapet to see for himself. The three riders had stopped a hundred paces from the Union position; the bugle sounded again. The bugler and the sergeant with the flag were riding spindly nags. The officer was mounted on a fine bay.

"Let me have that telescope," Sherman said, seized and held it to his eye. "By God—that is General P.G.T. Beauregard himself! He visited the college when I was there. I wonder what he is doing out there with a flag?"

"Wants to parlay, I guess," Appler said. "Want me to mosey over and see what he has to say?"

"No. If one general can ride out there I guess two of them can. Get me a horse."

Sherman dragged his skinny frame into the saddle, grabbed up the reins and kicked his mount forward. The horse picked its way carefully through the branches and litter of the battlefield. The bugler lowered his bugle when he saw Sherman approaching. Beauregard waved his men back and spurred forward toward the other rider. They came together and stopped. Beauregard saluted and began to speak.

"Thank you for agreeing to parlay. I am . . ."

"I certainly do know who you are, General Beauregard. You visited me when I was director of Louisiana State Military College."

"General Sherman, of course, you must excuse me. Events have been—" Beauregard slumped a bit in the saddle, then realized what he was doing and drew himself up sharply and spoke.

"I have just received telegraphed reports as well as certain orders. Before I respond I wished to consult with the commander of your forces here."

"At present I am in command, General." He did not go into detail why, since he did not want to discuss Grant's departure and his weakened position. "You can address me."

"It is about the British Army. It is my understanding that they have invaded the Federal states, that they are attacking south into New York State from Canada."

"That is correct. I'm sure that it has been reported in the newspapers. Of course I cannot comment further on the military situation."

Beauregard raised his gloved hand. "Excuse me, sir, it was not my intent to draw you out. I just wanted reassurance that you knew of that invasion, so you would understand better what I have to tell you. I wish to bring you intelligence of a second invasion."

Sherman tried not to reveal his distress at this news. Another invasion would make the defense of the country just that more difficult. But he knew of no other invading forces and did not want to reveal his ignorance. "Please go on, General."

Beauregard was no longer the calm and gently mannered Southern officer. His fists clenched and he had to squeeze the words out through hard-clamped teeth.

"Invasion and murder and worse, that is what has happened. And confusion. There were reports from Biloxi, Mississippi, that a Union fleet was bombarding the shore defenses there. Whatever troops that could be gathered were rushed there to stop the invasion. It was a night of rain and battle with neither side giving way. In the end we lost—and not to the North!"

Sherman shook his head, confused. "I am afraid that I do not understand."

"It was them, the British. Yesterday they landed troops to attack the defenses of the port of Biloxi. They were not identified until morning, when their flags and uniforms were seen. By that time the battle was over. And they were not simply satisfied with destroying the military. They attacked the people in the town as well, reduced it, burnt half of it. What they did with the women . . . The latest reports tell me that they are now advancing inland from Biloxi."

Sherman was shocked speechless, just managed to murmur under his breath. Beauregard was scarcely aware of his presence as he stared into the distance, seeing the destruction of the Southern city.

"They are not soldiers, but are murderers and rapists. They must be stopped, annihilated—and my troops are the only ones in a position to do that. I believe you to be a man of honor, General. So I can tell you that I have been ordered to place my soldiers between these invaders and the people of Mississippi. That is why I requested this meeting."

"Just what is it that you want, General?"

Beauregard looked grimly at his fellow officer, whom he had so recently engaged in deadly conflict. He thought carefully before he spoke.

"General Sherman, I know that you are a man of his word. Before this war you founded and led one of our great Southern military institutions. You have spent much time in the South and you must have many friends here. You could not have done this if you had been one of those wild-eyed abolitionists. I mean no insult, sir, to what I know to be your sincere beliefs. What I mean is that I can speak to you frankly—and know that you will understand how serious matters are. You will also know that in no way will I be able to lie to you, nor will you take advantage of anything that I might say."

Beauregard drew himself up and when he spoke there was a grim fury behind his drawling words.

"I am asking you simply—if you will consider arranging an armistice with me at this time. I wish only to defend the people of this state and do promise not to undertake any military incursions against the Federal Army. In turn I request that you not attack my weakened positions here. I ask this because I go to attack our mutual enemy. If you agree you can draw up whatever terms you wish and I will sign them. As a brother officer in arms I respectfully ask you for your aid."

This meeting, the invading British, the request were so unusual that Sherman really was at a loss for words. But he felt a growing elation at the same time. The armistice would be easy enough to arrange, in fact he would take a great deal of pleasure in doing so. His mission was to hold the ground he now occupied. He would far rather do that by joining a cease-fire than by bloody battle.

But even more important than that was the phrase that General Beauregard had used.

Mutual enemy, that is what he had said—and he had meant it. The very glimmer of a completely preposterous idea nibbled at the edges of his thoughts as he spoke.

"I understand your feelings. I would do the very same thing were I in your shoes. But of course I cannot agree to this without consulting General Halleck, my commanding officer," he finally said.

"Of course."

"But having said that, let me add that I have only compassion and understanding of your position. Grant me one hour and I will meet you here again. I must first explain what has happened, and what you propose. I assure you that I will lend my weight to the strengths of your arguments."

"Thank you, General Sherman," Beauregard said with some warmth as he saluted.

Sherman returned the salute, wheeled his horse about and galloped away. Colonel Appler himself seized the horse's reins when Sherman dismounted.

"General—what's it all about? What's happening?"

Sherman blinked at him, scarcely aware of his presence. "Yes, Appler. This is a matter of singularly great importance or the general would not have come forward as he has done. I must make a report. As soon as that is done I will speak with you and the other senior officers. Please ask them to join me in my tent in thirty minutes."

He went back down the slope to the encampment. But, despite what he had said, he made no attempt to go to the telegraph tent. Instead he went directly to his own tent. He spoke to the sentry on guard there.

"I am not to be disturbed until my officers assemble here. Tell them that they must wait outside. No one to be admitted to see me. No one at all—do you understand?"

"Yes, sir."

He dropped into his camp chair and stared unseeingly into the distance, his fingers combing distractedly through his thin beard. There was an opportunity here, one that must be seized and grasped tightly before it escaped. Despite what he had said he had no intention of contacting Halleck, not yet. He needed time to think this through without any distractions. The course of action that he was considering was too personal, too irrational for others to understand.

Of course it was obvious just what he should do. It was his military duty to telegraph at once, to explain what had happened in Biloxi and to ask for orders. Surely when the generals and the politicians understood what the British had done, why then they would certainly agree to the armistice. A common enemy. Better having the Southern army fighting the British rather than threatening attack on the North.

But how long would it take the politicians to make their minds up?

Too long, he knew that. No one would want to take responsibility for the drastic action that Beauregard was asking for. Commanders would dither, then pass the decision on up the line. Dispatches would be telegraphed until, probably, the whole thing would end up in Abe Lincoln's lap.

And just how long would that take? Hours at least, probably longer. And the decision must be made now. Hard as it was he must take the responsibility himself. Even at the risk of losing his career, he must decide. If this opportunity were missed it would never occur again. He must decide for himself and act on that decision.

And he knew what that decision must be. He went over every possibility, and still returned to the single course of action.

When his officers had gathered he told them what he was going to do. He measured his words carefully.

"Gentlemen, like the North, the South has now been invaded by a British Army." He paused until this fact had sunk in, then went on. "I have just talked with General Beauregard who asked for a cease-fire to permit him to take his troops south to do battle with the enemy. He called the invaders 'our mutual enemy' and that is true. A cease-fire would certainly be very much in order at this time. It is certainly to our benefit as well."

He looked around at the officers who were nodding agreement. But would they agree with him if he went further?

"I want to grant this cease-fire. What would you say to that?"

"Do it, General—by all means!"

"You must, there is no choice."

"Every redcoat they whup is one that we won't have to worry about."

Their enthusiasm came naturally, was not contrived or exaggerated. But how far could he go?

"I am glad that we are in agreement on that." Sherman looked around at his excited officers. Chose his words with great care. "I propose to render even greater aid to our common cause.

"If you agree with me, I am going to take a regiment of infantry and join General Beauregard in his attack on the British."

The silence lengthened as they considered the impact of what Sherman was proposing. This went far beyond a single battle, a single joined conflict. There was the possibility of course that nothing would come of this decision other than a single battle—or it could lead to even more momentous events almost impossible to consider. It was Colonel Appler who spoke first.

"General, you are a brave man to suggest this without working up through the chain of command. I am sure that you have considered that and considered all of the possibilities of your actions. Well I have as well. I would like you to take the 53rd Ohio with you. The President has always looked for any means to shorten this war, to make peace with the Confederacy. I am in complete agreement with that. Let us aid in stopping this adventure, this invasion of our nation's shores. Take us with you."

A spark had been lit that burned all of them with enthusiasm. Captain Munch shouted agreement.

"Guns, you'll need guns. My 1st Minnesota battery will go with you as well."

"Will the men go along with this decision?" Sherman asked.

"I am sure that they will, General. They will feel just as we do—drive out the invaders of our country!"

While the orders were being issued Sherman went into his tent and wrote a report describing the actions he was taking, and why it was being done. He folded and sealed it and sent for General Lew Wallace in command of the 23rd Indiana.

"You agree with what is being done, Lew?" he asked.

"Couldn't agree more, Cump. There is a chance here to do something about this war—although I am not clear just what will come out of it. After Shiloh and all those deaths I think I began to look at this war in a very different way. I do feel that what you propose to do is something that is well worth doing. Americans fighting Americans was never a good thing, even though it was forced upon us. Now we have a chance to do something bold—together."

PARTNERS IN COMBAT

"Good. Then you will take command here until I return. And take this. It is a complete report of everything that has happened here today. After we have gone I want you to telegraph it through to General Halleck."

Wallace took the folded paper and smiled. "Going to be busy around here for a bit. There are going to be some really great fireworks when this news arrives. I think it might be an hour or so before I'll be able to get this out."

"You are a sensible officer, Wallace. I will leave this matter to your discretion."

The guns were limbered up, the horses fastened in their traces. An opening was torn in the defense line so that they could ride through. The men of the 53rd Ohio had been informed of what he planned to do and their reaction was important. They stood at attention as he rode up—then burst into wild shouting. Cheered him when he rode slowly by, waving their caps in the air on the points of their bayonets. Morale was high and no one seemed to doubt the grave importance or the correctness of his decision. Would the Confederates see it the same way? He looked at his watch: the hour was up.

He and Colonel Appler rode out to meet the waiting General Beauregard with the eyes of the army upon them.

Sherman chose his words carefully, fearful of any misunderstanding. "This has been a difficult and most important decision, General Beauregard, and I want to assure you that it is a universal one. I have told my officers about the British attack and we are of one mind. I have even spoken to the troops about what I plan to do and I assure you every man in my regiments is in agreement. The North and the South do indeed now have a common enemy."

Beauregard nodded grimly. "I appreciate the decision. Then you do agree to a cease-fire?"

"Even more than that. This is Colonel Appler, the commanding officer of the 53rd Ohio. He, and every man in his regiment, agree with my decision as to what must be done."

"I thank you, Colonel."

Sherman hesitated. Was this the right thing to do—and how would Beauregard react? But there was no turning back now.

"There is more to this than just a cease-fire. We are riding with you, General. This regiment will aid you in your attack on the invading British."

The General left him in no doubt about his reaction to Sherman's decision. After one stunned moment of hesitation he shouted aloud and leaned over and grasped Sherman by the hand, pumped his arm furiously, turned and did the same with Colonel Appler.

"General Sherman you not only have the courage and courtesy of a Southern gentleman. But I swear by God on high that you are a Southern gentleman! Your years in Louisiana were not wasted ones. My call for aid has been exceeded in a manner I never thought possible. Bring your men. Bring your men! We march in common cause."

General Beauregard galloped off to ready his troops. He never had a moment's doubt about how they would react—and he was right. They cheered when he told them about Sherman's decision, cheered louder and louder and threw their hats into the air.

They were ordered into ranks and stood at attention as the blue column of Yankee troops, Sherman leading the way, marched toward them, out from the defensive positions. A drummer to the fore beat the step while the fifes played a sprightly tune.

Other than the thud of marching feet, the music of the fifes and drum, there was only silence. Would it work? Could men who had been fighting and killing each other now march side by side? Yes, Generals Beauregard and Sherman were in agreement. But the soldiers—what about the soldiers? A few days ago they had been murdering each other. How would they react now at such close proximity? No one could tell.

The sound of the drum and the shrill of the fifes, the shuffle of marching feet. There was a tension building up that Sherman did not like and he meant to do something about it. He urged his horse forward, bent and spoke to the fifes who stopped playing. They nodded to each other—raised their instruments to their lips and began to play again in unison.

The shrill sharp melody of "Dixie" pierced the afternoon air.

There was pandemonium. Shouts and cries and shrill whistles. The Confederates broke ranks without order—as did the Northerners. They laughed and shook hands and pounded one another on the back. Like their troops, the two generals shook hands again, this time in mutual triumph.

Dear God, Sherman thought, it might work—it was going to work after all.

The drums beat for attention and the soldiers slowly re-formed their ranks. Right faced in unison and marched off down the dusty road.

MARCHING TO BATTLE

Admiral Alexander Milne had gone to bed a happy man. His bombardment of the shore positions had surely aided in their eventual capture. The Americans had put up stiff resistance but in the end they had been destroyed. Because of the shallow sea, and the fact that the surf had ameliorated, unloading the supplies and the artillery appeared to be going remarkably well. By midnight the boats that were returning with the wounded also brought word of victory.

His responsibility for this phase of the operation was at an end; the continued success of the attack was now in other hands. The Duke of Cambridge was an extremely good soldier; a resourceful and experienced leader. With the landings and the attack a success he could be counted upon to hold the position. With the foothold established the breach in the American defenses would be widened. The blockade was broken and the cotton would flow to England once again. To pay for the weapons of war that the South could then afford to import. For the most part his job here was done. The fatigue of the past days, the stress and lack of sleep, were exacting their toll. His China wound was paining him, a reminder that he was pushing himself too hard. He left orders that he wanted to be on deck at first light, then retired.

It seemed that he had just closed his eyes when his servant quietly called to him. He sat up in bed and sipped his coffee slowly, made no effort to arise until the cup was empty; he was still very weary. Only when the coffee was finished did he shave and dress and go up on deck. Stars filled the black hemisphere of the skies, but there was the barest hint of gray in the east. Captain Roland was on the forward bridge and saluted him formally when he appeared.

"The storm passed during the night, sir. It is going to be a fine day."

"Any further reports from shore?"

"There was a counterattack which was repelled. General Bullers reports that victory is complete."

"Field guns and supplies?"

"All on the beach, sir. As soon as it is light they will be moved to the battlements."

"A most satisfactory engagement, satisfactory indeed."

It would not be long before Milne would deeply regret speaking those words. As the morning haze burned off he began to be possessed by a feeling of growing horror. The beach where the landing had taken place had open water to the right, and was much larger than it had seemed in the rain and fog the day before. In fact the beachfront curved back towards the harbor to the left, ran on down the coastline. He raised his telescope in the growing light, saw that behind the jut of land ahead there was a lagoon. Captain Roland gasped and spoke aloud what the admiral suddenly realized was the truth.

"That is not Deer Island—or any other island. That's the shore! Could we have made a mistake?"

There was the rumble of distant gunfire and they swung their telescopes in that direction. A ship was running down toward them; it was the sloop that he had stationed on their eastern flank, now approaching under full sail.

In her wake boiling out clouds of smoke was a pursuing warship.

"Beat to quarters," the captain ordered. "Raise steam. I must have full power."

Warrior had her guns run out and all sail set as well. She was just getting under way when the sloop rounded her stern and lowered sail now that she was under the protection of the ironclad. Her pursuer also slowed and went about, understandably not wanting to face the impregnable *Warrior* and her guns. As the ship's stern faced them a gust of wind caught her flag and spread it out. So close were they that no telescope was needed to identify her.

Stars and stripes. The American flag.

"Message to *Java* and *Southampton*," the admiral said. "Enemy in sight. Pursue and capture. Or destroy."

The captain of the British sloop had lowered a boat as soon as was possible, had come to report in person. He saluted as he came on deck.

"Report," the admiral said coldly. Fearing the answer.

"At dawn, sir, we saw an island and that ship anchored close offshore. Ran down close enough to see that there were fortified gun positions there. They fired on us as soon as they identified our flag. Then the warship upped her anchor and came after us. I checked the charts and, sir, I think that . . ."

His voice ran down and he coughed as though choking on his words.

"Out with it," the admiral snapped. The officer was pale under his tan. With great difficulty he spoke.

A YANKEE WARSHIIP FINDS *WARRIOR*

"I believe that . . . that the island was . . . Deer Island. When I discovered this I looked again at our charts. If you will look, sir, there on the shore, where we attacked. You can see that there is a small port, and right behind the port there are those buildings, next to where the landings were made. I have looked at all my charts and I feel . . . I think . . . that that is the city of Biloxi. Biloxi, Mississippi, which as you know is one of the Confederate states."

The sure knowledge struck the admiral like a physical blow: he reeled back and clutched the iron rail.

They had attacked the wrong fortress, invaded and destroyed property and lives in the wrong country. The mistake was his, none other. He must stop the attack: but it was far too late for that. He must try to make amends, do something. But there was nothing that he could do. The die was cast, fortune in jeopardy. The future was more than bleak for his career was in ruins, that was obvious, his life as he had known it was ended.

"I do not feel well," he said turning and shuffling from the bridge. "I am going below."

"But, Admiral—what shall we do? What are your orders?"

He did not answer them. But a few minutes later the sound of a muffled pistol shot was answer enough.

When the Duke of Cambridge climbed the boarding ladder to the deck of *Warrior* he was hurried at once to Captain Roland's quarters. Roland closed the door and turned to him, ashen-faced.

"Disaster . . ." he said in a hoarse voice.

"All too bloody right it is. You know we attacked the wrong bloody spot? You obviously do. Milne will pay for this, pay hard."

"He already has. The admiral is dead by his own hand."

"Well *I'll* not take the blame for this fiasco!" The duke slammed the table so hard that the bottles there leaped and clashed. "The army is advancing as ordered. I must see to it that they have reinforcements. The attack from Canada must be informed. I will wring victory from this rotten mess that you have created. What is that warship close alongside?"

"The *Java*."

"I'm taking her. You are senior captain here. Stay in command until the reinforcements arrive. And get it right or I'll have you reduced, dismissed. See if the navy can't get one thing right in this disaster."

* * *

Children ran alongside the marching troops, cheering and waving. The adults came out too, but not quite as sure of themselves as the children were. Riders had been sent ahead of the column to let everyone know what was happening. The blue uniforms and Union flags raised some eyebrows, but when they understood what was happening there was mutual enthusiasm.

"Give 'em hell boys!" an oldster called out from the porch of a roadside house.

"Yanks and Johnny Reb—well I never," a man on horseback said, then waved his hat. "Get them Britishers. I heard what they done and Hell is too good a place for them."

The two generals riding to the fore waved back.

"A fine reception," Sherman said. "I'll admit I had a bit of worry."

NORTH AND SOUTH—MARCH TO BATTLE

"I didn't," Beauregard said. "When they know why you are with us and where we are going—why you have only friends here. We won't be marching much longer, either. We're going to the railhead of the Mobile and Ohio Railway at Corinth." The two generals rode together at the head of their troops. "I've telegraphed ahead for all the engines and rolling stock that can be got together. Flatcars too for the artillery and boxcars for the horses."

"Any reports on the enemy?"

"Last reported on the outskirts of Handsboro. Now you

have to understand the geography of the Gulf Coast of this state. Biloxi is on the end of a long peninsula of land, ocean in front and the lagoon behind. Handsboro is at the land end of the peninsula. If the British plan to move north from there, why that is the best kind of news that we could have. Inland from the coast there is mostly pine slashes and sugarcane country. Before the telegraph operator in Biloxi was killed he got off a message. There were no troops of any strength nearby, but there was some cavalry at Lorraine. They're spreading out in front of what could be the enemy advance. People are being warned to clear out of the way. There are none of our troops anywhere close in front of them which is fine. I want them to continue their advance."

Sherman thought about this and a slow smile broke out on his face. "Of course. The last thing we want to do is face them head on and fight them on their terms. You want them to advance so we can get in behind them. Cut them off from Biloxi and their lines of supply. Maroon them in the center of a hostile countryside, then wipe them out."

"Exactly. Our strength will be in surprise. What we are going to do is bypass them by rail. There is a junction at Hattiesburg where two rail lines cross. We are going to change there to the cars of the Gulf and Ship Island Railway. Then straight south to Gulfport. In this way we will get behind them and cut them off. Hopefully separate them from their ships and their supplies. Run a noose around them—then kill them. That is what we are going to do."

Sherman nodded. "An excellent plan, excellent indeed."

They heard the shrill moan of the steam whistle from the train yard when they entered the outskirts of Corinth. The men were in great spirits and cheered as they marched. Smoke boiled from the diamond stack of the engine as she got up steam. Another locomotive waited on the siding ready to make up a second train as soon as the first one left.

"I don't want to divide our command," Beauregard said.

"A wise precaution," Sherman agreed. "I feel it would not be wise to march my bluecoats through Mississippi without you at my side. I suggest that we board one of your regiments and my 53rd Ohio on the first train. The rest of the men, guns and supplies to follow. We will all form up again at Gulfport."

The telegraph keys clicked steadily up and down the length of Mississippi. All normal railroad traffic was suspended and sidetracked to let the military trains go by. Through the heat of the day and into the evening the trains rolled south. There was some confusion at Hattiesburg when the change from one railroad line to another was made. But the soldiers worked together with good will; the loading finished after dark and the final leg of the journey began. The great kerosene headlight of the engine cut a swath through the darkness of the pine slashes. The soldiers, more subdued now after the tiring day, dozed on the seats and in the aisles.

Gulfport. End of the line and end of train travel. A Confederate cavalryman was waiting as the two generals climbed down from the car; he saluted them both.

"Captain Culpepper, he sent me here to wait for y'all. Said to tell you that those English soldiers have stopped for the night, no more than a couple of miles outside of Handsboro."

"How far are we from Handsboro?" Beauregard asked.

"Easy ride, General. Nor more'n ten, twelve miles."

"We have them," Sherman said.

"We do indeed. We march now. Get between them and Biloxi during the night. Then we shall see what the morning brings."

The USS *Rhode Island* did not try to outrun the British warships, probably could not. Instead she tied up at the wharf of Deer Island, guns rolled out and waiting, under the protection of the 30-pounders of the battery. The British ships nosed close, but beat a speedy retreat when the batteries fired a salvo that sent spouts of water close around them. When the British ships had rejoined the fleet, and showed no evidence of returning, *Rhode Island* slipped her lines and steamed east.

Before she had been forcefully impressed into the navy and sent to join the blockading fleet, the *Rhode Island* had been a coastal ferry. Her engines were old but reliable. With a good head of steam—and the safety valve tied down—she could do a steady seven knots. She was doing this now, her big side-wheels churning steadily, driving her east along the coast at her best possible speed.

"You saw them clear as I did, Larry, didn't you?" Captain Bailey asked—and not for the first time.

"Sure did, Captain, no missing a fleet that size," the first mate said.

"And the way that sloop sailed up toward us, bold as brass," the captain said. "That old Union Jack flapping away top of her mast. We're at war and there she was running right up to the guns of the battery. Commander should have held his fire a mite longer."

"I think he hit her a couple of times."

"May be. At least she skedaddled and led us right up to the others."

"Never saw an ironside like that English one before." The captain looked out at the coast of Mississippi slowly moving by. "What do you think? About another four hours to Mobile Bay?"

"About."

"I'll bet the admiral will be mighty interested in what we got to report."

"Every ship in the blockade there will be more than interested. Isn't the *Monitor* supposed to be joining them about now?"

"Should be. I read the orders. Supposed to join the others in the blockade just as soon as the new *Monitor*-class iron ship, the *Avenger*, got to Hampton Roads to take her place."

"I'll bet the boys on the *Monitor* will be more keen than anyone else. They must have been mighty tired of just being the cork in the bottle, looking out for the *Merrimack* to appear again. I hear she has a new commander?"

"Lieutenant William Jeffers, a good man. Poor Worden, wounded in the eyes. Shell hit the lookout slit, blew scrap into his eyes. Blind in one and the other not too good. Jeffers will be interested in our report."

"*Everyone* will be mighty interested as soon as word of all this gets to Washington."

AN ARMY DIES

The night was quiet and hot. And damp. Private Elphing of the 3rd Middlesex looked about in the predawn darkness, then loosened his stock. He was tired. This was his second night on guard just because he had got drunk with the others. And he hadn't even gotten near the women, had been too drunk for that. There were fireflies out there, strange insects that glowed in the night. Peaceful too, the easy breeze carried scents of honeysuckle, roses and jasmine.

Was something moving? The sky was lightening in the east so that when he leaned out from behind the tree he could clearly make out the dark figure lying in the underbrush. Yes by God—that was one and there were others as well! He fired his musket without taking time to aim. Before he could raise his voice to sound the alarm the bullets from a dozen rifled guns ripped through him and he fell. Dead before he hit the ground.

The bugles sounded and the British soldiers threw off their blankets and seized up their guns to return the fire that was now tearing into them from the scrub and trees next to their camp.

Emerging from his tent, General Bullers understood clearly from the severity of the firing that destruction might be just minutes away. The flashes of the guns and drifting clouds of smoke indicated that he was under attack by a sizable force. With cannon as well he realized as the first shells tore through the ranks of the defenders. And the attack was from his rear— they were between his forces and the landing beach.

"Sound the retreat!" he shouted to his officers as they ran up. A moment later the clear notes of the bugle call sounded.

It was a fighting retreat, not a rout, because these men were veterans. After firing at the approaching line of men they would fall back in an orderly fashion—and not run away. As dawn came they could make out the rest of the division in rough lines, falling back, firing as they went. But with every footstep they moved away from the beach and any hope of salvation. In small groups they worked their way to their rear, stopping to reload and fire again while their comrades went past them. They had no time to regroup. Just fight. And find a place where they could make a stand.

Sergeant Griffin of the 67th South Hampshire felt the bullet strike the stock of his musket so hard that it spun him about. The attacking line was almost upon him. He raised his gun and fired at the man in the blue uniform who rose up just before him. Hit him in the arm, saw him drop his gun and clutch at the wound. The soldier next to him shouted out a shrill cry and sprang forward his bayonet coming up in a long thrust— that put the point into the sergeant's chest even as he was raising his own weapon. The bayonet twisted free and blood spurted from the terrible wound. The sergeant tried to lift his gun, could not, dropped it and slid after it. His last wondering thought as he died was why his killer was wearing gray. The other soldier blue . . .

The attack did not falter nor hesitate. The British soldiers who tried to make a stand were wiped out. Those who fled were shot or bayoneted in the back.

A split-pine fence overgrown with creepers offered the first opportunity that General Bullers had seen to make any kind of a stand to halt the debacle.

"To me," he shouted and waved his sword. "Forty-fifth to me!"

The running men, some of them too exhausted to go much farther, stumbled and fell in the scant shelter of the fence. Others joined them and soon a steady fire, for the first time, began coming from the British lines.

The attackers were just as tired, but were carried forward by the frenzy of their assault. Beauregard quickly formed a line facing the defended fence row, stretched them out in the thick grass.

"Take cover, load and fire, boys. Keep it up a bit until you get your wind back and the reinforcements get here. They're coming up now."

Sherman had seen what Beauregard had done and gathered men about him until he had a sizable force. He saw that the field guns were being limbered up to advance to new positions. He dared not wait until they were ready to fire because Beauregard was in a dangerous position. He had to be relieved. The standard bearer of the 53rd Ohio was close to Sherman when he ordered them forward. The British defenders saw the line of advancing men and turned their fire on this new threat. Bullets began to tear through the grass around them.

Sherman heard a cry of pain and turned to see that the colorbearer had been shot, was falling. Sherman eased him to the ground and took the wooden pole with the stars and stripes from the man's limp hand. Held it high and signaled the charge.

The Union troops ran the last few yards and dropped to the ground among the Confederates who had been pinned down by the fire. Sherman, still carrying the flag, moved to join Beauregard who was sheltering in a small grove of trees with some of his officers and men.

"The guns are coming up," Sherman said. "Let them put some shells into the British before we attack again. How is your ammunition?"

"Holding up fine. The boys seem to enjoy bayoneting to shooting today."

Sherman looked about at the soldiers. Tired and weary, their faces and uniforms streaked with powder, they still looked a force ready to deal more destruction. The Confederate colorbearer was leaning his weight on the flagstaff to support himself. Sherman wanted to reload his pistol for this next attack, but he could not do this burdened with the flag. His thoughts were on the battle so, without conscious thought, he held the flag out to the Confederate soldier.

"Here you are, boy. You can carry two as easy as one."

The tired soldier smiled and nodded, reached out and took the flag, bundled it with the one he already had.

No one seemed to notice; they were readying themselves for the attack.

At that moment, in the midst of battle, no one perceived that the Stars and Stripes and the flag of the Confederacy were conjoined.

Flying together as the order was given and the soldiers swept forward.

A BATTLE TO THE DEATH

The Royal Marines had camped on the shore at Biloxi where they guarded the guns and stores. They had been alerted by the sound of firing to the west and were drawn up and preparing to march when the first of the retreating soldiers who had escaped the attack stumbled up. Major Dashwood strode to the staggering infantryman and pulled him around by his collar.

"Speak up—what is happening?"

"Attack . . . dawn. Surprised us. Got lots of guns, sir. Soldiers, masses of them too. General ordered retreat . . ."

"He didn't order you to throw away your weapon."

The major hurled the man to the ground and kicked him in the ribs with his heavy boot; the soldier screamed like a girl.

"I want all those defenses manned," the major said striding up the beach. "Get those boxes and bales up, use them for cover as well. Wheel those cannon about. See that the men do a good job and a fast one. Lieutenant, you are in command until I return. I am going out there to find out what is going on."

The horse, captured in the attack, was a wall-eyed brute and very skittish at the best of times. The major, with little riding skills, managed to clamber into the saddle with the aid of two marines. At an uncontrolled gallop he headed toward the sound of action. He found it quickly enough and managed to pull hard on the reins to drag the horse to a stop.

The cause was lost, that was obvious at a glance. English bodies covered the ground. They had taken many of the enemy with them—but not enough. The surviving British troops appeared to be surrounded and unable to escape. Surrounded by what was obviously a far superior force. He could counterattack with his marines. But they would be outnumbered as well—and certainly could not arrive in time to make any difference to the outcome of this battle. The intensity of the firing was dying down as the small circle of defenders grew ever smaller. A bullet kicked up sand nearby and he realized that he been seen by the skirmishers and was under fire himself. Reluctantly he turned the horse and galloped back to the beach.

When he saw that the defenses were manned and as strong as he could make them, he ordered the sailors to man one of the beached boats and made his way to the *Warrior*.

And total confusion. Boats from the other ships were crowded at the gangway and he had to wait until the senior officers went first. When he finally made it to the deck he saw that working parties were bumping into each other on deck, while others were aloft furling the mainsail to avoid scorching by smoke from the stack. The third officer, with whom he shared a cabin, was supervising the lowering of the aft telescopic funnel so he crossed the deck to him.

"Des, what's happening? Are we going to sail?"

"Yes . . . and no." He turned to bellow at a sailor. "You there—watch yourself! Lean into that line!" He motioned Dashwood aside, spoke quietly so the crewmen could not hear him.

"The admiral is dead—and apparently by his own hand."

"I think I know why."

"That island out there, you can just make it out on the horizon. That is Deer Island."

Dashwood looked from island to shore. "And how did our wonderfully efficient navy make this mistake? A slight error in navigation?"

Dashwood smiled coldly at the officer's discomfiture. "We discovered it this morning. General Bullers is now continuing the attack. I was to follow him as soon as the rest of the supplies are ashore. Now—I must report to the duke—"

"Gone on the *Java*."

"Then who is in command?"

"Who knows? The captain has called a meeting of senior captains in his cabin."

"I have some more bad news for them." He leaned close and whispered. "Buller has been attacked, defeated." He turned and went below.

Two of his marines were stationed at the cabin door and jumped to attention when he appeared.

"Captain ordered us, sir. No entry . . ."

"Stand aside Dunbar—or I'll strangle you with your own guts."

The arguing captains looked up when the marine officer entered.

"Damn it, Dashwood, I left orders . . ."

"Indeed you did, sir." He closed the door before he spoke. "I have the worst possible news for you. General Buller and his entire command are under attack. By now all of them have been killed or captured."

"That cannot be!"

"I assure you that it is. I went there myself and saw what was happening. One of the soldiers who escaped can confirm this report."

"Take your men—go to their aid!" The captain of the *Royal Oak* called out.

"Are you in command here, Captain?" Major Dashwood asked coldly. "My understanding is that with the admiral dead the captain of my ship commands my troops."

"All dead?" Captain Roland said, apparently numbed by the news.

"Dead or captured for certain. What do you want us to do, sir."

"Do?"

"Yes, sir." Dashwood was losing his patience at the dithering, but did not let his feelings show. "I've dug my men in on shore. With the guns they can resist an attack—but they cannot win it."

"What do you suggest?"

"Immediate withdrawal. Our military forces obviously did not accomplish their objective. I suggest that we cut our losses and retreat."

"And you are absolutely sure that our forces on land are destroyed? Or will be very soon?" one of the captains asked.

"You may take my word for that, sir. If you have any doubts I will be happy to take you to the scene of the battle."

"The supplies on shore, the cannon—what about them?"

"I suggest that we take what we can, destroy the rest, spike the guns. Nothing can be accomplished by staying a moment longer than we need. Now if you will excuse me, I must return to my troops."

Despite the urgency it took most of the day for a decision to be made. Dashwood had sent scouts forward and they reported that the battle was indeed over. They saw a small group of prisoners being led away. And the enemy divisions were forming. Skirmishers were already approaching and it was more than obvious what would happen next. The major walked back and forth behind the defenses, in a black rage at the indecision of the navy. Were his marines to be sacrificed too?

It was late afternoon before the very obvious decision was finally made. Destroy the supplies, spike the guns, board his men. The first boatload of marines had reached their transport when the lookout on *Warrior* reported smoke on the eastern horizon.

Within a minute all of the telescopes in the fleet were pointed in that direction. The smoke cloud grew larger and separated into individual columns.

"I count four, five ships, possibly more. Steaming on forced draft." Captain Roland's voice remained flat and emotionless despite the tension growing within him. "Isn't there a blockading fleet at Mobile Bay?"

"At last reports, a fairly good-sized one, sir."

"Yes. I thought so."

The leading ships were hull up now, white sails visible below the smoke. They were slowing to a halt well out of gunshot; a large battleship at the center of the line was swinging about.

"What on earth are they doing?" the captain called out. "Hail the lookout."

"Aye, aye, sir."

"It's a tow of some kind, sir. They've dropped the line to another vessel."

"What is it?"

A DEADLY ENGAGEMENT

"Can't rightly tell. Never saw nothing like that before."

The black form was so low in the water that details were not clear. It passed the other ships and slowly steamed toward the British. No one could make out what kind of ship it was, even when it drew close.

Black, so low in the water that its deck was awash, small. With a round construction in the center of its deck.

"Like a cheesebox on a raft," one of the officers said.

A chill possessed Captain Roland like nothing he had ever experienced before. He had read those very words in the newspaper.

"What can it possibly be?" someone said.

"Nemesis," he said, in a voice so low he could be barely heard.

The steam-powered wooden frigates of the American Navy opened into a half-circle to engage the British warships, carefully staying clear of the menacing iron ship. Only USS *Monitor* sailed steadily on.

The Americans were ready, guns charged and run out. Aboard the *Monitor* Lieutenant William Jeffers, in the armored bridge house, trained his telescope on the anchored ships. "We will attack the ironclad before she gets under way," he said. "She must be either *Warrior* or *Black Prince*. To my knowledge those are the only two iron ships that the British Navy has. Our agents have supplied complete details on their construction and design."

Warrior was swinging at anchor and getting up steam. The ship's stern was toward the attacking *Monitor* and her first officer gasped at what he saw. "The stern, sir—why it is not armored. There seems to be some kind of apparatus there, a winch, a frame of some kind."

"There is," Jeffers said. "I've read the description in the report. To lessen drag when she is under sail the screw is lifted clear of the water. So the stern is unarmored. As is the bow."

"We'll pound her out of the water!"

"It won't be that easy. The intelligence reports contained minute details about her construction. Her hull is made of one-inch-thick iron—but she is a ship within a ship. All of the main battery of guns are in the citadel, an armored box within the ship. Twenty-two of them, twenty-six 68-pounders and six 100-pounders. She outguns us in number but not in size of guns. Our Dahlgrens are weapons to reckon with. This citadel is made of four-inch wrought-iron plates backed by twelve inches of teak. She'll not be easy to take."

"But we can try?"

"We certainly can. Our shot bounced off the *Merrimack* because she had slanted sides. I want to see what a ball from an 11-inch Dahlgren will do against this citadel—with its vertical sides."

It was a fly attacking an elephant. The tiny iron *Monitor*, gushing smoke from her two stubby stacks, bustled toward the great length of *Warrior*. Somber and menacing in her black paint. Bulletproof lids covering the gun ports swung open and the muzzles of the big guns slid out. They were loaded and charged—and fired as one. A sheet of flame blasted out and the solid shot screamed across the gap between the two ships.

With no observable result. The turret had been rotated so that her guns faced away from the British ironclad. Most shot missed the low-lying target; the few that hit the eight-inch armor of the turret bounced away without doing any damage. *Monitor* chugged slowly on at her top speed of almost five knots. As she approached the great black ship steam hissed into the engine beneath the turret, turning the cog wheel that meshed with the gear under the base. The bogy wheels rumbled as the turret swung around so that both gun muzzles were scant feet from *Warrior*'s high flank.

And fired. Punching the cannonballs through the armor plate to wreak havoc and destruction in the gun deck. The guns recoiled on their slides, the tightened clamps squealing, metal to metal, as the massive guns were brought to a stop.

"Reload!"

The jointed shafts pushed the hissing sponges down the gun barrels. Then the charges were rammed into place, followed by the cannonballs held by steel claws, lifted by chain winches. Within two minutes they were reloaded and the sweating, filthy crewmen hauled on the lines to pull the guns back into firing position.

By this time *Monitor* had swung around the iron ship's stern with her guns almost touching the high rudder. Despite the force of guns in her main battery, there was only a single swivel gun mounted aft. This fired ineffectively.

Then the two heavy guns fired as one, smashing the round shot into the stern and through the single inch of iron of the hull. *Monitor* drifted there, engines stopped while the guns were reloaded. Marines lined the rail above her and bullets spanged against iron with no effect. Two minutes ticked slowly by. Clouds of smoke billowed from *Warrior*'s funnels as she got up steam. Her anchors were raised now and the massive black bulk began to turn to bring her guns to bear on her tiny attacker.

Then *Monitor* fired again. The ship's boat hanging in the stern there was smashed—and then the massive rudder.

Warrior's screw was turning now and the massive ship began to move away. With the rudder gone they could not turn, but at least they might escape the deadly attack.

With her guns silent *Monitor*'s crew could hear clanging impacts on the iron above their heads as the marines leaned over the rails and fired their muskets to no avail. But when the tiny Union vessel moved out from behind the stern and along the enemy's starboard side she faced the greater menace of the 68- and 100-pounders yet again. Muzzles fully depressed they fired on the roll as *Monitor* appeared in their sights. Iron pounded iron, crashing and clanging against turret and hull.

With no visible results. Round shot could not penetrate as *Merrimack* had discovered. But *Merrimack* had been immune to the return fire as well. Not the British. *Monitor* stayed in position alongside the ironclad, turret turned about as they reloaded. Reloading and firing every two minutes. *Warrior* finally had to stop her engines since she was heading toward shore. *Monitor* matched her every move. Firing steadily, punching through the armor of the citadel, destroying the guns and sending fragments of iron and wood scything through the gunners.

Around this two-ship action a naval battle was raging. It was a devastating conflict, wooden ship against wooden ship. However all of the ships of the American fleet were all steampowered—this gave them the fighting edge against those British ships driven by sail. The guns roared fire and shot, while in the distance the unarmed transports stood out to sea to escape the carnage.

With most of the British armorclad's main guns out of action, the unarmored American ships now approached and joined the battle against *Warrior*. Their smaller guns could not penetrate the armor—but they could sweep the decks. Her three immense masts were made of wood, as were her yards. Under the hail of shells from the Americans first the mainmast went, falling to the deck with a crumbling roar, her yards and sails crushing those below. Her mizzenmast went next, adding to the death and destruction. Canvas and broken spars hung over her sides blocking the gun ports so that the firing died away.

Monitor pulled away as Captain Jeffers nodded at the destruction she had brought. "A good bit of work. We'll leave her that last mast because she will not be going anyplace for awhile."

"If ever!" the first officer shouted, pointing. "*Narragansett* has grappled her by the stern—her marines are boarding!"

"Well done. With the iron ship out of the battle we have those wooden warships to think about. We must help the rest of our fleet. Free some of them to go after the transports. We must destroy as many as we can before they scatter. If they don't strike we'll sink them."

His smile was cold, his anger deep.

"This will be a bloody nose for the bloody British Navy that they will long remember."

A MOMENTOUS OCCASION

"I may have had worse days, John, though I really can't remember when."

The President sat in his battered armchair looking fixedly at the telegram that Nicolay had handed him. He was gaunt and losing weight, so much so that his shabby black suit hung loosely, wrinkled. Since Willie's death he was scarcely eating, barely sleeping. His dark skin was now sallow, his eyes surrounded by black rings. This new war was going very badly. A horsefly hummed angrily about the room, battering itself again and again into the glass of the half-open window. In the room just off of Lincoln's office the newly installed telegraph clattered away as another message was received.

"Bad news reaches me much faster now that we have that infernal machine so close and handy," Lincoln said. "Has the Secretary of War seen this?"

"Yes, sir."

"Well he will be over here soon enough I imagine. Those poor boys at Plattsburgh. A terrible sacrifice."

"They slowed the British down, Mr. President."

"But not for long. Port Henry is taken and in flames and no word from General Halleck yet."

"His last report said that he was forming a line of defense at Fort Ticonderoga."

"Are we doomed to keep on repeating history? As I remember it, didn't we run from the British there as well?"

"It was a strategic retreat that, rather unfortunately, began on the Fourth of July."

"I pray that Halleck does not repeat that particular maneuver."

"Grant's divisions may have joined them by now. That's a goodly force in the field when you put them together."

"Well they are not together yet. The British are chewing us up piecemeal. And what about that mysterious telegram from General Sherman? Any elucidation?"

"None that we can find out. Some telegraph lines are down and I am told that we are trying to reroute our communications. All that we have is a garbled message, something about southwards movement, and some sort of reference to General Beauregard."

"Keep trying, I don't like mysteries. Not in wartime—not at any time. And cancel those visitations for today. I cannot face the job-seekers who are a pestilential menace to my health."

"There's quite a crowd of them. Some of them have been waiting since dawn."

"I feel no sympathy. Inform them that matters of state must take priority, at least this once."

"Will you make a single exception, sir? There is an English gentleman here who has just arrived aboard a French ship. He has letters of recommendation from some of the most eminent men in France."

"English you say? A mystery and a most intriguing one. What is his name?"

"A Mr. Mill, John Stuart Mill. In his note that accompanied the introductions he writes that he has information that will aid in this war for American freedom."

"If he is an English spy, why then Fox will certainly want to see him."

"I doubt if he is a spy. The introductions refer to him as a natural philosopher of great merit."

The chair creaked as Lincoln leaned back and brought his long legs up before him. "I'll see him. In these days of desperation we must clutch at any straw. Perhaps the distraction will help me forget our disasters for awhile. Are there any clues as to what his information is that will aid our war?"

"I am afraid not. A bit of a mystery."

"Well—let us solve this mystery. Show the gentleman in."

Mill was a middle-aged man, balding and smooth-skinned, neatly dressed and most affable. He introduced himself, bowed slightly as he shook the President's hand. Then he placed the two books he carried on the desk and sat down, after first carefully tucking his coattails beneath him.

"Mr. Lincoln," he said in a solemn yet excited voice. "I have been an admirer of the American experiment for many years. I have followed your election practices and the operation of the lower house and the Senate, the judiciary and the police. While not perfect by any means, I nevertheless feel that in many ways yours is the only free country in the world—the only democratic one. I believe the world has seen enough of kings and tyrants and must find its way onto the road to democracy. With your noble cause under attack from my own country, a tragedy not of my doing but one that I must still apologize for. But this tragedy has goaded me into unexpected action—which is why I am here. I thought that when my dear wife died and my daughter and I retired to France, that I would write my books and bide my time until I could join her. But that is not to be. Necessity has drawn me from the quiet of my study and back to the world scene. I am here, if you will permit me, to aid your infant democracy and, and again, with your permission, help to guide it on the path to a prosperous future."

The President nodded in agreement. "Like you I feel that the American experiment is the last, best hope of Earth. You do indeed sound like a man inspired, Mr. Mill. But without intending any insult I am afraid at this time we need men that can fight more than those who can think. But, please elucidate and tell me how you will go about doing that."

Mill leaned forward and tapped the two books with his finger. "If you search carefully you will find the answer to that question in here, my *Principles of Political Economy*. They are yours, a small gift."

"You are very kind." Lincoln pulled the books across the desk and opened the first volume, smiling at the pages of dense type. "I have always been a great reader in natural philosophy. I greatly admire the theories of Francis Wayland whose work you surely know. Mr. Wayland believes that Labor is the source from which human wants are mainly supplied, labor before capital, capital exists as fruit of labor. But I digress. I look forward to studying your books. The pressures of this war permitting."

Mill raised his hand and smiled. "The war comes first, Mr. President. Put them aside for a quieter time. You will find that I and Francis Wayland are in agreement in many things. If you permit me, I can sum up my feelings and my theories most easily for you. Firstly, I have always supported your stance in this war since I recognize it as a struggle against slavery. But as an Englishman I have stood aside from this conflict feeling that I have no personal involvement. Now I feel that attitude has been wrong. I no longer can be a silent spectator. The invasion of your country by mine was a singularly wicked act and cannot be forgiven."

"You will find none here to argue with that, I assure you."

There was a quick knock on the door, then John Hay appeared holding a telegram and gravely concerned.

"Could I speak to you about . . . a highly sensitive matter, Mr. President."

"I will wait outside," Mill said, rising to his feet. "May we continue this conversation?"

"Of course."

Hay waited until the door had closed before he passed over the telegram. "I don't know what this is all about, sir, but if it is true it sounds a good deal better than the news from New York State."

Lincoln took the message and read aloud. " 'A group of Confederate officers crossed our lines under cease-fire agreement at Yorktown. They are now proceeding under escort to Washington. Leading them is General Robert E. Lee.' "

The President lowered the paper and Hay realized that he had never seen such a look of complete amazement upon his features before. Lincoln was ever the courtroom lawyer, the railroad lawyer who kept his emotions to himself. People saw the expression on his face that he wanted them to see. But not this time.

"Do you have the slightest inkling or fragment of information as to what this is all about? No, I thought that you didn't, and if the expression on your face is anything to go by you are as baffled as I am. Telegraph back to whoever sent this and ask for amplification. And you had better call the Cabinet together for an emergency meeting. This is . . . extraordinary. I'll finish my conversation with Mr. Mill. Come and get me when the Cabinet has assembled."

There was no making sense of the telegram. What was happening? And what about the mysterious communication from General Sherman? Was there a connection? So deep in thought was he that he was unaware that Mill had returned until a polite cough drew his attention.

Reseated, Mill got quickly to the point. "I have been thinking about your parting words to me as I left. About needing men who could fight, not men who could think . . ."

"I apologize if what I said disturbed you, since no insult was intended."

"Indeed no, sir, quite the opposite if truth be known. But you do need men who think, to plot the course into a successful future. I mind you of another Englishman, and indeed another philosopher. Thomas Paine, who wrote and theorized and argued the case for your American Revolution. He knew that the reason men fight wars is as important as the fighting itself. It is said that small men bring about progress by standing on the shoulders of giants. Paine and your founding fathers were indeed giants, and perhaps by standing on their shoulders this country can bring about a Second American Revolution that will build a new kind of future. This war cannot last forever, but *America* must last, survive and grow. Yours must be the guiding hand that sees to that survival. The place of the Negroes in your society is now an ambivalent one. This must be changed. And I know the way to do it . . ."

Lincoln was listening so intently that he was startled when his secretary knocked discreetly on the door.

"Mr. Mill. It is imperative that I attend a singularly important Cabinet meeting now. But you must return and amplify your suggestions. I heartily agree with your attitudes, and have the hope that perhaps you may be of great aid to me in solving some of my most difficult political problems."

* * *

The Cabinet meeting was a brief one.

"Without some more information," Chase said, "we have no way of making a decision on the matter."

"Perhaps they bring surrender terms?" Seward said hopefully.

"Hardly that," Lincoln told him. "We have no reason to believe that they want to end this war, not in so sudden and uncharacteristic a manner. When you consider the occasion you must realize that they are better placed at this moment than they have been since the war began. Why, they can just sit back and let the British fight their war for them. Then strike when they think we are at our weakest. Surrender is the least possible reason for this meeting. We must discover their intentions. We will meet with them, and I suggest that we have our military advisers there as well—since their mission consists only of military officers, or so I have been informed."

It had been deemed that the Cabinet Room would be too small for this meeting, not with the senior officers from the army and navy attending as well. They assembled in the newly decorated Blue Room, where Mary Lincoln had tea served to them while they waited. Hay stepped up quietly to the President's side.

"The only additional information we could get is that General Lee insisted on talking to you in person."

"Well he has my ear, he certainly does."

It was dusk before the cavalrymen and the carriages rattled up to the front entrance of the White House. The waiting military men stood, almost at attention, while the cabinet members who had been seated rose to their feet. The doors opened and General Robert E. Lee, Commander-in-Chief of the Confederate Army, strode into the room. An erect military figure, gray-bearded and grim of expression; over six feet in height, almost as tall as the President. He was followed by a small group of gray-clad and somber officers. Lee took off his hat and stepped forward to face Abraham Lincoln.

"Mr. President, I bring you a message from Mr. Jefferson Davis, the President of the Confederacy."

Lincoln's expression was under control now and he just

nodded, lips pursed with silent attention as Lee went on. He did not recognize the legitimacy of Jefferson Davis's title, but saw no reason to mention that now.

"If you would permit it, Mr. Lincoln, due to the confidential nature of my communication, I would like to be able to deliver it to you in private."

There was a troubled murmur from the listening men and Lincoln held his hand up until the room was silent again.

"Gentlemen," he said sternly. "I am going to honor this request. I am sure that the Commander-in-Chief of the Confederate armies is an honorable man and means me no physical harm."

"That is indeed correct, Mr. Lincoln. And I will leave my sword with my staff as some indication of my good will." He did just that, taking the scabbarded sword from its slings and passing it over to the nearest Southern officer.

The onlookers hesitated, but then stepped back when Lincoln turned toward the door. They opened a path and made way for the tall form of the President and the stern, upright figure of the general. The two men proceeded slowly from the room and up the grand staircase, if not arm in arm at least shoulder-to-shoulder. They passed the wide-eyed clerk at his desk and entered Lincoln's office. Lincoln closed the door and spoke.

"If you would be so kind as to be seated, General Lee. I am sure that it has been a tiring journey."

"Thank you, sir."

If it had been tiring Lee did not show it. He took off his gray field hat and placed it on an end table, then sat upright on the first few inches of his chair as Lincoln dropped into his.

"Your message, if you please, General Lee."

"Might I ask first, sir, if you have you had any word of the recent events in Biloxi, Mississippi?"

"None whatsoever."

"If you will excuse me, Mr. Lincoln, I don't mean to pry into your military matters, but this matter is most relevant to the Biloxi situation. In relation to this, excuse me for asking, but have you had a communication from your General Sherman?"

Lincoln pondered this one. Should he reveal Northern military matters to this most competent of Southern generals? Of course. This matter was infinitesimal compared to the presence of Lee in the White House. This was a time for honesty.

"A garbled and incomplete one that we could not understand. Do you know anything about that?"

"I do indeed, sir, and that is why I am here. Let me apprise you of the facts. As your country has been attacked by the British by land to the north, so has the Confederacy been invaded by sea from the south."

"You what . . . ?"

"A British invasion, Mr. Lincoln, sudden and severe and without any warning. It destroyed the battery and the defenses before Biloxi. Our men fought bravely but were outnumbered and many fell. Worse, sir, was the fact that the enemy pursued the soldiers into the town of Biloxi which they then burnt and destroyed. Not satisfied with wanton destruction these animals—I cannot describe creatures such as these as soldiers—also wreaked indescribable violation to the female population of that city."

The President fought to conceal his bafflement at this new development. He could only listen.

"Do you know, for—what reason did they do this?"

"We do not know why they did this, but we do know that this was done. Without declaration of war they have invaded our land, killed and raped and looted. Before the city was burnt the defenders did manage to telegraph what was happening. President Davis contacted General Beauregard in northern Mississippi, his troops were the ones that were closest to the invasion. Beauregard was ordered south, to proceed at once to face the British invaders. It is my understanding that General Beauregard requested a cease-fire from General Sherman so he could do battle with what he refers to as 'the natural enemy of both our countries.' "

"Then that was the message from Sherman. He must have granted the cease-fire."

"He did, and he did even more Mr. Lincoln." Lee hesitated for a moment, realizing the grave import of the words he spoke next. "He must have felt that this invasion was an invasion of our country, irrespective of North or South. For he did a very noble and courageous thing. Not only did he grant the cease-fire—but he took a regiment of his Northern troops south with Beauregard's division. They went by train and succeeded in outflanking the invading troops. The final communication said that they had attacked and defeated the British. Battling in unison. Johnny Reb and Yankee troops—side by side."

Lincoln's thoughts raced, trying to take in all of the implications at once. General Sherman had made a bold decision and an even bolder move. He had done it on his own without consulting his superiors. Would he have agreed if Sherman had asked his permission? Or would he have hesitated to make such a drastic and possibly far-reaching decision? He just did not know. Perhaps it was no accident that the telegram was garbled. Once Sherman had decided to act he would certainly know that there could be no turning back. Well, that was all water under the bridge now. But what could be made of this epic decision and most important victory? It was too soon to decide; he needed to know more about the situation. Lincoln looked shrewdly at the Confederate general.

"I gather that this information is not the message from Mr. Davis—but facts that I had to know first, in order to assess the message that he has sent."

"That is correct, sir. President Davis ordered me first to tell you about the conjoined battle against our British enemy, then to convey his heartfelt thanks for this greatly appreciated assistance. He formally asks if you would agree to a cease-fire on all fronts to begin as soon as is possible. When the cease-fire is operational it will enable President Davis and you to meet and discuss the portent of all that has happened."

Lincoln sat back and sighed a deep sigh—not realizing until that moment that he had inadvertently been holding his breath. When the import of the words sank home he was possessed of a feeling of elation, stronger than any he had ever experienced before. He could not sit still but sprang to his feet and paced the room. Turned and seized the lapels of his jacket to conceal the trembling of his hands, fought to keep his voice firm when he spoke.

"General Lee—I cannot begin to impart to you the strong emotions that possess me at this moment, the newly-kindled hope that, at least to some degree, the killing and slaughter of this terrible war may stop. I have said countless times, in public and in private, that I would do anything, go anywhere, take whatever action was needed to stop this war. You must convey the word to Mr. Davis that the truce is to begin at once, as soon as all of our armed forces have been informed."

"The President suggested that the truce begin at midnight tonight, since our troops must be notified as well."

"Agreed, General, heartily agreed. Then—to equally practical matters. Did Mr. Davis have any suggestion as to where our meeting might take place?"

General Ulysses S. Grant hated any delay, no matter how short. But the locomotive's water tank was almost empty and they needed to take on coal as well. The cars rattled over the switch points into the siding on the southern outskirts of Ticonderoga, New York. The city itself was obscured by an immense pall of smoke; gunfire rumbled in the distance. Grant climbed down from the car just behind the engine and lit a cigar. He would have liked a drink of whiskey as well but he knew better.

"Send a runner up to the telegraph office in the station," he told an aide. "There may be another message from General Halleck. You can let the troops down for a stretch—but tell them that they can't stray more than fifty yards from the train."

It had been a half a day since there had been word about the invasion and the enemy to the north. After defeating the Plattsburgh defenders the British Army had moved south into the Hudson Valley. They had paused just long enough to burn Port Henry then had continued their advance south. Halleck had telegraphed that his militia and volunteer regiments were going to make a stand at Fort Ticonderoga. That was the last that they had heard. Two more trains, filled with troops from the west, were an hour behind this first one—and hopefully more to come. Grant knew that he had to get these reinforcements to Halleck without delay.

A train whistle moaned up the line to the north and in a moment an engine chuffed into view. An engine with a single boxcar attached. It slowed as it approached the troop train and Grant saw the uniform of an army officer in the cab. As the engine braked and squealed to a stop the officer swung down to the ground. Clumsily because his bandaged right arm was in a sling. As the wounded man hurried toward the group of officers Grant could see, through the open door of the boxcar, that it was filled with wounded soldiers. The bandaged lieutenant stopped in front of Grant and half-saluted with his left hand.

"General . . ." he said, then stopped. He was filthy and bloodstained, his eyes were wild, his hand shaking slightly. Grant spoke quietly, kindly.

"What is your outfit, Lieutenant?"

"14th New York, sir."

"You were with General Halleck's forces?" The wounded man nodded dumbly. "I want you to tell me about the battle."

Some of the fear left the man's eyes and he pulled himself up. "Yes, sir. We took up defensive positions centered on Fort Ticonderoga. Scouts said that the enemy were coming on in force. They hit us just after we had dug in. I got a ball through the arm right off. First there was the cannon, a real barrage. After that they came at us in lines, firing as they attacked. Too many of them, too many. Don't know how long we held out, didn't see it myself. He told me, Major Green, told me to get the wounded into the train. He died. Then everything seemed to fall apart at once, soldiers running, redbacks chasing and killing . . ." He swayed, then regained control. "We loaded some wounded, no time, the trainmen only hooked up the one car. They broke us, the major said, soldiers running in all directions. I saw them." He closed his eyes, almost fell. Grant's aide reached out and steadied him. His eyes opened and he spoke, whispering, scarcely aware of the group of officers before him.

"Major Green told me. The general, General Halleck. He saw him die in the attack . . . then the major died too."

"Board the men," Grant ordered. "If there is no doctor with

the wounded in that boxcar, see that one is found for them. With medical supplies. Let's go."

Grant was already staring at the map when the others boarded. He looked around at his officers, then tapped the map with a thick finger.

"Here," he said. "Here is where we make the stand—and stop them. Stopped them there once before. Saratoga. Good defensive country. But we are going to have to block them and hold them with just what we have. Reinforcements will be on the way, but we don't know when they will arrive." He puffed furiously on the cigar.

"We hold, do you understand that? We are falling back now because we have no choice. But this is the last time. We will make a stand. After that we do not give way and we do not retreat. The only way they are going to advance is over our dead bodies."

The whistle sounded and they swayed as the train clanked into motion and began to pick up speed.

In reverse. Back down the track. Grant hated this, hated to retreat but had no choice.

But this was going to be the last time.

THE WORLD TURNED
UPSIDE DOWN

"I don't think that we are going to need all of the cavalry now," Lincoln said, looking down from the window at the mounted soldiers clattering up the drive to the White House, dark silhouettes against the rising sun. "Not in the light of the most astounding recent developments."

"I spoke almost those very words to the major in charge," Hay said as he packed his ledgers into the carpet bag. "He was most firm in response—until he has orders to the contrary, he said—when you go out of this building you are to be surrounded by his troopers at all times. That assassin came close enough to put a bullet through your hat last month when you were out strolling by yourself. There are still a lot of people out there with a grudge against Old Abe."

"Well, I imagine that you are right. Have we been able to contact General Sherman yet?"

"We have indeed," Nicolay said. "Since we connected our telegraph wires to the Confederates' telegraph system at Yorktown we have opened a whole new world of communication. General Sherman has already been picked up by the U. S. S. *Itasca* at Biloxi and is on his way to the meeting. There was some concern at first when our ship approached the harbor—particularly when a cannon was fired. But it was only a salute since they were the first to know that our troops helped to revenge their destruction. In fact it was hours before they could get away from the reception for Sherman."

"A relief to hear. So the ceasefire is more than holding.

Now then, let us away as well before Seward or Cameron get wind of our early departure."

"Perhaps the Secretary of State . . ." Nicolay said hesitantly; the President interrupted.

"My mind is made up, Nico, you know that. If Jefferson Davis and I cannot work out an agreement between ourselves, no passel of politicians is going to be of any help. Do you realize what an opportunity has befallen us?"

"I can think of nothing else, sir, and didn't sleep a wink last night."

"Nor I, my boy, nor I. Have there been any more reports about the ceasefire?"

"Went into effect at midnight. There have been a few accounts of sporadic shooting on both sides, from troops who hadn't received the word. But all that has died away now."

"Excellent. So we shall see if a little yachting voyage might relax and refreshen us."

The President led the way out of the office, with his heavily-laden secretaries following. The White House was silent, everyone asleep except the soldiers on guard. Lincoln mounted his horse while his secretaries put their bags into the carriage. Despite being six feet, four inches, most of the President's height was due to his long legs. Now in the saddle he was surrounded by a solid wall of human flesh and invisible among the massed troopers. They trotted steadily out onto Pennsylvania Avenue, past the redolent canal and on to the Potomac.

Once aboard the steamer *River Queen* the President felt much better. He sat on the bench by the rail and pulled his legs up and wrapped his arms around them as he watched the lines being cast off. The engine throbbed smoothly and the green hills of Virginia moved slowly by.

"There will be Confederate troops waiting at West Point Depot," Nicolay said, almost muttering to himself as he pulled at his wispy beard.

"I imagine that there will be, Nico, since their army is stationed there. And I am sure that they will also greet Jeff Davis with great enthusiasm when he arrives by train from Richmond. It was my decision to meet on Southern territory because they were forthcoming enough to send Lee and his men into ours. General Sherman had no hesitation in joining them and marching through the South, so I can do no less. But we are sailing in neutral waters and neutral we must remain. If I will be in any peril from the Confederates, why then a handful of troops or a few guns on this ship would make no difference. No, we must rely instead on the spirit of goodwill instilled by General Sherman. He was the one who stood in direst peril and he is to be admired for his strength and courage. He seized the nettle, did his duty as he saw it—and made this meeting possible."

"Why did they do it?"

Lincoln knew who the *they* was since the same question was paramount in all their minds.

"As yet, we do not know. The captured British soldiers, like soldiers in any army, just followed orders. I hear that an officer has also been captured, but he is badly wounded. But for whatever reason the British attacked the South we must accept the fact that they did and make the most of it. This opportunity will not occur again. I pray only that Jeff Davis be of the same mind as the rest of us."

The shore shimmered in the summer heat haze, but there was a cool sea breeze moving across Chesapeake Bay so they traveled in comfort. Only when the little ship turned into the York River did the heat return. The river here was more than wide enough for easy navigation, and only narrowed after it had passed the landings at West Point Depot. The ship's engine shut down as they drifted slowly towards the dock at the depot. The lines were thrown, but instead of boatmen or longshoremen grabbing on, gray-coated soldiers hooked them over the bollards. Hay shivered at the sight of them, seized by the sudden thought that perhaps this was all some kind of desperate ruse to kidnap and kill the President. But, no, he had seen General Lee with his own eyes.

Word must have been sent ahead when the yacht was first seen in the river for there was a carriage now coming towards the landing. The Southern soldiers, in their motley and patched uniforms, had been drawn up and stood at attention. President Lincoln stood at the rail, patting his old, tall hat into place.

If there was ever a moment of historical significance this was surely it. In the midst of a terrible war there was suddenly peace. The guns were silent, the fighting stopped. Now the leaders of the two warring sides, which less than a day ago had been locked in mortal conflict, were prepared to meet each other in peace.

The carriage pulled up on the wharf and the top-hatted and elegantly clad figure that climbed down now could only be one man. Jefferson E. Davis, the elected President of the breakaway new nation. He conferred briefly with the officers who awaited him. Then he strode alone confidently towards the companionway that had just been pushed ashore. There he stopped for an instant.

President Lincoln who was waiting at the other end did not hesitate but walked down to meet him. For the first time since the war had begun he was standing on Southern soil. The long moment of silence was broken when he spoke.

"Mr. Davis, it was a brave and courageous thing you did to arrange this meeting. I thank you."

"I thank you, Mr. Lincoln, for your instant response and for your bravery in coming here deep inside Virginia."

Lincoln smiled at that. "I am no stranger to these parts. My grandfather, Abraham, for whom I was named, was from Virginia. So I feel that I am coming home."

"I know that, Sir, since I was born here as well. Our birthplaces are less than a hundred miles apart, I do believe. I am normally not a superstitious man, but I cannot feel but that there is a hand of destiny here."

There was silence and a certain hesitation. Too much in the past separated them. Lincoln, the man who had brought war and destruction to the South. Davis, slave-holder and oppressor. But this must change—this had to change.

Both men strode forward at the same instant. By common and instant decision they clasped hands. Nicolay felt the breath catch in his throat, seeing this, yet not believing what he was seeing.

"Do come aboard, sir," Lincoln said. "And out of the sun."

Nicolay stepped aside when the two presidents turned, climbed the companionway and stepped aboard the ship.

"We shall use the main salon and we will not be disturbed," Lincoln said. Both secretaries nodded in silence. "That is not until General Sherman arrives and meets with General Lee. You will then please tell them to join us then."

With a guiding and friendly hand to the shoulder Lincoln escorted Davis into the low-ceilinged and comfortable salon and closed the door behind them.

"Would that I were but a fly on the wall in there!" Nicolay said, wringing his hands in real anguish. Hay nodded agreement.

"We will hear in good time. Now—let us seek some protection from the fury of this Virginia sun."

Despite the heat of the day the portholes in the cabin were closed so what was said here could not possibly be overheard. Lincoln shrugged out of his jacket and dropped into the comfortable armchair that was bolted to the deck. Davis hesitated, started to open his jacket, then rebuttoned it. Perhaps formality might be put aside, like so many other things that had made this meeting possible. But he was a formal man who could not shake the habits of a lifetime. The jacket remained on. He hesitated, then took a pair of strongly tinted spectacles from his jacket pocket and put them over his severely inflamed eyes.

"The war in the north, Sir," he said. "Is there any news?"

"None other than that a desperate battle is now under way. Before engaging the enemy General Grant telegraphed that he had retreated to prepared positions. He added that he would not retreat again nor would he be beaten."

"You must believe him," Davis said. "We did not at Shiloh. It took 10,000 of our dead to prove him right."

"And 12,000 of ours killed in the doing thereof." The thought drove Lincoln to his feet, to stride awkwardly the length of the small cabin, then back. "I am filled with a sense of wonder and of hope. We are facing together a common enemy—"

"Which in order to subdue and destroy we must unite in common cause."

"I could not agree more. We must seize this ceasefire and turn it somehow into a peaceful union that will enable us to fight our joint enemy. Will your Southern troops enter into such an agreement?"

"With enthusiasm. Firstly, despite the horrors and death that this war between the states has thrust upon them, up until now it has been a war of soldier against soldier. All this has changed. A foreign power has not only invaded our land but has ravished and murdered Southern womanhood. This must be avenged."

"And so it shall be. And a fine start was made when our conjoined troops attacked and destroyed the invaders."

"But not all of them. Many fled the beaches and escaped by sea. While your ironclad and warships were engaged in battle a good part of the enemy fleet scattered despite the efforts by your ships to capture them. Thus the invaders escaped a second time. They will surely be used to reinforce the British invasion of New York State."

"Will you join us and do battle with them there?" Even as he spoke the words Lincoln realized how filled with portent they were, how grave and world-changing the answer might be. Davis's response was instantaneous.

"Of course we will, Mr. Lincoln. Anything else would be a blemish to Southern honor. Good men of the North under General Sherman's command died in the Battle of Biloxi and we must honor their memories as well. We ask no others to fight our battles—but will happily join our fellow countrymen in this invasion of our common shores."

Lincoln dropped into his chair, as exhausted as if he had split a cord of wood. "You understand the import of what you have just said?"

"I do."

"Instead of killing each other, we take common cause to kill those who invade our country."

"That is my understanding. And since we are now united in a single army we must consider the prisoners of war taken by both sides."

"Of course! Our first joined order will be to throw open the prison gates so they can return to their homes. This will not only be a practical and humanitarian thing to do. But also symbolic of our changed relationship. As long as we trust each other our plan must succeed."

Abraham Lincoln ran his long fingers through his desperately tangled hair as though to pummel the thoughts that raced through his brain.

"Jefferson, after what we have said to each other I feel compelled to speak to you of my most innermost thoughts, my most heartfelt hopes. I would have this Union as one again, but will not speak of that now. More important I would seek to finally put an end to this terrible war where brother kills brother. When it began I am sure that neither of us knew what horrors there were to come. Now we have a sudden peace and unity that will prevail whilst we battle a common enemy. An enemy whom we will certainly defeat. And then . . . ?"

Davis's mouth was a firm hard line. "And then your abolitionists will begin their baying and threatening again. The causes of this war are still there and will not go away. We will lay down our lives—but not our honor. There are people in the North who will not allow that. When our common enemy is defeated they are going to turn on us again. They drove us from the Union once before and I know that they will have no hesitation in doing it a second time."

"While your plantation owners will promise to lay down their lives, and the lives of many others, for the God-given right to enslave other men."

"That is true. Our way of life and our Southern cause is the rock upon which we stand."

"You can still say that after the 22,000 dead at Shiloh? Must brother go on killing brother until our land is soaked in blood?"

Davis took off his tinted spectacles and touched his handkerchief to his damp eyes. "They are not killing each other at this moment," he said.

"Nor shall they ever begin again. Let us put aside for the moment the things that divide us and dwell instead upon what unites us. We fight together and we must find a way to continue this unity. I for one will do anything to prevent our recent civil war from flaring up again. It shall not be! I have put editors into jail—and some are still there—to silence the voices of those who fought against my policies. I can clap the baying abolitionists into jail just as easily if they threaten our new-found unity. Can you do the same?"

"I have jails as well, Mr. Lincoln, and will fill them as well with those who threaten this same unity. But the question still remains. What about the slaves? I am a slave-owner and, I feel, a good man. A good owner. I take care of them because they are incapable of taking care of themselves."

Lincoln shook his head slowly. "We must try, at least try. A way has now been found for a temporary cessation of the war between the states. A way must also be found to make that cessation permanent. A road to peace must exist. We must find that road and march down it. We must be firm in our resolve to find that way. Meanwhile we know what we must do, to silence any opposition, silence those who would destroy this new-found unity, then perhaps a way can be found, *must* be found, to assure that this vengeful war does not start again. But I feel—no—I *know* that what we have decided here must not be spoken of outside the confines of this room. Our military alliance to repel the invaders, yes, that will be shouted aloud. This will be a noble and patriotic war and none will question that. But about this other matter, which for the moment we should agree to call the search for the future of peace, nothing must be said."

"On that we are in complete agreement. Common cause will unite us and satisfy those that must do battle. That we are entertaining the possibility of an even more difficult and far-reaching goal must be kept secret lest it be compromised."

They clasped hands at that and felt the elation of a mutual hope that the possibility existed, just the tiniest possibility now, that sometime in the future, out of the ruins of the old Union, a new Union might yet be formed.

Lincoln went to the fiddled sideboard, where a pitcher of cool water had been placed, and poured two glasses full. He drank deeply from his—then lowered it suddenly.

"I know someone who can help us in this common labor. An Englishman, a natural philosopher by the name of John Stuart Mill. I think that he was sent by a compassionate Providence to aid us in our hour of need. He is a man of great international standing who has written a very learned book on what he calls political economy. A great thinker who may be the very man to guide us on this path to our mutual goal."

"An English traitor?"

"No, indeed—he is a loyal member of mankind. He speaks for our cause of freedom just as his countryman, Thomas Paine, spoke for our freedom during the Revolution. He is staying with his daughter in Washington. He is of the firm belief that the American system is one that should be admired and duplicated. He began to speak of the recent war and how it could be ended. He is not a charlatan but a gentleman of vigor and intelligence. It is my hope that he can aid us."

"Mine too if what you have said is true."

"We must take him under advisement at the earliest opportunity . . ."

There was a light tapping on the door.

"We were to be disturbed only when our generals arrived," Lincoln said. He emptied his waterglass before going to unlock the door.

"They are here," Nicolay said.

"We will see them now. And have these portholes opened before we combust."

The slight form of William Tecumseh Sherman, garbed in a rumpled and battle-soiled blue uniform, was quite a contrast to the elegantly turned out Commander-in-Chief of the Confederate Army. Jefferson Davis jumped to his feet when the two officers had entered the room, then strode quickly to the Union General and seized him by the hand. Davis did not speak but the intensity of his emotions was obvious. Lincoln spoke for both of them.

"I share Mr. Davis's feelings, General Sherman. We all do. And we thank you for what you did."

"I did my duty," Sherman said in a quiet voice. "To my country and all of its citizens. Now, if you please, what word of Grant?"

"No news yet—other than that he is under attack at Saratoga. He said that he will not give way."

Sherman nodded agreement. "Nor will he. Have reinforcements been dispatched to aid him?"

"I have sent what was available. More will be on the way as soon as new operational plans are made," Lincoln said and turned to Davis who nodded.

"Mr. Lincoln and I have agreed that the ceasefire will be extended to enable both our armies to unite in battle against the British invaders."

"May I make a suggestion?" General Lee asked.

"Of course," Jefferson Davis said.

Lee rested both hands on the pommel of his sword, spoke slowly and carefully, well aware of the great import of his words.

"There must be unified command if we are to be successful in this operation. That will not be an easy thing to do. I am sure that my men would be most reluctant to serve under General Grant who has slaughtered them by the thousands. And I am sure that the same would be true of Northern troops who might be asked to serve under a Southern general. So it is obvious that the various regiments and divisions must keep the commanders that they have now. I am perfectly willing to remain in command of the Southern forces, as I do now. But there must be a Commander-in-Chief who will be respected by the soldiers from both armies, who must follow his orders without a moment's hesitation. I have talked of this with General Beauregard and we are of the same mind. As far as the officers of the Army of the Confederacy go there is but a single officer who could take that command."

"I am in agreement," Jefferson Davis said. "That commander must be General Sherman."

Sherman held his hand up. "I appreciate the honor, and I thank you. But General Lee far outranks me . . ."

"Rank in war is determined by winning," Lee said. "You fought and held at Shiloh and I understand that you were rewarded with a promotion for that. Now you have risked life, career, everything to aid us. I don't think that the Northern armies would accept a Southerner in the top command. But they will accept you—as will we."

"You are perfectly correct, General Lee," Lincoln said. "Since General Halleck's death General Grant has been in command of the forces now arrayed against the British. As you may have heard, General McClellan is in the hospital with fever. I have relieved him of his post as General of the Armies and have assumed that command myself. It is now, with great pleasure, that I relinquish that title to General Sherman. And more than that, since he will be in command of two armies his rank must reflect that fact. As well as being Commander-in-Chief I recommend that he be named General of the Combined Armies as well."

"I concur, Sir," Davis said. "It is fitting and deserved."

Robert E. Lee turned to the Union officer and saluted. "I am at your command, General Sherman."

Sherman returned the salute. "For the sake of our unified armies and the cause they fight in, I accept. Now—let us plan what must be done to attack the invaders. To demolish them in battle and thrust them back from our country. If it is war they want, why they shall have it in a sufficiency."

SHARPSHOOTERS!

"The west flank, General—they're coming over the wall!"

General Grant's uniform was torn and dirty, his face black with smoke. He swayed in the saddle with fatigue; he had just returned from repelling another British attack. He pushed both hands down on the pommel of his McClellan saddle to straighten himself up.

"I want every second man from this line to follow me," he ordered. "Let's go boys! The way they been dying today they ain't going to go on like this forever."

He drew his sword and led the way, his exhausted horse barely able to stumble over the rough ground, beat down by the smoke and heat. And there they were, dark-green uniformed soldiers with black buttons, a fresh regiment thrown into battle. General Grant drew his sword and shouted wordless encouragement as he led the attack.

He avoided the bayonet, kicked it aside with his stirruped heel, then leaned over to slash the man across the face. His horse stumbled and fell, and he dragged himself clear. The melee was hand-to-hand and a very close run thing. Had he not brought his relief troops the battery and revetments would have been taken, punching a hole in the line they were fighting so hard to defend.

When the last green-uniformed attacker had been killed, his body dumped unceremoniously over the wall, the American forces still held the line. Battered, exhausted, filthy beyond belief, with more dead than living: they had held.

And that is the way the day went. The enemy, as tired as they were, kept attacking uphill with grinding strength. And were repelled with only the greatest of effort. Grant had said that his line would not break and it did not.

But at what a terrible cost.

Men who were wounded, bandaged, went back to fight again. Used their bayonets lying down when they were too fatigued to stand. It was a day for heroism. And a day for death. Not until it began to grow dark did the defenders realize that this day of hell was over. And that they had survived, fewer and fewer, but enough to still fight on.

The firing died away at dusk. Visibility faded in the gathering darkness, made even more obscure by the hovering clouds of smoke. The British had withdrawn after their last desperate attack, leaving behind the tumbled redcoat corpses on the ridge. But for the exhausted American survivors of the day-long attack there could be no rest, not yet. They lay aside their muskets and seized up spades to rebuild their defensive earth-works where British shells had torn great gaps. Boulders were rolled up and heaved into position. It was well past midnight before the defenses were up to Grant's expectations. Now the weary soldiers slept where they fell, clutching their weapons, getting what rest they could before dawn saw the British attacking yet one more time.

General Grant did not rest, could not. Trailed by his stumbling aide-de-camp he went from one end of the defenses to the other. Saw that ammunition was ready for the few cannon remaining, that food and water were brought up from the rear. He looked into the charnel house of the field hospital with the pile of dismembered arms and legs beside it. Only when all had been done that could be done did he permit himself to drop into the chair before his tent. He accepted a cup of coffee and sipped at it.

"This has been a very long day," he said, and Captain Craig shook his head at the understatement.

"More than long, General, ferocious. Those British know how to press home the attack."

"And our boys know how to fight, Bob, don't you forget that. Fight and die. Our losses are too heavy. Another attack like this last and they could break through."

"Then in the morning. . . ?"

Grant did not answer but drank his coffee—then looked up sharply at the distant sound of a train's whistle.

"Is the track still open?"

"Was a couple of hours ago. I had a handcar run back down the line to check it. Telegraph wire is still out of service though. It seems that either the Brits don't have their cavalry out behind us or they just don't know the military value of the train."

"May they never learn!"

There was the scrabble of running feet and a soldier appeared in the firelight, throwing a ramshackle salute.

"Train comin' into the siding, General. Captain said you would shore like to know."

"I shore do. Troops."

"Yes, sir."

"About time. Captain Craig, go back with this man. Get the commanding officer and bring him to me while they are unloading."

Exhausted but still not able to sleep, Grant took more coffee and thought about the stone crock of whiskey in the tent. Then forgot about it. His days of drowning troubles that way were long past; he could face them now. He frowned as he noticed that the sky was growing bright, relaxed only when he realized that it was the newly risen moon. Dawn was still some hours away.

Footsteps sounded in the darkness—and a sudden crash and a guttural curse as one of the approaching men tripped. Then Captain Craig appeared followed by a tall, blond officer who limped slightly and brushed at his uniform. He was an amazing sight among the battle-stained survivors with their ragged uniforms. The newcomer was bandbox perfect with his stylish green jacket and light blue trousers, while the rifle he carried was long and elaborately constructed. When he saw Grant he stopped and saluted.

"Lieutenant Colonel Trepp, General. 1st Regiment United States Sharp Shooters." He spoke with a thick German accent. Grant coughed and spat into the fire. He had heard of these Green Coats but had never had any of them under his command.

"What other regiments are with you?"

"None that I know of, General. Joost my men. But there is another train running a few minutes behind us."

"A single regiment! Is that all I am sent to hold back the entire British army? Carnival soldiers with outlandish guns." He looked at the strange weapon that the officer was carrying. Trepp fought hard to keep his temper.

"Dis is a breech-loading Sharps rifle, General. With rifled barrel, double trigger and telescopic sight—"

"All that isn't worth diddily-squat against an enemy with heavy guns."

Trepp's anger faded as quickly as it had come. "In that you are wrong, sir," he said quietly. "You watch in the morning what we do against them guns. Just show me where they are, you don't worry. I am a professional soldier for many years, first in Switzerland then here. My men are professional too and they do not miss."

"I'll put them in the front line and we'll see what they can do."

"You will be very, very happy, General Grant, that you can be sure of."

AMERICANS UNITED—AGAINST THE INVADER

The sharpshooters filtered out of the darkness and worked their way down the battlements. Only when they were gone did a waiting soldier approach Grant. When he was close to the fire Grant saw by his uniform that he was an infantry officer.

"Captain Lamson," he said, saluting smartly. "3rd Regiment USCT, sir. The men will be unloading soon—we had to wait until the train ahead of us was moved out. I came ahead to let you know that we are here."

Grant returned the salute. "And very grateful I am. You and your troops are more than welcome, Captain Lamson. What did you say your unit was?"

"Sergeant Delany, step forward please," Lamson called out and a big sergeant stepped into the firelight. He had a first sergeant's stripes on his sleeves and saluted with all the vigor and correctness of that rank.

Grant automatically returned the salute—then paused, his hand half raised to his hat brim.

The sergeant was a Negro.

"Second Regiment USCT reporting for duty," he called out in best drillfield manner. "Second Regiment United States Colored Troops."

Grant's hand slowly fell to his side as he turned to the white officer. "You can explain?"

"Yes, General. This regiment was organized in New York City. They are all free men, all volunteers. We have only been training a few weeks—but were ordered here as the nearest troops available."

"Can they fight?" Grant asked.

"They can shoot, they have had the training."

"That is not what I asked, Captain."

Captain Lamson hesitated, turning his head slightly so that the firelight glinted from his steel-rimmed spectacles. It was Sergeant Delany who spoke before he did.

"We can fight, General. Die if we have to. Just put us into the line and face us toward the enemy."

There was a calm assurance in his voice that impressed Grant. If the rest were like him—then he could believe it.

"I hope that you are right," he said. "They will have the opportunity to prove their worth. We will certainly find out in the morning. Dismissed."

Grant realized that he meant the words most strongly. Right

now he would put a regiment of red Indians—or red devils for that matter—into the battle against the British.

The enemy lines had been reinforced during the night. The pickets reported hearing horses and the sound of rattling chains. At first light Grant, who had fallen asleep in his chair stirred and woke. Yawning deeply he splashed cold water onto his face, then climbed to the parapet and trained his field glasses on the enemy lines. Before them, on the right flank, a battery of artillery was galloping up in a cloud of dust. Nine-pounders from the look of them. Grant lowered his glasses and scowled. He had used the 1st Regiment USCT to fill in the gaps where his line was the weakest. Colonel Trepp had stationed his men at intervals along the defense positions and he was waiting close by for instructions. Grant pointed at the distant guns.

A DEADLY SHARPSHOOTER

"You still believe that you can do anything against weapons like that?"

Trepp shaded his eyes and nodded. "That will not be a problem, General. Impossible of course without the right training and the right weapon. For me, I do not exaggerate when I tell you that it is a very easy shot. I make it to be just 230 yards." He lay prone and settled the gun butt against his shoulder, squinted through the telescopic sight.

"It is still too dark and we must be patient." He spread his legs apart for a more comfortable position, then looked again through the telescopic sight. "Yes, now, there is enough light."

He slowly pulled down the long trigger that cocked the smaller hair-trigger. Took careful aim and gently touched the trigger. The gun barked loudly and pounded into Trepp's shoulder.

Grant raised his glasses to see the officer commanding the battery rear up. Clutch his chest and collapse.

"Sharp Shooters—fire at will," the colonel ordered.

It was a slow, steady roll of fire as the sharpshooters who lay prone behind the battlement fired, opened their rifle breeches to load bullets and linen cartridges, sealed and fired again.

In the British line the gunners were unfastening the trails of their guns from the limbers, wheeling them about into firing position. While they did this they died, one by one. Within three minutes all of them were down. Next were the horse holders, killed as they tried to flee. And finally, one by one, the patient horses were killed. It was butchery, the best butchery that Grant had ever seen. Then a British gun fired and the shell screamed by close overhead. Grant pointed.

"Easy enough when they're out in the open. But what about that? An entrenched and sandbagged gun. All you can see is the muzzle."

Trepp rose and dusted off his uniform. "That is all we need to see. That gun," he ordered his men, "take it out."

Grant looked through his glasses as the reloaded gun in the center of the British lines was run back into firing position. Bullets from the sharpshooters began to hit in the sand all about the black disk of the muzzle and spurts of sand almost obscured it; then it fired again. When it was reloaded and run back into position yet again the bullets tore into the sand around the muzzle.

This time when the cannon fired it exploded. Grant could see the smoking wreck and the dead gunners.

"I developed this technique myself," Trepp said proudly. "We fire most accurately a very heavy bullet. There is soon enough sand in the barrel to jam the shell so that it explodes before leaving the muzzle. Soon when the attack begins we will show you how we handle that as well."

"Truthfully, Colonel Trepp, I am greatly anticipating seeing what you get up to next."

The destruction of the artillery seemed to have impressed the enemy commander, because the expected attack did not come at once. Then there was sudden movement on the far left flank as another battery of guns was pulled into position. But Trepp had stationed his sharpshooters in small firing units the length of the line. Within minutes the second battery had met the same fate as the first.

The sun was high in the sky before the expected move came. To the rear of the enemy lines a small party of mounted officers trotted out from the distant line of trees. They were a good five, perhaps even six hundred yards away. There was a ripple of fire from the American positions and Grant called out angrily.

"Cease firing and save your ammunition. They are well out of range."

Trepp was speaking to his marksmen in German and there was easy laughter. The colonel aimed carefully then said softly, *"Fertig machen?"* There was an answering murmur as he cocked the first long trigger. *"Feuer,"* he said and the guns fired as one.

It was as though a strong wind had swept across the group of horsemen, sweeping them all from their saddles in a single instant. They sprawled on the ground while their startled mounts quieted, lowered their heads and began to graze.

A single gold-braided, scarlet-coated figure started to rise. Trepp's rifle cracked and he dropped back among the others.

"I always take the commanding officer," Trepp said, "because I am the best shot. The others take from left to right as they wish and we fire together. Good, *Ja?*"

"Good, *Ja,* my friend. Are your marksmen all Swiss?"

"One, two maybe. Prussian, Austrian, all from the old countries. Hunters there, damn good. We got plenty Americans too, more hunters. But these boys the best, my friends. Now watch when the attack comes. We shoot officers and sergeants first, then the men carrying the little flags, then the ones who stop to pick up flags. They always do that, always get killed. Then we shoot the men who stop to shoot at us. All this before their muskets are within range. Lots of fun, you will see."

Despite losing many of their officers the British pushed the charge home, roaring aloud as they rushed the last yards. Most of the troops on both sides had fired their final rounds and the battle was joined with bare bayonets. Grant looked at his new colored troops and found them holding the line, fighting fiercely, then even pursuing the attacking redcoats when the charge lost its momentum. Fight and die their sergeant had said—and they were doing just that.

Perhaps this battle was not lost quite yet, Grant thought.

The little steamer, *River Queen,* that had been so empty on the outward bound trip from Washington, was as filled as a Sunday excursion boat on her return voyage. Jefferson Davis, Robert E. Lee and all their aides filled the salon. The air was thick with the smoke of cigars and excited talk: there was good attendance in an alcove where a keg of whiskey had made an appearance. Abraham Lincoln retreated to a cabin with his secretaries, and General Sherman, to write the first of the many orders that must be issued. General Lee was called to consult with them and the atmosphere here became so close after a bit that Lincoln retreated to the deck where the air was fresher. The ship slowed as they approached the harbor at Yorktown where General Pope and his staff were waiting. Soon their blue uniforms were mixing with the gray of Lee's officers. All of these men had served together at one time and knew each other well. Now they put the war behind them. Men who had been separated by the conflict were comrades once again. Seeing the President standing alone, General John Pope left the others and went to join him.

"The best of news, Mr. President. The telegraph line is finally opened to Grant's command. They have held!"

"Welcome news, indeed John."

"But they held at a terrible price. He reports at least 16,000 dead, more wounded. The reinforcements are getting through to him, the regiment of sharpshooters was first, then the New York Third. More are on the way. As soon as the cease-fire with the Confederates went into effect almost all the troops from the Washington defenses were pulled out and sent north. The first of them should be reaching Grant later today. I have another division on the way. We are getting plenty of men to the railheads, that is not the problem. Trains are. Just not enough available to move all the men that are needed."

"You keep at it. Any problems with the railroads, let me know. We will see what kind of pressure we can apply. Grant must have all the reinforcements available—and he must hold until our joint forces can relieve him."

"General Grant sent you a personal report on the fighting. With an added note to the army. He wants more troops like the New York Third."

"He does? Now tell me—what is so special about them?"

"They are Negroes, Mr. President. We have other black regiments in training—but this is the first to have seen battle."

"And their behavior under fire?"

"Exemplary according to Grant."

"This war of invasion seems to be changing the world in many and unusual ways."

The water became more choppy as the steamer left the York River and headed northeast into Chesapeake Bay, toward the mouth of the Potomac River. These were busy waters and at least two other ships could be seen close by. Low on the eastern horizon were even more ships, white sails and smears of black smoke against the blue sky. Lincoln pointed them out.

"More of the blockading fleet being withdrawn, I imagine."

"They would not have received their orders yet," General Pope said. "Only those in port that could be reached by telegraph." He signaled to an aide to bring his telescope, raised it to his eye.

"Damnation!" he said. "Those aren't American ships. Union Jacks—I can see them! That is a British fleet!"

"Which way are they going?" Lincoln called out, feeling a dreadful anticipation. "Send for the captain."

The ship's first officer came down from the bridge and saluted. "Captain's compliments, Mr. President, but he would like to know what he should do. Those are British warships."

"We know—but we don't know which way they are going."

"Same heading as ours, the mouth of the Potomac River. Towards Washington City. All but one of them.

"One of the battleships has altered course and is coming our way."

PRESIDENTS IN PERIL

There was a feeling of tension released, and even pleasure and happiness, in Whitehall as they went through the reports that the packet had brought from Canada to Southampton.

"I say," Lord Palmerston called out, waving a paper in the air. "General Champion reports that the Yankees appear to be putting up only the poorest of defenses. Plattsburgh taken and the troops marching on, advancing steadily. Jolly good!" And his gout had eased as well; the world had become a sunnier and more beneficent place.

"And this from the admiralty," Lord Russell said. "The fleet in the Gulf Coast attack should have completed their task by now. They are expecting the first reports of victory very soon. From the Washington City attack as well. The navy showed great foresight and tactical acumen there. I must say that the Admiralty has more imagination and tactical ability than I ever gave them credit for. Perfectly timed. Waited until the reports came in that troops were being pulled out of the defenses of the capital. Then, while the American soldiers rush to defend their borders—attack the heart of their homeland. They will soon be brought to heel."

Palmerston nodded in happy agreement. "I do agree. And I know that I can confide in you, John, that at times I have been a bit worried. It is one thing to talk about war—another thing completely to take the first step and open battle. I like to think that I am a peaceable man. But I am also an Englishman and will not suffer in silence when insulted. And this fair land has been insulted, gravely, gravely. And then there is the fact that Wellington was so positive that we should not go ahead with the war. That worried me. But, still we pressed on. But now, by hindsight, I can see that this war has all been right and proper, almost preordained."

"In truth, I am forced to agree. I look forward to the next reports with utmost expectation."

"As I do, old friend, as I do. Now—I must to Windsor to bring these good tidings to the Queen. I know that she will share our pleasure at the good news. Preordained, preordained."

Captain Richard Dalton, 1st U.S. Cavalry, had not seen his family in over a year. If he had not been wounded at the battle of Ball's Bluff he might have gone another year without getting home. The piece of shrapnel that had lodged in his right shoulder hurt bad enough, hurt even more when the surgeon cut it out. He could still ride pretty well, but it would be some time before he could raise a sword or fire a gun. His C.O. had been willing to grant him sick leave so, despite the almost constant pain, he felt himself a lucky man. He was still alive when a lot of his men were not. The ride south from the capital was an easy one, his welcome when he opened his front door worth all the pain past, pain to come. Now the sun was warm, the fish were biting, he and his seven-year-old son had almost filled the creel in a few hours.

"Daddy—look at our ships! Ain't they great?"

Dalton, almost dozing in the warm sunlight, looked up at the mouth of the inlet where it met the Potomac.

"Sure big ones, Andy." Ships of the line, hurrying upstream under sail and steam. White sails filled, black smoke roiling from their funnels. It was a grand sight indeed.

Until a puff of wind caught the flag on the stern of the third vessel in line, spread it out before flapping it about the staff again.

Two crosses, one over the other.

"*The Union Jack!* Row for shore Andy, just as fast as you can. Those aren't our ships, not by a long sight."

Dalton jumped onto the bank as soon as the bow grated on the sand, bent to tie it up one-handed.

"Go on Andy. I'll bring the fish—you just run up to the barn and saddle up Juniper."

The boy was off like a shot, along the lane that led to their house at Piney Point. Dalton secured the boat, then grabbed up the fish and followed him, found Marianne waiting at the back door, looking troubled.

"Andy shouted something about ships—then ran into the barn."

"I've got to ride to the depot in Lexington Park, they have a telegraph there. Got to warn Washington City. We saw them. British warships, an awful lot of them, heading upriver toward Washington. Got to warn them."

The boy led the big gray out. Dalton checked the tightness of the girth, smiled and tousled the lad's hair. Grabbed the pommel with his left hand and swung himself up into the saddle.

"I'll be back as soon as I can. Soon as I tell them that the war is on its way to the capital."

Mary Todd Lincoln laughed aloud with happiness as she poured the tea. Cousin Lizzie, who was new to Washington, was not impressed by the local ladies and was so funny when she strutted across the room, flouncing an invisible bustle.

"Why I tell you—I am not making this up. They just don't have *style*. You don't see ladies in Springfield or Lexington walking like that—or talking like that."

"I don't think that this is a real Southern city," Mary's sister, Mrs. Edwards said. "I don't think it knows what it is, what with all those Yankees and politicians infesting the place." She took the cup of tea from Mary. "And, of course, none of them are Todds."

The sisters and cousins and second-cousins all nodded at this. They were a close-knit family and it was Mary's pleasure to have them visiting her. Just for a change the talk of the war was taking second place to gossip.

"I am so afraid for Mr. Lincoln and this mysterious meeting that no one will tell us about," Cousin Amanda said. "An Abolitionist going into the deep South at this time!"

"You mustn't believe everything you read in the vampire press," Mary said firmly. "They are always after me as being pro-Southern and pro-slavery when y'all know the truth. Of course our family kept slaves, but we never bought them or sold them. You all know my feelings. The first time I saw a slave auction, saw them being whipped—why I became as much of an abolitionist as a Maine preacher. I've always felt that way. But Mr. Lincoln, the thought of his being an abolitionist is so absurd. I don't think he knew anything about slavery until he visited me at home. And he has the strangest idea about slaves. Thinks that if you bundle them all off to South America that would solve the problem. He is a good man but not knowledgeable about the Negro. But he does want to do the right thing. What he believes in—is the Union, of course. And justice."

"And God," Cousin Lizzie asked, a twinkle in her eye. "I do believe that I haven't seen him in church at all during this visit."

"He's a busy man. You can believe in God without going to church. And vice versa, I must say. Have some more tea? Though some argue with that." Mary smiled, sipped her tea and sat back.

"Now you didn't know him when he first ran for Congress because that was many years ago. The man running against him for the office was a hellfire and brimstone Methodist preacher who always tried to make out that Mr. Lincoln was an infidel. Then one day he saw his chance when he was preaching in church and Mr. Lincoln came in and sat in the back. The preacher knew what he had to do and he called out 'All of you who think you are going to Heaven, you rise.' There was a bustle as most of the congregation got up. Mr. Lincoln did not stir. Then the preacher asked for all those who expected to go to Hell to stand. Mr. Lincoln did not stand. This was the preacher's chance.

"'So then, Mr. Lincoln—where do you think you are going?'

"Only then did Mr. Lincoln stand up and say, 'Well—I expect to go to Congress.' And he left."

Most of them had heard the story before, but they still laughed. The tea was nice, the little cakes sweet, and the gossip even sweeter.

There was a sharp knock at the door of the Green Room and it was thrown open.

"Mother, I must tell you—"

"Robert, such a hurry, that's not like you." Her son was down from Harvard for a few days; no longer a boy, she thought. He had filled out during the year that he had been away.

There was more than one giggle and he flushed. "Mother, ladies, I am sorry to burst in like this. But you must all leave the Presidential Mansion at once."

"Whatever do you mean?" Mary asked.

"The British, they are coming, they are attacking the city."

Mary did not drop the teapot, but forced herself to set it down gently instead. A lieutenant ran in through the open door.

"Mrs. Lincoln, ladies, we got a telegraph, they were sighted in the river, they are coming! The British—a flotilla, coming up the Potomac."

There was silence. The words were clear—but what did they mean? British ships in the Potomac and moving on the nation's capital. There were hurrying footsteps in the hall and Secretary of War Stanton pushed in; he must have rushed over from the War Department building just across the road.

"You have heard, Mrs. Lincoln. The British are on their way. I blame myself for not thinking of this—someone should have. After their attack from the north we should have seen history repeating itself. We should have realized, thought more about 1812, they seem to fight their wars in a most predictable way."

Mary suddenly realized what he was talking about. "They attacked Washington then, burnt the White House!"

"They did indeed and I am sure that they intend to repeat that reprehensible deed yet again. You must get your son down here at once. We should have a little time yet, pack some light bags . . ."

"I'll fetch my brother," Robert said. "You get the ladies moving."

She was too disturbed to think straight. "You want us to flee? Why? Mr. Lincoln has reassured me many a time about the defenses that guard this city from attack."

"Did guard, I am most unhappy to say. With the onset of the cease-fire we felt that they could be withdrawn, sent to the aid of General Grant. I blame myself, for I of all people should have considered all of the consequences, that is my duty. But like all the others I thought only of the fate of Grant and his troops. Almost all of the Washington garrison is now on its way north. Even the Potomac forts are undermanned."

"Recall them!"

"Of course. That is being done. But time, it takes time. And the British are coming. Gather your things, ladies, I beg of you. I will arrange for carriages."

Stanton hurried out past the waiting officer who turned to Mrs. Lincoln again. "I'll send some troopers to help you, ma'am, if that's all right."

"Come, Mary, we have things to do," Cousin Lizzie said.

Mary Lincoln could not move. It was all too sudden, too shocking. And she felt one of her headaches coming on, the big ones that put her to bed in a darkened room. She closed her eyes and tried to will it away. Not now, not at this time.

"Stay here a moment," Mrs. Edwards said, putting a protective arm about her sister. "I'll get Keckley, Robert is fetching Tad. I'll have her bring the bags right down here. Then we'll think about packing some things. Lieutenant—how much time do we have?"

"One, maybe two hours at the most before they get here. No one seems to rightly know. I think it's best we get going now."

Robert led Tad in; the boy ran to his mother and put his arms around her. Mary hugged him back, felt better for it. Keckley, more of a friend now than the Negro seamstress they had hired, looked concerned.

"We have some time," Mary said. "To get away from the White House before the British arrive. Help the ladies pack some clothes for a few days."

"Where will we go, Mrs. Lincoln?"

"Give me a moment to think about that. Please, the bags."

Everyone in Washington seemed to know about the approaching ships and panic was in the air. All of the church-bells were ringing, while men on horseback galloped through the streets, a menace to those on foot. In the street just outside the White House a horse had gotten out of control, maddened by the frenzied whipping of her owner, and had crashed carriage and driver into the iron fence about the grounds. The man sat on the cobbles, holding his bleeding head and moaning. On any other day passersby and guards would have hurried to his aid; today he was ignored. The panic was spreading.

The Secretary of War was not the kind of man who lost control easily. Once he had arranged transportation for Mrs. Lincoln, and put a reliable officer in charge of the operation, he put them completely out of his mind. And the rest of the war as well. The defenses of the city took first priority. A glutton for work, he stood behind his tall desk, without a chair, and issued the orders for the defense of the city.

"Any word of the President?" William Seward, the Secretary of State, asked as he hurried in, pushing his way through the crowd of officers.

"Nothing that is new," Stanton said. "You know just what I know, since he left the same message for both of us. He slipped away from here at dawn to meet with Jeff Davis, took the steam yacht. We have had a wire since saying that they are returning together on the *River Queen*. Since the Vice-President, Hannibal Hamlin, is in New York, until we hear different the Cabinet is in charge and I want it that way. Maybe the President is lucky to be out of the city."

"Maybe he has been unlucky and ran into those British ships. It would be a black day for the country if he did."

Seward was less than sincere in this hope. *He* was the one who should have been President; only Republican party infighting had prevented that. If the British did capture Lincoln, why that would be a certain kind of justice indeed. He would not have to wait until the next election to take up the reins of government. He was the more qualified man for this important job.

Stanton hurried off to confer with his officers, while Seward paced the room thinking of the possible bright future the war had thrust upon him.

Unlike the civilians in the streets the military was under control and doing the work they had been trained for. The defenses were alerted and what reserves were available were sent to reinforce them. The troop trains had been contacted, stopped, would be returning.

"Not in time," Stanton said. "The British will be here and gone before they get back. We'll have to make do with what we have. I have men clearing out the files from the White House, bringing all the records over here. This is a sound building and we are going to defend it if the enemy gets this far. We don't know their plans but they are easy enough to imagine if you know your history."

"That was 1814," Seward said. "That time they came up the Patuxent River and attacked by land. Are they doing that again?"

"No, no landings reported. This appears to be strictly a seaborne invasion up the Potomac. In 1814 everyone fled the city and the invaders had an easy time of it. They burnt the Capitol and the White House before they left. But it won't be so easy this time. The generals say that if we can defend a few strongpoints that it may be possible to hold out until relief arrives. The civilians are doing a fine job of evacuating themselves so that is not going to be a problem."

Less than an hour later the first batteries of guns opened fire on the approaching battleships.

Bow on, a bone in its teeth, the British warship charged toward them.

"Go back to Yorktown," Lincoln said. "There are troops and batteries there."

"I don't think that we should, Mr. President," the captain said, his telescope to his eye. "Hard to starboard," he shouted and the President grabbed at the rail as the steamer heeled as it began a tight turn. The captain pointed at their pursuer, at her full sails and black-billowing smoke.

"She's a fast one, lot faster than this old girl. And she'll forereach us if we turn back. That is she will be coming up at an angle and would get to us long before we got to Yorktown. But now she is on a stern chase and it will take a lot more time for her to catch up with us."

"Where are we going?"

"Fortress Monroe. Dead ahead. The British will never follow us under those big guns."

Deep in the hold the stokers poured with sweat as they shoveled. Under the highest head of steam she could carry the screw thrashed the green waters of the bay. Ahead was the tip of the Yorktown Peninsula, growing ever closer.

As was their pursuer. Bows on, closer and ever closer. A sudden puff of white smoke blossomed and vanished; there was no sign of where the shell landed.

"Ranging shot," General Lee said. "Or a warning to stop."

"They can't possibly know who is aboard," Sherman said. "Or we would have had the whole fleet after us."

"We can hide below," Hay said, his teeth almost chattering with fear; military glory had never been for him.

"You and I could, John," Nicolay said. "But why should we bother? I don't think even the British shoot civilian captives. In any case, if they do stop us, we would certainly be of no interest to them."

A DEADLY PURSUER

"Indeed true," Hay said pointing at the uniformed men around the President. "They'll never believe their luck. Not only Lincoln but all of his commanders-in-chief. This cannot happen! It all cannot end like this. With the ceasefire in place, plans made, a new war, a new world waiting." Fear was replaced by anger. But what could be done?

Very little, all aboard agreed. The officers stamped about the deck easing their swords in their scabbards, fingering their revolvers. The ship had a small store of arms and these were brought on deck. But how could they fight against the guns of the warship? Flight was their only option. Top speed—and pray that the old boiler held together, that no vital piece of machinery carried away.

The army officers were like caged lions, pacing and muttering in angry frustration. Wanting only to attack and kill their pursuers, they could only wait impatiently and watch the enemy ship's steady approach. Lincoln left them, sought the quieter haven of the bridge. The sailor at the wheel a solid rock of concentration, correcting every slight sideward movement, aiming toward the headland. On the far side of it was their haven; Fortress Monroe. The captain murmured into the

THE ATTACK BEGINS

speaking tube, talking to the chief engineer. Lincoln stepped onto the flying bridge, looked aft. Was shocked to see how close their pursuer had come in the few minutes he had been inside.

White bow wave surging. At some unheard command thin black silhouettes suddenly appeared on both her flanks.

"Run her guns out," the captain said; he had joined the President on the bridge.

"She looks very close," Lincoln said, running his fingers through his beard.

"She's too close, Mr. President. I don't want to say this but I have to. She's too fast for us. We're not going to make it, sir."

"Certainly there is a chance."

The captain pointed to the tip of the Yorktown Peninsula ahead; waves broke lazily on the sandy beach. "We will weather the point all right. But it's maybe eight miles more down the coast to the fort. That warship will catch us up before we've gone half that far. Sorry, sir. We have done what we can—this old ship has as well. There is nothing more that can be done. We have all the steam up, almost too much. Short of blowing up our boiler we've done our best."

Then the British ship fired. The shells fell short. Now. But the range was closing.

So close, so very close. Lincoln pounded his fist against the side of the cabin. It could not be. The war just could not end like this, with humiliation and disgrace. Too much was at stake, too many young men had died. Now that there was a possibility that the war between the states might end, the stupidity of this chance encounter was almost too much to believe. But it was true. The British ship was growing ever closer: the end was in sight.

The wheel came over and the ship heeled as they weathered the point, sailing so close to the shore and the marshland beyond that they were practically in the breakers. The *River Queen* seemed to gain a bit as the larger British warship stood further out to sea, needing more depth beneath her keel.

But it wasn't enough. From his experiences as a river boatman Lincoln could tell that there was no escape. They would be overtaken long before they reached the security of the fort and its guns. For a moment the warship seemed to be going away from them, showing her flank bristling with cannon. Then she turned once more to the pursuit, bows on and coming fast.

Lincoln could not look at this certain destiny. He turned toward the bow as the eastern portion of the coast opened up. With the dark smudge of Fort Monroe at its farther end.

"My God!" the captain gasped.

"My God, indeed," Lincoln agreed, and felt his tight clasp on the rail loosen.

For there, not a mile away, was an ironclad warship. Smoke pouring from her funnel, heading toward them.

And most glorious sight of all—the Stars and Stripes that were streaming out from her masthead.

WASHINGTON CITY
ATTACKED

Royal Oak led the way, a sixty-gun ship of the line. In line astern were two other great ships. *Prince Consort* also with sixty-guns, and following her was *Repulse* with fifty-nine. They slowly came around the bend in the river and the city of Washington was open before them. The fighting ships drew close to the shore while the troop transports moved toward the Virginia side of the river. As soon as the British ships were within range the battery of American field artillery on the shore, and the guns of Fort Carrol, opened fire. The sound of the explosions echoed through the empty streets of the city; acrid smoke drifted in the hot air. The gunners shouted with pleasure as they saw their shells strike home in the high oak flanks of the warships.

Their voices were drowned in the thunder of the ship of the line's broadside. Thirty guns fired as one and *Royal Oak* rolled with the recoil. The artillery battery ceased to exist. The undermanned fort grew silent as the heavy guns pounded it.

Other guns on the shore were firing now, with little effect against the thick oak of the British ships. They drifted closer to the embankment, turning as they came so the gun layers could pick out the individual batteries and guns. There were few enough defenders to begin with, fewer still after the first minutes of firing. None remained intact fifteen minutes later as the first of the transports approached the shore.

There was a spatter of defensive fire from the American

soldiers there, answered at once by British guns firing grape-shot. Marine marksmen in the rigging added to the carnage. The signal flags went up and the big troop transports threw their sails over and tacked across the river to the shore. Sailors jumped down lines to secure them and gangways were slung down.

By the time the first troops were marching ashore, the pocket of resistance had been all but wiped out. Urged on by the shouts of the sergeants, two columns were quickly formed up and then marched out briskly. One in the direction of the Capitol—the other directly towards the White House. History was repeating itself with a vengeance.

Secretary Stanton looked down from the high window of the War Department at the troops advancing down Pennsylvania Avenue. There was shouting from the hall behind him and the sound of running feet.

"Sir," a voice called out and he turned to see the red-faced and sweating Captain Docherty. "We got the presidential party to safety, got my men back here as quick as I could."

"Where did you take them?"

"Mrs. Lincoln said they would be safe in Mrs. Morgan's house in Georgetown. Good a place as any. Locked in and all the windows bolted. I left a corporal and two men though, just in case."

"What are the streets like?"

"Empty, pretty much. Houses all locked up. But there are more and more men about, carrying guns."

"What do you mean?"

"City folk. Got their women and kinfolk to safety then began to get angry, I guess. This may be the capital of the country but it has always been a Southern city. These people don't like being invaded, particularly by the British."

"Any chance of forming them up?" General A. J. Smith said, turning from the window. More shots were sounding from the street below.

"No way—but they're doing all right from what I seen. Most of them are sniping away at the redcoats like they was at a turkey shoot. Rise up and let go, then slip away. Don't know how much good they're doing against the regulars, but I've seen the redcoats fall."

Soldiers were firing from the windows now at the British advancing through the street below. A burst of counterfire took out the glass from the window and Stanton retreated to the far wall out of the line of fire.

"What do you see, General?"

The officer was ignoring the occasional bullet that crashed into the room, even leaned out to see better. "Those Kentucky troops, the ones stationed in the White House, they're putting up quite a defense. Keeping the lobsterbacks pretty clear—by tarnation, good shooting!"

"What?"

"There was a rush, a squad with burning torches, they were cut down before they could reach the portico. But it can't last, we're too outnumbered."

With the firing now concentrated on the White House, Stanton was emboldened enough to come closer to the window. The streets below swarmed with enemy troops. They ringed the Mansion and were slowly closing in. Disaster was certain. He wondered if they would be burning the Capitol as well.

The USS *Avenger* was the U.S. Navy's newest acquisition, steam-powered and iron-hulled, with engines powerful enough to push her through the sea at fifteen knots. Heavily armed, with four 400-pound Parrott guns mounted in double turrets she was a shark of the sea. Commodore Goldsborough himself was in the pilot cabin when they saw the little steamer come around the tip of the Yorktown Peninsula, less than a mile ahead. The first officer had his glasses on her.

"I know that ship, Commodore. *River Queen*. Assigned to the army, does packet service—"

His voice broke off as the large warship surged into view behind the smaller vessel. A warship moving at great speed, her guns run out and spouting a great column of smoke.

"British!" the Commodore said when he saw their flag. "Beat to quarters. Prepare for action. Open port lids and run out the guns."

"Solid shot, sir?"

"No, the new explosive shells. She's seen us and she's going about—but they're not going to get away."

But the British ship was not retreating. With her guns already run out she was prepared for battle and was ready for it. She was no longer following the *River Queen* but was turning to engage this new enemy who had suddenly appeared across her bows.

Both ships had their boiler pressure close to the red. Their closing speed was almost thirty-five miles an hour. Within two minutes the mile that had separated them had diminished to a hundred yards. Through the slits in the iron pilot box the American officers could see the men manning the guns on the enemy ship, the officers on the bridge there peering down toward them.

"Starboard your helm," Goldsborough ordered. "Helmsman, steer fine, pass her to port. Steady."

When the great warship had turned and gone thundering by them, the captain of the *River Queen* had eased the pressure in his laboring engine and had turned in the other ship's wake. The men in the salon were roaring with relieved laughter, shouting with excitement as they poured on deck to watch the spectacle. President Lincoln had the perfect view of the action through the bridge window.

"You will never see the likes of this again," the captain cried out. "Never again!"

For an instant it looked as though the two warships were going to strike each other, bow to bow. But no, they slid past just yards apart. And as they passed the guns on the British battleship roared out at point-blank range, one after another.

With absolutely no effect. The solid shot slammed into the iron turrets and bounced away. Sheets of flame joined the two ships together, smoke billowing high.

Then *Avenger* fired. Four shots only, one after the other, fired at point-blank range, the noise like the thunder of a summer storm.

Then the ships were past each other and in those brief moments the battle had been engaged—and ended.

The *Avenger* swung about in a great arc. By the time she had turned in her own wake the ship was ready for battle

again as the reloaded guns, one after another, were run back
into position. There were burns and great smears and gouges
in her armor plate where shells had struck and exploded. But
she was still fit, still ready to do battle.

There was no need.

In the time it had taken for the two ships to pass each other
the wooden British warship had been holed and was aflame
from stem to stern. There was scarcely time to lower the boats
as the rigging and sails caught fire; the terrified crewmen
hurled themselves into the ocean to escape the flames.
Corpses and upended cannon were strewn on her deck. There
was a muffled explosion deep in her hull and gushing steam
added to the horrors aboard her as the boiler exploded.

Avenger slowed her engines as she approached the enemy,
guns ready and alert. Yet not a shot was fired. With all resistance ended the enemy lay heavy in the sea, almost unseen
behind the flame and smoke that roared from her.

Goldsborough nodded with satisfaction. "Lower the boats
to pick up those survivors in the water."

The little steamship had come close to the warship now and
Lincoln's orders kept the *River Queen*'s signalman busy. As
soon as the import of his message reached Commander Goldsborough the word was quickly passed and one of the boats,
oars flashing, raced for the smaller vessel. Lincoln climbed
wearily down from the bridge to speak to his assembled
officers.

"Gentlemen, I think that we have experienced the nearest
thing to a miracle that we will ever see in our lifetime."

"Amen to that, brother!" called out one of Lee's officers, a
preacher in civilian life.

"We have little or no time to waste. We all saw the fleet that
is now sailing on Washington. And we know how defenseless
that city is at the present time. Providence has provided us
with this magnificent vessel that might put a halt to that invasion. General Sherman and I will go aboard the *Avenger* and
sail with her. You will follow in this ship. We will meet again
in Washington." He looked down at the boat that now, oars in,
was tying onto their ship.

"There is danger, Mr. President. I am a soldier and it is my duty to move into battle. But you are the leader of our country, your life far more valuable than mine," General Sherman protested. Lincoln shook his head.

"I have a feeling, General, that for this day at least Providence is on our side. Let us go." He went to the ladder and descended, one of the sailors helping him into the boat. Sherman could only follow.

Commodore Goldsborough came out of the hatch and onto the shrapnel-strewn deck and saluted when they climbed aboard. Old, gray-haired and overweight, he was still a man of fighting spirit.

"Thank you for the timely arrival," Lincoln said. He looked at the blazing wreck and shook his head. "A single broadside did that . . ."

"We used explosive shells, Mr. President. The aft battery was charged with the new incendiary shells that we were testing out at sea. They are filled with an inflammable substance that is said to burn for thirty minutes without the possibility of being quenched. I wish we had more of them for I would say they are a great success. But welcome, sir, welcome aboard. You as well, General Sherman." He turned and shouted commands in a voice that could be heard in a gale; the engines rumbled deep below. He coughed, cleared his throat, and continued to speak but in a far more conversational manner.

"I tied up at Fort Monroe less than two hours ago, to take on coal. Then telegraphed reports began coming in about the presence of the enemy fleet in the Potomac. As far as I know mine is the only ship of strength in these waters. I dropped my lines and, well, you saw what happened next. I must thank you for bringing that British ship to my attention."

"We must thank you, Commodore, for your timely arrival and most convincing treatment of our pursuer. Now—to Washington."

"To Washington, Mr. President. Full speed ahead."

When the War Department was not directly attacked, General Rose had ordered scouts to slip out of the back windows. They desperately needed to know what was going on. The

first one to return was ordered to report directly to Secretary
Stanton.

"What is the city like, Corporal?"

"Pretty quiet, nothing moving except where them British
troops are. Everyone locked up and quiet. I think I saw the
Capitol on fire, and it had been hit by gunfire, but couldn't get
close enough to be sure. Then I got as near to the river as I
could. All our guns wiped out, many of our men too. Redcoats still landing, lots of them spread out, but lots of them
shot dead."

THE IRONCLAD SAVIOUR!

"What do you mean?"

"Local folks not taking kindly to them. And it looked like
every farmer that could ride a mule headed for the city when
these ships went by on the Potomac. They got a line of men
stretched out and firing—with more arriving every minute."

"Enough to stop the British?"

"I don't believe so, sir. Those troops are regulars and there
is an awful lot of them."

"Mr. Stanton—it looks like they're getting into the White
House now!"

It certainly appeared to be the end. The defensive fire had
died down and the first enemy troops were battering at the

sealed front door. The troops inside were firing through the shattered windows to no avail.

Above the scattering of shots a bugle could be clearly heard. Sounding the same call over and over.

"That bugle call—what is it?" Stanton asked worriedly.

The general shook his head. "I'm afraid that I do not know, sir. It is not a call used in the United States Army."

"I know, sir," the corporal said. Every eye was on him. "I'm in a signals unit, we know all the British calls as well.

"That's *retreat*, sir, that's what they are sounding. Retreat."

"But—why?" Stanton asked. "They are winning. Have our troops rallied and attacked . . ."

"Not troops!" General Rose cried out. "Look, there in the Potomac!"

In the patch of river, just visible past the verandas of the White House, a hulking dark form moved into view. Guns ready, the stars and stripes flapping from her staff.

An American armor-clad; the salvation of the city.

"Your orders, Mr. President," the Commodore said.

Lincoln was bent over and looking out through the slit in the armor that covered the bridge. It was hot, close in here. What it would be like when the guns fired and shells struck outside he did not even want to imagine. There was a good chance that he might find out in the coming minutes.

"What do you suggest, Commodore?"

"Wood, sir. All wood and no iron on any of the warships. You saw what happens when wood fights iron."

"I did indeed. Can you call upon them to surrender?"

"I could, but I doubt that it would be appreciated. Those ships came here to fight and fight they will. See, they are already swinging about to get their guns to bear."

"The ships with the troops—you will spare them?"

"Of course—unless they refuse to surrender and try to escape. But I think they will be reasonable after they see what happens to the others."

Smoke rolled out from the *Prince Regent*'s guns and there was a mighty clang of metal upon metal that sounded through the ship.

"Return fire," Goldsborough ordered.

The Battle of the Potomac River had begun.

The British had their defensive tactics forced upon them: they were compelled to keep their warships between this armored enemy and the unarmed transports tied up along the shore. The retreating troops were being boarded as fast as they could, but it would still take some time. Time that would have to be bought with men's lives.

They sailed in line against the single enemy, crossing the T just as Nelson had done at Trafalgar. This would concentrate the gunfire of each ship in turn against a single target. But success at the Battle of Trafalgar had seen wooden ships fighting wooden ships. Now it was wood against iron.

Prince Regent was first in line. As she passed the ironclad gun after gun fired at close range. The solid shot just bounced off the armor plate; the explosive shells could not penetrate. There was no return fire until the rear turret of *Avenger* was even with the waist of the British ship. The two guns fired and the massive iron shells from the 400-pounders crashed through the oak hull and on into the crowded gun deck.

Royal Oak was next and she took the fire of the other turret and suffered the same fate as her sister ship. Guns unmounted, men screaming and dying, tangled rigging and sails down.

It took two minutes to reload the big guns. Every minute one of the turrets fired and death crashed into the British squadron. The ships fought and died, one by one, a small victory bought at a terrible price. But the first transports had slipped their lines and were heading downriver.

Men ran along the bank, cheering and shouting, letting off the occasional shot against the retreating ships. A British warship had her rudder blown away and drifted helplessly in the current; the watchers cheered even louder.

Guns were still firing upstream from the drifting ship as it slowly drifted out of sight. Smaller guns firing at erratic intervals. And every two minutes the louder boom of the 400-pounders.

"We are winning, Mr. Lincoln," Goldsborough said. "No doubt about that."

"Has this ship suffered any damage?"

"None, sir—other than our flagstaff being shot away. They got Old Glory and they will pay a terrible price for that."

THE TASTE OF VICTORY

The Battle of Saratoga was in its third bloody day. The troops that had been trickling into the American positions had been thrown piecemeal into the line as soon as they arrived. And they held, just barely, but they held. The fighting was hand-to-hand; the cannon could not fire for fear of hitting their own troops. Then, at noon, some of the spirit had seemed to go out of the British troops. They had been brave enough, had fought hard enough—but all to no avail. They hesitated. General Grant saw it and knew what he had to do.

"We counterattack. All of the freshest troops. Push them back, hurt them."

With a roar of pleasure the American troops attacked for the first time. And the British fled.

Badly hurt in their frontal attack the enemy were now changing their tactics. A few cannon fired at the Americans as a grim reminder that they were still there. But other events were in progress.

The weary and dusty officer approached and saluted General Grant.

"Scouts report plenty of movement on the left flank, General. Some cavalry, maybe even some guns. Looks like they are trying to flank us, attack from our rear."

"Well that's what I would do in their position. I just wonder what took them so long to think about it." He turned to his staff officers. "What about the food and water?"

"When the last reinforcements arrived we pushed them into the line and pulled some of our veterans out. Had them eat, then bring the grub back to the other men. Worked fine—and we have plenty of ammunition to boot."

"I certainly hope so. The enemy is not going to give up easily."

"I passed an officer back there, General. Cavalryman. Wants to find you."

"Cavalry you say! I want to talk to him as well."

The mounted officer was just swinging to the ground when Grant came up—and stopped dead in his tracks. He had read the telegraphed reports about the second British invasion and the fighting in Mississippi, but the overall reality of the situation had not penetrated to him in the heat of deadly battle. Now he saw before him the gray coat and golden sash of a Confederate officer. The tall, richly-bearded man turned to face him and his face lit up with recognition.

"Ulysses S. Grant, as I live and breathe!"

"You are a welcome sight, Jeb, most welcome indeed."

They shook hands and laughed with pleasure. The last time they had met had been at West Point. Since then they had gone different ways. Grant was a general of the Union Army. J.E.B. Stuart was the greatest cavalry officer that the Confederacy possessed.

"We rode the cars as far north as we could, then cut across country. Some of the farmers took some pot-shots at us, didn't hit anything though. I suppose they thought we were British. I heard what Cump did for us in Biloxi. I figured that I could return the favor for an old friend."

"A favor greatly appreciated. My scouts report enemy action on our left flank."

"Now do they, rightly enough. My boys are watering the horses and resting them a bit. As soon as that is done I think we'll sort of mosey around there and see what we can find. Have you seen any of these yet?"

He pulled a carbine from the long holster slung from his saddle and held it up.

"While we were passing through the Philadelphia junction this supply officer sought us out. Said he was shipping these arms to the troops and since we were the nearest bunch we got first look in. That was mighty friendly of the man and we do appreciate it. This is a Spencer rifle that loads from the breech and is a wonder to behold. Look at this." Stuart pulled a metal tube from the wooden butt of the gun and held it up.

"There are twenty bullets in here, all metal with percussion caps on the end. They can be fired one after another, just as fast as you can work the cocking lever and pull the trigger. The brass just jumps out and the next bullet goes into battery. Let a shot off then do the same thing again. I am shore glad that we got them now. I don't think I would have enjoyed it a time back if we had to ride into the muzzles of these things."

Grant turned the gun over and over with admiration, handed it back. "I heard that they were going into production, never saw one before though. Could have used a few thousand of them right here."

"A perfect cavalry weapon. My boys just a-thirsting to try them out."

"Good luck."

Stuart galloped away to join his troops while Grant turned back to the grim business of defending their positions. And killing the British.

Private Poole of the 16th Bedford and Hertfordshire was not a happy man. For two years his regiment had been stationed in Quebec, in Canada, in that wildest of wild countries. Frying in summer, freezing his arse in winter. Then this war. First the long march to the landings, then the boats down the lakes. Easy enough that, but the last march south in the heat was something else again. A pleasure after that to rest a bit before getting stuck in to kill Yankees. Run right over the first lot they did and it wasn't much more work to take out the second bunch. But the easy victories were over now. The fighting had been fierce and the British losses heavy. More than one of his butties dead now. To make matters worse in the last engagement his musket had exploded, seared the side of his head it had. That was a wound for the doctor, for sure. Sergeant didn't see it that way. Told him to rub some grease on it and get back into the line. Gave him a musket from a dead man. Useless thing, Brown Bess, the same gun that had licked Napoleon. But that was a long time ago and he missed his rifled Enfield musket.

"Column halt. Fix bayonets. Left face."

The sergeant walked behind them, checking their packs and weapons with his tiny, cold eyes.

"We are going to attack," he said. "We are going to stay in line and advance together and I'll have the skin off the back of any man who falls behind."

He probably would too, Poole thought gloomily, and rued the day he had listened to the recruiting sergeant when he came round the Horse and Hounds. Buying drinks for all. Telling them about the wonderful life in the army. The Queen's shilling and a new life in "The Old Ducks" he had told them, that was what the regiment was affectionately called. Not much affection now.

THE LIGHTNING STRIKE OF SOUTHERN CAVALRY

"Forward—"

At the same instant the command was spoken the soldiers became aware of the sound of galloping hooves from the scraggly forest of trees that lined the road. Louder and louder.

And then came the screams. A demented, high-pitched warbling cry that raised the hackles on their necks. There were shouted orders and they were just turning to face the enemy when the cavalrymen were upon them.

Gray-coated cavalry that shouted, screamed as they attacked. Firing as they came, firing over and over. Bursting through the British infantrymen, turning to attack again. And still firing. Not appearing to reload at all but pouring out a continuous withering fire that tore through their ranks.

It was brutal slaughter. The British lines just melted away before the rolling, ceaseless hail of bullets. Some of the infantrymen fired back, but very few. The horsemen stayed where they were, still shooting. They did not seem to stop, just kept blasting a blizzard of bullets into the men before them.

When they rode back through the British lines a second time there was nothing for them to fire at. Cavalry sabers slashed down at any movement among the fallen soldiers. As they cantered away into the cover of the woods they left only silence behind them.

Private Poole lay on his unfired Tower musket, a bullet through his arm. He waited long minutes until he was sure that the cavalry had gone, then pushed the dead weight of the sergeant off his back. Climbed unsteadily to his feet and looked horrifiedly about him at the destruction. Stumbled back down the road to escape it.

The sole survivor.

On the other side of the Atlantic an unseasonal summer storm was rolling across England. Streams swelled and burst their banks as rain lashed the countryside. Lightning flared behind the crenelated towers of Windsor Castle; thunder rumbled. The two men who emerged reluctantly from the carriage hesitated for a moment—then hurried over to the shelter of the doorway where they waited. Liveried servants helped Lord Palmerston to the ground and half carried him to the entrance to join the others. His gout had improved slightly, but walking was still painful.

Doors opened before them as they progressed through the castle, to the final chamber where they were all to meet.

The Duke of Cambridge, newly returned from America and resplendent in the full dress uniform of the Horseguards, turned as they entered.

"Capital—just the fellers I wanted to see. Come in, dry yourselves, have some of this sack," he waved his glass at the sideboard. "Just the thing in this poxy weather."

By no word or deed did he refer to the disastrous failure of the American Gulf Coast invasion. And none dared query him. He had remained in seclusion while the American newspapers crowed about the wonderful victory. When he emerged and once more assumed command of the armies there was no one so bold as to mention anything about the matter. It was part of the past; he looked forward to a brilliant future.

There were murmurs of greeting, most polite since the Duke was not only the Queen's cousin as well as being Commander-in-Chief of all the British armies. They looked with interest at the lean officer who stood beside him, almost skeletal in comparison to the Duke's portly figure. Instead of a stock or cravat they could see that the man's neck and throat was covered with bandages and he held his head at a stiff angle. The Duke nodded in his direction.

"You may know Colonel Dupuy of the 56th West Essex? Home on a spot of sick leave, font of information on the colonials. Speaks well of their weapons and he appears to be most contemptuous of ours. Wants to spend money, a good deal of money I dare say. There Colonel, that chappy there is the one you want to speak to. Name of Gladstone, Chancellor of the Exchequer."

"My pleasure, Colonel. I hope you are recuperating well."

"Fine, thank you, sir." His voice was a hoarse whisper.

"And what is it that you want to spend our nation's gold on?"

"Guns, sir," Dupuy said. "Modern rifles, breech-loaders at that." He touched his throat. "Of the kind that did this. At a range of hundreds of yards."

"You, sir," Palmerston rumbled angrily, "you feel that your country has been amiss in supplying its military?"

"No, your Lordship, I did not intend that. I meant that the military, myself included, has accepted the status quo and not thought enough about modernization. Do you realize that some of my men actually use Tower muskets?"

"Brown Bess won wars," the Duke said.

"Won, sir, in the past, sir. Fifty, a hundred years ago. One of my officers was so contemptuous of the weapon that he went so far as to say, humorously of course, that he preferred the good English longbow. Far better and more accurate than a musket. Four times the rate of fire. Does not discharge smoke that gives away a soldier's position."

"Quite a wit," Palmerston said, angered at the levity. "Are your officers always this impertinent?"

"Rarely. This one won't repeat his impertinence. He fell at the Battle of Plattsburgh."

"You mention only weapons," Lord Russell said. "Do you also take fault with our morale, our organization, our abilities to fight?"

"Don't misunderstand me, your Lordship. I am a professional soldier in the most professional army in the world—and proud of it. But put simply, bullets win battles. If an enemy fires ten bullets at me in the time it takes me to fire one—he is then as good as ten soldiers. Which means that there are no longer level terms in combat. A hundred against a hundred means my hundred against their thousand. That is an engagement that cannot be won."

"Training is what counts," the Duke said. "That and morale. We have the morale and the training and the resolution to fight and win in every part of the world. This Empire was not built by men of little resolve. We have not lost in the past and we shall always win in the future. This minor setback will be overcome. The enemy will be trounced and we shall be victorious. We lose battles—but we do not lose wars. A temporary setback can lead to a future victory. If the enemy were to plead for peace we might grant it. But only so that we could return in even greater force later. In the end we will triumph."

He stared around angrily waiting for someone to contradict him.

In the silence that followed they welcomed the announcement that Her Majesty had arrived. They turned and bowed her presence to her chair. Queen Victoria was garbed all in black; black gloves and tiny black veil, she mourned and would forever mourn her lost Albert. Since his death she had become more and more unstrung. Her face was puffy and blotchy and she had put on more weight. Members of the court worried about her sanity. She nodded at the Duke of Cambridge.

"I understand that it was you who called this meeting?"

"I did indeed. Matters of policy to discuss, serious ones. But first, if you please, I would like you to hear a personal report on the war that has affected me as no dispatch or written command has. A verbal report by one who has fought in it. Colonel Dupuy."

"Well then, speak up. What of the war, Colonel?"

"I regret, ma'am, that I bring only bad news."

"I am sure of that!" she said shrilly. "There has been too much of this of late, far too much."

"I regret deeply that I must add to your disquiet. Your Majesty's soldiers and matelots have fought most valiantly, I assure you of that. But we are outgunned on land, overwhelmed at sea. I assure Your Majesty that brave men have done their best, courage has not been lacking—but the material of war has . . ."

His voice was even hoarser and he touched his throat with his fingertips as though in pain. The Queen raised her hand.

"Enough! This man is injured and he should have attention—not an audience before the Queen. Have the colonel helped out, see that he is rested. It hurts Us to see a brave man who has suffered for his country, in this parlous state."

She was silent until the colonel had backed tremorously from the room, then rounded on the Duke.

"You are an imbecile! You brought that man here to embarrass Us, to make some vague and obscure point that completely escapes me? I want you to know that We are not amused."

The Duke of Cambridge was not fazed at all by her anger. "Not obscure, dear cuz, but painfully clear. We are stalemated in this war and appear to be suffering great losses on the Northern Front. I want your Prime Minister and his cabinet to be sure that they understand that fact. And I have even worse news. This colonial war seems to have spread. We have reports that regiments of the Confederacy have joined the Union in attacking our troops."

"That cannot be!" Queen Victoria shouted, her face twisted with anger.

"It is true."

"They cannot be that duplicitous. This war began because

of their two wretched diplomats who are still in enemy hands. When we fight to defend them they react in some sly, Yankee way. Are you telling me that they have combined to defeat Our will?"

"They have. Perhaps it was due to a diversional attack we launched in the south of the country—we will never know."

Only silence followed this preposterous statement; none dared to speak. History is written by the powerful. Blandly and easily the Duke spoke on.

"So now that we are acquainted with all the facts we can determine the course of the future."

"My patience is at an end," she shrieked. "Tell me what is going to happen!"

"A decision must be made. A choice is quite simple. Peace—or barring that—a wider war."

The Queen's patience, never very good, was at an end and she was screaming. "You speak of peace after the humiliation We have suffered? You speak of peace with these colonial creatures who killed my dear Albert? Are we, the greatest Empire the world has ever seen, are we to humble ourselves before these backwoods rebels, these murderous swine?"

"We need not be humbled—but we should consider opening negotiations to discuss peace."

"Never! And you gentlemen of the Cabinet, do you hear what I have said?"

Lord Palmerston hesitated before he spoke. "I think that I speak for the others when I say that the Duke raises some strong points . . ."

"Does he indeed!" The Queen shouted, her voice shrill and angry, her face purple with rage. "But what of the country, what of the people and their desire to teach this upstart nation a lesson that it will never forget? I speak for them when I say that surrender is out of the question. There is such a thing as pride to be considered."

The Duke of Cambridge nodded his head in compliance to her will.

"Of course we will not surrender. But we need more than pride to fight this new kind of war. If we are not to have peace—we must then gird ourselves for a far greater effort. At sea we must have armor-clad ships, on land modern weapons. The Empire must be called on for assistance, for men, for the money that we must have, to build the forces that we must have if, in the end, we are to be victorious."

Lord John Russell forced himself to speak. "Your Majesty, if I may. This is a moment of great decision and all of the facts must be weighed coolly and calmly. I firmly believe that there should be no lasting conflict between Your Majesty's government and that of the United States. We come from common stock, speak the same language. Surely the road to peace must be considered as well as the road to war." He bowed and stepped back.

Gladstone had some knowledge of the sums that were needed for any continuance of the war—as well as the depleted state of the treasury. It was not his place to speak but he looked pleadingly at Palmerston. The Prime Minister nodded grimly.

"Majesty," he said, "we must consider what Lord Russell has said. We must also think of the financial cost of what we are discussing—and it is beyond belief. I believe that all options must be examined. Negotiations for a just peace could be opened, the possibility of apologies might be assumed . . ."

Her rage had cooled somewhat while the others spoke. In fact her voice was almost toneless now, as though a different person occupied her body. "Far too late for that. We do not consider peace an option at this time. And the possibility of failure does not exist. If the Americans must be taught a lesson let it be a strong one. Confer with my ministers and prepare proposals for this mechanical sort of war that the enemy seems to be fighting. What they can do we British can certainly do better. For is this not the heartland of science and engineering? Where Britain leads the world must perforce follow. If we are seen to bend the knee to this rag-tag wild country we can expect only scorn from the crowned heads of Europe. We shall not submit. Britain and the Empire will only be stronger for this exercise. For centuries we have ruled the waves and so be it into the foreseeable future."

She folded her hands firmly in her lap. Jaw set with grim

determination she looked around at the assembled men, challenging them for argument or dissent. The silence lengthened and no one spoke.

"Well then—you are dismissed."

THE SECOND
AMERICAN REVOLUTION

The President of the Confederacy and the President of the
United States had fallen into the pattern of early morning
meetings. It had started by chance, when they wished to prepare a common agenda before a joint Cabinet meeting, had
become the habit since then. Jefferson Davis would take his
carriage from Willard's Hotel, just down Pennsylvania Avenue at 14th, and enter the Mansion to climb the stairs to Abraham Lincoln's office. Nicolay would serve them with coffee,
then close the door and stand guardian in the outer office to
assure that their privacy was not compromised.

Davis drank some coffee before he spoke. "I have had a
very pleasant correspondence from William Mason. He asks
me to thank you most profoundly for the special order for
their release. He has returned to the bosom of his family, as
has John Slidell. Along with the letter was a box of fine Havana cigars."

"You must thank Captain Wilkes, the officer who captured
them, for he was the one who reminded me of their incarcera-
tion. In the midst of a war begun, ostensibly at their seizure,
no one but Wilkes seemed to have remembered them at all,"
Lincoln said, pushing a sheaf of telegrams across the table.
"These arrived a few minutes ago. The counterattack by our
forces has begun. Although it is still too early to get details of
what is unfolding, I think that I can truthfully say that we can
be sure of the outcome. Our fresh troops against their weary
ones—and I am sure that we vastly outnumber them as well.
They must retreat, or stand and die."

"Or both," Davis said, blowing on his coffee to cool it. "I do perhaps have some pity for the common soldiers who serve such reckless masters. But not enough to wish strongly for any other outcome. Perfidious Albion must be struck a fatal blow that will send her reeling so hard that she will have no choice but sue for peace."

"But not too soon," Lincoln said, raising his hands as though to keep this outcome at bay. "We are both in agreement that while the battles rage this country is united as one. So we must consider once again what will happen after the last guns are silenced. There is someone waiting next door that I would like you to meet. A man of great wisdom whom I have mentioned before. A man who has brought me new ideas, a new dimension that I feel affects our mutual theater of operation. He is the natural philosopher I told you about, the one who is a practitioner in the arcane art of economic theory."

"I know nothing of it."

"Nor did I until he explained. With his aid I feel we can find a way to settle our differences, to bind up our wounds and take this country into a proud and united future."

"If he can do that, why then I do declare that he is a worker of miracles!"

"Perhaps he is. Certainly he values liberty above country for he is, of all things, I might remind you, an Englishman."

Davis did not know what to say, for the arcane matters of finance and economics were beyond him. He was a soldier forced into politics while his only desire was to lead in the field. He only stirred and rose when the gray-haired philosopher came in. Lincoln introduced him to Jefferson Davis, and they spoke politely until Nicolay had gone out and sealed the door. Only then did the President address himself to the problems that faced them.

"You know, Mr. Mill, that your country has now invaded the South just as it did the North?"

"I do. Nor can I understand it nor explain it. I only pray that your conjoined forces can resist these attacks."

"We as well, sir," Lincoln said, then hesitated. His long fingers twisted together just as his thoughts twisted with how

much he should reveal. Everything, he finally decided, there
was really no choice. If Mill were to aid them, then he must be
privy to all their thoughts, their every decision. "The warring
sides in our civil war have mutually agreed upon an armistice
to enable us to do battle with our mutual enemy. This country
is as one again—but we are afraid that this situation will only
prevail as long as battle rages. However, I must be frank, and
tell you of our fears and hopes for the future, while asking you
to reveal to no one what we speak of today."

"You have my word, Mr. President."

"Our thoughts are simple. When this war against the invaders is hopefully won—can we keep the peace that we now
enjoy between our recently warring states? And can we, in
some way, also find a way to end the dreadful war between the
states that now has been suspended?"

"Of course you can." Mill spoke quietly and assuredly, with
a frank pleasure and certainty in his words. "If you are strong
in your resolve I can point you to the path that will make that
peace possible. I shall resist any attempt to lecture you gentlemen, but there are certain facts that I must point out that must
be considered in detail. We must remember the past so that
we do not repeat it. I come from a Europe that is constrained
by its past as your country is not. You will recall that but a
few short years ago there were dangerous political stirrings in
Europe. She is old and her ideas are old."

He paced the room as he spoke, raising one finger at a time
to enumerate the points that he was making.

"At this time the French government was wholly without
the spirit of improvement and wrought almost exclusively
through the meaner and more selfish impulses of mankind.
The French people wanted change and were willing to man
the barricades and die for a better future. But what happened?
The regime of that fat, middle-class king, Louis Philippe,
could not handle the crisis. He fled to England as the working
men of Paris rose up as one and raised the Red Flag over the
Hôtel de Ville. And what was the response to that? The Paris
mobs were put down by the National Guard with ten thousand
casualties. Louis Napoleon then ended the Second Republic
and founded the Second Empire.

"In Belgium the frightened king offered to resign. In the end the government let him stay—and he rewarded them by abolishing the right of assembly. In Germany barricades went up. The troops were then called out and the rebellious citizenry were shot down. Prussia still has no parliament, no freedom of speech or right of assembly, no liberty of the press or trial by jury, no tolerance for any idea that deviates by a hair's breadth from the antiquated notion of the divine right of kings."

"You make some very strong points in your observations," Lincoln said.

"I do—and I am correct. Look at the other countries. Mobs rioted in Italy which was, and still is, no more than a hodgepodge of anachronistic principalities. Russia under the Czars is the cornerstone of despotism in Europe. Prague and Vienna had popular uprisings like Paris, and the mobs seized control of cities. They were shot down by the military.

"Compared to all this the conditions in England have been positively idyllic. But now the British have embarked upon this foolish war, this terrible gamble, this threat to the elected government of the only sizable democracy in the world. Tiny Switzerland does not represent the noble future of the human race—but a reborn United States of America could."

The two Presidents looked at each other in silence, weighing the words and their import.

"I for one have never considered these matters in this light," Davis said. "I think we take our country for granted and accept these favors as being naturally received."

"Very much of what we consider natural is mutable," Mill said. "The natural rule of Britain over her American colonies was changed by those rebellious colonists themselves. I do not regress when I talk to you of economic law. If you but follow where I lead you will come to the heart of the problem that you face.

"You must realize that the true province of economic law is production and not distribution as many have believed. This fact is of monumental importance. The economic laws of production concern nature. There is nothing arbitrary about whether labor is more productive in this use or that, nothing capricious or accidental in the diminishing powers of productivity of the soil. Scarcity and the obduracy of nature are real things. The economic rules of behavior that tell us how to maximize the fruits of our labors are as impersonal and absolute as the laws that govern chemical interaction."

Jefferson Davis looked bewildered. "I find these matters beyond my comprehension."

"I assure you that they are not. But follow for a moment where I lead. The laws of economics have nothing to do with distribution. Once we have produced wealth we can do what we want with it. We can place this wealth as we please. It is society that determines how it is shared—and societies differ. You in the North are proving this law for you know that there is no "natural" law determining how men treat men. The means of production can be changed, slavery can be abolished and production will still continue."

Davis shook his head angrily. "I beg to differ with you. The economy of the South is based upon the institution of slavery and we could not exist without it."

"You could exist—and surely will. The principle of private property has not yet had a fair trial. Now it has one in the war that you were fighting over the true definition of property. I put it to you that human beings cannot be property. The laws and institutions of Europe still represent its violent and feudal past, not the spirit of reform. Only in America can this vital experiment in change be made. My model society has a goal different from any of the good men who came before me. I believe that social behavior can be changed, just as you must believe, or you would not be fighting this war for liberty."

"Liberty for the South is not the same as liberty in the North," Lincoln said.

"Ahh, but it is. You are referring to slavery of course. But we must look at the economic record. Slavery as an institution has been on the decline since 1860. Slavery and cotton can only prosper when land is cheap and fertile. Cotton prices have been going down and the depletion of cotton land has been going on for some time. Is this not true, Mr. Davis?"

"Unhappily it is so. Before this war slave prices were drop-

ping, many of my fellow planters found that having a large
number of slaves was a burden."

"The handwriting is on the wall. Despite all the furor over
it there never was a chance of slavery spreading west—the
land is not suited for it. Slavery is a cumbersome and expen-
sive system, and can show profits only as long as there is
plenty of rich land to cultivate and the world takes the produce of crude labor at a good price. I believe that it has now
reached its limit. Since the blockade of the Southern coasts
began the world has been seeking out other sources for their
cotton, in countries such as Egypt and India."

"Slavery will not go away by us just telling it to," Lincoln said.

"Then we must generate an atmosphere where it is no
longer needed. You are now engaged in a war against an empire. It will soon be an economic war and you must look to
your resources. This country is blessed with all the natural resources you need and they must be exploited. The South must
become as industrialized as the North to manufacture the material of peace—and war."

"And the slaves?" Davis asked.

"Must no longer be slaves," Mill said firmly. "But the
planters must be paid for their slaves who are freed. The
amount is small compared to the amounts spent on continuing
this battle. Less than one-half of a day's cost of war would pay
for emancipating all the slaves in Delaware. Cost of eighty-
seven days of war would free all slaves in border states and
the District of Columbia. Slavery will not vanish overnight,
but the first steps must be taken. And one of these steps must
be a law that no more slaves will be born."

"I don't understand," Lincoln said; Davis also looked
bewildered.

"Just that. You gentlemen must see into law the ordinance
that children born of slaves will be free. Therefore within a
generation the practice of slavery will be gone. First a bill
must be passed ordaining this change and ordering it to commence, while an amendment to your constitution is voted on."

Davis shook his head. "I do not like this, Mr. Mill, not a
littly-bit. This will not be an easy thing to do and the people

of the South will not take to it at all. And, speaking frankly, I am not sure that I do approve of it. You are asking the men of the South to change everything, to alter a way of life and everything that we believe in. That is not fair nor is it acceptable. But what sacrifice is the North going to make?"

"Sacrifice?" Lincoln shook his head wearily. "We have made the sacrifice in blood—as have your people. Tens of thousands dead and the soil of this land drenched in that blood. If there had been another path to take I would happily trod upon it. But there wasn't. We must not talk about a way of life we are losing—but of one that we will be gaining. A country united again. A rich and industrious country where there will be no need for slavery. Jefferson, I beg of you. Do not let this opportunity slip away because of your need to keep other men as property."

"The President speaks the truth," Mill said. "I realize that it will be hard for you to do—but do it you must. You can do it and you will do it."

Lincoln ran his fingers though his hair and nodded his head. "As the lady said when she started to eat the whole watermelon, I don't know if I can do it or not, but I'm sure going to give it the best try I can."

Davis hesitated, then nodded grim agreement. "For all our sakes I will try. When Mr. Mill explains these matters it makes sense. But will it be the same when I return to my plantation? Where will I find the words to explain what will happen when I speak with other plantation owners?"

"I will give you the words, Mr. Davis," Mill said. "There is a clarity of design here that once perceived must be believed."

"I pray that you can do that," Lincoln said. "We will follow this course and at the same time we will not forget that while we are doing this we must also see that the war is won as well."

Some of the American regiments had marched north, up the length of the Hudson Valley, their supply wagons churning up the dusty roads behind them. Others had come by troop train, from the deep South and the Far West. The cavalrymen flanked the regiments on the roads, their weary mounts trotting with lowered heads after the fatigues of the journey. On

WILL VICTORY PREVAIL?

they came, a river of blue uniforms, a flood of butternut-gray. They were grim in purpose: firm in their resolve. The invaders would be pushed back, driven from the soil of these re-united United States.

Trestles had been set up in the shade of a grove of oak trees, boards placed on them and the maps spread out. General of the Armies, Supreme Commander-in-Chief, General William Tecumseh Sherman, looked around his gathered officers and nodded greeting.

"I feel that I am among friends again, and sincerely hope that you all share that feeling."

There were nods and smiles.

"It is very much like being back at West Point," General Robert E. Lee said.

"Agreed," General Ulysses S. Grant said. "And I much more prefer my fellow cadets fighting at my side than against me."

"And fight is what we will do," Sherman said. "Fight and win." He touched a map with his index finger and the watching officers leaned close.

"General Grant, you will continue to hold the line here as you have done so well up to now. When will your reinforcements be in place?"

"By dawn at the very latest. As the fresh regiments take over I'm withdrawing the veterans. They have been badly knocked about."

"Fine. With your reinforcements you will hold in strength. You should have no real difficulty repelling any attacks. But you will hold and not advance from your positions for the moment. The opening attack will be yours, General Lee. Your troops will swing around from behind our left flank, here, and proceed to hit the enemy the mightiest blow that you can. We have enough guns now to soften them up with a barrage. When it lifts—you go in. The British will be outflanked. They will be faced by your army to the west of them. Grant's entrenched army here to the north—and the river to the east of them. They'll find no peace there because the flotilla of ironclads will arrive tonight. Their guns will be part of the bombardment. When you strike they will be forced to retreat or be destroyed. And the instant they fall back General Grant's troops will attack as well."

Robert E. Lee smiled grimly as he swept his hand across the map. "So we'll hit them here, here and here. If they stand they are destroyed. If they retreat north, as they must do, our cavalry will be out there to give them greeting. A simple plan, sir, and one that I heartily approve of. After this night's rest the troops will be mighty refreshed and more than ready for the attack."

Ulysses S. Grant nodded solemn agreement. "We have been too long on the defensive, gentlemen, and it grows very wearisome. I take great delight in going on the offensive at last." He bit the end off a long black cigar and scratched alight a match, blew a cloud of smoke up toward the oak leaves above. "We'll smoke them out and attack and then attack again. Very few of them will find their way back to Canada if we do this correctly." Sherman nodded in agreement.

"So shall it be. I have never led officers with such commitment, or commanded men with such mighty resolve. Tomorrow we will put this commitment and resolve to the test of fire. There is no justice in battle, no certainty in war. But we are as prepared as ever we will be. In the morning I think—I *know*—that every man in this army will fight. And fight to win."

At their next meeting President Lincoln had some welcome news for Jefferson Davis.

"I have prepared a message for Congress, outlining the

straightforward agreements that we have reached. I'll discuss it with my Cabinet today and have it read to the Congress this afternoon."

Davis nodded. "I'll await the result. Then return to Richmond for the same task with the Confederate Congress. We must finish our discussions now while the war rages, come to conclusive agreement while feelings are at their highest."

Lincoln pulled his watch from his fob pocket and looked at it. "With this course in mind I have asked Gustavus Fox to join us here in a few minutes. He is an Assistant Secretary of the Navy, although in reality he has a far more important role in government. Mr. Fox travels a good deal, to many places where he meets with his many friends. He sees to it that we know far more about America's enemies than they know about us."

Davis sipped the coffee and smiled wryly. "I thought that the excellent Mr. Pinkerton headed your secret service?"

Lincoln smiled as well. "If he did it would not be secret long—nor much of a service. I believe that your people convinced his agents that the forces facing General McClellan were twice what they really were."

"Not twice, Abraham, thrice."

"No wonder Little Napoleon was always so reluctant to attack. No, Fox amasses information and assesses it—and so far it has always proven to be correct. Come in," he called out when there was the expected knock on the door.

Fox entered, bent slightly toward the two men.

"Mr. Lincoln. Mr. Davis, it is my pleasure to meet you at last. If you will permit, gentlemen, I will give you some detailed information about our enemy." He took a folded sheet of paper from his tailcoat pocket and read from it.

"In England, Scotland and Ireland, the keels of nine large ironclads have been laid. They are of a new design, borrowed heavily from the French *La Gloire*. She is an ironclad wooden ship that can remain at sea for a month cruising at eight knots. Her maximum speed is thirteen knots and she mounts 26 cannon, 68-pounders. A formidable warship, as will be the British copies."

"How long before any of them are launched?" Lincoln asked.

"Too early to tell precisely—since the construction techniques are so novel, the yards are inexperienced in this kind of work. It took twenty months to build *Warrior*. So I would guess six to nine months in the earliest. The British are also providing armor for their larger ships of the line, replacing the top two decks of four of them with iron plating. Now, small arms. They have finally noticed the importance of the breech-loading rifle. They are perfecting a design of their own by modifying the 1853 rifled Enfield into a breech-loading conversion called the Snider."

He selected another sheet of paper. "Because of the distances involved some of my information is incomplete as yet. I do know about India though. A number of British troops are at seaports waiting for transport. There are also Indian regiments among them. Gurkhas, Dogras and Sepoys. Some of them have never been out of India before and their ability might be suspect. Others have fought Britain's imperial wars and are a force to be counted with. But all possible dissidents in the army there were eliminated after the Mutiny. So we must consider Indian troops as a definite possibility."

After outlining all the other preparations for extensive war, he produced clippings from the British press.

"The public is behind the government in this—all of the way if you can believe the newspapers. My people there assure me that this is true and no exaggeration. No voice is raised to speak of peace, not one newspaper even dares use the word. New regiments are being raised, yeomanry called to arms. Taxes raised as well, now up to thrupence in the pound. Be assured, gentlemen, that Britain is very serious about pursuing this war."

"And so are we," Davis said with firm assurance. "On this we are united."

"If you are, may I be so bold as to suggest that you meet a gentleman who is waiting downstairs. His name is Louis Joseph Papineau."

"That name is familiar," Lincoln said.

"You will know why when I tell you more about him. But

first I must ask you gentlemen—what do you plan to do with our British enemies?"

"Defeat them, of course," Lincoln said; Davis nodded firm agreement.

"Then let me then outline what the future may hold for us," Fox said. "We will defeat them at sea, where their wooden ships are no match for our iron ones. Then on land. Our massed attacks will drive them back into Canada from whence they came to invade this country. And then, gentlemen? What will happen next? Do we sit complacently as we face an armed enemy on our northern border, one that is free to grow in strength? An army that can be reinforced and bolstered by all the might of the British Empire. Do we watch quietly while they build an army that will surely attack this country again—if there is no treaty of peace?"

"It is an uneasy future you predict, Mr. Fox, and something that must surely be considered," Lincoln said, running his fingers through his beard.

"One decision you might make would be to meet the gentleman now waiting outside. Mr. Papineau is a French Canadian—"

"Of course!" Lincoln sat up suddenly. "He was the one who led the rebellion in Quebec in 1837. The British put it down and he fled."

"Then you will remember as well that he wanted to establish a French republic on the St. Lawrence. Canada is not the placid, happily governed state that the English would have us believe. In that same year William Lyon Mackenzie led a similar revolt in Upper Canada against the ruling officialdom. This desire for freedom and independence is still strong despite the Act of Union joining Upper and Lower Canada. The French Canadians, with some justification, believe that the act was aimed at intimidating and controlling them. Mr. Papineau has been in Canada, talking with his countrymen. He assures me that the French Canadians are as eager as ever for their freedom. If they were aided . . ."

"You are indeed a devious man, Mr. Fox," Davis said. "You have not spelled it out, but you have us now thinking on the future course of events. Not only in this country, but on this continent. These are serious matters. I don't think the good folk of this country would sleep well at night with Canada brimming with armed British ready to invade again at any time."

"Instead of those sleepless nights our countrymen might very well look in favor at the alternative," Lincoln said. "Which is a democratic Canada, linked by fraternal ties to her sister republic to the south. It is something surely worth thinking about. Let us have your Messr Papineau in so we can hear what he has to say for himself."

WORDS TO CHANGE
THE WORLD

The blue-clad soldiers had fought hard this day. No longer satisfied with holding their lines, they had eagerly surged in attack when the bugle call sent them forward. Out of the shattered remains of the defenses at Saratoga they came, to fall upon the retreating British, already battered by the attacking Confederate Army. But it had not been an easy battle to win, because the invading soldiers were professionals and did not panic or run. They held their positions and kept up their fire. Only when their lines were threatened with being overrun did they make a fighting retreat. Nor could the attackers afford to make any mistakes. Any weaknesses in their own defenses would be instantly taken advantage of; the British troops were capable of turning and lashing out like wounded animals.

Though the outcome of the day's battles should have been certain, the contest was still fierce and deadly. Through the fields and forests of New York State the fighting had raged, large conflicts and smaller, even more deadly ones. It was now late afternoon and the Union soldiers of the New York 60th lay in the shade of the stone wall and took what rest they could. A fresh regiment of Maine riflemen had passed through them and for the moment they were out of the battle. This did not mean they could afford to be unwary, since the front was now very fluid. There were bypassed British units still about, and new regiments arriving.

Private P. J. O'Mahony was one of the men placed outside the perimeter on guard duty. He cocked his gun when he heard the sound of horse hooves from the road on the other side of the wall; the jingle of harness as men dismounted. He rose up slowly and looked through a chink in the wall, then carefully uncocked his rifle before he stood and waved his hat at the gray-uniformed horsemen there.

"Hello, Reb," he called out to the nearest trooper. The man reined up and smiled a gap-toothed grin.

"Hello yourself, Yank." He dismounted and stretched wearily. "Got my canteen tore off riding through the scrub. I'll be mighty grateful for a swaller or two of water if you can spare it."

"Spare it I can, and have it you shall. Sure and you've come to the right place. In the spirit of generosity I must tell you that it is two canteens that I carry."

"You never!"

"I do. One filled with water—the other with poitheen."

"I can't rightly say that I ever heard of no poy-cheen."

"It is the national drink of all Irishmen across the ocean in that green and distant land. Though I do believe it is far superior to your normal beverage, you'll have to judge for yourself. I've heard it compared to a drink you may know, name of moonshine . . ."

"Tarnation, but you are sure a nice feller! Furget what I said about the water and pass me the other one like a good soldier."

The cavalryman drank deep, sighed and belched happily. "Now that is the sweetest shine that I have ever tasted, that's for sure. And my daddy had one of the best stills in Tennessee."

Private O'Mahony smiled proudly. "That's because it's Irish, boyo, none other. The secret of its making brought to this new world from the ould sod. And we should know. For this proud regiment that you see before you is the 69th New York—and every mother's son of us Irish."

"Irish you say? I heard of it. Never been there. Hell, I never been out of Tennessee until this war started. But as I do recollect it was my grand-pappy, on my mother's side, they said that he come from Ireland. Guess that kind of makes us like kin."

"As indeed I am sure that it does."

"You-all eat ramrod bread?" the cavalryman asked, taking

a darkish chunk from his saddlebag and holding it out. "It's just plain old cornmeal plastered on a ramrod and cooked over the fire."

O'Mahony munched happily and smiled. "Jaysus—if you lived on nothing but boiled potatoes and salt water for half of your lifetime you wouldn't be asking questions like that. It's a poor country, old Ireland, made ever poorer by the bastard English who occupy her. It is with the greatest pleasure that we have the chance to fight them now."

"I shore do agree with that. Another little swaller OK? Thank you kindly. Guess you know more about the British than I do, being from over there and everything. But Willie Joe, he can read real good, he read to us from the newspaper. About what them British did down in Mississippi. Makes the blood right boil it does. I shore am glad we caught up with them today. Got 'em in the flank, hit them hard."

"It's a fine body of men, you are, with some good horse-flesh as well . . ."

"Saddle up." The order sounded down the road.

"That was mighty good likker," the cavalryman called out as he mounted his horse, "and I'll never forget it. And you want to pass the word to your sergeant that we been running into some companies of riflemen down the valley apiece. They was on the way south, reinforcement looks like. They fresh and they mean as rattlesnakes. Take care, you hear."

Private O'Mahony duly passed this information on to the sergeant who in turn told it to Captain Meagher.

"More redbellies—a blessing from the Lord. Let us find the bastards and kill them all."

Meagher meant it. He had been a revolutionary in Ireland, a Fenian, the underground movement that was fighting for Ireland's freedom. He had been battling the English for most of his adult life. On the run all of the time and watch out for informers. In the end he had been caught because of the price on his head that was so large it became irresistible in that poverty-stricken country. Once in jail the charges against him mounted up, so much so that the sentencing judge felt no qualms about giving him the most severe sentence on the books. In Anno Domini 1842, early in the reign of Queen Victoria, he had been sentenced to be hanged. But more than that. Before the noose had killed him, he was to have been taken down from the gallows to be drawn and quartered while still alive. But a more lenient review court had taken offense at his medieval sentence and had commuted it to banishment for life in Tasmania. For nearly twenty years he had labored in chains in that distant land, before making good his escape and fleeing to America. It was understandable that no man had greeted war with the English with more exuberance than he had.

"Get the lads moving, Sergeant," he ordered. "This neck of the woods is clean of the English for the moment. Let's see if we can join up with the rest of the division before dark . . ."

A sudden burst of fire sounded down the line. There was shouting and more firing as a picket ran through the trees.

"Sir, redcoats, a fecking mob of them."

"Over the wall, me boys. Take cover behind these stones and show them how Irishmen can fight."

The enemy were appearing from among the trees now, more and more of them. Private O'Mahony took aim with his brand new Spencer rifle and put a bullet through the nearest one.

"That's the way," Captain Meagher shouted happily, firing again and again. "Come on you English bastards, come and meet your maker."

An English officer heard the shout and smiled grimly at the Irish accent. Up until this moment it had been a good war for Lieutenant Saxby Athelstane. His attachment to the irregular Canadian cavalry, which he had so loathed, had turned out to be a godsend. His report of the treacherous and deadly night attack by the Americans had gone right to the top of the chain of command, to the Duke of Cambridge; the Commander-in-Chief himself. He had been called back to headquarters and queried for details of the invasion, and had been more than happy to supply them. His gallantry against great odds had been noted, and the general himself had ordered his promotion to captain.

With the promotion came a new regiment, to replace an officer carried away by fever. The 56th West Essex Regiment, which had been transferred from Bermuda to reinforce the invading army. Although nicknamed The Pompadours, they were a tough and seasoned lot and Captain Athelstane found it a pleasure to lead them into battle.

He cupped his hands and shouted back. "I say, is that Fenians that I hear? You should have stayed in the old sod, Paddy, instead of coming to the New World to be killed."

Dark figures slipped forward as the firing intensified.

It was an unfair and uneven battle with the Irish outnumbered over three to one. But they had their rifles and their spirit—and their hatred. They brought down more than their own number of the enemy as they died. Not one of the Irish tried to escape, not one surrendered. Out of ammunition in the end they fought with bayonets. Meagher laughed with pleasure as an English captain pushed through the struggling soldiers and attacked him with his sword. With practiced skill he stepped forward with his left foot and, with a single thrust under his attacker's sword, he ran the startled officer through the heart.

Meagher twisted the bayonet as the officer fell, pulled it from his body and turned to the attack. In time to see the muzzle of a musket leveled at him—to flare fire into his face. The flame blackened and burned his skin, the bullet struck his skull, threw him to the ground blinded by blood, unconscious. An English soldier clubbed to death P. J. O'Mahony, who had just killed his sergeant.

Only a handful of Irishmen still remained alive when the gray-clad cavalry swept down the road, firing as they came. The surviving English troops sought safety in the forest.

Captain Meagher groaned as consciousness brought fierce pain to his bruised head. He rubbed the blood away so he could see, sat up and looked around at the carnage, the dead Irish soldiers. Very few had survived. There were no wounded among them—for they had all been killed as they lay. There were tears in his eyes as he looked at the destruction.

"You fought like men and died like men," he said. "This day will not be forgotten."

* * *

In the ordinary course of events President Lincoln would write his address to Congress, then have one of his secretaries carry it over to the Capitol, where a clerk would read it out for him. He considered this, then realized that this time it must be different. This time he wanted the Congress to understand the depths of his feeling; he wanted to gauge as well the quality of their response. At no time during his short term as President had he felt that a speech of his was of such great importance. He knew that Mill had opened their minds, pointed the way toward a bright future. President Davis was in complete agreement and they had laid their plans accordingly. Now the speech was done.

"Seward has had his say," the President said, slowly going through the sheets of foolscap one last time. "Even Welles and Stanton have read this. All the lawyers in the cabinet are worried because what I propose to do flies in the face of the Supreme Court decision in the Dredd Scott case. I told them that these little legalistic quibbles would have to wait until after the war. But I have considered and made emendations when they were needed and now the work is complete."

Lincoln put the speech into his stovepipe hat, clapped it onto his head and stood.

"Come Nicolay, walk with me to the Congress."

"Sir. Would it not be wiser to go by carriage? Less tiring and, surely, the *gravitas* of the situation warrants a more formal entry."

"I always get worried when someone uses one of those foreign words, as though simple old English, as spoken by a simple old rail-splitter, was not good enough. Now what is this gravy-tas I'm supposed to have more of?"

"I mean, Mr. President, that you are the most important man in Washington City and your deportment should echo that fact."

Lincoln sighed. "I'll take your carriage, Nicolay, mainly because I've been tired of late. I've had little rest."

And little food, his secretary thought. Plagued by constipation the President took more of his blue mass medicine than he did of vittles. Sometimes he had only a single egg for dinner that he just pushed around and around the plate. His dark skin was sallow now, and his always-rumpled suit even more rumpled as it hung from his skeletal frame. Nicolay went ahead to get the carriage.

The platoon of cavalry accompanied them so it was indeed an arrival at the Congress that was appropriately impressive. The doorway of the building was charred and reeked of smoke where the British had attempted to fire it before their retreat. Lincoln walked among the Congressmen, having a few words with old friends, even stopping for a talk with bitter enemies. Walls must be mended; he must have the firm and committed backing of Congress. And the people.

He spread the notes before him and, in a high voice, began to speak. As he talked his voice steadied and lowered and became convincing in its integrity.

"As I speak to you now Americans are fighting and dying to preserve the freedom of this country. A foreign power has invaded our sovereign shores and the goal we must seek, through force of arms, is to repel that invader. To do this the two warring sides have agreed on an armistice in the war between the states. I now ask you to aid in formalizing that armistice, and to go beyond it, to seek a way to avoid any continuance of the terrible intercine warfare that we have passed through. To do this we must consider that aspect of our history, the existence of slavery, that was somehow the cause of this war. To strengthen, perpetuate, and extend this interest was the object for which the insurgents would rend the Union even by war, while the government claimed no right to do more than to restrict the territorial enlargement of it. Yet both sides read the same Bible and pray to the same God, and each invokes His aid against the other. It may seem strange that men should ask God's assistance in wringing their bread from the sweat of other men's faces. But—let us judge not lest we be judged.

"It is time now for us to remember that all American citizens are brothers of a common country, and that our greatest ambition must be to dwell together under the bonds of fraternal feeling. We cannot escape history. We of this Congress and of this administration, will be remembered in spite of ourselves. We know how to save the Union. The world knows that we do know how to save it. In *giving* freedom to the *slave* we assure freedom for the *free*—honorable alike in what we give, and what we preserve. We shall nobly save, or meanly lose, the last, best hope of Earth. Therefore I urge the Congress to adopt a joint resolution declaring that the United States ought to co-operate with any state which may adopt gradual abolishment of slavery, giving to each state pecuniary aid, to be used by such state in its discretion, to compensate for the inconveniences public and private, produced by such a change of system. Furthermore it shall be held that any state that agrees to this will be deemed a State of this Union and thusly eligible to send representatives to this Congress.

"Each and all of the States will be left in complete control of their own affairs respectively, and at perfect liberty to choose and employ, their own means of protecting property, and preserving peace and order as they have been under any administration.

"In addition there will be no increase in the number of slaves in this country. No more slaves will be imported from abroad. And no more slaves will be born here. From this date forward any children born of slaves will be free. Within one generation slavery shall be banished from our land.

"With malice towards none, with charity for all, with firmness in the right, as God gives us to see the right, let us strive on to finish work we are engaged in, to bind up the nation's wounds, to do all that we may achieve and cherish a just and a lasting peace, among ourselves, and then with all nations.

"I am loath to close. I mind you of the more than twenty thousand American dead at the Battle of Shiloh. American must not kill American ever again. We are not enemies, but friends. We must not be enemies any more. The mystic chords of memories, stretching from every battlefield and patriot grave, to every living heart and hearthstone, all over this broad land, will yet swell the chorus of the Union, when again touched, as surely they will be, by the better angels of our nature.

"The Union must again be one."

As the President concluded the hushed silence with which the Congressmen had listened to him was broken by a mighty roar of approval. Even the most ardent abolitionists, long seeking punishment of the slave-masters and the rebellious, were carried away by the spirit of the audience.

The motion to prepare a bill was carried unanimously.

DEFEAT—AND
A NEW FUTURE

The Battle of the Hudson Valley was drawing to a close. And there was disaster in the making for the exhausted British troops. English, Scottish, Welsh and Irish soldiers were mixed together now. They had cohesion of a sort, they obeyed their officers because they knew they were all determined on one thing. Escape. But this was not an easy thing to do because the American forces were growing as theirs were reduced in number. With the armies of Grant and Lee pushing close behind them, the British had no choice but to flee north. But there was still no escape. The American cavalry harassed their flanks and cut up their supply trains. By the time they had reached Glens Falls their numbers had been halved by wounds, death and surrender. The last became the only option for the ordinary soldier when all the officers and non-commissioned officers were dead, all the ammunition used up. There was no dishonor for an exhausted man to drop his weapon and raise his hands to the sky. Rest, surely, food and water possibly. Road's end, definitely.

Some of the reinforcements fought on. The 62nd Foot had come late to this war, had actually returned from India to be refitted and sent across another ocean to do battle. They were tough, professional soldiers, who had fought in Afghanistan and other embattled countries at the extreme edges of the British Empire. They were accustomed to attacks by irregular horsemen so stood up well to cavalry harassment. They fought in retreat as they did in advance. Since they had never contacted the main bodies of the pursuing armies they were relatively unscathed.

Their commanding officer, Colonel Oliver Phipps-Hornby, was proud of his men and wished he had done better by them. Lake Champlain had promised succor. The boats that had brought them here from Canada would return them the same way. But the scouting patrol he had sent ahead returned with the most depressing news possible.

"Gone, sir," Lieutenant Harding reported. "Not a boat in sight at the landings or along the shore."

CERTAIN DEATH—OR SURRENDER

"You are sure?"

"Positive, Colonel. There were some wounded at the landing, with a surgeon, they had been evacuated to the rear some days ago. One of the wounded, a sergeant, told me that the boats had been there, waiting for us, but they were driven away by enemy artillery. They must have approached under cover of darkness because he said that the firing began at dawn. Some of the boats were sunk, all the rest fled north. The sergeant said that the enemy artillery then limbered up and went north after the boats. There was also some infantry with them, maybe just a regiment."

"I don't understand—how could this happen? The enemy is south of us, flanking us as well. How could they also be to our rear?" The colonel was baffled, wiping at his long mustachios as he tried to digest this dire news. The lieutenant opened a folded and dusty map and pointed.

"Here, sir. I think that this is what happened. You must remember that this is a large country with very few decent metaled roads, unlike Britain. What really connects the different states is the railway network. Look here, see how dispersed and widespread it is. A line here and here, another here. Now, if you will look at Plattsburgh, where we fought through last week. You see this railroad track that begins there and goes south and west through New York State and on to Pennsylvania. It is just possible that the American troops and field batteries could have been sent by train to go around our flank."

"But our troops still occupy Plattsburgh."

"Doesn't matter. The enemy could detrain anywhere near here and move south behind us, and they could have reached Lake Champlain here. Once in position they opened fire to drive off our boats. Then they followed them back along the lake to keep them from returning."

"These trains, a bloody nuisance. Though I must admit that these colonials make very good military use of them."

"Your orders, Colonel?"

The quiet words brought Phipps-Hornby back to the present. The intensified firing to the south meant that an attack in some strength was in progress. As politely as possible Lieutenant Harding had pointed out that the regiment was still in danger.

"Outlying parties, fire and retire. We'll pull back to the last defensive position on that ridge. Issue the command."

Fire and retire the bugles sounded. With practiced skill the men of the 62nd disengaged from the enemy and pulled back through the other defenders. Line after line of them until they were all in the prepared positions.

Lake Champlain was behind them and, apparently, the entire American army was across their front. Soldiers in Blue and Gray were taking up positions in the fields that they had just crossed. More and more units moving around to their flanks. While file after file of British prisoners could be seen marching off dejectedly toward the enemy's rear.

On a hillock behind the enemy lines the colonel could see a gathering of mounted officers. Under two flags still, but united in every other way. Not for the first time did he wonder how all of this could have happened. What should have been the simple invasion of a weakened and warring country, appeared to be ending in this debacle.

A bullet tore through the shoulder of his jacket, ripping the epaulet away, and he dropped instantly to the ground. Too many officers had paid with their lives by exposing themselves to the enemy marksmen. At a thousand yards they still exacted a bloody toll.

General Sherman had his glasses on the enemy, sweeping along their defenses. He saw that an officer there was doing the same thing, when he dropped suddenly from sight. The United States Sharpshooting Corps had wreaked havoc among the enemy leaders and was still doing its deadly work. They stayed behind the first line of troops and advanced with them. Whenever the enemy went to ground and the line became static they went forward to practice their murderous skill.

Behind the entrenched enemy could be seen a blue patch of Lake Champlain, the goal of the retreating troops, the end of the battle surely. Sherman knew that what he had caused to be done had to be done. The enemy had to be defeated—and now it was. Suddenly he was very tired of the killing. He lowered his glasses and turned to his commanding generals, joined together now for the first time since the battle had begun.

"Gentlemen, war is hell and I for one have had enough of it for the time being. Their wounded are scattered all along the lake shore and that regiment on the ridge appears to be the only sound unit left. Get a flag of truce over to their commander and see if we can arrange a surrender, before more of our good boys are killed. I care not for the enemy lives, but would grieve at any more loss of American ones right now. The men deserve some reward for the magnificent battle that they have fought."

"I am in agreement to that," General Lee said.

"And I," said Grant. "And I also would like to have a good talk to that commanding officer. I have not seen one of them over the rank of lieutenant alive since our attack began."

Lincoln was looking through the newspapers, shaking his head with sadness.

"There is a shadow over this land, Nicolay. In the midst of happiness at our victories there is this note of great sadness. A New York company wiped out almost to a man. Apparently because they were Irish. Can this be possible?"

"Not only possible—but highly probable, Mr. President. Certainly the Irish in New York City think that is what happened, and they should know. Almost all of them were born in the old country. If there could possibly be a good side to this massacre, it means the end of draft riots there. Not only have they stopped rioting but the Irish are volunteering in large numbers, fit and angry men . . ."

"He's done it!" Hay cried out as he threw the door open, waving the sheet of paper. "Sherman has wiped out the invaders, seized thousands of prisoners. The battle is over, the invasion ended."

"That is wonderful news indeed," Lincoln said, letting the newspapers drop to the floor as he seized the telegram. "This is most important and timely. Send it on to Jeff Davis at once. He will be as overjoyed as we are, and badly in need of any support."

The telegram that President Jefferson Davis received not only filled him with an immense happiness and a feeling of relief—but was most opportune as well.

"It could not have come at a better time," he said, striking the most fortuitous sheet of paper with his hand. His carriage was at the door waiting to take him to the Cabinet meeting that he had called at the Council Chamber in Richmond. He planned to go over with them the details of the speech he wanted to give at the Confederate Congress and the agreements he proposed to put forward. This would not be an easy thing to do. But it might be easier to get them on his side when he told them of the great victory that had just occurred. The Battle of the Hudson Valley was over, the last of the invaders had surrendered. And it was Southern troops as well as Northern troops who had effected defeat of the enemy. Biloxi had been avenged. He must remind them of that and hopefully carry them along with his new proposals in the heat of success. A new and most decisive political battle was about to begin. He needed all the support he could get from his Cabinet if it was to be fought in the manner that he and Lincoln desired.

One slave helped him on with his coat, another opened the door and handed him up into the carriage. Slaves, he thought as the driver cracked his whip and they started off at a merry clip.

Solve the slavery question and the Union was saved.

But that was not going to be a very easy thing to do.

Most of the Cabinet were already there when he arrived. Rotund and stubby Judah P. Benjamin, the Secretary of State, was talking to James A. Seddon, the Secretary of War. Seddon, tall, lean, dressed in black and wearing a black skullcap, looked more Jewish than Benjamin did, although he was a Virginia aristocrat. Davis looked to them for support: Seddon had once even advocated arming the Negroes; thinking the unthinkable. He was an intelligent enough man to think positively and possibly override inborn prejudices.

Seddon should aid him, but Davis was not so sure of Christopher G. Memminger from South Carolina. He was Secretary of the Treasury and had a wicked temper. As had Stephen Mallory, the Secretary of the Navy. He was the son of a Connecticut Yankee and had helped his mother run a boarding house for sailors in Key West. This surely had not been easy; but he was a quick man with his fists.

The door opened and John H. Reagan, Postmaster General, came in with Thomas Bragg, the Attorney General.

"I see that all members of the Cabinet are present," Jefferson Davis said, seating himself at the end of the long table. He took the folded sheets of his speech from his jacket pocket, started to put them on the table, then changed his mind. He knew it by heart and he wanted to watch their reactions to his proposals. He opened the table drawer and put it inside, next to the revolver pistol that he kept there.

"Gentlemen—do any of you have any urgent business that we need to hear before we get to the substance of the meeting?"

"Need more money in the Treasury," Memminger said, and there was a murmur of laughter. The Treasury was always short of funds.

"Any other?" Davis asked, and the rest of the Cabinet members shook their heads. "Good. Then to the matter of the proposed bill. The North has given us certain assurances that we must consider deeply before we think of the assurances that we must give in return. There must be the end of all abolitionist attacks and propaganda. That is essential."

"Not only essential, but vital," Bragg said. "Particularly when we try to persuade the planters to sell their slaves."

"I agree . . ."

Davis broke off as the door to the hallway was swung open so hard that it crashed against the wall. Leroy P. Walker, the former Secretary of War stormed in. Davis had dismissed the tall Alabaman from his Cabinet and in doing so had made an enemy for life.

"This is a private meeting and you are not welcome here," Davis said.

"Of course it's private 'cause you and the other traitors are trying to sell the South down the river like some ol' nigger woman."

"How do you know what we are doing here?" Davis said, mouth tight with cold anger.

"I know because at least one of you ain't a traitor and told me what you were planning."

"Walker—you are no longer a member of this chamber and you are not wanted here," Mallory shouted, jumping to his feet and striding forward.

"Maybe I ain't—but you going to hear what I say first. Now—stand clear!" Walker shouted as he stepped aside quickly so his back was to the wall. "Now you listen while I speak—and listen good."

He took a long cavalry pistol from inside his jacket and pointed it at them.

Seddon spoke slowly and calmly in his deep Virginia accent. "Put that away, Leroy. This is the Conference Chamber of the Confederacy and not some white trash saloon."

"You hush and listen to me—"

"No!" Mallory shouted, lunging forward and grabbing him by the arms.

They struggled, cursing, and the gun fired with a muffled crack.

"Shot me . . ." Mallory said weakly and he fell to the floor.

Jefferson Davis had the table drawer open and was taking out his pistol.

Walker saw the movement, turned and fired. Just as Davis pulled the trigger of his own gun.

There was stunned silence after the two shots; gunsmoke drifted across the chamber. Walker lay dead on the floor with a bullet hole in the center of his forehead.

They rushed to Davis, stretched him on the floor. His eyes were closed and his jacket was soaked with blood. Reagan opened an immense clasp knife and cut his shirt and jacket away. The bullet had entered his chest just below his shoulder blade and was oozing blood.

"Use this," Seddon said, taking a large white kerchief from his tailcoat pocket; Reagan pushed it against the wound.

"Will someone go for the surgeon!"

Davis sighed and opened his eyes, looked up at the men grouped around him. "Walker . . . ?" he asked weakly.

"Dead," Judah Benjamin said, kneeling at his side. "Memminger has gone for the doctor."

Jefferson Davis looked up at the circle of worried men. They had to carry on, finish the work that he had begun. Good men all of them, supporters and friends. Some not too bright, some very bigoted. Who could he rely on? His eyes stopped moving and rested on the rotund figure and concerned face of Judah P. Benjamin. The brightest of the lot. The peacemaker. Would he be able to work for the greater peace of the country?

"Take care of things, Judah," Davis said, trying to sit up.

"You are the one who can sow accord—and you are the brainiest one here. See that this war is ended and peace is made." He raised his voice a bit. "Have you all heard me? Do you agree with me?" One by one they nodded in silence as he looked around the circle. "Then the matter is settled. I have faith in Judah Benjamin and you must have too . . ." His eyes closed and he dropped back to the floor.

"Is he . . . dead?" someone asked in a hushed voice. Benjamin leaned his head close to Davis's mouth.

"Breathing still. Where is that doctor?"

Two days later Judah P. Benjamin rose to speak before the assembled Congress of the Confederacy. He had studied Jefferson Davis's speech, improved it where he could, made sure that all of the proposals were outlined in the greatest detail. Now he must read it with the greatest sincerity. The Congressmen *must* be convinced.

"You all know what occurred at the fated meeting of the Cabinet. Two men dead, Jefferson Davis wounded, possibly mortally. His last conscious words were for me to speak for him, and I do that now. He asked me to read this proposed speech and do my utmost to convince you all that this is the wisest and sanest course to follow.

"As all gathered here know, the Congress of the United States has agreed to reunite this country in a manner that will be satisfactory to all and repellent to none. You all will have read the bill and pondered on its significance. If we here, in Congress assembled, agree upon its merits we will declare, in essence, that the War between the States is over. Brother will no longer kill brother.

"In all this wretched struggle it is mournful to reflect that the real difficulties spring more from the selfish passions of men rather than from the necessities of the case. In border states slavery is already declining from natural causes. If only intemperate and too often unprincipled abolitionist agitation of the subject for electioneering purposes in the North would stop, slavery in the border states would disappear in five years. The President of the United States has assured me that it will.

"War causation tends to be explained in terms of great forces. Something elemental is supposed to be at work. It is not. People stumble into war for many reasons—some of which they are not even aware of. Now a war that has occupied us has ended by the invasion by a more threatening enemy.

"This war that is now suspended by a cease-fire was not started by slavery or anti-slavery, states rights or Lincoln's election or slavery in Kansas. If you wish to take one word to explain it it would be none of these. It would be fanaticism—on both sides—misunderstanding, misrepresentation, or even politics.

"I therefore ask you to take action on the proposal of the United States Congress. I ask you to look into your hearts and seek agreement. How you decide here will affect thousands alive, millions still unborn. Your decision will essentially end this Confederate Congress, but it will also see the rebirth of a wounded country. We will sit side by side with our brothers from the North to save these United States from a greater threat. Do not forget that in our hour of peril they came to our aid. They were not asked, they volunteered. With their aid—and the deaths of their soldiers—a blood pact was signed that Biloxi would be avenged. And so it has been. Let us seize on this fact and remember it—and try not to dwell upon the war that has now been put aside by armistice. Let us search our hearts and find an honorable way to extend that armistice and put the war behind us. I formally request you all to vote to accept the proposals put forward by the Congress of the United States."

There was no overt reaction when Judah Benjamin stopped speaking. There was a mutter of comment, then one voice louder than the others broke through.

"Judah Benjamin you are a damned Judas—like the other Jew who betrayed our savior—selling out your birthright, your friends and family, your country—for damn Yankee promises." It was Lawrence M. Keitt, the fire-eating Congressman from South Carolina, a slaveholder, very rich and very sure of the right of his cause.

"I sell out nothing, Congressman Keitt. But I do resent your tone, and reject your racial insults. If we were not fighting the British invaders I would call you out to defend my honor. But we have all seen how disastrous it is to mix guns with politics. That I do not challenge your insulting slurs means that I must be strong and not be provoked—as all of you must be as well. We must put personal feelings and honor aside in order to reunite this country."

Keitt grew even more angry at this. "And I resent your tone and your arguments. My slaves are my property and no man will take them from me. And as for my honor, sir, I value it just as you do yours. I will be happy to face your gun, now or at any other time."

"Do you threaten me, Mr. Keitt?"

"More of a promise than a threat." But the arrogance in his voice belied the words. He loosened his pistol in his tailcoat pocket. Benjamin pointed at it.

"You have brought a gun into this Congress to enforce your threat? You do this after what has happened to Jefferson Davis?"

"A gentleman does not go about unarmed—"

"Sergeant at arms," Benjamin called out. "Arrest this man for his threatening behavior."

He had planned for this and the squad of soldiers was ready. All of them veterans of battle, all returned home to recuperate from wounds. All grimly eager to see the end of this war. Keitt shouted angrily and pulled out the pistol—but was quickly disarmed and half-carried, half-dragged from the hall.

There was much argument and raised voices at this, but Benjamin would not permit dissension to rule.

"The dead, think of the dead. Do we really want to begin over again a war that has been brought honorably to an end? Must we once again pick up the guns that have been peacefully laid down, and once again begin killing each other? Have we learned nothing from the deaths of our loved ones? You are the ones who must decide—and posterity will never forget what was decided here this day."

One by one they were won over until, at close to midnight, the final vote was made to accept the conditions of the Congress.

It was carried by the smallest of majorities.

A single vote. But it was enough.

The War of Secession was over at last.

A DIRTY WAR

The frigate *Speedfast* had not been the first British warship to be engaged by the *Avenger* during the brief and deadly Battle of the Potomac. Two others had taken the full impact of her broadsides. The fact that only one of the American warship's guns had been reloaded and run out when the two vessels exchanged fire was all that spared her. A single 400-pound shell had torn though her. The *Avenger* had steamed on to attack the rest of the flotilla—leaving *Speedfast* with dead crewmen, dismounted guns, her wheel and helmsman blown away. Captain Gaffney was an experienced and proficient officer. While his ship drifted helplessly down the river he had the wrecked masts cut away and relieving tackle rigged to the rudder. It was a clumsy arrangement but it worked. Shouted orders were relayed from the bridge; sailors belowdecks pulled on the ropes to move the rudder. Maneuvering was slow and arduous, but it could be done. The battle was far upstream behind them by the time *Speedfast* got up steam again and was brought back under control. Much as he wanted to, the captain knew that it would have been suicide to rejoin the one-sided battle. *Speedfast* had no choice other than to turn her bow downstream in the wake of the escaping transports, to limp sluggishly back to sea and to her home port in Kingston, Jamaica.

An investigating board had cleared Captain Gaffney of any misconduct in leaving the scene of battle. Despite this he felt humiliated by the engagement. Now, refitted and repaired the *Speedfast* was back at sea again. Her mission, as Gaffney saw it, was a simple one.

Vengeance.

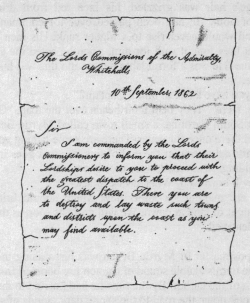

*The Lords Commissions of the Admiralty,
Whitehall,*

10ᵗʰ September, 1862

Sir

*I am commanded by the Lords
Commissioners to inform you that their
Lordships desire to you to proceed with
the greatest dispatch to the coast of
the United States. There you are
to destroy and lay waste such towns
and districts upon the coast as you
may find available.*

Lieutenant Wedge, the commander of her marine detachment knocked and entered the captain's cabin.

"We are hitting back," Captain Gaffney said. He was an angry man. Angry at the enemy who had wrecked his ship and killed his men. He was well aware of the greater military disaster that was befalling Britain, but his feelings about that were distant and controlled. He would willingly join in that battle and do the best that he, his men, and his ship could possibly do. That went without saying. But now, on this mission, he would take great pleasure in wreaking personal revenge upon the country that had so personally tried to destroy him.

"These are our orders," Gaffney said, holding up a single sheet of paper. "They are from the Secretary to the Lords' Commissioners of the Admiralty. Succinct and to the point and I am sure that they will be followed with a great deal of pleasure. You may read them."

"Understood, sir. And to be obeyed with the greatest of pleasure, sir!"

Wedge's hair was grizzled, his face red from drink or rage—or both. He had been passed over for command too often and would never rise to a higher rank. His men hated him, but they fought well for him, since he hated the enemy even more. He was a formidable fighter and this was his kind of battle.

"Do you have a site in mind, Captain?"

"I do. Here." They bent their heads over the map. "On the coast of South Carolina, a small town called Myrtle Beach. I called in there once for water. There are some fishing vessels, and a railroad station at the end of this line that goes inland. The buildings, as I recall, were mostly wooden."

"They'll burn well. When do we attack?"

"We are making six knots now which should bring us within sight of land at dawn. We will go in as soon as the target is identified."

The postmaster of Myrtle Beach was just raising the flag when the unmistakable sound of cannon fire boomed from the direction of the harbor. By the time he had hurried to the corner, to look down the road to the shore, dark clouds of smoke were roiling up above the roofs. There were screams now and people running. The fishing boats tied up in the little harbor were all burning. Boatloads of soldiers in red uniforms were coming ashore. Beyond them the dark hull of a warship brightened suddenly with the flames from its guns and an instant later the front of the First Bank of South Carolina exploded outward.

The postmaster ran. Through the crunch of broken glass to the train terminal, throwing open the door to the telegraph office.

"Get this out on the wire! The British are here, burning and blowing up everything. Firing cannon, landing soldiers. The war has come here . . ."

The burst of musket fire hurled the postmaster back onto the telegraph operator, threw them both dead to the floor.

Lieutenant Wedge and his marines stamped across the floor in their heavy boots and on into the empty station beyond. A black, diamond-stack locomotive waited on the tracks there:

the crew had fled. A trickle of smoke rose from the stack; steam hissed lightly from a valve.

"Just what I had hoped to find. Bring up Mr. McCloud."

The captain had agreed at once when the marine lieutenant had suggested that the ship's engineering officer accompany them ashore. Wedge pointed at the locomotive when the engineer appeared.

"Can you take care of that thing? Blow it up. Will you need black powder?"

"Not at all, sir. A steam engine is a steam engine, none much different from the other, at sea or on land. I'll just stoke her red hot, close all the outlet valves—and tie down the safety valve. After that the boiler will take care of itself."

The town was in flames, the fishing boats burnt down to their waterlines, the townsfolk who had not escaped were dead in the streets. A satisfactory morning's work, Lieutenant Wedge thought as he climbed back to the deck of the *Speedfast*. He turned to look at the burning buildings when there was a great explosion and a white cloud of steam shot up out of the black clouds of smoke.

"What was that?" Captain Gaffney asked. "A powder store?"

"No, sir. A steam engine blowing itself to kingdom come."

"Well done. Be sure to mention that in your report."

"Another town burnt, Mr. President," Nicolay said. "Myrtle Beach, little place on the South Carolina coast. And at least seven American merchant ships have been attacked and seized at sea. Even worse, there have been two more armed incursions across the Canadian border. A most serious one in Vermont. People are in panic up there, leaving their homes and fleeing south."

"These are terrible things to hear, John. Terrible. Soldiers fighting soldiers is one thing, but the British have declared war against our entire population. Go to the Congress at once, report what is happening to the clerk there. They should be voting on the proposals today and perhaps these cruel events can add a little fire to their resolution."

Nicolay ran most of the way to the Capitol, arrived gasping for breath. Gave the reports to the head clerk and dropped into a chair. Congressman Wade, the fire-breathing abolitionist, was on his feet and in fine oratorical form.

"Never, and I repeat never, will I put my name to this proposal that will so weaken our resolution to do away with the evil institution of slavery as soon and as rapidly as possible. Men have died, battles have been fought on this principle. Simply freeing the slaves is not enough. That their masters should be *paid* for freeing them is an insult. God has called for the punishment of these evil men. They must be hurled down from their high station and made to suffer just as their helpless Negroes suffered at their hands. It would be treason if we allowed them to escape God's justice . . ."

"You dare speak of treason!" Congressman Trumbull shouted, on his feet and waving his fist, apoplectic with anger. "You betray your country and betray all the young men, both of the North and the South, who gave their lives to rid this country of the foreign invaders. Now we hope to bind up the wounds of war and unite against this common enemy and you want to prevent that. I say that any man who speaks as you do is the *real* traitor to this country. If it were within my power I would see you hanged for your treasonous cant."

This session of Congress was loud and vituperative and ran far into the night. Only exhaustion finally ground the discussion to a halt. With the acknowledgment that it would continue the following day. They would stay in session until agreement of one kind or another was reached.

Far from Washington, in the most northern part of the State of New York, an armed column of soldiers was moving briskly through the night. This was the smallest command that General Joseph E. Johnston had had in many years. And the strangest. The infantry regiments, the 2nd and 13th Louisiana, had served under him in the past. They were mostly from New Orleans and the surrounding parishes. Lean and hard; tough fighting men. The four artillery batteries had joined up with them in Pennsylvania. They were good and well trained soldiers. But he was still not used to having Yankees under his command.

A NIGHTTIME MISSION

And then there were the supply wagons. Not only the military ones, but the five others driven by Missouri mule skinners. Silent men who chewed tobacco constantly and spat with deadly accuracy.

If General Robert E. Lee himself had not met with Johnston to tell him in detail what needed to be done, he might have begun to doubt the sanity of the operation. But once General Lee had explained the overall concept of the strategy he had agreed at once to take command. Within twenty-four hours of their meeting his troops, guns, wagons and horses had come together in the marshaling yards. It was after midnight and raining hard, the rain hissing on the metal covers of the kerosene lamps, when they had boarded the waiting trains. The wagons had been pushed aboard the flatcars, the horses coaxed and pulled into the boxcars, the weary troops more than willing to fill the passenger cars. After that the only stops had been for coal and water as they rolled north. To Woods Mills, New York, a rail junction where two lines crossed. And perilously close to enemy-occupied Plattsburgh.

"I want scouts out on all sides," General Johnston ordered. "Cavalry down the roads that we will be taking."

"We've got us a volunteer here," a cavalryman said. "Came riding up when he saw who we were." A burly man on a large horse came forward out of the darkness into the light of the lantern.

"The name's Warner, gentlemen, Sheriff Warner and this here is my badge."

The general looked at it and nodded. "Lived here long, Sheriff Warner?" the general asked.

"Born here, traveled a bit, served in the cavalry during the Indian wars, General. Had enough of the army by that time and I come back here. Nothing much here but farming and I didn't take to that. Sheriff died of the pox and I got his job. If there is anything I can do to lend a hand—why I am your man."

"You know the local roads?"

"Know them better than I know the back of my hand. I could find my way around anywhere here in the dark with my eyes closed."

"Well we prefer that you to do that with your eyes open. You can go with these men here." General Johnston pulled the lieutenant aside as he started to follow his men. "Keep an eye on him and the roads you take. You can never be too careful."

But the sheriff proved to be a man of his word. They bypassed the sleeping Plattsburgh and the British units stationed there without being seen.

With Sheriff Warner showing the scouts the way, they had crossed unseen south of this city during the night, and by morning were moving steadily along the shore of Lake Champlain to ambush the boats.

And it worked exactly to plan. The dawn attack with the cannon, the destruction of some of the craft, the flight north of the rest. Then his command had turned in their tracks and followed the boats north. But there was a fair wind from the west and the boats were soon hull down and out of sight. Which was fine, very fine indeed. The trains were waiting for them when they got back to Woods Mills and the tired men and horses were happy enough to board them once again. The civilian wagons that had been left behind were still aboard the train, the mule skinners as surly and silent as ever.

In his headquarters car General Johnston met with his officers.

"A job well done, gentlemen," Johnston said. "Night-time movements with a mixed force is always difficult. I must commend you how it all worked out."

"Come a danged long way, General, if you don't mind my

speaking out plain," Colonel Yancey said, pouring himself a large glass of corn whiskey. "Just to blow up a few bitty boats, then turn around and march away."

"I do agree with you, Colonel—if that was the only goal of this operation," Johnston said, holding up a sheaf of telegrams.

"These were waiting for me at Woods Mills. Our troops have broken the enemy all along the Hudson front. The British are on the run. And any of them that manage to reach the landings at the lake will find their transport gone. Soon they'll all be in the bag. We did exactly what we set out to do to cut off their retreat. But, I can tell you now, the boats were the smallest part of this action. Although what we did was most consequential, it was really part of a bigger plan that will be set into action very soon. The most important events are coming up now."

The general smiled as sudden silence filled the car. He took his time pouring whiskey into his own glass and sipping a bit of it. He had a most attentive audience.

"I refrained from telling you about this any earlier because our true purpose could not even be hinted at. General Lee swore me to silence—and I now ask the same of you."

"Permission to interrupt, sir," Captain DuBose said, then continued when the general nodded his head. "Was there any other news in the telegrams? Have you heard any more about the state of Jeff Davis?"

"Indeed there was information in this last batch. Alive and recovering—but very weak. Good news indeed. Now— back to the war. This was a fine operation, gentlemen, I congratulate you. Yancey was absolutely right. We did come a long way to blow up a few bitty boats. That is done. It was the perfect cover for the action that we will be taking now. We are now on this train which is definitely not going back to Pennsylvania." The cars rattled and swayed through a set of switches, driving home his point. "We are on a different track and heading for our final destination, the city of Ogdensburg. If any of you are not clear about Yankee geography I can tell you that Ogdensburg is on the shore of that mighty river, the St. Lawrence. And of course you know what is on the other side of this river . . ."

"Canada!" Captain DuBose shouted, jumping to his feet. "Canada with the *salaud* English clumped up there thick as fleas on an old dog. We cannot be here by chance. Is that it, General? We are here to make things very bad for the English?"

"Yes, gentlemen, that is it."

TAKING THE WAR
TO THE ENEMY

Lincoln looked around at the members of his Cabinet, and shook his head in disbelief. He pulled his bony legs up before him, resting his heels on the edge of his chair, and wrapped his arms around them. "Why I have not seen as many long faces since my last visit to a livery stable. We should be celebrating victory gentlemen, not looking as though we have suffered dismal defeat."

"The war is at a stalemate," Secretary of War Stanton said. "Sherman has stopped at the Canadian border. The British sink our merchant ships at sea, then land and pillage our shores at will. They justify these actions by saying that a state of war still exists between their country and ours. This is nonsense. They invaded us. Congress declared that a state of war did exist only after their invasions. Now that they have been hurled back from our land, have been defeated at sea—what cause do they have for these continued murderous attacks on our citizenry?"

"None whatsoever, seeing that they have agreed to discuss peace," Seward said, with equal gloom. "But despite this agreement the Prussian talks progress not at all. Adams has presented our terms, which are reasonable indeed, but nothing pleases Palmerston or his lackeys. The British representatives in Berlin still make impossible demands for reparations, apologies, everything they can think of—other than seriously discussing peace. I feel that the Tory government is determined to press on with this war and only agreed to the talks to quiet the opposition parties in Parliament."

"Let us then talk of the good news," the President said. "The Reconstruction Bill has passed the lower house and will surely be approved by the Senate. When I sign it into law we will see the beginning of the end, hopefully, of our internal war. As regards the broader conflict I assure you that our generals are not standing still. If the British do not want peace then they shall see enough war to give them their fill. I have the distinct feeling that they will be far more surprised than we will be at the developments in the near future."

"What do you mean?" Seward asked. "As Secretary of State I should be privy to all war plans."

"You should be—and so should I," the President said. "But there are also times when you should play poker with your cards close to your chest. The city of Washington is populated by foreign agents, eager to seek out any tiny nugget of information and sell it on. But you should at least know that certain operations are in progress. Orders have gone out, carried by hand since we found numberless taps, people listening in, on our telegraph wires. I, personally, do not know the details of these endeavors, so no one in this Cabinet should feel put out. What I can tell you is that the British in Canada are due for some interesting experiences in the very near future."

FREDERICK DOUGLASS

There was a secretive smile on his face when he left the Cabinet Room, almost mischievous. It might be safe to tell them what was in the wind, but Chase was a great gossip. Seward would undoubtedly tell his daughter; word might leak out. Better to just not talk about it no matter how put out the Cabinet might feel.

Hay met the President in the hall as he left the Cabinet Room.

"The delegation of Negroes is here now. I let them into the President's Office to wait. Told them you would be there as soon as the Cabinet meeting was over."

"I will see them now. Do you have any inkling of what they have in mind?"

"None at all, although I did make inquiries as you asked me to."

"Then we shall see, we shall see." He turned the knob and went in.

The men stood when Lincoln entered. The well-dressed Negroes took this meeting very seriously, and looked with great interest at the man who was having the most drastic effect upon their lives.

"I believe that I have met some of you before at an earlier conference."

"You have, Mr. President," their leader E. M. Thomas said. "We had a most interesting discussion with you in this very same room."

"We did indeed. As I recall your group then was less than enthusiastic about Congressional approval for the plan for Negro settlements in South America."

Lincoln spoke without rancor, although the formation of the settlements had been a favorite of his. Then he realized that there was a newcomer in the group whom he had never seen before. A burly man with a thick growth of hair, a pointed beard—and the most concentrated and intense scowl that he had ever seen on a human face. The man pushed by the others and put out a muscular hand.

"I am Frederick Douglass, Mr. President," he said. Shaking the man's hand was like seizing a slab of wood.

"I of course know of you by reputation, Mr. Douglass. It is time we met."

"Time indeed. The Reconstruction Bill that you presented to the Congress is as important as the Constitution itself. It is the first step along the road that will lead to the freedom of my people. Your stature among the Negroes, both in the North and South has never been equaled by another human being.

Uncle Linkum, as the slaves call you, places you upon a pinnacle in Zion. Every other boy baby is now named Abraham in your honor."

"Indeed . . ." the President said, for once at a loss for words. The others in the group murmured in agreement to Douglass's words.

"That is why you must do more," Douglass said with grim intensity; the murmurs of approval turned to gasps of shock. "Once you have set your foot upon the road of freedom you must walk the entire length of it. To the very end where my people must have the same rights as your people. To be free in every way, free to own their own property and free to vote in free elections."

There was shocked silence among the listening men at the strong words addressed to the leader of the country. One of them pulled at the sleeve of Douglass's jacket; he shrugged the man off.

Lincoln tugged at his beard, his face expressionless. "You make your views quite clear," he finally said. "Now I suggest that we take our seats and see where this frank discussion might lead. In some of your speeches that I have read I note that you have a pretty poor opinion of this country that you want to join."

"I do now—but that could change."

"I surely hope so. I don't see how a person who hates the Fourth of July can be a true American."

If possible, Douglass's perpetual scowl deepened. "I said that this holiday has no meaning for black Americans. Nor does it. Slavery brands your republicanism as a sham, your humanity as a base pretense, your Christianity as a lie."

"In the slave states what you say is true. But soon slavery will be at an end."

"It is my strongest wish to see that day. But it is my fear that the deeply prejudiced slave owners and planters will not surrender their slaves that easily. That is why we have come to meet with you this day. To bring you our aid. You must enlist the help of the former slaves to assure their own freedom. The black churches are united in the South and you must seek their cooperation. Other black organizations are also offering hope."

Lincoln nodded. "We shall. I am also organizing a committee to oversee the enforcement of emancipation."

"I should indeed hope so. How many Negroes will be on that committee?"

"I hadn't considered . . ."

"Then consider it now!" Douglass said, jumping to his feet. "If the committee for administrating equality does not have equality then you are lost before you begin. I thereby ask you to appoint me to that committee. What say you, sir?"

"I say," Lincoln drawled slowly, "I say that you have a very positive personality, Mr. Douglass, and a very forceful one. Some might say that your temerity borders on effrontery, but I shall not be so bold as to say that. I do not know what your career ambitions are in life, but I do say that you would make a good railroad lawyer."

The small jest released the tension in the air; some of the group even smiled. A slight nod of Douglass's head was more of an acknowledgment of a worthy opponent than agreement. Before he could speak again the President went on.

"I shall take your words to the committee when it is formed and tell them of my agreement with your position."

The meeting ended on this conciliatory note. Lincoln, ever the professional politician, had neither given ground nor made any promises that could not be kept. Although he did believe that Douglass's suggestions were for the good. The cooperation of the freed slaves was a necessity.

The flat fields on the banks of the St. Lawrence River were ideal for an encampment. The last wheat had been cut and the stubble was crisp underfoot. The air was beginning to warm up under the pale sun, but there was still a scattering of snow in the furrows from the previous night's flurries. Winter was drawing close. The tents were quickly set up and camp made.

Private Ducrocq was leading the colonel's horse; he joined the horse handlers from the artillery on the track down to the water. It was nice here, except for the cold it reminded him very much of the Mississippi near Baton Rouge. Even the

flatboat out there on the river was much like the ones he had
poled through the muddy waters at home. He looked with interest as the oarsmen turned it toward the shore as it came
closer, then grounded close by the drinking horses. The
solid, gray-haired man standing in the bow stepped carefully
ashore. He looked around at the horses and soldiers and nodded happily.

"C'est l'armee Americaine, n'est-ce pas?" he asked.

"Oui, certainment. Etes-vous Français?" Ducrocq replied.

*"Certainment pas, mon vieux! Je suis Français Canadien.
Je suis ici pour parler à votre officier supérieur, le Général
Johnston."*

Ducrocq pointed out the officers' tents in the field above.
Louis Joseph Papineau thanked him and went up the bank.
The soldier looked after him and thought what a strange accident it was to meet someone speaking French up here in the
cold north so far from home. Then he laughed aloud.

Even a simple *garçon* from the bayous knew that there
were few coincidences like this in war. French Canada was
just across the river—and two regiments of French-speaking
American soldiers were on this shore. And then there were
the gun batteries and the heavy-laden wagons. Something
very interesting was in the wind.

"Rifles," General Johnston said, pointing into the open
box. "The very newest Spencer-breech loading, repeating rifles. They fire ten shots before they have to be reloaded. They
are different, of course, from muzzle-loading rifles. But not
difficult to master. Our soldiers have had recent experience
with them and will be happy to show your men how to use
them with the greatest efficiency."

"That will take some time, General. Unhappily most of my
loyal followers come from small towns and farms and speak
only French."

"I think that you will pleased to discover that will not be a
problem. Canada is not the only part of North America where
French is spoken."

"Of course! The Louisiana Purchase. You have troops from
that area, around New Orleans."

"We do."

QUEBEC IN PERIL

"I should have realized when I was answered in French by one of your soldiers. I thank you for the guns—and for your willing instructors."

"I have also been ordered to aid you in any way that I can. The battle plan and attack will be yours, of course. But you will be fighting regular troops and I can assure you that you will need cannon to assure victory."

A steam whistle sounded in the distance, then once again. Johnston pulled his watch from his pocket and looked at it.

"Accurate to the minute. I wish that all operations of war went this well."

They emerged from the tent as the warship came around the bend, two more steaming in her wake.

"Cargo ships from Lake Ontario. They had the armor plate and guns added in Rochester. Originally built to stop any waterborne British invasion—across the lakes. But I think they will be just as good on the attack as on the defense."

Papineau was wild with delight and would have embraced and kissed Johnston if the general had not stepped quickly back.

"I am overwhelmed, *mon général*. Before, when we had our rebellion I had only men, boys really, armed with their fathers' hunting guns. So we lost. Now I have these so marvelous weapons you bring. Your soldiers, big cannon—and now this. I tell you Montreal will fall at a single blow, for there are only a few hundred English troops in the city. And I have agents there already, talking to the local Canadian militia who have no love for the *Anglais*. They will rebel, follow us to a man."

"And they will be reinforced by my troops. Since the British are raiding south from Canada, I have no compunction about invading your country."

"It is no invasion. You are most welcome. I see this action as brother aiding brother."

"We will have to cross the river. Where do you suggest that we land?"

He spread out a map and Papineau examined it closely, then pointed to a spot.

"Here. There are flat meadows and an old timber dock, just here, so landing from your ships will be quite easy. Also— this small forest shields the landing from the city which is around this bend in the river. It is not a long journey and my men know all the paths and roads. A march could be done during the night, to be in position to attack at dawn."

"Agreed. That is just what we will do."

A steam whistle sounded as the ironclads swung in toward the landing; the troops cheered and went down to greet them. Papineau's eyes were unfocused, as though he were seeing the incredible events of the future taking place before him.

"First Montreal—and then on to Quebec. We will succeed, we must succeed. Canada will be French once again."

General Johnston nodded as though he agreed. Though in truth he had little thought of Canada, French or not. He was fighting this war to lick the British. If an uprising in French Canada could help destroy the enemy, why then he was very much in favor of it. In war you use any weapon to hand. In this he was very much in agreement with his new commanding officer, General Sherman. You fight wars to win.

Far to the south, in a far warmer clime, a brief but fierce engagement was coming to an end. The only fortifications in the British West Indies were on the islands of Jamaica, Barbados and St. Lucia. The two smaller islands, important coaling stations, had fallen quickly to the American attackers who then pressed on to Jamaica. The headquarters of the Imperial West India Station had always been considered impregnable to attack by sea. The harbor of Kingston had heavily reinforced gun positions guarding its entrance; any enemy ship attempting to enter would be destroyed by fire.

Any wooden ship that is. General Ulysses S. Grant had experience at reducing gun batteries with ironclad gunboats, at Forts Henry and Donelson. Now he had the *Avenger* with her twin turrets, each mounting two 400-pound Parrott guns, far heavier than the guns he had used before. From the deck of the steam frigate *Roanoke* he had watched emplacement after emplacement pounded and destroyed. Some of the gun emplacements were shielded by stone walls that fell slowly when struck by solid cannonballs. For these the *Avenger* used explosive shells that blasted great openings in the defenses, destroyed the artillery behind them. The defenders kept firing to the last—and every cannonball bounced harmlessly from the ironclad's armor.

When the last gun was silenced the wooden-hulled *Roanoke* had led the troop transports into the harbor. Resistance was slight—as expected. Spies had revealed that the garrison in Newcastle consisted of only four companies of the West India Regiment. The other regiments, infantry, Royal Engineers and Royal Artillery had been sent to the American campaign. The remaining regiment had been dispersed about the island and could not be assembled in time to prevent the Americans from landing. When the port had been taken and Government House seized, Grant had finished his report on the operation and taken it personally to Commodore Goldsborough on *Avenger*.

"Well done Commodore, well done."

"Thank you General. I know that you have experience of combined army and navy operations, but this was an education to me. Is that the report for the President?"

"It is."

"Excellent. I shall have it telegraphed to him as soon as I reach Florida to take on coal. I will get my ammunition and powder that I need in Baltimore, then continue north. At full speed. It is hard to realize in these salubrious islands that winter has arrived."

"There is much to be done before the snow comes and the lakes and rivers freeze. General Sherman has his troops in position by now and is just awaiting word that you are on your way."

"I am, sir, I am—with victory in my sights!"

THE BATTLE OF QUEBEC

The air was filled with the clatter of the telegraphs, the scratch of the operators' pens as they transcribed the mysterious, but to them knowledgeable, clickings. Nicolay seized up one more sheet of paper and hurried to the President's side.

"Montreal has been seized with unexpected ease. The ironclads bombarded the Royal Battery below the city, and the Citadelle above. The battery was destroyed and the Citadelle so knocked about that Papineau's men took it on the first attack."

"What about those Martello towers that General Johnston was so concerned about?"

"Papineau's agents took care of that. The towers were manned by the local volunteer regiment of gunners—all French Canadian except for their officers. When the battle began they threw their officers out of the gun ports and turned their guns on the British. Within an hour of the first shot the defenders had either surrendered or ran. The Canadians are now in command."

"Wonderful—wonderful! The doorway to Canada opened up—while Grant and Goldsborough have cleansed the West Indies of the enemy presence. I hope that I am not tempting fate when I say that the end may be in sight. Perhaps with a few more military disasters the British will reconsider their delaying tactics in Berlin. They must surely begin to realize that their disastrous adventure here must eventually end."

"There is certainly no sign of it in their newspapers. You have seen the ones the French ship landed yesterday?"

"I have indeed. I was particularly enamored of that fine likeness of me with horns and pointed tail. My enemies in Congress will certainly have it mounted and framed."

The President stood and walked to the window, to look out at the bleak winter day. But he did not see it, saw instead the bright islands in the Caribbean no longer British, no longer a base for raids on the American mainland. Now Montreal taken as well. Like iron jaws closing, the military might of a reunited United States was cleansing the continent of the invaders.

"It will be done," the President said with grim determination. "General Sherman is in position?"

"He marched as soon as he received the word from General Grant that Jamaica had fallen and that *Avenger* was steaming north."

"The die is cast, Nicolay, and the end is nigh as the preachers say. We offered peace and they refused it. So now we end the war on our terms."

"Hopefully . . ."

"None of that. We have the right—and the might. Our future is in General Sherman's most competent hands. Our joined armies are firm in their resolve to rid this country—if not this continent—of the British. I suppose, in a way, we should be grateful to them. If they had not attacked us we would still be at war with the Southern states. A war of terrible losses now thankfully over. Perhaps all hostilities will soon end and we can begin to think of a land at peace again."

The kerosene light hung from the ridgepole of the tent, lighting up the maps between the two generals. Sherman leaned back and shook his head.

"General Lee—you should have my job, and not the other way around. Your plan is devastating in its simplicity, will be deadly and decisive when we strike the enemy."

"We worked this out together you will remember."

"I have assembled the forces—but the battle tactics are yours."

"Let us say I have had greater experience in the field—and almost all of the time defending against superior forces. A man grows wise under those circumstances. And you are also forgetting something, Cump. Neither I nor any other general could take your place in command of our joined forces. No other Union general could command Southern troops and Northern troops at the same time. What you did for us in Mississippi will never be forgotten."

"I did what had to be done."

"No other man did it," Lee said firmly. "No other man could have done it. And now that war between the states is over and, with God's aid, it will soon be nothing but a bitter memory."

Sherman nodded agreement. "May you be speaking only the truth. But I know the South almost as well as you do. Will there not be bitterness over the act to free the Negroes?"

Lee looked grim as he sat back in his camp chair, rubbed his gray beard in thought. "It will not be easy," he finally said. "It is easy enough for a soldier to do, to follow commands. So we have the military on the side of justice, on the enforcement of the new laws. And the money will help see that all of the changes go down easily since most of the planters have been bankrupted by the war. The money for their slaves will put them back on their feet."

"And then what?" Sherman persisted. "Who will pick the cotton? Free men—or free slaves?"

"That is something we must ponder upon—certainly the newspapers write of nothing else. But it *must* be done. Or all the death and destruction will have been in vain."

"It *will* be done," Sherman said with great sincerity. "Look how our men have fought side by side. If men who had recently been trying to kill each other can now fight shoulder-to-shoulder—certainly men who did not see war can do the same."

"Some did not feel that way when the Congress of the Confederacy met for the last time."

"Hotheads—how I despise them. And poor Jefferson Davis. Still attended by the doctors, his wound not healing well."

Lee sat quiet for long minutes, then shook his head. "All that we have talked about, I am sure that it will work out well. Money for the planters. Jobs for the returning soldiers as the South begins to industrialize. I think that all of these tangible things will work, that slavery will be ended once and forever in this country. It is the intangibles that worry me."

"I don't follow you."

"I am talking about the assumed authority of the white race. No matter how poor they are, what kind of trash, the Southerner doesn't think but *knows* that he is superior to the Negro just by the color of his skin. Once things have settled down and the men are home they are going to look at free blackmen walking the streets—and they will not like it. There will be trouble, certainly trouble."

Sherman could think of nothing to say. He had lived in the South long enough to know that Lee was speaking only the truth. They sat in silence then, wrapped in their own thoughts. Lee took out his watch and snapped the lid open.

"It will be dawn soon, time for me to join my troops," Lee said, climbing to his feet. Sherman stood as well—and impulsively put out his hand. Lee seized it and smiled in return.

"To victory in the morning," he said. "Destruction to the enemy."

After General Robert E. Lee left, General William Tecumseh Sherman looked once more at the maps, once more went over the details of the attack. His aide, Colonel Roberts, joined him.

From the south bank of the river the city of Quebec loomed up clearly in the light of dawn. Sherman lowered his telescope and looked again at the map.

"It is just a little over a hundred years since Wolfe took the city," he said. "Appears that little has changed."

"If anything the defenses are stronger," Colonel Roberts said, pointing at the upper city on the headland of Cape Diamond. "The walls and gun batteries have been built up since then. I would say that they are impregnable to frontal attack."

"A frontal attack was never considered."

"I know—but there was ice on the river last night."

"Just a thin film. The St. Lawrence rarely freezes before the middle of December, almost two weeks from now. What we must do will be done today."

"At least we don't have to land men at Wolfe's Cove and

have them climb the path to the Plains of Abraham—as Wolfe did."

Sherman did not smile; he found nothing humorous in war. "We shall not vary from our agreed plan of operation unless there is sufficient reason. Are the ironclads in position?"

"They went by during the night. Shore observers report that they are anchored at the assigned sites."

"General Lee's divisions?"

"Cleared out some British positions on the Isle of Orléans above the city. His troops are now in position there and on the St. Charles side of the city."

"Good. There is enough light now. Start the attack on the gun positions at Point Lévis. Report to me when they are taken and our guns are in position."

Sherman raised his telescope again as the telegraph rattled the command. An instant later the deep boom of cannon could be heard to the south, mixed with the crackle of small arms fire.

The British would be expecting an attack from the north, across the Plains of Abraham, the flattest and easiest approach to Quebec. Their scouts would have reported the advance of General Wallace's divisions from that direction. So far, everything was going as planned. The armies north and south of the city, the ironclads in the river, the guns all in position.

There were shouts from the field behind the telegraph tent, a rattling and clatter as the wagons swung off the road. Almost before they had stopped the trained team of soldiers had started to pull out the crumpled yellow form and stretch it along the ground. Soon the sharp stench of sulfuric acid cut through the air as it was poured into the containers of iron filings. The lids slammed down and within minutes the hydrogen gas generated by the chemical reaction was being pumped through the rubberized canvas hose. As the balloon inflated more and more men grabbed onto the lines: it took thirty of them to keep it from breaking free. When the line was attached to the cage the observer and the telegraph operator climbed in. As the observation balloon rose the telegraph wire dangled down to the ground, all eight hundred feet of it.

General Sherman nodded approval. Now he had the eyes of

a bird, something generals had been praying for for centuries. The iron frame of the telegraph in the wagon tapped out the first reports from the operator above.

It appeared that everything was going smoothly and to plan.

Within an hour the American cannon, and the captured British cannon, were firing their first shells into the besieged city.

GENERAL SHERMAN'S EYE IN THE SKY

"Can't anything be done about that bloody contraption?" General Harcourt said, then stepped back as a shell struck the parapet nearby sending stone fragments in all directions. The yellow observation balloon hung in the still air, looking down into the besieged city.

"Sorry sir," his aide said. "Out of range of our rifles—and no way to hit it with a cannon."

"But the blighter is looking right down into our positions. They can mark the fall of every shell . . ."

A messenger ran up, saluting as he came. "Captain Gratton, sir. Reports troops and guns from the north. A field battery already firing."

"I knew it! Plains of Abraham. They can read history books as well. But I am no Montcalm. We're not leaving our defensive positions to be shot down. Going to see for myself." General Harcourt swung into his saddle and galloped off through the city streets, with his staff right behind him.

The city of Quebec was now surrounded by guns. Those parts of it that could not be reached by gunfire from the opposite banks of the river were attacked by ironclads in the river. Some of these had mortars that lifted a 500-pound shell into a lazy arc up above the battlements, to drop down thunderously into the troops behind it. No part of the defenses was safe from the heavy bombardment of the big guns.

The ironclads were constantly on the move, seeking out new targets. Three of them, those most heavily armed, came together at exactly eleven o'clock, leaving the St. Lawrence and entering the St. Charles River that passed the eastern side of the city. At that same moment the yellow form of a second observation balloon rose from behind the protection of the trees and soared high into the air behind the warships.

The cannonade increased, explosive shells dropping with great accuracy on the defenses on this flank of the city. The telegraphed messages from the observation balloon were passed on to the gunships by semaphore.

When the bombardment was at its fiercest, the battlements blinded by the pall of smoke, General Robert E. Lee's men attacked. They had landed on the city side of the river during the hours of darkness and had remained in concealment under the trees. The dawn bombardment had kept the British heads down so their presence had not been detected. The Southern force reached the crumbled defenses just as the British General Harcourt, on the far side of the city, was told of the new attack. Even before he could send reinforcements the attacking riflemen had gone to earth in the rubble and were firing, picking off any British soldier who stood in their way.

A second wave of gray-clad soldiers went through them, and still another. The rebel yell sounded from within the walls of Quebec; the breech had been made. More and more reinforcements poured in behind them, spreading out and firing as they attacked.

They could not be stopped. By the time General Sherman had boarded the ironclad to be ferried across the river there was no doubt of the outcome.

An entire division of Southern troops was now inside the city walls, spreading out and advancing. The defending general would have to take men from his western defenses. General Lew Wallace's division had a company of engineers with them. Coal miners from Pennsylvania. Charges of black powder would bring down the gates there. Trapped between the pincers of the two armies and hopelessly outnumbered, the only recourse for the British was to surrender or die.

Within an hour the white flag had been raised.

Quebec had fallen. The last British bastion in Southern Canada was in American hands.

VICTORY SO SWEET

The cabinet meeting had been called for ten o'clock. It was well past that now and the President still had not arrived. He was scarcely missed as the excited men called out to each other, then turned their attention to Secretary of the Navy Welles when he came in, asking for the latest news from the fleet.

"Victory, just victory. The enemy subdued and overcome by force of arms, crushed and defeated. The islands of what were once called the British West Indies are now in our hands."

"What shall we call them then?" Edwin Stanton, the Secretary of War said. "The American East Indies?"

"Capital idea," William Seward said. "As Secretary of State I so name them."

There was a rumble of laughter. Even the stern Welles chanced a tiny smile as he ticked off points on his fingers.

"Firstly, the British are deprived of the only bases they have close to our shores. They have no port for their ships to be stationed in—whatever ships they have left—nor coal available for their ships' boilers should they hazard more attacks from across the ocean. The murderous raids on our coastal cities must now cease."

"But they can still raid from Canada." Attorney General Bates was always one to find the worst in anything.

"If you substitute *did* for *still* you would be closer to the truth," Edwin Stanton said. "The successful rebellion by the French nationalists has deprived them of their base in Montreal. The enemy flees before the advance of General Sherman's victorious troops. Even as we speak he is drawing the noose

319

around Quebec. When that noose snaps tight the British are doomed. Their troops will have to flee north and east to Nova Scotia where they hold their last naval base at Halifax . . ."

He broke off as the door to the Cabinet Room opened and President Lincoln entered. Just behind him was Judah P. Benjamin.

"Gentlemen," Lincoln said, seating himself at the head of the table. "You all know Mr. Benjamin. Please welcome him now as our newest cabinet minister—the Secretary for the Southern States."

Benjamin bowed his head slightly at the murmured greetings, shook the Secretary of State's hand when Seward generously extended it, took his appointed seat.

"In previous meetings," Lincoln said, "we have discussed the necessity of representation from the South. A few days ago Mr. Benjamin stepped down as appointed leader of the Confederacy when the last meeting of the Congress of the Confederacy was convened. He will tell you about that."

There was a tense silence as Judah P. Benjamin spoke to them in his rich Louisiana drawl, a tone of unhappiness in his words.

"I will not lie to you and say that it was a pleasant time. The more level-headed gentlemen of the South were no longer present, some of them are already here in Washington and sitting in the House of Representatives. I will not go so far as to say that only the hotheads and the firm-minded were left, but there was indeed a good deal of acrimony. Some of them felt that the honor of the South had been betrayed. Motions were made and passions ran high. I am sorry to report that two more Congressmen were arrested when they threatened violence. In the end I had to bring in veteran troops who, having seen the bloody hell of war, would not let these men stand in the way of peace. Their commander was General Jackson who stood like a stone wall before the dissenters. Unmoved by pleas or curses, firm in his resolve, he saw to it that the last meeting of the Confederate Congress ended peacefully."

He stopped for a moment seeing something they did not see. A country he had served, now vanished forever. He saw the South perhaps, soon to be changed beyond all recognition. He frowned and shook his head.

"Do not think that I weep for the fallen Confederacy. I do not weep, but can only hope, pray, that we can put the division of the states behind us. I ended the meeting, had those ejected who tried to remain, declared that the Confederate Congress had now ceased to exist. And then had the building sealed. I think I have done my part in the healing process. I now call upon you gentlemen, and the Congress of the United States to do yours. Keep the promises you have made. See that there will be an honest peace. If you do not do that—why then I have been part of the biggest betrayal in the history of mankind."

"We will endeavor with all our will and strength to do just that," the President said. "Now that the states of the South are sending representatives to Congress the wounds of our recent war must heal. But there will be problems in the process, none here would be so foolish as to deny that. During the past weeks I have worked closely with Judah P. Benjamin and have formed a bond. We are of like mind in many ways, and believe in the same future.

"To assure that future we must speak as one. This Cabinet must be firm in its resolve. Reuniting this country and binding up our wounds will not be easy. There are already reports of friction in the Southern states, about the purchase of slaves. We want to make sure that if and when problems arise they can be dealt with by Mr. Benjamin, who is not only knowledgeable in these matters, but is also respected and trusted in all parts of the former Confederacy."

"There will always be hotheads and malcontents," Benjamin said, "Particularly in the South where honor is held in great esteem and blood does run warm. The troubles that the President refers to are in Mississippi and I have already had correspondence about the matter. Simply put, it is the Reconstruction Act. While the details of purchase of slaves is spelled out, the prices to be paid are sufficiently vague to cause trouble. I intend to go to Mississippi at the soonest opportunity to thrash out details on the spot. We must make policy that is favorable and agreeable to all. If I can produce a workable agreement with the Mississippi planters I know that other plantation owners throughout the South will adhere to whatever rules we draw up."

"Excellent," Lincoln said. "This is the keystone of our agreement and it must work and work well." He folded his hands before him in an unconscious attitude of prayer. "Our problems will multiply with time. In the past we have thought only of survival, of winning the war. With the armistice we ended one war to enable us to fight another. Here too we had but a single track to follow. We had to destroy our enemy and force him from our land. With the aid of our Creator we are doing that. But what of the future?"

He closed his eyes wearily, then snapped them open and sat erect. "We are no longer on a single track. Ahead of us are branch lines and switches that lead in many different ways. The mighty train of the Union must find its way through all hazards to a triumphant future."

"And just exactly what will that be?" William Seward said. There would be a presidential election and his ambition for that office was well known.

"We don't exactly know, Mr. Seward," Lincoln said. "We must seek guidance in that matter. Not from the Lord this time, but from a man of great wisdom. He has shared this knowledge with Mr. Davis and myself, and recently with Mr. Benjamin, and was of great aid in preparing the Emancipation Bill. I have asked him here today to speak with you all, to answer grave questions like the last one. We will send for him now." He nodded to his secretary who slipped out of the room.

"We have heard of your adviser. English is he not?" There was dark suspicion in the Attorney General's voice.

"He is," Lincoln said firmly. "As was this nation's other great political adviser, Tom Paine. And, I believe, as were the founding fathers of the Republic. That is the ones who weren't Scotch or Irish. Or Welsh."

Bates scowled at the laughter that followed, but held his peace, unconvinced.

"Mr. John Stuart Mill, gentlemen," Lincoln said as Hay showed him in.

"You can read the future?" the Attorney General asked. "You can predict what events will and will not happen?"

"Of course not, Mr. Bates. But I can point out pitfalls in your path to the future, and point out as well achievable goals." He looked around calmly, very much in control of himself and of his words. "I wish to get to know you all much better. You gentlemen are the ones who will shape the future, for you and the President are the guiding stars of this country. So I will speak generally of these goals and what can realistically be obtained, and will then be happy to answer particular questions about your aspirations.

"I will speak to you of the importance of representative government, of the necessity of freedom of discussion. I am opposed to uneducated democracy, as I am sure you all are. These are abstractions that must never be forgotten, goals that must be achieved. But your first goal must be economic strength. You will win this military war. You will find it harder to win the peace, to win the economic war that must follow."

Stanton's brow was furrowed. "Do you speak in riddles?" he asked.

"Not at all. When you fought this war against the British you also fought a war against the British Empire. Have you ever looked at a map of this Empire, where the countries that sustain it are marked in pink? That map is pink, gentleman, and it is pink right around the world. There is a 25,000 mile circuit of the world where the British flag flies. The pink covers one-fifth of the Earth's surface, and Queen Victoria rules one-quarter of the world's population. The Empire is strong so you must be stronger. I know my countrymen and I know they will not suffer a defeat of the nature that you have forced upon them. I do not know what action they will take, but they will be back. So you must be prepared. The easy days in the South are at an end—although I realize that much of the way of the South is a myth and her people actually labor well and long. Your land is rich and your people, North and South, know the meaning of work. But the South must be just as industrialized as is the North. Subsistence farming does not make a country rich. The South must produce more than cotton to add to the national wealth. If you have the will you have the means.

There is wealth in the soil, wealth to feed all of this country's citizens. Wealth as well in iron, copper, gold.

"You must take this wealth and build a strong America. You can do this if you have the will. Seize the opportunity and lead the world by your example. The people of oppressed countries will see in you a glowing example of representative government. And, as my dear wife and daughter have pointed out to me, half of the citizens of the world are women. I owe much to them. Whoever, either now or hereafter, may think of me and the work I have done, must never forget that it is the product not of one intellect and conscience, but of three. Therefore you must one day consider the cause of universal franchisement."

"Would you make that clearer?" Salmon Chase rumbled. "I do not understand your meaning."

"Then I will elucidate. All here must surely believe in the bond that unites man and woman. Marriage is an institution that unites both sexes equally. For one cannot exist without the other. Women of intellect can match their male counterparts. They are equal before the law. They can own property. But in one thing they are unequal. They cannot vote."

"Nor shall they ever!" Edward Bates called out.

"Why not, may I ask?" Mill said calmly.

"The reasons are well known. Their physical inferiority to men. Their nerves, their inconsistency."

Mill would not be moved. "I feel that you belittle them, sir. But I do not wish argument now. I simply say that one day universal enfranchisement must be considered if this country is to be a true democracy representing all of its citizens. Not right now, but the issue cannot be avoided forever."

"In the South we hold our women in great esteem," Judah P. Benjamin said. "Though I hesitate to say that allowing them to vote would affect that esteem in a negative manner. And if one follows your logic to the very end—why you will next be thinking of allowing the Negro to vote?"

"Yes. In the long run the ideal universal suffrage must be taken under consideration as well. To be truly free a man must be sure that others are free. When others are chattels, either women or Negroes or any other group, then freedom is not complete. A true democracy extends freedom to all of its members."

He paused for breath and touched his kerchief to his lips. Before he could continue there was a discreet knock at the door and secretary Hay entered.

"President Lincoln, members of the Cabinet, please forgive this interruption. But I know that you will want to hear the contents of this telegram." He lifted it and read.

"Quebec is taken, the enemy is routed. Signed, General Sherman."

In the silence that followed the President's quiet words were clearly heard by all present.

"It is over then. The war is won."

A UNION TRIUMPH

Oh the sound of it! Oh the glory of it!

Men shouted, children shrieked, churchbells rang on every side. People cheered themselves hoarse, then croaked on, happily unaware.

Victory shouted aloud, cried aloud, sung aloud. The British power broken with the fall of Quebec. The streets filled as the word was passed. *Victory!* The day, which had started damp and cold, turned warm with the warmth of victory, shone with the sun of success.

The crowds gathered outside the White House, calling loudly for the President.

"I must go out and talk to them, Mary," Lincoln said.

"Not in that old wrinkled black suit, not on this day of jubilee."

She prevailed upon the President to put aside his soiled and rusty black suit for at least this one day. The new suit was black swallow-tailed and made of the finest broadcloth, his linen shirt white and crisp, his foulard the finest silk from Paris.

"I am so proud of you, Father," Mary said, clasping her hands and smiling. He returned her smile, pleased to see it there, for she had rarely smiled since Willie's death. She had also abandoned her black garb, at least for this day, and was wearing a white silk ball dress decorated with hundreds of small black flowers.

They went hand in hand to the balcony and the crowd roared its approval. There was nothing he could say: if he spoke none could possibly hear. But they waved and smiled until, after some minutes, they felt the chill. Also the first of many carriages was coming up the drive as they went inside.

The Cabinet members had found their way to the Green Room, where they were joined by a troop of senior Senators from the Hill. The walls echoed with the sounds of mutual admiration and good cheer. Hay pushed his way through and caught Lincoln's eye.

"It's the Russian Ambassador."

"The baron with the unpronounceable name?"

"Yes, sir. Baron Stoeckl. He wants to offer his congratulations."

"After what the British did to the Russians in Crimea I imagine he does."

The baron was elegantly garbed and bore a soup plate–sized golden decoration around his neck. He seized Lincoln's hand and worked it like a pump handle, so strenuously did he do this that his wig threatened to be displaced.

"May I extend my congratulations, Mr. President, my heartiest congratulations on your victory in the field of battle." He stepped aside and indicated the elegantly garbed military man behind him. "May I introduce you to Admiral Paul S. Makhimov who is here with flagship, a coincidental but wonderfully timed visit."

The admiral had a calloused hand and a firm grip, but a limited command of English. "You sink the sheeps, I sink *Angleski* sheep. *Da!*"

"The admiral is referring to his victories at sea during the last war."

Lincoln extracted his hand with some difficulty and nodded agreement. "We have indeed sunk a great number of ships."

A touch on his arm drew him away. "Mrs. Lincoln would like you to join her in welcoming the guests," Nicolay said.

As more and more well-wishers crowded into the White House an impromptu reception line was being formed. Lincoln greeted them all with a quick word or two and a handshake. Mary, who did not relish the thought of touching so many people, held a bouquet before her in her folded hands. Nodded and smiled.

Politicians and their ladies for the most part, although there were some generals, and the one Russian admiral; most of the military officers were still in the field or at sea. There were of course the foreign dignitaries and ambassadors, as well as local residents of note.

"It is a proud day," Miss Bettie Duvall said.

"It certainly is," Mary Todd Lincoln said, her voice now more Southern-Todd than Yankee-Lincoln. "Have you been keeping well?"

The softness of her words belied the sharpness of their content. After first being put under house arrest in Washington for the outspokenness of her Confederate views, Miss Duvall had finally been sent south along with the widow Greenhow, who now stood beside her. This was after it was discovered that not only were they outspoken sympathizers—but that they had been active as well as spies for the South. Imprisoning women of their class and advanced years had been out of the question. Sending them back to the impoverished wartime South had been punishment enough.

"Most well. Our boys have done it—haven't they?"

"Most certainly they have. Soldiers of the North and South fighting side by side to hurl back a foreign invader. It is a wonderful day."

They all smiled and, at least for the moment, the past was put behind them. This was a night of victory and not of malice.

The room was soon crowded and hot and Mary's head was beginning to hurt. She whispered to her husband and slipped away. He shook the proffered hands diligently, but scarcely looked at the visitors.

"A day of victory for American arms," the officer said. Lincoln glanced down at the short, uniformed man standing before him, shook hands once, then let go.

"I sincerely hope that you have recovered from your fever, General McClellan."

"In every way," Little Napoleon said firmly. "And prepared once again to serve my country in the field of battle." No hint in his voice of his procrastination in avoiding battle, or his losses when battle was finally and hesitantly joined.

"Indeed I am sure you are. But I relinquished the title of Commander-in-Chief that I assumed with your illness. That title is now held by one far more efficient than I in military prowess." With perhaps a suggestion in his voice that General Sherman was far more efficient than McClellan as well. "You must address yourself to our most victorious commander when he returns from the battlefront."

Everyone wanted to talk to the President this night, even former Navy Lieutenant Gustavus Fox who, intelligence services put aside for the moment, was in naval uniform to honor the occasion. He signed to Lincoln as he took the arm of a short man in dark garb, who carried an ebony cane as well as an air of calculated indifference.

"Mr. President. May I present you to the new French ambassador, the Duc de Valenciennes."

The duke bent very slightly from the waist in condescending acknowledgment. Lincoln shook his soft hand like a pump handle before the Frenchman could extricate it.

Fox smiled and said, "The Duke was explaining to me just why his country has landed another thirty thousand troops at the Mexican port of Vera Cruz just a short while ago."

Valenciennes dismissed this minutia with a flick of his hand. "A matter of business only. The Mexican government has not been honoring its commitments nor repaying certain loans to the French."

"You go about your bill collecting in a most impressive way," Lincoln said.

"It was on the fourteenth of December last year that French troops landed in Vera Cruz, was it not?" Fox asked.

This was also dismissed with a trifling wave. "Business, just business. We were aided by the Spanish who were calling in the same loan. As well as, I believe, some seven hundred British troops. Also there to collect a loan."

Lincoln nodded. "I do remember a bit about that. But the British were causing a lot of trouble about one of their ships, the *Trent*, at the time so I let my attention waver. But you have all of my attention now. I do believe that Mexico has a new constitution that is based on the American one—is that right, Mr. Fox?"

"Indeed it is. Done in 1857."

"Which I guess makes her a sister republic. Thirty thousand troops is an awful lot of bill collectors calling on our sister. I think that the Monroe Doctrine covers matters of this kind. Mr. Fox, could I have a complete report about this?"

"Of course."

"My congratulations upon your military victories," Valenciennes said, suddenly eager to change the subject. "Might I meet with your Mrs. Lincoln to add to those congratulations?"

"I think she has retired, but I will be sure and tell her what you said."

Fox led him away and Lincoln smiled. While his attention was distracted by the war with the British, there had been trouble coming in through the back door of the United States. Well, he was looking the right way now.

It was well past midnight by this time and the excitement showed no sign of abating. Lincoln worked his way through the crowds of well-wishers and climbed the stairs, heard the clacking of the telegraph from the office beside his own. Nicolay was there sorting through a thick wad of papers.

"Mostly congratulations, sir," he said. "As well as suggestions of what we should do to the defeated enemy, some of them very instructive. And the usual entreaties for appointments."

Lincoln settled into his armchair with a sigh. "What of the prisoners? How many thousands do we have?"

"Not tallied yet—but there are sure to be even more after the fall of Quebec. The Irish prisoners have welcomed our farming program and will stay in this country. They feel that they would be far better off working the land here rather than back in their impoverished country. Though some are too young for heavy work I am sure that they will all fit in. There are Irish boy soldiers of only eight and ten. Volunteered for the British Army they say. That or starve. There is still no decision on the English prisoners."

"What do you mean?"

"The offer of farm work and the possibility of homesteading was meant only for the Irish. But there are now English volunteers who prefer staying on in this country to returning home."

"Let's have them, I say. One's good as another. But I am to bed, Nico. It has been quite a day."

"It certainly has."

But not quite over yet. Gideon Welles was waiting in the president's office, stroking his great fluffy beard as he looked out of the window. He turned when Lincoln came in. "A day that will live forever in history." Being a former journalist, he sometimes spoke in newspaper headlines.

"It certainly will. It has been a long time since the British have been so thoroughly beaten."

"It is the first time, I do believe. England was last invaded in 1066. Since then she has not been invaded and has fought a good number of wars. She gobbled up Wales, Cornwall, Scotland and Ireland and became Great Britain. Not satisfied with that she has plundered her way right around the world and in doing so has founded the British Empire. I fear for our navy, Mr. President."

"As Secretary you should. But is there anything in particular that troubles you?"

"Peacetime bothers me. We have just laid the keels of eight more iron ships. Will there be the money available to build them?"

"There must be. We will tread softly in this world—but we will not go unarmed. A strong navy and a strong army will assure our safety."

"People will complain about taxes and Congress will listen to them."

"Congress will listen to me as well. No one in the Cabinet is in any doubt about our economic needs for the future, that Mr. Mill has pointed out."

"There are distant rumbles of discontent."

"As long as they stay that way, why fine. But none shall stay the course of the mighty battleship America as she sails into her successful future. Those that man her must speak with one voice, seek one goal."

"They must sail with a fair breeze—or jump overboard."

"Precisely. There have been Cabinet changes in the past—" Lincoln turned to address his Secretary of War, who was just now entering the office, "you will not forget your predecessor Simon Cameron."

Stanton laughed. "Nor will I forget his fate—ambassador to Russia."

"A well deserved fate as you know, since you had to clean up the mess he made of the navy. But let us leave these matters for the morn—and enjoy this night of victory. When the Cabinet meets tomorrow it will be time enough to discuss our peacetime future."

DAY OF VICTORY

The warship *Avenger* arrived just two days before General Sherman. She made landfall on the Nova Scotia coast at Cape Sable, then steamed north. Her arrival at the seaport of Halifax caused instant alarm. The two British frigates in the port raised steam and headed out to sea as soon as the American warship was identified. If there had been some wind they might have escaped, using a combination of screw and sail. But it was a still, cold December day and their sails hung in limp festoons. The newly-built *Avenger* had engines that were far superior to theirs. Once again iron mastered wood and the *Chatelain* was battered and wrecked after a single barrage from the warship's two turrets. The master of the British frigate did not strike his colors even though nothing could be gained by fighting on. *Avenger* did not bother to ask the frigate to strike and disdained further battle to go in pursuit of her sister ship. The captain of the *Courageous* was more prudent, or practical, or simply realized that nothing could be gained in unequal battle. He struck as soon as the first shots had been fired. A boarding party was sent to her and took command, bringing the frigate back into the port she had so recently fled. *Avenger* looked on, guns ready, as the captured ship hove to, then threw a line to the battered *Chatelain* and took her under tow. Following orders the *Courageous* stopped her engines as soon as they had entered the outer harbor, then dropped anchor there. *Avenger* passed them and moved slowly toward the shore. As soon as she was within range the batteries of the harbor defenses opened fire.

Cannonballs threw up columns of water in the sea around

the American ironclad—and bounced off of her eight-inch-thick armor. Seemingly indifferent to the attack the *Avenger* did not return the fire of the batteries as she patrolled the waterfront. Nor did she fire on the merchantmen and transports tied up there. Instead she moved to the center of the harbor where she dropped anchor and came to rest.

The nearest gun battery at the harbor mouth fired again. This time there was a response. The 400-pound shells from a single turret blew the battery into a jagged ruin in an instant. No other batteries fired.

"What the blazes is that thing doing?" the Duke of Cambridge asked. No one volunteered an answer. He stood on the balcony of his headquarters in Government House, wrapped in furs to ward off the bitter chill. He had only arrived a few days previously to take charge of the American operation. Urged to do so by his cousin, the Queen. The presence of the Commander-in-Chief of the British Army may have helped morale and rallied the troops some; it had had no apparent effect upon the operation of the war.

All the news was bad.

"First that disastrous adventure in the American South. Naval defeat in the Potomac. General Champion killed in battle. Our West Indies bases taken—Quebec fallen. And now this. You, Clive, you're supposed to be the brainy one. Can you explain it?"

Brigadier Clive Somerville hesitated. The answer seemed obvious enough.

"Go on, then," the Duke urged.

"Well, Sir—I imagine that warship is the cork in the bottle. The Yankee ironclads were reported in the St. Lawrence heading for the sea the last we heard."

"The ice will stop them."

"Not hard enough or thick enough yet to stop a steam powered iron ship. And I am sure that the enemy troops are marching close behind them."

"Cork in the bottle, you say?"

"Yes, Sir. That armored ship of the line could bombard the city, drive us out if they wanted to. I think that they like us just as we are."

The Duke of Cambridge looked at the dark form of the warship again and shivered. "Damn cold out here. Let's to the fire. Someone find me a large brandy." He led the way inside.

Soon after dawn the next morning the small flotilla of ironclads appeared out of the mist. They anchored next to the *Avenger*, which launched a boat as soon as they had dropped anchor. A portly form in a heavy cloak climbed slowly down and was transported to the leading ironclad. Very soon after that a boat started toward shore. A soldier in the bow held a white flag aloft.

"Send someone down there," the Duke ordered and reached for his brandy glass. His staff officers talked uneasily among themselves as they waited. The Duke was still seated when the messenger returned, followed by a gray-garbed officer. He was turned out smartly in a gray uniform, gleaming boots, gold sash with a bold feather in his hat. He stopped before the Duke and saluted.

"General Robert E. Lee," he said. "Of the United States Army."

"What do you want?" the Duke snapped.

Lee looked him up and down coldly as he sprawled in his chair. There was more than a little contempt in his voice when he spoke.

"I want to speak to the commanding officer here. Who are you?"

"Watch your tone or I'll have you run through!"

"This is the Duke of Cambridge," Brigadier Somerville said quietly. "He is Commander-in-Chief of the army."

"Well now, I think that will surely do for being in charge. I have a message from General Sherman, Commander-in-Chief of our forces. He would like to meet with you to discuss terms of surrender."

"I'll see him in hell first!" the Duke shouted, draining his glass and hurling it into the fireplace. Lee was unmoved, his soft Southern voice unperturbed.

"If you refuse this meeting all of the ships, military and civilian, in this harbor will be destroyed. This city will be burnt. Our army, less than a day's march away, will make prisoners of any survivors and we will send them in chains to the

United States. I must advise you that you have no choice in
this matter."

Brigadier Somerville broke the impasse once again.

"The Duke will see General Sherman here . . ."

"No." All warmth was gone from Lee's voice now. "The
meeting will take place at the waterfront in exactly one-half
hour's time. The Duke is instructed to have no more than
three officers with him."

Lee did not salute again but turned on his heel and stamped
from the room. The fire crackled as an ember burst: this was
the only sound.

On the bridge of *Avenger* Commander Goldsborough glanced
up at the ship's clock, then raised his telescope again. "Ahh,
there at last. A portly officer wearing furs, three others."

"Time to go," Sherman said grimly.

The two boats moved swiftly to the shore. There was some
delay as Commodore Goldsborough was half-lifted ashore.
Then more than a dozen officers stepped onto the dock before
General Sherman appeared. They opened ranks, then strode
behind him as he walked across the cold stone towards the
waiting men. A thin scud of snow swirled around them.

"I am General William Tecumseh Sherman, Commander-
in-Chief of the United States Combined Forces. I understand
that you are the Duke of Cambridge, Commander-in-Chief of
the British Army."

The chill air had damped some of the Duke's bellicosity.
He nodded abruptly.

"Good. The only course open to you is unconditional surrender. You will be relieved of all your guns, weapons and
arms. If you do that you have my word that all of your men
and officers will be allowed to board the transports and will be
allowed to return to England. You and your staff will not go.
You will accompany me to Washington for discussions with
the American government about war reparations. There will
be payments in gold as partial recompense for the destruction
you caused to American cities, as well as the unwarranted
deaths of her citizens."

"I'll see you in hell first!"

"No you will not." Sherman barely controlled his fury, his transparent eyes cold as death. "You brought this war to our shores and will pay the price for that audacious act. Your forces in the field are destroyed or captured, your naval bases taken. The war is over."

The Duke was now blazing with fury. "The war will never be over as far as I am concerned. Hear me you contemptible Yankee upstart—you are not taking on some pipsqueak little country. You have offended the greatest country in the world and the greatest Empire. You do that at your peril."

"Our peril? Has it not been drawn to your attention that you have lost this war? As you have lost here on this continent before. If you are any student of history you will know that America was once a British colony. You were forcefully ejected from our shores. You forgot that lesson in 1812. And now you have forgotten it yet again. We fought the Revolutionary War under many different flags and banners. Now we have but one for we are united as we never have been before. But I must remind you of one of our revolutionary battle flags. It depicted a snake with the legend 'Don't Tread on Me'. Remember that for the future. You have tread and you have been defeated. To save America we have taken up arms against invasion and hurled you back.

"To save America we will do the same again, whenever we are threatened."

General Sherman stepped aside until he was facing the other three officers.

"You have an hour to decide. One hour. Then the bombardment begins. There will be no more discussion of this matter. Your surrender is unconditional."

He started to turn away, then swung back. There was no warmth in his smile or his words.

"I personally prefer the second way. For the sake of my country I would happily blow you all away, every ship, every soldier, every officer, then blow away your Politicians and your Queen.

"The choice, gentlemen, is yours."

The snow grew heavier, the day darker, the wind more chill as the American officers returned to their ship and the British officers were left in silence.

DAY'S END

The Duke of Cambridge had stayed in his cabin ever since the Cunard steamer had departed from Washington City. Stayed below in the stuffy fug, looking unseeingly at the shadows thrown by the paraffin light rocking in its gimbals. Only when the swaying of the lamp became more regular, the movement of the ship rolling steadily from side to side, did he grow conscious of his surroundings. This was the motion of the great Atlantic rollers; they must be out of the river now and standing out to sea. He rose, tightened his collar and put on his jacket, went up on deck.

The air was warm and salty, a June day to relish. Brigadier Somerville was standing at the rail; he turned and saluted when the Duke came up to him. They leaned on the wooden rail and looked in silence at the American coastline vanishing behind them. The Duke turned away and grimaced, preferring instead to look at the sails and the laboring sailors rather than the shores of the United States.

"Let the political johnnies take over," he said. "I have done my bit. It has been jaw-jaw for far too long now."

"You have indeed done your bit, Your Grace. You extracted terms far better than those originally proposed."

"Like extracting teeth at times—and just as painful. But don't diminuate your contribution, Somerville. I faced them across the conference table. But it was your words and your arguments that carried the day."

"Happy to be of service, sir," he said, bowing slightly and changing the subject. The ruling classes of Britain looked down upon the brainy ones and thought little of a man who

339

flaunted his intelligence. "The armies are safely home, prisoners soon to be released, a messy affair there at an end. As you said, the politicians can cross the T's and dot the I's. The entire matter is well ended."

"Is it?" The Duke hawked deeply and spat into the ocean. "Speaking from a military point of view it was a disaster. Our invading armies thrown back. Disaster at sea. Canada all but lost to us—"

"The English in Canada are loyal. They will not join the French in this new republic."

"They will be hard-pressed not to. And if they go—what do we have left then on this continent? The frozen colony of Newfoundland, that is what. Not what one would call an overwhelming presence in the New World."

"But we have peace—is that not enough?"

"Peace? We have been at war ever since my cousin first mounted the throne. Queen Victoria's little wars, I have heard them called. Wars of necessity as the British Empire expanded around the world. We have won them all. Lost a battle here and there—but never a war. And now this. It leaves a bad taste in one's mouth."

"We should treasure the peace—"

"Should we?" The Duke of Cambridge rounded on Somerville, his jaw tight with anger. "If you believe that, well then, sir, you are in a damned minority, sir. The American newspapers crow about their great victory and the people strut about like cocks on a dungheap. While at home there is a continuous growl of resentment that will not cease. Yes, this armistice and this sordid peace were forced upon us. But this does not mean that we have lost the greater battle of Great Britain's place in this world. Our country is intact, our empire fertile and flourishing. We have been insulted, all of us—insulted!"

"But there is nothing that can be done now. The war is over, the soldiers returned, the reparations to be paid . . ."

"It is never over—not while the stigma of defeat is upon us. Keels of ironclad warships are being laid even as we speak. In Woolwich the forges glare as guns and other weapons are produced. And our people are not happy, not happy indeed."

Brigadier Somerville spoke quietly, tonelessly, attempting

not to state his own position in this matter. "Then what do you suggest, sir? We will rearm, that is being done now as you say. Armies can be raised, armed and made ready. But then what? There is no cause to start another war."

"No cause? You have witnessed our humiliation. Something must be done. What—I don't know. But we shall confer upon this, yes we shall. That pipsqueak general, what was his name? Sherman. Had the bloody nerve to threaten a peer of the realm. Bloody snake and don't tread on me and all of that. Well I have tread on many a snake and feel no fear in doing so again."

The Duke turned and looked back at America now vanished in the hazy horizon. He felt the blood rise to suffuse his face as he remembered the defeats and the humiliations. It was more than one could possibly bear. His anger bubbled over and he shook his fist in the direction of that vile country.

"Something can be done—something *will* be done. This matter is not over yet. That I promise with all my soul and body. This is not the end."

AFTERWORD

Stars & Stripes Forever could be a true story.

The events depicted here actually happened. President Lincoln did have a very secret, secret service that was headed by the Assistant Secretary of the Navy, Gustavus Vasa Fox.

A Captain Schultz, purporting to be from the Russian Navy, did turn over plans of the British breech-loading Armstrong cannon to the gunsmith, Robert Parker Parrott.

The British government, newspapers and public were incensed by the *Trent* Affair. That government did send troops and guns to Canada and seriously considered the invasion of the United States.

The speeches reported here, as well as the newspaper articles, are all a matter of record. The threatening headlines and bombastic newspaper articles published during the crisis appeared exactly as they are quoted.

Captain Meagher, the Fenian rebel, was indeed condemned to be hung, drawn and quartered by the British government. The sentence was later changed to transportation for life to Australia. He was imprisoned in Tasmania, but escaped and went to America where he served in the Union Army.

During the War of 1812 the British did issue the order, in the very words recorded here, to land and destroy property and take the lives of American civilians.

The United States Sharpshooting Corps were excellent shots. Enemy cannon were destroyed by them in the manner indicated here.

Jefferson Davis's letter to the Governor of Louisiana is a matter of record.

There were over 22,000 soldiers killed at the Battle of Shiloh.

The battle between the *Monitor* and the *Virginia* was the first encounter by two iron ships in the history of warfare.

Lincoln's words on slavery are true and taken from the records. John Stuart Mill's views on liberty, on American democracy and the state of decay in Europe are quoted at length from his works.

The American War Between the States was the first modern war. Rapid-firing, breech-loading guns and rifles were introduced early in the hostilities.

One week after the battle between the *Virginia* and the *Monitor* the North began construction of twelve more *Monitor*-class ironclads. They were to be armed with incendiary shells that were "filled with an inflammable substance which, when the shell is exploded, burns for thirty minutes without the possibility of being quenched."

Observation balloons used electric telegraphs to report troop movements, while the railroads played a vital role in moving armies and supplies.

When the Civil War ended the combined armies of the North and the South contained hundreds of thousands of trained soldiers. Not only could this combined force have destroyed a British invasion, but they could undoubtedly have won in battle against the combined armies of Europe—not defeating them one by one but could very well have defeated them even if they had united all of their forces.

Modern warfare began in the Civil War, although it took many years for the rest of the world to realize this.

Events, as depicted in this book, would have happened just as they are written here.

HARRY HARRISON

WINTER—1862

THE UNITED STATES OF AMERICA
Abraham Lincoln *President of the United States*
Hannibal Hamlin *Vice-President*
William H. Seward *Secretary of State*
Edwin M. Stanton *Secretary of War*
Gideon of the Welles *Secretary of the Navy*
Salmon P. Chase *Secretary of the Treasury*
Gustavus Fox *Assistant Secretary of the Navy*
Edward Bates *Attorney General*
John Nicolay *First Secretary to President Lincoln*
John Hay *Secretary to President Lincoln*
William Parker Parrott *Gunsmith*
Charles Francis Adams *U.S. Ambassador to Britain*
John Ericsson *Inventor of USS Monitor*
Captain Worden *Captain of USS Monitor*

UNITED STATES ARMY
General William Tecumseh Sherman
General Ulysses S. Grant
General Henry W. Halleck
General George B. McClellan *Commander Army of the Potomac*
General Ramsay *Head of Ordnance Department*
Lieutenant General Winfield Scott *Commander West Point*
Colonel Hiram Berdan *Commander U.S. Regiment of Sharpshooters*
General Benjamin F. Butler

Colonel Appler *Commander, 53rd Ohio*
General John Pope *Army of the Potomac*

UNITED STATES NAVY
Commodore Goldsborough
Charles D. Wilkes *Captain of USS San Jacinto*
Lieutenant Fairfax *First Officer of USS San Jacinto*
David Glasgow Farragut *Flag Officer, Mississippi Fleet*
Lieutenant John Worden *Commander USS Monitor*

GREAT BRITAIN
Victoria Regina *Queen of Great Britain and Ireland*
Prince Albert *Royal Consort, her husband*
Lord Palmerston *Prime Minister*
Lord John Russell *Foreign Secretary*
William Gladstone *Chancellor of the Exchequer*
Lord Lyons *British Ambassador to the United States*
Lord Wellesley *Duke of Wellington*
Lady Kathleen Shiel *Lady-in-Waiting to the Queen*

BRITISH ARMY
Duke of Cambridge *Commander-in-Chief*
General Peter Champion *Commander of British Invasion Forces*
Major General Bullers *Infantry Commander*
Colonel Oliver Phipps-Hornby *Commander 62nd Foot*
Lieutenant Saxby Athelstane *Cavalry officer*
General Harcourt *Garrison Commander of Quebec*

BRITISH NAVY
Admiral Alexander Milne
Captain Nicholas Roland *Commander of HMS Warrior*
Commander Sydney Tredegar *Royal Marines*

CONFEDERATE STATES OF AMERICA
Jefferson Davis *President*
Judah P. Benjamin *Secretary of State*
Thomas Bragg *Attorney General*
James A. Seddon *Secretary of War*

Christopher G. Memminger *Secretary of the Treasury*
Stephen Mallory *Secretary of the Navy*
John H. Reagan *Attorney General and Postmaster General*
Stephen Murray *Secretary of the Navy*
John Slidell *Confederate Commissioner to France*
William Murray Mason *Confederate Commissioner to England*

CONFEDERATE ARMY
General Robert E. Lee *Commander-in-Chief*
General P.G.T. Beauregard
General Albert Sidney Johnston

CONFEDERATE NAVY
Flag Officer Franklin Buchanan *Captain CSS Virginia*

AN INTERVIEW WITH HARRY HARRISON

Harry Harrison's career as a science fiction writer has virtually spanned the history of the genre. Born is Stamford, Connecticut, in 1925, he grew up reading Astounding Science Fiction in the Borough of Queens in New York City. Following WWII, in which he served as gunnery instructor in Laredo, Texas, volunteering every month for overseas service, Harrison attended a number of art schools, then worked for some years as a commercial artist and art director. From this he moved on to publishing and editing, sold articles and stories, and started his first novel. Finding New York City an impossible place in which to write, he and his wife, Joan, and unprotesting year-old son, Todd, moved to Mexico in 1956. From there to England in 1957. To Italy in 1958. After a quick visit to New York in 1959, where daughter Moira was born, the family moved to Denmark in 1959. The peripatetic Mr. Harrison, at present, resides in Ireland. He is the author of more than forty novels, among them The Stainless Steel Rat books, the acclaimed West of Eden trilogy, *Make Room! Make Room!* (made into the movie *Soylent Green*), and, most recently, *Stars & Stripes Forever*, the first in a new alternate history series. His books have been translated into twenty-seven languages, including that perennial favorite, Esperanto. He received the Nebula Award in 1973.

We spoke with him recently about his distinguished career, his memories of the past and thoughts of the future, his long love affair with alternate history, and cannibalism.

* * *

Q: What was it like to be an SF writer in the '40s and '50s? The Hydra Club, John W. Campbell, Jr., and Astounding— was there a sense among the people involved that you were creating something special and important, making up the golden age as you went along?

A: I grew up as an SF fan in the golden age of the '30s. The war interrupted. Back in NY after the war I was not sure if I wanted to draw or write. I chose art. But I was also deeply involved in SF. I drew comics, illustrated magazines, including SF, and did a cover for two Lewis Padgett novels for Marty Greenberg of Gnome Press. He took me to a meeting of the Hydra Club—the group of professional SF people in NY. I was right at home there. I did artwork for Damon Knight's *World Beyond*, Horace Gold's *Galaxy*, and Danny Keyes's *Marvel*. (Danny went on to write *Flowers for Algernon*, among others.) I was so much at home with the SF professionals that I eventually became chairman of the club. I slid from illustrating comics to editing writing for, and publishing, comics. When the comics died in the late '40s, I slid sideways into editing SF and other pulps. These were the golden years of SF. Every writer either lived in NYC or came through there. We all knew each other, and there was plenty of cross-fertilization. The money wasn't much, rates were low, but we were inventing a whole new world.

I grew up reading Astounding, and John Campbell was like a god to me. The greatest pleasure was to work with him, have lunch with him, hear his ideas. And sell him stories. My first six novels were done as serials for Astounding, then sold for books later on. John and I differed greatly on many things, mostly politics. But he respected my views. So much so that he asked me to edit a volume of his editorials. Which I did, but not without a good deal of infighting. Only by threatening to take my name off the cover did I finally convince him that I would not permit inclusion of his far right, exaggerated anti-Communist pieces. I shall miss him.

Q: How has science fiction, and its audience, changed since the Golden Age?

A: Well. Yes, major changes. None for the better, I am sorry to say. Today's reading audience is pretty dumb and unknowledgeable about SF. (And too prone to read abysmal fantasy.) But the same can be said for the editors, and the writers. The writers of the '40s are snuffing out one by one and no one is replacing them. I shall keep the flag flying and go down with all guns still firing.

Q: Damn the torpedoes . . . ! The New York SF scene that you describe was a major literary movement that has yet to receive its due—from mainstream critics, at least—although the influence of those writers/editors began to make itself increasingly felt outside the SF community from the '60s on, until today it's permeated much of popular culture.
A: That old devil, Kingsley Amis, once described science fiction as going from *"Beowulf* to *Finnegan's Wake* in fifty years." That is, from the first crude, barely literate pulps to writers getting more involved in form than content. This is true, but a simplification. This kind of writing is but one rivulet in the estuary that SF has now become. From the broad, mighty river of the Campbellian Astounding years, the river has now branched into countless separate streams. Just look at the diversity: not only the academic forms favored by the Chip Delaneys, but fantasy, horror, alternate history, future war, heroic fantasy, Arthurian legendry, female fantasy, and more. This is good in that new writers can explore tempting fields of endeavor, bad in that so much is produced that good new writers can easily be ignored. Not to mention established writers who see their sales diminish as more and more titles are loaded into the field. Or fields. I don't think this growth rate is sustainable. With too many titles chasing too few slots, there will be a night of long knives—or a slow hemorrhaging to death—someday soon.

Q: As someone whose career has stretched from the Golden Age to the end of the millennium, what kind of future do you see for SF?
A: SF is filled with false predictions; I will not attempt to join mine to their number.

Q: Tell us how Slippery Jim DiGriz, a.k.a. the Stainless Steel Rat, got his start.
A: I was writing narrative hooks for practice. The term goes back to the pulp magazines. You started your short story manuscript over halfway down the double-spaced first page. A "narrative hook" was something so intriguing that you "hooked" the editor into turning the page. At that, he would buy the story since he rarely read that much of a submitted manuscript. (The first four paragraphs of the first Rat book is that hook.) I was intrigued by my hook, so I wrote a story to explain it. And another. Amplified into a book. Then a sequel. Then on. It was never planned that way. I have just finished the tenth and last Rat book. Even good things have to end.

Q: Do you have a favorite opening line or hook among all your books?
A: No, because an opening line is a thing of flux for me. Years ago I copied out fifty opening lines of books I admired. I found out an interesting fact. They were all different. Since then I have simply started my novels. Then, when finished, in the light of what was to come, I have gone back and rewritten the opening page. Polishing it well in the light of the shadows cast by coming events.

Q: You've worked with two of the most influential editors in SF—John W. Campbell, Jr., and Brian Aldiss—men with very different, one might almost say antithetical, editorial sensibilities and conceptions of what SF could or should encompass. Can you describe what effect your experiences with them had on your writing?
A: Brian and I met and became close friends. We are very different kinds of writers but very much in agreement as editors and critics. We started the first critical SF magazine, *SF Horizons*. And did fifty anthologies together. In the very beginning we agreed not to differ. That is, we both liked every story we printed. If one of us had reservations, the story was out. Working with Brian was a revelation. In our constant examination and evaluation of other writers, there must have been some effect on our works.

Q: Did you ever collaborate as writers?
A: We did try once. Brian had started a story where, I don't remember how, all the oceans dry up. I carried on with it and it died a natural death. It wasn't his novel, or mine, and just didn't work.

Q: Two words: Soylent Green.
A: Yes, well. Simply, a mostly fair adoption of a very good and seminal book: *Make Room! Make Room!* (He said humbly.) The first book, fiction or nonfiction, to deal with the problem of overpopulation. The producer, Richard Fleischer, and Chuck Heston wanted to do it as an overpopulation book. MGM didn't think the topic was important enough. They only bought it because it was about cannibalism.

Q: Not that there's anything wrong with cannibalism! Has history borne out the concerns you raised in Make Room! Make Room!*?*
A: I was correct right down the line, because all of my predictions on population and overconsumption were taken from specialist studies. The powers fighting birth control are still fighting, and killing, in the name of saving life. Birth rates are falling in the West, not because of morality, but because of selfishness. Instead of a new baby, people prefer a bigger TV and better holidays. This started first in Germany, and now many countries have hit zero population growth or lower. Selfishness also means that we are almost totally indifferent to zooming Third World population growth, followed by land destruction and famine. The little wars only exacerbate the existing situation. When plagues start reaching us from Africa we might take some notice.

Q: Many of your novels and novel series feature alternate worlds or histories: Tunnel Through the Deep, The Hammer and the Cross, *the Eden books . . . You're not just jumping on the alternate history bandwagon with* Stars & Stripes Forever. *What is it about the form that appeals to you as a science fiction writer?*

A: I didn't know there was a bandwagon! As you say, I've been there before. I am a great fan of Alternate History (AH) and have always written it. It's important to remember that AH is the only kind of SF that H. G. Wells did not write. He invented the rest: time travel, invasion from space, et cetera. But not AH. Therefore, this is a field of human endeavor that has not been staked out. The rules are to be invented as you go along. There is not much good, or even bad, AH around because to do it well it requires a lot of work. And all writers are naturally lazy. AH requires months, years of research. You have to like it to do it. My interest in the Civil War goes back to the '40s. My library is quite large. *Rebel in Time* came out of this, while I was still shaping *Stars & Stripes*. It has really been cooking for thirty years or more.

Q: In Stars & Stripes Forever *you postulate a Machiavellian attack by Britain against America in the midst of the Civil War. Can you tell us a little about the history, and the alternate history, that went into the book?*
A: Some years back I did my sums and realized that not only was the Civil War the first modern war, but the combined forces of North and South would make up a modern army that could engage all of the other armies of the world at one time. And win. This knowledge stewed along there until the time was right. Serendipity. I had the background material and rudiments of the plot. When I dug into the material I had and put things together—there was the story. I'm glad I waited this long because I am hitting at the right time. With the end of Communism, the U.S. has lost a goal . . . which was just "anti." We have to rethink the future. By going into the past I have produced one possible answer.

Q: Rethinking the future by going into the past—a phrase combining the science fiction writer with the historian! As opposed to rethinking the past by going into the future, which one could say is the raison d'etre *of much SF, from Asimov's* Foundation Trilogy *onward.*
A: I have said that AH is the newest and best thing on the SF horizon. When Doc Smith's galactic wars were new, along

with Isaac's Foundation, they were good fun indeed. But that was fifty years ago. Attempting to revive them now is a mug's game. The life is gone from the corpse, and no matter how many volts you pump into it, it is still a corpse. SF became popular—and great—because it had no limits and was set to explore anything. That challenge is still there and is what is important. Not retreading tried ideas.

Q: Even a historical novelist such as Patrick O'Brian, whose books are justifiably renowned for their scrupulous fidelity to historical fact, confesses to having "taken great liberties . . . within a context of general historical accuracy." How does this apply to writers of alternate history such as yourself?
A: Great liberties? No. An AH writer cannot take liberties with fact; at least, not up to the point where the story begins—the twist that changes history. Only then can history be bent and mutated. But always dealing with the real past and projecting changes into a possible, and new, future.

Q: Exactly. It seems to me that AH in its "pure" form (if such a beast exists!) consists of taking the cards dealt by history, reshuffling them, and dealing them out again, then playing the hand through without introducing a wild card. Postulating as a history-altering event a British attack on a war-torn USA and CSA is a different order of "alternate" entirely from having a killer asteroid strike during the Battle of Gettysburg.
A: I beg to differ with your poker analogy. The cards are not reshuffled in AH. There must be truth, solid truth, up to the nexus where change begins. In the case of *Stars & Stripes*, Prince Albert's death occurs just a few weeks earlier in time. Then we watch the ripples spread out from this change: how, one after another, events are altered, small changes growing into larger ones until there is a new history that is just as realistic as the one in the history books. This is directly opposed to the killer asteroid you mentioned. That is the easy way out. Showy perhaps, but very easy to write. The slow slog of slightly altered history and the widening of events from that tiny change is the way I much prefer to go.

Q: You currently live in Ireland. Do you consider yourself to be an expatriate writer?
A: I left America in 1956 because I needed time and space to write my first novel. Mexico was cheap and fun: I could write and enjoy a different society. It is not that I left the States for any reason; I went to another country for a lot of reasons. I went to England, then Italy, then Denmark (seven years), then Ireland because there was a great joy in seeing new languages, cultures, what might be called inspiration. I am still an American writer, as *S&S* proves.

Q: Can you tell us what you're working on now?
A: I've just finished *The Stainless Steel Rat Joins the Circus*, the tenth and last Rat book. And I have delivered the final manuscript of *Stars & Stripes in Peril*. This, and the last in the trilogy, *Stars & Stripes Triumphant*, should see me well into the next millennium.

Q: Going back to Soylent Green, *are there any plans for other movies based on your books?*
A: The Rat books have been under option for twelve years. And every year we expect to do it. Closer to cinematic reality is *The Technicolor Time Machine*. Mel Gibson optioned it awhile back. A screenplay has been done by Marshall Brickman, who had written a number of Woody Allen films. Allen has agreed to play the second lead. If all goes well, production should start this fall.

Q: Woody Allen and Mel Gibson? Alvy Singer meets Mad Max? Now that's what I call alternate history!
A: It should be great fun. If you remember the novel, the second lead was a con man film producer, guilt-ridden, stumbling into an unknown future. Perfect for Woody Allen. And Mel will be your perfect Viking. He told me that he hates Vikings. Perfect role for him since he projects self-hatred so well in some of his roles.

Alternate History fiction asks,
"What might have been . . . ?"

Del Rey Books asks,
"Why not find out?"

Check out
www.randomhouse.com/delrey/althist
for the exciting world of possible pasts.

If you enjoyed *Stars & Stripes Forever*, you
won't want to miss the sequel . . .

STARS & STRIPES IN PERIL
by Harry Harrison

Coming in hardcover from Del Rey
in October 2000, the official
Alternate History Month.